THE HUNTING MOON

TOR TEEN BOOKS BY SUSAN DENNARD

THE HUNTING MOON

SUSAN DENNARD

TOR
TEEN

TOR PUBLISHING GROUP
NEW YORK

THE HUNTING MOON

Copyright © 2023 by Susan Dennard

Map art by Tim Paul, © 2022 Susan Dennard

A Tor Teen Book
Published by Tom Doherty Associates / Tor Publishing Group
120 Broadway
New York, NY 10271

www.tor-forge.com

Tor® is a registered trademark of Macmillan Publishing Group, LLC.

The Library of Congress Cataloging-in-Publication Data is available upon request.

ISBN 978-1-250-19414-5 (hardcover)
ISBN 978-1-250-33059-8 (international, sold outside the
U.S., subject to rights availability)
ISBN 978-1-250-19416-9 (ebook)

Our books may be purchased in bulk for promotional, educational, or business use. Please contact your local bookseller or the Macmillan Corporate and Premium Sales Department at 1-800-221-7945, extension 5442, or by email at MacmillanSpecialMarkets@macmillan.com.

First Edition: 2023

Printed in the United States of America

0 9 8 7 6 5 4 3 2 1

For Erin,

a nerdy Monday who has a caring Sunday heart

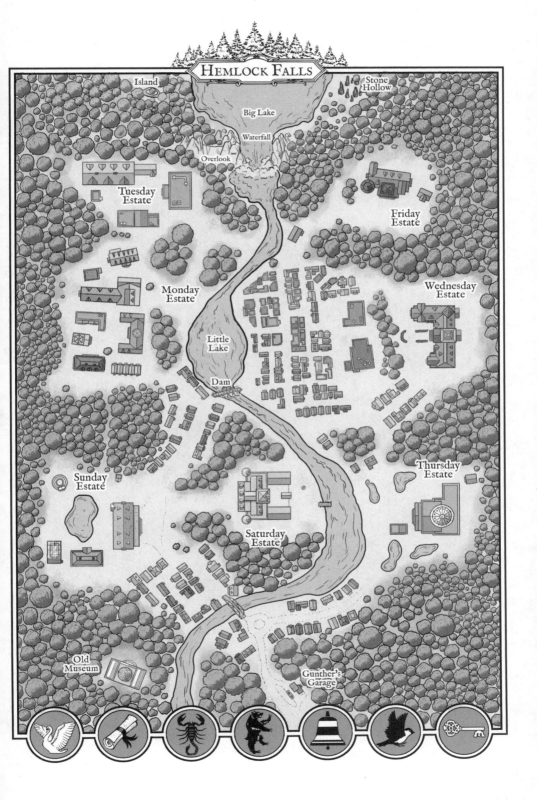

THE WITCH

On the girl's twelfth birthday, the Dianas come for her.

They send the usual crow with a locket in its beak to her window because there is a chance that, like the girl's sister, she will want to join them. The witches are about three weeks too late, though, and when the girl sees the crow outside, she doesn't open her window. She doesn't take the locket.

As much as she hungers for the flames of magic to burn through her fingertips, she has no interest in trading one controlling society for another.

Culture runs thicker than blood. Her best friend's father used to say that, and the girl knows it's all too true. Suffocatingly so, like coffin walls burying you alive.

She doesn't need them, the witches or the Luminaries, because she has the spell her sister left behind before she was betrayed. And she has a plan. A careful, meticulous plan that will take her years to finish . . .

And that will finish anyone who dared hurt her sister.

One by one. Insects wriggling in a web.

One by one, payback for the pure heart of the forest.

THE NIGHTMARE

The boy awakens beside a hemlock tree in the forest. He doesn't know how he got there or how long he has been lying there. He still wears his pajamas—the ones with Wolverine on them—and his feet are filthy and frozen.

His heart drops to his bowels. He yanks in his legs to stand, but terror stiffens his joints, his low back, his skull.

The forest, the forest, *why* is he in the forest? And what if someone finds him here?

His bare feet knock something as he grapples upward. It is a wolf's jawbone. *The* wolf's jawbone that first appeared in his bedroom four days ago and told him the forest would be coming for him.

The boy knows now exactly what it must mean, exactly *how* it came for him. He doesn't understand why, he doesn't understand the mechanics, and he can't remember anything of what came the night before. Yet he feels the truth of what he has become dwelling deep inside of him.

He is no longer a sparrow, he is a wolf.

He is no longer a boy, he is a nightmare.

He snatches up the jaw. It is slick with something that might be blood or might just be mist mixed with the red clay beneath his toes. Then, with the curved bone clutched tight in his grasp, he runs east toward the rising sun.

He prays this is the right way home.

This story begins with a funeral in a town where the locals don't bury their dead. After all, the forest nearby has such a nasty habit of waking the bodies back up again.

This particular corpse is a stranger to Winnie Wednesday. She knew *of* Grayson Friday, of course. He was the person who first busted into the old museum on the south side of town and turned it into The Place to Party. He also used to sneak into the clans to steal banner sigils just to show that he *could*. And then there was that one time when, according to local legend, he stole a Tuesday Hummer and drove it right off the dam—while he was still inside.

Yet for all that Winnie knows *of* Grayson, she never, not once in her life, actually talked to the guy, with his peat-brown hair and his bright green eyes.

Now, she never will.

"You okay?" Mom asks, squinting at Winnie's face. She and Winnie are in the forest, walking toward the Big Lake's western shore.

"Yep," Winnie lies. "I'm fine." It's not a good lie, and Mom definitely doesn't believe it.

"You don't have to come."

"I do." Winnie avoids her gaze. For Jay, she needs to come. She is his friend again, so she should be here. Grayson Friday was *his* Lead Hunter, after all.

"You can go home," Mom presses, "and I'll get a ride with Rachel—"

"No." Winnie snaps this harder than she intends. People are coming up the path from behind; she doesn't want to deal with them. She's as close to a local celebrity as Hemlock Falls gets these days thanks to Johnny Saturday calling her "the Girl Who Jumped" on a news segment five nights ago. Everyone wants some of her shine.

Because ten nights ago, Winnie completed her third trial; saved Emma Wednesday's life with a banshee claw; jumped off the Big Lake's waterfall; and got bitten by a werewolf while somehow not absorbing the werewolf's nightmare mutation and turning into one too.

It's exciting stuff, worthy of a penny dreadful (or a repeated slot on the nightly news) . . .

Except half the story is missing.

Emma wouldn't have been in the forest if she knew how bad Winnie really was at hunting. Winnie only jumped off the waterfall because the Whisperer—a nightmare *no one* believes in—chased her there. And as for the werewolf bite . . . Well, Winnie can't remember that part. Almost everything from after she'd plunged into the water is forgotten, erased, missing.

Which just makes this whole celebrity thing even worse. It's a *constant* reminder of the gaping hole inside her brain.

"Take these," Mom says, cutting into the spiral that consumes Winnie's thoughts almost hourly these days. She slides the Volvo's key from her pocket. "If it gets to be too much, just leave, okay?"

"It won't be too much," Winnie counters, although she does take the keys and push them into her own pocket. If for no other reason than to end this conversation.

Like Mom, Winnie wears all black underneath her jacket, although her black jeans have faded more to heather gray at this point. Her feet, bound in the combat boots she wore on her second trial, stomp out a steady and graceless rhythm down the path. Mom's tread lands more lightly behind her.

Eventually, she and Mom clear the trees and the entirety of the Big Lake opens before them. The waters are dark at this morning hour, the surface rippling and writhing like basilisk scales—all moving south, toward the waterfall. Spindrift rises off the precipice like flies off a dead body.

"Hey," Mom says, gripping at Winnie's biceps. Winnie flinches. "Let's go back."

Winnie has stopped walking. She hadn't realized it. Her feet just . . . aren't moving. "No." She wags her head. This is weird. She, Winnie, is being weird, and she needs to get a hold of herself.

It's not like she's never been to a hunter's funeral before.

Twenty steps bring Winnie and Mom to the amorphous cloud of people clustered at the Big Lake's silty edge, two bacteria sucked into a colony. It's more Luminaries than Winnie would have expected at a funeral for the smallest clan, although Tuesday scorpions do inflate the numbers. They cluster around the edges in their camouflage fatigues, weapons strapped across their bodies.

Winnie can't tell if they're here for the ceremony or because this is where their daily route just happens to take them. Their faces are hidden in the glossy brown, carapace-like helmets they always wear.

Menacing helmets. Little shields meant to hide something.

These are the Alphas—a special branch of the martial Tuesday clan who deal with any nightmares that escape the forest. Or, as the Alphas have been deployed lately, to surveil the forest for daywalkers.

Conversation drones around Winnie. She hears someone mention the werewolf and how it must be brought to justice. Then someone else complains that the Council can't get its shit together—and hey, did you see Johnny's interview with Dryden last night? What a disaster. But at least the Masquerade hasn't been canceled.

Winnie gets whiplash just from listening. *Werewolf, werewolf . . . Masquerade! Werewolf, werewolf . . . Masquerade! Darkness, darkness, light!*

She should be used to it by now.

It has been eight days since she told the truth to Aunt Rachel about the banshee head. Eight days since Aunt Rachel told Winnie not to tell anyone. And eight days since Winnie was forced to accept that no one—absolutely *no one*—in this town cares that she and Emma Wednesday almost died.

People have even asked Winnie if it was fun jumping off the waterfall.

Fun jumping to her almost death. *Darkness, darkness, light!*

Winnie yanks off her glasses and frowns down at the lenses. They're clean, but she scrubs at them anyway until Lizzy Friday clears her throat.

Then Winnie shoves her glasses back on to watch the funeral. Her heart beats faster than it should.

Lizzy stands at the lakeshore, waves lapping gently a few steps behind her, tiny tentacles feeling for their next meal. She wears a simple black button-up tucked into functional black slacks, and she looks more like a traffic cop than leader of the Friday clan now mourning her lost. In one arm, she holds a ceramic urn.

"Thanks for coming," Lizzy says, and the crowd goes silent. Now there is only the waterfall's roar to fill the afternoon sky. "Grayson would have liked knowing he was this popular." She smiles; a few people laugh.

"Grayson died doing what he loved," Lizzy continues. "He died a hero protecting us from the forest. And although no one outside Hemlock Falls will ever know it, he died protecting them too."

Grayson's mother chokes at those words. She stands at the front of the crowd, her back ramrod straight like she's still bracing for bad news. Like she hasn't yet heard her only son is dead, but she knows the message is on the way.

Mom and Ms. Friday went to school together; Grayson is only a little older than Darian.

Was only a little older than Darian.

For two years, Grayson has been Lead Hunter for the Fridays. Now he will be one more name among the thousands hammered into a wall in city hall downtown, and on the next Friday night—just six days from now—the new Lead Hunter will take his place in the forest.

The new Lead Hunter stands near his aunt on the shore, his head bowed. He doesn't move as Lizzy speaks. He is still as the forest. Still as a corpse preserved in the morgue.

His suit jacket is too short in the sleeves, suggesting he borrowed it, and Winnie doubts Jay has slept in over twenty-four hours. Grayson only died last night, his body so mangled Jay had to identify it by the ring on a nearby finger.

Winnie wonders who gathered up the pieces of Grayson for burning. Funerals have to happen fast in Hemlock Falls, before the forest can make a revenant.

She hopes no parts of Grayson got left behind.

"Integrity in all," Lizzy says, ending her eulogy with the Friday clan's motto. "Honesty to the end. May Grayson Alexander Friday find peace in his long sleep at the heart of the forest."

Everyone murmurs those words back.

Everyone except Winnie.

Because Grayson Friday isn't sleeping. He isn't finding peace. And whatever he was two days ago, now he is nothing more than fish food floating in an aquarium.

C H A P T E R

2

Winnie waits until all the eulogies are over and Grayson's ashes have sunk into the unfeeling deep. Only then does she go to Jay. He has moved away from the lake and tucked himself into the shadows of an old hemlock. If Winnie hadn't watched him shuffle from the shore, she might never have noticed him hiding there.

He looks like he often does, eyes bloodshot and face haggard. If Winnie didn't know he'd just been on the hunt, she would assume he'd been out all night drinking. His hair is still damp—as if he only just left the shower, where he scrubbed off all the remains of forest and death.

"Thanks for coming," he tells her. His eyes are misty gray today, rimmed with red. She suspects he has been crying.

Questions boil inside Winnie: *Please, tell me you saw the Whisperer. Please, tell me it wasn't the werewolf and I'm not crazy. A werewolf didn't do this. Please, tell me it was the Whisperer.*

Winnie swallows those words, greasy and hot. She can't acknowledge them right now, not when Jay is simply trying to survive a day that weighs too heavy.

"I'm . . . really sorry," Winnie says instead. "If you need anything, you, uh . . . you know where to find me."

Jay nods, distracted, and fidgets with his dad's watch. His gaze skates behind Winnie, to where a line is forming. Hunters and clan members wanting to offer their sympathies . . . but also to offer their congratulations. After all, when one Lead Hunter leaves, another must step in.

Jay's shoulders sink half an inch. The boy who does nothing but shirk responsibility is now faced with a metric ton of it. He has to manage clan training; he has to coordinate schedules and gear and safety; he has to guide hunters into the forest every Friday night, knowing they could end up like Grayson.

And that he could end up like Grayson too.

"Jay," says a new voice, creaking and thin. Winnie turns to find Jay's great-aunt Linda pushing in and reaching for Jay's hands. So Winnie offers him a tight smile and moves on.

A quick scan reveals Mom in conversation with an Alpha named Isaac Tuesday who graduated when Darian did. Mom's eyes shine. She's glad to be here, even if it's for a funeral, because she believes in the long sleep and the balance and the death that's a part of life.

And don't I believe in that too?

"Hey, Winnie."

Winnie twists around to find that Aunt Rachel has pushed through the crowd to stand beside her. She is dressed almost identically to Mom, and Winnie can't help but wonder if maybe they bought their outfits at the same time—back when they not only had hunted together, but had also been best friends.

"Hi." Winnie tries for a smile. It falls flat.

"Did you know Grayson?" Rachel cocks her head toward the lake, as if the ashes somehow still contain bits of him.

They don't.

"No," Winnie admits. "I just . . . thought I should support Jay." *And what a great job I've done at that.* "I guess you knew Grayson?"

"Yeah. Lead Hunters—we consult pretty regularly." Rachel sighs and stuffs her hands into her coat pockets. "He was good. *Really* good. It's, uh, scary how fast things can turn on you." As she says this, Winnie can practically see the nightmares in Rachel's eyes. All the times when she—like Winnie—really should not have made it out of the forest alive.

After a few seconds though, Rachel rolls her shoulders, curt efficiency taking hold of her posture. As if her very skeleton is saying, *There is no time for the shadows. Compartmentalize and move back toward the sun.*

"Listen," Rachel begins, "it's totally fine if you don't want to join the Wednesday hunt right now—"

The way she says this does not make it sound totally fine.

"—but the clans need help with corpse duty. We've got so many dead nightmares to deal with these days, given the amped-up hunter numbers. Think you can join the crew on Thursday morning? You don't have to be in charge again, but we could really use the help."

Winnie has two thoughts in that moment. First, that she absolutely doesn't want to spend any more time than she has to with Rachel's son, Marcus, who will undoubtedly be there for corpse duty on Thursday morning.

Second, that she isn't sure she wants to return to the forest if it's going to keep making her feel this way. *It won't, though. You're just being weird and this is just a one-off.*

Except . . . was the waterfall always so loud?

Rachel clears her throat. Winnie realizes she has been staring into space. Possibly glaring into space too. She blinks. "Yeah. I can do that, Aunt Rachel."

"Great." Rachel rubs her hands together. "I appreciate that. And of course, whenever you're ready to join me on the hunt, you just let me know. No pressure."

But also definitely some pressure.

As Rachel strides away, Winnie is struck yet again by the utter polarity of it all. Rachel just nudged her niece to join in the exact activity that led to Grayson's brutal death . . . *at* Grayson's funeral. And right now, although Winnie is a whole thirty paces away from Jay, she can hear an unfamiliar voice booming out: "Congratulations, young man. Youngest Lead Hunter in Hemlock Falls. You must be so proud."

No, Winnie thinks as she stomps away from it all to seek solitude in the parking lot. *He's not proud. And jumping wasn't fun. And Grayson isn't sleeping. And the Nightmare Masquerade should not be happening in two weeks.*

Yet even as those thoughts slice through Winnie's brain one after the other, bright, burning meteorites, she knows that the better thoughts—the better questions she really should be raising—are: *What is wrong with me? Why can't I compartmentalize like everybody else?*

And why am I not acting like a Luminary?

Winnie isn't at the Volvo for long before Mom joins her. One look at Winnie's face with her front teeth clicking and her cheeks flushed from too many emotions, and Mom opts to preserve her silence.

Thank god. Winnie doesn't know what she'll say if she has to speak right now. She feels like a piece of Grayson Friday got stuck inside her. Like his ashes were grenade shrapnel and now they're wedged in so deep, she'll never dig them out again.

Or maybe it's just the growing realization that she isn't very good at being a Luminary.

Or maybe she's just hungry and she shouldn't have skipped breakfast.

"You're driving," Mom says, and though the last thing Winnie wants to do right now is concentrate on getting the Volvo into second gear without stalling halfway up the hill onto the dam, she also needs the distraction.

And to her surprise, it's actually sort of soothing. *In goes the clutch. Change gears. Out goes the clutch.* There's a rhythm to it that slows her heart. *In. Change. Out.*

Fallen branches litter the side of the gravel road that leads south out of the forest. Then they're passing the Tuesday estate, all bare-bones practicality—more bunker than fancy mansion.

"You want to talk?" Mom asks when they successfully make it past the Monday estate without any gear-shift problems, a morning fog weaving through the college campus–like grounds.

"Yeah," Winnie answers eventually. "Everything's okay. It was just . . . a lot." She hopes Mom interprets this as the funeral in general; she really doesn't want to talk about Jay's misty eyes or the way the waterfall sounded too much like death.

Fortunately, Mom does misinterpret. "I would be lying if I didn't say I'm relieved you're not hunting yet, Winnebago. If your trial had gone just a little bit differently . . ."

Mom doesn't finish the thought, and she doesn't need to.

"Until this werewolf is killed," Mom continues, "I'll be grateful you're not in the forest. You're still not planning to hunt any time soon, right?" She fastens Winnie with a laser-eyed stare, and Winnie's fingers tighten on the steering wheel until her knuckles turn white.

Because there it is, right there. One more piece of festering shrapnel: not even her own mother believes her about the Whisperer, and it's thoughtless little comments like this one that keep giving her away.

God, I hope they catch this werewolf, she said last night after Dryden's interview on the news.

To think, it's just out there walking among us. That comment came last Thursday.

And: *I am so, so glad the werewolf didn't get you, Winnie.* That was from last Sunday, Winnie's third day home from the hospital.

Winnie doesn't turn her head. She doesn't meet Mom's eyes. "No," she says with as little inflection as possible. "I don't plan to hunt any time soon."

Winnie and Mom clear the last of the trees. To their left, the Little Lake is almost blue this morning. It is the opposite of the Big Lake. Cheerful instead of oppressive, welcoming instead of cruel. Winnie can't help but wonder if Grayson Friday really did drive into the water there. If so, does that mean a Hummer is still sitting at the bottom of the lake right now?

Winnie kind of hopes it is. For some reason, that just feels right: a statue no one can see for a man no one will ever speak to again.

CHAPTER

3

Werewolf, were-creatures: Human by day and monster by night, these rare daywalkers blend in easily and are indistinguishable from other humans in their daytime form. Also, wrongfully accused of killing Grayson Friday.

Whisperer: This nightmare is a new creature native to the American forest. No one believes it is real except for Wednesday Winona Wednesday, despite ample evidence that the monster exists.

Since Mom is due for a shift at the grocery store, Winnie will be driving herself to Sunday training (*alone*, yikes). But first she is meeting her brother Darian. He has already canceled their usual Saturday dinner tonight—which he did last weekend too—so Winnie roped him into at least grabbing a coffee with her. Proof-of-life sort of thing.

Coffee-scented warmth whooshes against Winnie as she pushes through the front entrance into Joe Squared. A sign proclaims that the establishment was VOTED BEST COFFEE SHOP IN HEMLOCK FALLS!

Considering they are also the *only* coffee shop in Hemlock Falls, the distinction doesn't mean much.

Never graceful on a good day, Winnie offers an especially spectacular display of awkward as she peels out of her leather jacket, knocks her glasses to the floor, and ends up getting her golden moon locket caught in her hair when she doubles over to retrieve said glasses. These are her newer pair, finally repaired so that they sit straight atop her nose—though not for long if she keeps dropping them.

Her face is aflame when she finally approaches the counter.

"What can I get you?" Jo, one of the the two owners, asks.

"Um . . ." Winnie wets her lips. She is overwhelmed by the menu, embarrassed by her failure to de-jacket, and still reeling from the weirdness of the funeral. "Just . . . a coffee? Black? I, uh, have a tab."

"Oh?" This seems to surprise Jo, who's eyes widen behind her cherry-red glasses. They are very cool glasses, which depresses Winnie because her thick black frames seem extremely *un*cool by comparison. "What's the name?" Jo asks.

"Um, it's probably under Wednesday." Winnie swallows. "Winnie Wednesday. And if it's not under that, then it'll be Mario Monday—"

"Holy crow." Jo slides her very cool glasses down her nose. "You're Winnie Wednesday? I thought you looked familiar, but it's been so many years since I really saw you. What with the, uh, *you know.*" She twirls a hand in the air, as if Winnie's exile from the Luminaries was just a *thing* that *happens* now and again. Like heat waves or bad hair days.

"Oh." Winnie hadn't realized Jo had ever noticed her pre-exile.

"You're all over the news," Jo continues. "The Girl Who Jumped, they're calling you. And a werewolf bite too. Incredible." Jo's focus drops to Winnie's arms, and Winnie is glad she opted for long sleeves today. Otherwise the faint scars hatch-marking her right forearm would be visible, and she already feels enough like a lab specimen when she walks around Hemlock Falls.

Fortunately, Jo doesn't seem to expect an answer. "You know what?" She rubs her hands together. "I'll name a drink after you. What do you like? Whipped cream? Cinnamon? Soy milk? Whatever your palate prefers, we'll sell it. The Girl Who Jumped! I can even add green food coloring on top, to match that dress you wore. It *was* green, right?"

Winnie doesn't know how to answer this. This is like the funeral all over again, but worse. *You almost died! Let's commemorate that traumatic event with food coloring!* Jo herself had to have her leg amputated after a droll encounter. So shouldn't she, of all people, be less . . . well, *impressed* by all of this? And maybe a bit more horrified?

Apparently not, since as Jo twists away, grabbing for a box of almond milk, she says: "Maybe the Girl Who Got Bitten instead? Johnny used that one last night. Did you hear it?" She flings a backward glance at Winnie.

And Winnie is forced to shake her head. She had *not* heard it, and she hates that title even more than the first one. Because at least she *remembers* jumping. Getting bitten, though? That memory never recorded inside her brain, so every time someone brings it up, Winnie is forced to play a cruel version of that matching game where you flip over cards and try to recall where two identical ones are hiding . . .

Except Winnie can't ever find a match, so she just keeps flipping over cards and losing, losing, losing.

"What about no drink instead?" Winnie suggests.

Jo snorts. "You can't call a drink No Drink, Winnie. People will think they're ordering air."

Winnie screws her eyes shut. This is getting worse by the second. She should have gone straight to the Sunday estate after the funeral. She should have told Darian she'd meet him another day, preferably at his place, where no one in Hemlock Falls can recognize her or complain about the werewolf or squee about the Nightmare Masquerade.

For several minutes, the only sound is the grinding of fresh beans, then the steaming of almond milk, and finally the high-pitched *shhhhh* of whipped cream. Until Jo is suddenly back before Winnie and shoving a mug her way.

The cream on top is very, *very* green.

"Give it a try." Jo winks. "And let me know what you think of the Girl Who Jumped. Or . . . maybe I'll call it the Jumping Girl? Because, you know, coffee hypes you up."

Winnie nods. As much as she would like to say, *I actually prefer black coffee please,* she takes the mug with both hands. It's warm against her numb fingers. "I'll sip this . . . over there." She dips her head toward a table.

"You do that." Jo nods knowingly. Then taps her forehead. "And I'll keep noodling drink names."

Darian is late. This isn't particularly surprising, given that his entire life is dictated by Dryden Saturday right now—and Dryden's life is dictated by the furious town, the "dangerous werewolf" on the loose, and the Nightmare Masquerade he refuses to call off.

Old Darian, however, was never tardy, so when he finally does arrive, it's clear he is distraught by the thirteen minutes that Winnie had to wait on him. "Oh my god," he breathes, dropping into the chair across from Winnie. "I am *so* sorry I'm late. Everything is such a mess these days, Win."

Darian himself is something of a mess too. His collar isn't draped evenly over his sweater vest, and there's a black smudge on the bottom of his glasses that might be ink or also might be the exhausted ether of his soul.

"Did you see last night's interview?" he asks, combing a hand through his hair—and not helping the already lopsided application of his hair gel.

Winnie nods. "It was . . ."

"An epic shit show? A hurricane of hell? A massacre of misery?"

Winnie winces. Darian has clearly tipped onto the *severely stressed* side of the continuum if he's using alliteration, and when he reaches for her coffee, she doesn't interfere.

He gulps back green whipped cream. Then freezes, cheeks bulging as his face curdles to the same shade (which *was* actually quite close to the true emerald of Winnie's dress). He swallows very slowly, very carefully. "What," he says when his mouth is finally empty, "did you order?"

Winnie doesn't answer. She simply rises in silence, fetches a glass of water from the cooler by the entrance, and offers it to him upon her return. Darian downs it in one swallow.

"That is disgusting," he says, and Winnie nods her agreement. She only needed one sip to know she would never drink it again.

"More water?" she offers, but Darian shakes his head. And for the first time since arriving, he seems to notice that Winnie isn't looking so great herself.

"Funeral," he says, smacking his forehead. "I'm such a jerk. How did the funeral go?"

"Not great," she admits, and she finds her fingers grabbing for her locket . . . then releasing because the locket brushes too closely to her own mental compartment marked DAD. It's a box she has kept closed for eight days, ever since cracking his secret message: *I was framed.* She is absolutely not about to open it here.

"Did you know Grayson?" she asks, adding an extra padlock to the box.

"Yeah," Darian replies, brow wrinkling with a frown. "Though only as much as person *could* know Grayson Friday."

"What does that mean?"

"It means he was popular."

"And you weren't?"

"No." Darian flashes a glare. "I mean, *yes,* I was quite popular, thank you . . . until . . . you know. The incident."

Winnie does know; she also knows that Darian wasn't popular. At least not like Grayson Friday was. Darian had friends and was generally liked, but he wasn't the life of the party—and certainly not the one hosting the parties every night of the week.

"Grayson knew everyone," Darian continues, "and everyone knew Grayson. Except no one really *knew* Grayson, if that makes sense. He joked a lot. Was nice to people unless they were a teacher. And he partied or pranked pretty much every night of the week. But I couldn't tell you anything more about him. He was a hard person to describe, and at the end of the day, I don't think anyone *really* knew him. And now . . ." A bob of one shoulder. "No one will."

"No one will," Winnie repeats, half sigh, half invocation, as if such words will somehow make his ashes sink faster inside the lake.

Darian reaches across the table to grab Winnie's hands, and when Winnie meets his eyes, she sees the slightest gloss has gathered over them. "I'm glad you're not hunting yet, Win. We almost lost you once, and that was more than enough."

"Yeah," Winnie says, praying he isn't about to say what Mom said. That he isn't about to add more grenade shrapnel to her heart . . .

But then it comes. Because of course it does. Darian has always been skeptical about the Whisperer's existence, even if he has never directly declared this to her.

"I know it's been chaos getting the tests coordinated, but I promise we'll catch that monster soon. Tuesday Alphas are combing the forest constantly, we've got double the hunter numbers at night, and the testing site by the pier should be ready to go in the next day or two."

Darian gives a reassuring squeeze before finally releasing Winnie's hands and leaning back. He doesn't seem to notice that his sister has turned as immobile as a statue before him.

"We'll be coming to the Sunday estate to test you and all the other students directly, and honestly, it should only be a matter of days before we have this werewolf cornered. It can't run forever. It is *going* to pay for what it did to you and Grayson and—"

Darian's phone rings, interrupting him as his voice is rising and his face is flushing with uncharacteristic fury—fury Winnie knows is on her behalf because as far as he believes, this werewolf almost ended her life.

A small part of Winnie appreciates that fire. A larger part, though, just wants some blessed relief. A heart can't survive with this much shrapnel in it.

"Crap," Darian says once he finally has his phone fumbled free and can read the caller ID. "I have to take this. I'll see you later, okay, Win? Be good." He pushes to his feet, already swiping the phone to life. "Yes, Dryden, what is it?" He briefly crooks over to give Winnie a kiss on the top of her head. It's a surprising and uncommon show of affection for their family.

He's been doing a lot of that since she left the hospital, and Winnie wishes it made her feel better. She wishes the grenade's blast radius hadn't been quite so wide.

Darian leaves Joe Squared with a distracted wave. Winnie doesn't wave back.

Several minutes after Darian's departure, as Winnie is dropping her mug of now brownish-green slush into a bin near the counter, Jo steps up beside her. "What'd you think of it?"

"No," Winnie says. It's a little breathy. She wags her head. "No."

Jo cringes. "More noodling?"

"No." Winnie shoves her glasses up her nose. "No more noodling, please. I don't like fancy drinks or whipped cream. I just wanted a black coffee."

Jo nods thoughtfully. "Okay, okay. I think I hear what you're laying down." She snaps her fingers. "I've got it! How about we name a cup of drip coffee the Winnie and it can be half off on Wednesdays?"

Winnie's posture slumps. She sighs. At this point, everyone in Hemlock Falls might as well have cotton stuffed in their ears for all they listen to her. And after her encounter with Darian just now, Winnie is too defeated to keep fighting. "Sure," she says. "Let's call it the Winnie. Half off on Wednesdays."

"Excellent." Jo grins. "Oh, and hey," she adds at Winnie's now-departing back. "You can have all Winnies for free! Your mom and your brother too!"

4

The last thing Winnie wants to do right now, while green whipped cream sloshes inside her organs alongside Grayson's eulogy, is go to the Sunday estate for training. But she has also worked so hard to become a Luminary again that she has no plans to mess that up by skipping the required weekend classes. So despite still wearing her funeral clothes, Winnie parks the Volvo on the Sunday estate and lumbers into the red brick building, her backpack feeling heavy despite its near emptiness.

She has missed first period—a fact over which she will shed precisely zero tears. Luminary history with Professor Samuel and a bunch of younger Luminaries (including her cousin Marcus) is her least favorite part of the day.

Her favorite part, meanwhile, is the class she now slinks into: nightmare anatomy with Professor Il-Hwa. She arrives with a few minutes to spare before the tardy bell will ring, and a quick scan of the room finds the twins and Fatima near the windows; Erica Thursday sits at the back.

Winnie accidentally makes eye contact with Erica, earning a cool nod—which is basically the *only* interaction Erica ever offers. Winnie can't lie that she had hoped for more since she cornered Erica at the Thursday estate six days ago. She isn't sure what she'd hoped for exactly, but definitely more.

Then again, cool nods of acknowledgment are a million times better than the liquid-nitrogen glares Erica bestowed on her for the four years previously.

"Hey," Winnie says as she drops into her usual desk beside Emma and behind Bretta. Fatima sits in front of Emma, so they form a little square.

"Hey," Emma replies, which prompts Bretta and Fatima to twist Winnie's way too. "How was the funeral?"

Emma's left leg is wrapped in a silicon webbing that acts as a breathable and waterproof cast. A set of crutches lean against her desk. She wraps the rubber tops in different scarves every day to match her outfit, and today's is cobalt blue to complement her blue-and-green baby doll dress.

The color brings out the cool undertones in her umber skin, and she has wrapped a similar scarf around her braids.

"The funeral wasn't great," Winnie answers honestly. She digs her fingers under her glasses to rub at her eyes. "Jay is pretty devastated."

Winnie was the only student to attend the funeral. *For Jay,* she told herself when she asked Mom to let her go. Now, though, she has to wonder if it wasn't *For me.* Some morbid need to learn more about the werewolf, the Whisperer, the death that so easily could have been her own . . .

And it's not like she did much good supporting Jay in the end, did she? She was just the Girl Who Jumped, clinging to the funeral's edge like a parasite before fleeing back to the parking area when it all got too hard.

"Of course Jay is devastated." Fatima wags her head, and her turquoise hijab flutters against her gray polka-dot sweater. "He's now the youngest Lead Hunter in Hemlock Falls. Like, *ever.*"

"Poor Jay." Bretta offers a genuinely sympathetic sigh. Her corkscrew curls bounce as she hugs her arms to her chest. She wears a pair of faded jeans and a hot-pink T-shirt, while her sneakers are so white, they have to be brand new. "Should we do something for him? Flowers don't really seem like his sort of thing."

"No." Winnie huffs a sigh. "Honestly, I don't think there's anything we *can* do. It's kind of the worst situation possible, but—"

"Heeeeeeey, Girl Who Jumped." Casey Tuesday plops on top of Winnie's desk like a spidrin dropping from a tree branch. Winnie has no idea where he came from. All that's missing is the web. "We're having a party tonight at the old museum, and you've *got* to be there."

"*Please,*" chimes Peter Sunday, who materializes behind Winnie with the same nightmarish speed and silence—as well as a cologne that is laid on just a little too thickly. "All of you gotta come."

Fatima glares at Peter, then at Casey. Bretta rolls her eyes while Emma, always the nicest of the friend group, says, "I don't know. Your parties always go so late."

"But this is for that guy who died," Casey insists.

And Winnie stiffens in her seat. "You mean Grayson Friday?"

"Yeah, him." He grins at Winnie as if they're friends. As if they have *always* been friends and he didn't spend the past four years tormenting her.

Peter wears the same expression—one that can only be described as *smarmy*—and Winnie wants to shred the puckered lips right off his freckled face. It was only two weeks ago that he sang *Happy birthday, Diana spawn* at her in homeroom and then laughed when Dante Lunedì told her not to steal his finger bones. Now Peter looks like he'd gladly give her his finger bones and some toe bones too.

"Did you actually know Grayson?" Winnie asks.

"No." Casey shrugs one shoulder. "But we always have a party to honor fallen hunters. Plus, this guy is the one who made the old museum into *the old museum*. So we've gotta have a party for him, you know? It's just the right thing to do."

The way he says that with such moral superiority—as if he knows anything about honoring anyone—makes Winnie's fingers curl into fists.

Although her fingers straighten right back out when Emma says, "Maybe we'll go." Then Bretta sighs and says, "We'll think about it, okay?"

Fatima chimes in a heartbeat later with a voice that is very like her mother's councilor voice: "Now go away please, boys, because the adults are talking and we don't want you near us."

Casey and Peter obey—Casey with a flip of his shaggy hair and a "Cool, we'll see you tonight," Peter with a mock salute. They remove themselves as quickly as they'd arrived.

"Oh no, please don't say you *actually* want to go, Emma." Fatima shakes her head at Emma.

"It's for Grayson Friday." Emma looks both sheepish and defensive, scratching ferociously at her calf through a gap in the cast's webbing. "We've always gone to the hunter parties before. And yes, I realize Casey and Peter suck"—she flashes Winnie a commiserating eye roll—"but I think this is the right thing to do. He died, and we should respect that."

"Is this because of Jay?" Fatima asks suspiciously. "Because I'm pretty sure he and Winnie are a thing—"

"We are *not* a thing," Winnie spurts. Heat sears onto her face and she dips over the aisle toward everyone. "I already told you that."

"I know, but . . ." Fatima shrugs as if to say, *I do not believe you, Winnie Winona Wednesday.* And judging by the sideways smirks on Bretta's and Emma's faces, they don't believe her either.

And Winnie finds her fists re-forming. Not because of the girls' knowing grins or the substance of Fatima's words, but because Winnie feels like she did at the funeral all over again. Like she's back beside the thunderous falls while people fume about the wrong nightmare and congratulate a Lead Hunter who doesn't want to be one.

Stop being weird, she shouts at herself. *This isn't the way a Luminary reacts!* In fact, having a party for a dead hunter is peak Luminary. As is having a coffee named after her. It's like Grandpa Frank once told her, *That's why we're called the Luminaries, Winnie: we are lanterns the forest can never snuff out.*

"Let's go," Emma begs as Professor Il-Hwa steps into the classroom. "Please? Like Casey said, it's the right thing to do."

Bretta nods as if this explanation is fully acceptable, and Fatima sighs in defeat. "Fine, but if my mom catches me sneaking out, I'm blaming the three of you."

"Wait," Winnie hisses—right as Professor Il-Hwa clears her throat at the front of the room. "We have to sneak out? What time is this party?"

"Oh, sweet Winnie." Bretta pats her arm gently. "We'll pick you up at midnight."

Winnie finds it hard to focus on Professor Il-Hwa's lecture. Not even a thorough breakdown of the circulatory systems of kelpies can hasten the two-hour period along.

Kelpie: A shaggy water creature, it is horselike in shape, but close examination reveals algal hair and a bulbous body best suited to high-pressure depths.

She takes occasional notes—*similar to tuna, moves blood warmed by muscles to heart*—but her pencil more often slides to the margins of her ruled paper. She draws droll hands first. Just the bones, so many, each perfectly in its place. Winnie has always found it soothing to sketch them.

It doesn't soothe today.

So she shifts to the lesson's subject. She saw a kelpie up close only ten days ago. She hacked right through its two bilateral tentacles. Its face, waterlogged and humanoid, had a single row of fangs glistening in the night.

Winnie will never forget that glisten.

She'll also never forget how the kelpie bellowed, a sound that felt fathoms deep and centuries ancient.

Most of all, though, Winnie won't forget how the Whisperer came out of the trees only a few hundred steps later. She'd been so preoccupied by the manticore also bearing down—and then the werewolf knocking her out of the way . . .

Winnie scratches through her drawing of the kelpie. A vicious silver line to hack away its agonized face. Then she scratches through the droll hand, and finally, she scratches through the date scribbled at the top of the page. ~~April 6~~.

Grayson's funeral, she scrawls instead. *RIP.*

When the bell finally rings, the twins and Fatima confirm that they'll see her at midnight—which, *wow,* seems so far away—before they all separate. Emma, Bretta, and Fatima all head for history class. Winnie, meanwhile, aims for the locker room. She is still four years behind; she still has to endure her cousin's smug, entirely too punchable face every single day.

Like a watered-down Beetlejuice, simply thinking Marcus's name three times seems to summon him. As soon as Winnie steps from the locker room in her black tracksuit, a cool spring breeze sweeps over her, carrying an arrangement of birdsong . . . and Marcus is right there.

"Hey, cuz."

"Oh my *god,*" Winnie replies, letting loose all her exasperation from the day. She won't be rude to Casey or Peter—at least not before she, Mom, and Darian are *officially* back in the Luminaries—but Marcus? He's family. Horrible, obnoxious family.

"What do you want?" She picks up her pace down the stone path that leads to the elaborate obstacle course.

"I hear there's a party tonight at the old museum. Can I come?"

"No." Winnie glowers at him. It has no effect. "You're fourteen. You cannot come to a party."

"You're only sixteen."

"That's a pretty big difference." To demonstrate this, Winnie drags her hand from the top of her forehead down to the top of his. Her hand has to drop several inches. "Your voice hasn't even changed yet."

His cheeks brighten to a satisfyingly arterial red. "So? Doesn't mean I can't party."

"It *absolutely* means you can't party."

"Why are you such a jerk?"

"Why are you so annoying?"

"I'll tell my mom if you don't let me go."

"Thereby proving my point." Winnie snorts. The beginning of the obstacle course is visible now, a long stretch of muddy track zigzagging into a high-walled maze, beyond which are a series of platforms connected by ropes and swinging tires. "I don't care if you tell your mom," Winnie continues. "I really doubt she'll do anything. She probably partied at my age too."

Marcus's blush turns into something fiery. His eyes—dark brown like Winnie's—sink into a scowl. "Just because you're the Girl Who Jumped doesn't mean you can treat people badly. I liked you more before." He sticks out his tongue, behaving like the absolute child he still is, and strides away to join two of his cronies at the starting line.

Winnie gapes after him, a combination of righteous anger and genuine hurt mingling in her stomach. Part of her wants to chase after him and demand he take the words back. But most of her knows that would only amount to immature fire fighting immature fire. So instead, she tows off her glasses and cleans them.

Scrub, scrub, scrub. Her training tee's cotton rubs against polycarbonate.

"He's a prick."

Winnie's attention snaps sideways. Coach Rosa has appeared beside her, moving silently like the hunter she is each Sunday night.

"He's a prick," Rosa repeats. "He'll grow out of it though." She pauses. Then adds, "I mean, I think he will. Probably."

Winnie laughs and shoves her glasses back on.

"In the meantime, Winnie"—Rosa pats her shoulder—"let him eat your dust on the obstacle course. That'll teach him not to mess with you." She squeezes once before releasing Winnie and striding away. In mere moments, a whistle is at Rosa's lips and she's hollering for everyone to *get in rows at the starting line!*

And Winnie finds a warmth is surging up from her chest. A phoenix emerging from the burning ashes of her morning.

For four years, Marcus has been nice to Winnie in private and then an utter *prick* to her the instant someone else was around. She let it slide off her like water off cockatrice feathers—just like she did with all her bullies. The Casey Tuesdays and the Dante Lunedìs and the Peter Sundays and even the cryo-freezing ice queens like Erica. After all, there was nothing Winnie could do; she just had to endure her outcast punishment and serve her time.

But like Marcus said, she's the Girl Who Jumped. She gets invited to parties now; she has a coffee named after her and gets featured on the local news. She might not *officially* be a Luminary again as deemed by the Council, but everyone in town is welcoming her back as if she already is. There are avenues open to her that haven't existed in four years—places she's welcome to go and people who will not only talk to her, but actively want to.

Winnie isn't a helpless outcast anymore.

She can use that. She *should* use that.

One of the key defense mechanisms of a phoenix is to shine so brightly, their predators are temporarily stunned and unable to pursue.

At that thought—at a line from her ever-reliable Nightmare Compendium—the last of Winnie's ashes clear away. She suddenly finds herself looking forward to the party at the old museum, because from now on things are going to be different. All the Marcuses and Caseys and Peters will eat her dust as she pulverizes them on the obstacle course.

She *can* compartmentalize. She *is* a Luminary, burning bright and stunning people so they cannot see what hides within her flames.

5

Winnie is so nervous that even though she knows she should try to sleep an hour or two before the twins arrive—because otherwise, tomorrow is going to suck—she just can't seem to.

She has snuck out before. She did it barely two weeks ago for her first trial. It's not hard, thanks to the position of Darian's window over the roof. But that escape was for forest-related excursions; it felt virtuous, in other words. All she had to do was point to the bear banner on the back of her bedroom door and say, "I was doing it for the cause, Mom! *Loyalty!*"

Sneaking out to go to a party, however . . .

That'll be a lot harder to explain if she gets caught.

If Mom notices Winnie's zipped-up, stiff-backed version of herself that night, she gives no indication. She's too excited about news she got this afternoon: "Rachel really thinks it'll happen on Wednesday," she says over their pizza dinner. "She really thinks we're going to officially be back in the Luminaries on Wednesday."

"Voes vee?" Winnie asks through a mouthful of cheese and pepperoni. "Vat's villy exciting, Ma." She means it too, and her excitement over the party ticks up another notch.

When Mom finally goes to sleep, Winnie crawls into bed, where she stares silently at her shadowy popcorn ceiling and listens to a crow occasionally caw outside. It sounds grumpy.

At eleven thirty, Winnie creeps from her freshly washed covers to get dressed. She has no idea what to wear to an event like this, so she decides her usual daily fashion is sufficient: jeans, a T-shirt, sneakers. She does at least forgo her Save the Whales hoodie for her still-so-new-it-smells-like-heaven leather jacket that Emma and Bretta gifted her on her birthday.

At ten to midnight, Winnie slips through Darian's room, squeezes from his window, climbs down the roof onto the shed, and finally descends to solid earth. The same crow cackles at her; it sounds like it's on the front porch. *Careful, human, or I'll wake your mama!*

Winnie keeps glancing toward the window that belongs to Mom . . . but no face ever appears and no lights ever wink on. She reaches the sidewalk undetected, her heart pounding far harder than the exertion calls for. It doesn't slow when she hunkers to a seat on the curb either, to await the twins.

Cold air twines over her.

She is shivering by the time the twins do arrive a few minutes later in their dad's minivan. A window rolls down, and Bretta's curls gleam; she has added blue streaks. "Hey," she whisper-shouts. "Get in!"

Winnie shoots a furtive glance at Mom's window. Nothing. Silence and shadow and that darn crow over the window's eave. So Winnie slings into the back seat. It's delightfully cozy inside; it smells like the lilac perfume Emma usually wears.

Winnie yanks on her seat belt. "Your parents just let you take the van and go?"

"Nah," Bretta says as she accelerates with the buttery smoothness of an automatic vehicle. "Mom is out of town training a new networker, and Dad sleeps like a droll."

Winnie laughs at that. She has met the twins' dad, Kevin, once before, and she can easily imagine him draped over his bed, snoring like a droll—not that Winnie has ever actually *heard* a droll snoring. But it's a detail noteworthy enough to make it into the Compendium: *Vibrations from droll sleep exhalations can be felt up to two hundred feet away.*

As Bretta guides the car through neighborhoods and intersections, past stop signs and darkened houses, Winnie's heart doesn't calm like she thought it would once she'd finally Houdini'ed from her bedroom. Instead, it beats harder. Faster. A little fist that wants to punch right through her throat.

Bretta talks about when her third trial might be—how much it sucks that she and Fatima can't do it now because of the werewolf. Emma tells her to be patient; Bretta retorts she isn't a Sunday, thank goodness.

"If I *could* be any other clan, though," she adds, "I would one hundred percent choose Saturday. They have all the fanciest stuff."

"Not me," declares Emma. "I like being a Wednesday. We've always got each other's backs. Winnie—what about you?"

"Huh?" Winnie grunts from the back seat. She was only half listening.

"Winnie would choose *Friday*," Bretta says with a mischievous giggle. "To be with her *man*."

"Oh stop." Emma pokes her sister in the biceps before twisting around toward Winnie. "Unless . . . *is* he your man, Winnie? That was a very insistent 'no' you gave us in anatomy today."

"I plead the Fifth," Winnie replies because she has no idea what else to say. It is physically impossible to insist any more strongly than she did a few hours ago. "Now if *I* had to choose a clan, I would go for Monday—"

"I knew it," Bretta cries. She bangs the steering wheel. "I knew it! Didn't I say 'Backlit' was about her, Em?" *Bang!* "Also 'pleading the Fifth' is a non thing, Winnie, so it won't work here. More details, please!"

Winnie's seat belt suddenly feels tight. The heat suddenly feels less cozy, more cloying. Because here it is again—that juxtaposition of darkness grating up against the light. The three of them are literally on their way to a party honoring a guy Jay watched get ripped apart by . . . well, probably the Whisperer.

Yet right now, Bretta is more fixated on the possibility that Winnie and Jay are hooking up.

Winnie rubs at her forehead. She would be squealing and sighing and pestering Emma or Bretta if they were in her shoes, wouldn't she? Certainly, old Winnie would have—the Winnie of four years ago. Maybe even the Winnie of two weeks ago.

And the Winnie of two weeks ago would have also been really excited to have a coffee named after her, and really, *really* excited for the coming Nightmare Masquerade.

"Hey," Emma says, piercing into Winnie's thoughts with a tentative smile in the rearview. Unlike her sister, she seems to sense Winnie isn't loving this new conversation. "There should be a bag in the back seat. Do you see it? Because it's for you."

"For me?" Winnie pokes around in the dark until, sure enough, she finds a duffel bag propped against the opposite door. Outside, streetlamps flash past. The only light there is on the southernmost edge of town. It feels like they're moving at warp speed in a spaceship.

"What's in it?" Winnie asks, hauling the bag toward her—and genuinely grateful for the change in subject.

"Better clothes," Bretta says at the same time Emma offers, more politely, "A different outfit."

"Aw, come on," Winnie groans, unzipping the bag. "My wardrobe isn't that bad."

"Your wardrobe is *so* that bad," Bretta replies. "And ten bucks says Fatima will have brought you an outfit too."

"Har-dee-har." Winnie rolls her eyes. "Glad to know you all hate my clothes so much."

"But we don't hate *you*," Emma replies.

"Sure you don't." Winnie withdraws a very tiny black T-shirt, and her jaw sags. "Good lord, ladies, this is way too small."

Bretta snorts. "That is literally the point."

"If you got it," Emma agrees, "flaunt it!"

"I don't think I got it then." Winnie squints at the shirt. It's so small, she's not even sure it will stretch beneath her boobs.

"Everyone's got it." Bretta flips on the turn signal; the van slows at a gap in the night-dark trees to their left. "It's a state of being, Winnie."

"Then I *know* I don't got it."

"Ah, but"—Emma wiggles her eyebrows in the rearview—"you *will* as soon as you put that shirt on. Trust us. You're the Girl Who Jumped, and all eyes deserve to be on you."

All eyes deserve to be on you. That is exactly what phoenix-Winnie wants, even if it suddenly seems terrifying. Like truly: Who willingly shows this much skin? As far as Winnie can tell, it's just more places for nightmares to slash their claws into.

"If we were in the forest, yes," Bretta replies when Winnie voices her concerns aloud. "But this is a party, Winnie. A Luminary party. And trust me: that shirt is enormous compared to what some people will be wearing."

Bretta isn't lying. When she pulls them into the museum's old parking lot, Winnie instantly spies at least three people wearing what can only be described as bikini tops.

They must be freezing.

Bretta pulls the van into one of the few spots left. If Grayson would have been pleased by the turnout at his funeral, then he would be positively *thrilled* by the turnout at his party. Music and lights and teenagers—and older people too, like Darian's age—spill out of the museum's front doors.

Decades ago, this was the first city hall in Hemlock Falls, housing the original Council. But when the new, modern hall was built, this Art Deco building was handed off to eager Sunday professors determined to turn it into an educational experience for the town . . .

Until they abruptly shut it down six years ago. No one ever learned why, but the rumor was *politics*—namely that Dryden didn't like how much better the Nightmare Masquerade events at the museum were than the grand finale ball at the Saturday estate, so he made sure not only to shut down the Sunday party . . . but then to shut down the entire freaking establishment.

Peak Dryden, right there.

The museum's tall arched windows are gray and boarded up, and the glass dome in the center of the roof is dark, save for the occasional burst of light to blast through. A distant beat thrums, while the scraggly hedges now lean and sway against the gray walls as if they're as drunk as the partiers within.

Winnie hastily changes in the van's back seat. The shirt isn't *quite* as small as she feared, stretching all the way to her midriff. While the black jeans also included in the duffel reach high enough to leave only two inches of skin exposed. When she pulls on her leather jacket again, it covers anything she doesn't want seen. A few necklaces and bracelets await at the duffel's bottom, but Winnie doesn't take those. Clothes are easy to keep track of; jewelry, however, she's genuinely afraid she might lose.

By the time she tumbles from the car, freshly dressed, it's to find that Fatima has joined the twins. She holds up a brush. "Allow me."

Winnie sighs, but doesn't argue. She even musters a laugh—albeit tiredly—when Bretta points out, "I believe I won ten bucks." Sure enough, Fatima *has* brought clothes for Winnie to wear.

Black, of course. Everyone, Winnie now sees, is in black. She actually would have stood out more in her original outfit than she will in this Barbie-doll-sized tee.

"We're just smoothing the frizz," Fatima assures as she drags the brush through Winnie's hair. "And adding some braids . . . and a little hair spray . . ." A cloud of chemicals envelops Winnie like forest mist. "*Et voilà!*" She grips Winnie's shoulders and swivels her around to stare at her reflection in the car window.

Winnie doesn't look *that* transformed, but the frizz is gone, and Fatima has braided a few strands of hair on one side. It's part fairy princess, part hippie earth goddess, part subtle way to keep the hair out of her eyes.

Winnie doesn't disapprove.

"Thanks." She gives Fatima a shivery grin—it's so *cold* standing out here—and Fatima beams back. The braces on her bottom teeth sparkle in the colorful lights from the museum.

"Let's go," Bretta declares, scooping her arm into Winnie's. The velour of her long-sleeved shirt seems to shimmer against Winnie's leather. "Emma, if you take too long on your crutches, I *will* leave you behind."

"I expect nothing less!" Tonight, Emma's crutches have black scarves to match her knee-length dress. Fatima, meanwhile, struts along in black high-heeled ankle boots and a long, fitted black sweaterdress. If the twins look like they're here to party and dance, Fatima looks more like she has come to read poetry and nibble crudités.

For all Winnie knows, maybe you can actually do that here. The museum is so much *bigger* than she remembers—and far more crowded than any time she ever visited as a girl.

They pass people outside, chattering away while vape smoke and regular smoke coil around them. Some hold bottles, some have cans, some clutch bright red Solo cups, and Winnie is pretty sure she spots nightmare contraband passing around too. Melusine scales, ground phoenix feathers, and maybe even diluted banshee tears.

Where do they get it? she wonders, trying to keep abject horror off her face. She is cool. She is hip. She is a Luminary and it is just *totally* normal to break the rules on the use of extracted nightmare parts.

Another part of her wants to go study all that contraband. After all, you can use powdered phoenix feathers as an alternative to gunpowder in a pinch, and melusine scales? *They provide all the euphoric feelings of melusine blood,* the Compendium says, *but with only limited active healing properties.*

The scales are also hard as steel yet light as air, so Winnie has always wanted to examine one under a microscope.

No such luck tonight, though. Instead, she follows her friends inside, where body heat and a booming beat cascade against her. It's as overpowering as jumping off the waterfall, but also far more welcoming than her sledgehammer crash into the river below.

Voices echo in the welcome rotunda, where a staircase curves upward to the museum's second floor. A life-size skeleton of a droll used to hang here, and though the bones are long gone, the wires that held it still dangle. Disco balls spin from each one, and Winnie wonders if Grayson installed those. She wonders if all the spray-paint streaks on the walls and steps and banister were his handywork too.

She knows so little about him.

People shout at Winnie as she passes—sometimes her name, but more frequently, *Hey, Girl Who Jumped!* She recognizes a few, but most are just faces steeped in disco light, passed and gone before she can match a voice to a face.

She finds herself looking at each person anyway, searching for familiar ashen skin marked by two gray eyes.

Bretta finally navigates them into a long room that once served as a gallery for nightmare illustrations. It used to be Winnie's favorite room, and Dad would patiently sit at a bench in the room's center while she scoured and sketched and studied.

The walls are bare now, and the bench long gone. Winnie frowns at where it used to be—at where folding tables now sag beneath liquor bottles and punch bowls. It is more alcohol than Winnie has ever seen in her life. Literally. Even Gunther's just outside town doesn't have this much booze.

"The punch is really good," shouts a new voice, pushing into step beside

Emma. It's Katie Tuesday, her red hair in pigtails and her black miniskirt caroming around her thighs. "Xavier made it this time, so it's not too strong." As if to demonstrate this, she offers her Solo cup to Emma.

But Emma shakes her head. "No drinking for me tonight. I'm still on meds for the leg."

"Ah, too bad. Bretta?"

"I'm driving." Bretta grins. Then grabs at Winnie's elbow. "But Winnie here might want something."

Winnie's eyes widen. "No." Then a slightly less emphatic (because she is cool! she is hip!): "I'm good. Thanks." She wants to summon some obvious reason for abstaining, but she can't find one—*I have school tomorrow* is a bit too dorky. And *I don't drink because my family acts like circus clowns after consuming alcohol* doesn't sound great either.

Fortunately, Katie doesn't seem to care, and after verifying Fatima is also abstaining, she bounces off. "To the conservatory!" she exclaims. "If you can't take your trials yet, at least you can dance! Come on!" She beckons dramatically for all to follow, and since Bretta, Emma, and Fatima obey, Winnie does too.

They aim for a door in the room's corner. The music gets louder with each step, though it's not the conservatory they find on the door's other side. Just a hall filled with couches and a lot of vape smoke that smells like weed. After that room, though, they finally reach the glass double doors into the old conservatory.

This was always Dad's favorite space in the museum, with all the plants dripping and dangling, frilly and frondy. *It feels like stepping into a nineteenth-century estate,* he would say, and Winnie hates that she has now thought of him twice in the span of five minutes. She's not here to think of secret messages in birthday cards or locked mental compartments crammed with the past. She's here to burn so bright she stuns the world around her.

It *does* give her a slight jolt of satisfaction, at least, to know how much Dad would hate the way the glass-walled conservatory looks now, its elaborate tiles barren of pots and plants. This was a room built for stillness and green; now it is packed with bodies who dance and dance and dance to scare the nightmares away.

6

Winnie is boiling before she and her friends are to the fringes of the dance floor, so she slips off her jacket. Then glares when Dante Lunedì looks at her as if he likes what he sees. And although dancing has never really been her thing, Winnie will do it by golly, and burn this whole place to the ground if she has to.

Or that is the plan until Peter Sunday shows up and starts howling at her.

Literally, howling as if he were a wolf under the moon.

Winnie's dancing pauses. Her face scrunches up. "Because you got bitten!" Emma shouts over the music.

Oh, of course. Except Winnie doesn't like that. She doesn't like it at all, and when other people start howling too—when even her friends start howling and someone she can't see shouts, "Show us your scar!"—Winnie discovers spiders are hatching inside her skin.

This is worse than the funeral. Worse than being on the nightly news or having Marcus tell her he liked her more before. It's like being stuck on the Tilt-A-Whirl ride at the Masquerade's Floating Carnival. Nothing feels right side up. Everything is warped and wobbly. And suddenly Winnie's plan to burn bright feels so naive, so *stupid.* Because oh my god, what is she even doing here? Dancing and laughing and pretending that everything is fine? It hasn't even been twenty-four hours since Grayson died, but she's acting like she already forgot him.

Everyone is acting like they forgot him, even though this is supposed to be his memorial party.

Aroo! Aroo! People howl around Winnie, faces streaming into a Whisperer-warped smear of teeth and eyes and body heat. Except the Whisperer might not be real, and Winnie might have made the whole thing up.

"Show us your scar!" Casey shouts in a pause between howls. A few people are looking at her, but most don't even seem to know why they're howling. "Show us where it bit you, *arooo!*"

No, Winnie cannot stay here. She is going to be sick.

"I need . . . air," she pants at Emma, fanning her face as if her sudden overheating is from the dance floor. "I'll be . . . back."

"Want company?"

"No." Winnie says this too harshly. But she doesn't want company. She *really* doesn't. "I'll find you soon."

Then Winnie pushes away from her friends, from their warmth and their light, and sets off in search of the shadows she knows are always lingering nearby.

Although years might have passed since Winnie visited the museum, she remembers how to get to the bathroom on the second floor. She just prays it is empty and still operational. She wants to splash her face with cold water. She wants to calm her chattering teeth.

She finds an emergency exit stairwell. It shuts loudly behind her. The boom of the party briefly quiets. There are people in the stairwell, trudging up and down or making out against the wall like this is a perfectly acceptable place to do such a thing.

And against Winnie's very best judgment and very *deepest* wishes, her brain reminds her of something Jay said almost two weeks ago: *There are better places than the forest to make out.* She hopes he didn't mean here.

Then she scolds herself for caring.

On the second floor, she pushes into a long hall filled with beer pong tables and board games—all crowded with people, none of whom seem to be talking about or even thinking about Grayson Friday. Would he have loved knowing so many people turned up? Or would he have felt like Winnie, grating and scratchy and light-headed because none of it feels right?

Aroo, aroo! Show us your scar!

Was it fun to jump?

No, it wasn't fun. It wasn't like a Marvel movie or an Assassin's Creed game. In fact, it was all *so awful* that Winnie's brain erased most of it from her memory.

She is practically jogging through the room now, keeping her head down and hugging her leather jacket in a tight ball against her stomach. No one notices her, and she soon escapes onto the top of the main stairs in the rotunda. Here the noise is so intense, it's like the waterfall all over again, but this time with the sledgehammer and the pain and the sense that she will drown.

Worst of all, Winnie feels static scraping at the back of her neck. A little charged feather warning of thunder this way. *The Whisperer,* her body thinks, locking up so tight she can't breathe. *The Whisperer is here.*

Fortunately, Winnie's brain is smarter than her body. The Whisperer is not here; the Whisperer might not even be *real* if everyone else is to be believed; and it's just the noise and heat and chaos playing tricks on her.

"Breathe," she whispers to herself, pushing across the rotunda and into the next room. It's smaller, an antechamber that used to have statues of the first councilors in Hemlock Falls. Now it's empty, save for a single easel set up in the middle. On it, in crude permanent marker, are the words *We will miss you, Grayson Friday!* As if he just retired after forty years at the local bank.

All that's missing are some store-bought cupcakes.

Winnie stalks close to the easel. Taped below the words is a photograph, clearly printed from someone's inkjet. Despite the crap quality of the image, the energy of Grayson still exudes. His hair is thick and wavy in the photo, his green eyes bright even in this dark room. And his grin is that of a guy who gives zero craps about anything.

Winnie swallows. Her teeth are still clicking, but slower now. The spiders are less intense. *I'm sorry,* she thinks at Grayson's handsome face. *I'm so, so sorry.*

If only she had pulled her lanyard sooner during her second trial, then maybe someone else would have seen the Whisperer in real life too. Or maybe if she'd been more aggressive with Dryden Saturday in the auditorium eleven days ago . . .

She has gone over that encounter a hundred times, a thousand. Maybe at the end of the conversation, if she had shouted more or pushed harder at Mario and Darian to back her up, then *maybe* Dryden would have listened.

Or maybe if she'd just held on to Lizzy's camera a little bit longer during her third trial, then she could have captured actual footage of this dimension-warping chain saw of a nightmare. Then Johnny Saturday could be playing *that* every night instead of talking about how Winnie survived a werewolf bite.

And god, as screwed up as it is, Winnie almost wishes she could somehow lure the Whisperer out of the forest and right into downtown Hemlock Falls.

Then everyone would see.

Then everyone would believe.

Instead, here she is at a party while Saturday hunters and Tuesday scorpions risk their lives in the forest *at this exact moment* that people dance and laugh and booze themselves into oblivion. Even Emma, who almost died ten days ago at the claws of a harpy and spent a week in the hospital . . .

It's like nothing happened. Like Emma isn't wearing a cast and using crutches. Like Winnie didn't inject her with banshee venom and leave her in a bloodied coma on the forest floor.

That's why we're called the Luminaries, Winnie: we are lanterns the forest can never snuff out.

Are they really lanterns though, Grandpa Frank? Or is this just denial? Just numbing and pretending and wearing virtues like shields against nightmares that definitely do not care?

"Hey."

Winnie whips sideways to find Erica Thursday standing beside her. She hadn't heard the other girl approach. Erica's sharp heels were lost to the thrum of music and crush of voices.

Her black hair is pulled into a bun so tight, it tugs at the skin around her russet-brown eyes. In the poor light, her amber skin has lost its warm undertones, while her ever-perfect makeup appears unusually minimalist tonight—no fake lashes or sharp contouring. In fact, it looks as if she might be wearing only black eyeliner and lip gloss. Even her outfit is minimalist: a black turtleneck and black jeans.

Winnie pushes at her glasses. "Hi." She doesn't know why she's surprised to see Erica here. Erica is popular; Erica does what Luminaries are expected to do. She is a future councilor in the making.

But there's something about Erica's eyes right now—a brief parting of her usual stage curtain—that isn't what Winnie expects to see.

Grief.

Winnie blinks. "Did you know Grayson?"

Erica's lips compress. She is staring at the crude memorial poster. "Not really."

"Oh." And yet, Winnie is certain she senses sadness. It's tightly leashed and Erica almost has it under control. But not even four years apart can erase how well Winnie knows her.

Erica might look different, might wear makeup like a model on the runway and dress so stylishly, she'd make an influencer weep with envy, but she is still *Erica.*

Then it hits Winnie. *Of course.* "They threw a party for Jenna, didn't they?"

Erica's breath catches. The leash loosens ever so slightly—just a quick shudder in her chest. "Grayson did, yeah. He . . . even invited me."

"You were twelve."

"I know." Erica snorts. But it isn't an angry sound. If anything, it's amused. "I wanted to go too, but I made the mistake of asking my mom."

Winnie gasps. "No you didn't."

"I totally did." Erica's eyes—so dark in these shadows—flit Winnie's way. "Mom was furious. Even more furious than I would have expected, and I'm pretty sure she tried to stop Grayson from throwing the party." She shakes her head. "He didn't, though."

From what little Winnie knows of Grayson, this sounds on brand.

"Does she know you came tonight? For him?"

"Of course not. You think I have a death wish?" Erica lifts a single eyebrow. "Mom thinks I'm spending the night at Angélica's."

"And Angélica's mom thinks she's spending the night with you?"

"Something like that." Erica smiles. It isn't big, but it's genuine, lifting the edges of her mouth and crinkling into her eyes. "I did tell Papá, though. He, uh . . . well, you know him. He's more okay with this sort of thing."

Winnie does know Erica's dad, Antonio Jueves, and he is the literal opposite of Erica's mom in all ways: gentle where Marcia is harsh, lighthearted where Marcia is serious, and generous where Marcia is withholding. In fact, Erica, Jay, and Winnie all used to joke that he was the *Antonio-nym* to Marcia.

Winnie does not make that joke now. Although it does occur to her that, *Oh my god, we're having a civil conversation.* Not just civil either, but actually friendly. Erica isn't being her usual ice queen self—a perfect replica of Marcia—and Erica was even the one to initiate this conversation in the first place.

It also occurs to Winnie that she feels better. She doesn't feel so sweaty; the nauseated spiders have passed; and the howling has faded in her ears. Maybe it wasn't such a mistake coming to this party. If she can find a quiet spot, she can probably survive a few more hours here.

As if reading her mind, Erica dips her head toward the corner, to where a window hangs open and a draft steals through. "Maintenance access," she says by way of explanation. "Ladder goes all the way to the roof."

Then she bows her head, not quite an ice queen so much as a princess bidding adieu.

Winnie smiles.

Erica almost smiles back.

7

The ladder onto the roof is far more precarious than Winnie was antici-
pating. It's not the worst thing she has ever climbed—that distinction
goes to the hemlock tree Jay showed her in the forest. The one she
barely ascended in time to escape vampira fangs.

Which is also where she watched the Whisperer decimate those same
vampira as easily as a chain saw through grass.

Maybe because this *isn't* the forest and this *isn't* a climb to save her life,
the ascent feels a hundred times more terrifying. Each rung rattles and the
wind whips against Winnie, thick with music and sharp with cold. She
pulled her jacket back on before climbing, but failed to zip it up—a mistake
she deeply regrets. If she falls into the haze of blue shadows below, her ice
block of an abdomen will shatter into a hundred pieces.

Winnie isn't sure why she keeps climbing. She wanted a splash of cold
water to her face, not a potential fall to her death from the museum.

But it's like Erica set her a challenge, and now she has to see it through.
She also can't help but wonder what sort of place Erica might retreat to. Her
uniform of three-inch heels would not be well suited to this ladder.

Soon enough, the ladder reaches a metal landing that hugs the rooftop's
edge. Winnie hauls herself onto the platform, then hops three iron steps
onto the gently sloping roof.

Where she discovers that someone else is already there.

He lies on his back, one leg crooked up while the other hangs down. He holds a vape, and a beer bottle stands at attention nearby, its cap intact and condensation gathering on the glass like a rainstorm. To Winnie's surprise, he still wears his suit from the funeral, though the jacket is off and now he's just in the white button-up tucked into black pants.

Even in the darkness, Winnie can see that his eyes are glossy and bloodshot, and it occurs to Winnie in a vague sort of *aha!* that the lines of him are fuzzier than she's used to. As if he's a drawing she has only just begun shaping, mere pencil markings on a page.

Maybe, all those times she thought Jay was high, he wasn't.

Right now, he is unquestionably high.

Jay's eyebrows lift at the sight of Winnie, but he doesn't sit up. "You are the last person I expected to see coming up that ladder." His voice is rough; Winnie can't tell if it's from the vape or grief.

Probably both.

"Sorry to disappoint you." She almost turns around right there. But then decides even a stoned Jay is better than being howled at by fake werewolves.

She can't help but wonder, though, if Erica knew Jay was up here when she pointed out the open window.

And she can't help but wonder what it would mean if Erica did know. This is *definitely* a better place to make out than in the forest, and though Winnie hates herself for it, an uncomfortable heat surges up her neck at the thought of all the various people Jay might have brought here over the years.

She stomps across the roof. Her jacket swings open; night air sweeps against her stomach.

And she's pretty sure Jay's eyebrows rise an inch more at the sight of her skin.

To her vast annoyance, the heat in her neck reaches her face as she drops to a seat beside him.

In a rustle of black wool and white cotton, Jay finally deigns to sit up. He smells like weed. Wind pulls at his hair. "Beer?" He offers Winnie the bottle.

"Of course not," she snaps.

Which only makes him laugh, a sound like a wintery forest sigh. "What are you doing here, Wednesday Winona Wednesday?"

"Don't use my full name." She glares. "And what do you mean? It's a party. People attend parties."

"I *mean*," he drawls, "this is not exactly your scene."

"I'm a Luminary again. Therefore, it is my scene, Jay No Middle Name Friday."

"Is it though?" He takes a long drag on his vape. Holds the breath in his lungs. Then extends the vape Winnie's way.

Her glare deepens to vicious.

And he smiles, chest still expanded and breath still held. "That," he offers eventually as vape smoke drifts out over his teeth, "is what I'm talking about."

"Ugh, Jay." She jerks her gaze away from him and stares out over the trees. She was so distracted by him, she hasn't even bothered to take in the view.

And what a view.

Woods stretch toward the river before opening up to reveal a sliver of glossy water. The moon's reflection drags long, a waxing crescent turned lucent snake. Then it's more trees and the sky, big and open and for once not clotted by clouds.

Meanwhile, far at the edges of what she can see, Winnie spots the lights of downtown, twinkling and warm. Little promises that you can be safe there, that the forest can't get you if you'll only step inside.

But none of them can be trusted. They're just swamp fires pretending to be fairies, and they're even worse liars than Winnie is.

She hugs her knees to her chest. "I'm sorry I don't like smoking and drinking," she mutters. "It just doesn't appeal to me."

"And that's fine," Jay replies. He sets the vape aside. "It's one of the things I like about you."

"I didn't know you liked anything about me."

He grunts, a noncommittal sound that stings more than it should, and for several minutes, they sit in silence. Winnie watches the horizon, and Jay watches her. She *knows* he watches her because she can feel his eyes studying her profile while she gazes at the lying lights of downtown.

She isn't cold anymore.

Until eventually, she can't handle the staring a moment longer. She twists toward him. "So is this your famous make-out spot?"

Jay's eyebrows shoot to his hairline. "I'm sorry, what?"

"You told me that there were better places to make out than in the forest. Is this one of them?"

"Oh shit," he says, swooping up his beer and twisting off the cap. "What a thing to ask me, Winnie." He gulps back a long swallow. When he finally lowers it, a smell of yeast and sugar drifts Winnie's way. It's a welcome reprieve from the weed.

She wishes it were bergamot and lime.

"Winnie," he says, squaring his torso her way. "This is not one of my make-out spots."

"Ah, too bad." She shrugs. Then realizes a heartbeat too late how her words must sound.

Jay realizes too, and somehow his eyebrows rise even higher.

"I mean," Winnie quickly amends, "it's too bad for the world. Not for me."

"Right."

"*Right,*" she insists. Then, because she is desperate to change the subject, she says, "Tell me what Grayson was like."

Jay's jaw clenches. His muscles lock up. And for several seconds, Winnie is worried that she crossed some invisible force field and dug too close to the secret heart of him.

But then his answer emerges: "Fearless."

Ah. One more thing Grayson and Jay have in common then.

"Did he really steal a Hummer and drive it off the dam?"

"Yeah, he really did." Ever so slowly, Jay's muscles release. He grabs the bottle for another swig. "Don't you remember? It was all anyone talked about for days." *Drink. Swallow. Return bottle to rooftop.*

"They didn't talk about it to me." Winnie pulls off her glasses and frowns at the lenses, glinting in the night. "Outcast, remember?"

Jay winces. "Right. And it wasn't on the news."

"Why not?"

"Because it happened on Grayson's second trial, which the Saturdays were overseeing."

"Ah." The Saturdays—i.e., *Dryden*—do not appreciate negative attention. "Did they punish him?"

Another swallow. "No." Jay stares out over the trees. "I don't know why either. They even let him pass the trial—and obviously he became a hunter. But it was weird. The whole thing was just . . . weird. And now?" Another swig. Another head shake. "Now I'll never know why."

"I'm sorry, Jay." Winnie reaches out a hand, as if to take his. But then she stops halfway. Her fingers fall useless to the frozen roof.

"Me too." His gaze flicks to her hand. One heartbeat. Two. Wind whips against him, pulling up his hair. Until finally, he reaches out and takes her fingers in his own. Then he slowly levers himself back onto the shingles and stares up at the sky.

His grip is cold and damp from the beer bottle. For some reason, it makes Winnie think of the forest when it rains.

Jay's chest rises. His chest falls. He doesn't look at Winnie again, nor does he speak. The only sound is the music from the conservatory, the shouts and the laughter and the *darkness, darkness, light* of the Luminaries within.

Eventually Winnie joins him, lying back upon the roof beside him, her hand still clutched in his. And together, they watch the night pass and pretend that whatever this is between them is totally normal, totally fine and that the forest isn't lurking only a few miles away. Or that there isn't a four-year history trailing behind them, filled with hurt and loss and unanswered questions that Winnie can never wholly forgive him for . . .

Right now, Jay grieves, so right now, Winnie will stay with him, this lost boy in a suit that doesn't fit and a new title that fits him even less.

8

I t is almost 2:00 A.M. before Winnie finally gets home. She is so tired, her brain hurts. Her ears hurt too from all the noise. And that crow still sits on the roof and laughs at her while she sneaks back in. But Winnie has no trouble falling asleep and staying there as soon as she curls into bed.

She dreams of a wolf howling upon a rooftop.

Then she dreams of the Whisperer, hunting her through the forest while a full moon beams down—except that in this dream it has a new name. One that comes to her on banshee tears, sliding down her cheeks.

Pure Heart. Trust the Pure Heart.

She has no idea what that means. *Pure Heart* isn't in the Compendium any more than *Whisperer* is.

When the telltale *bzzzzzz* of her alarm sounds at eight, Winnie awakens with a smell like burning plastic in her nose. Her head throbs from too little sleep. She slams down the snooze button. Ten more minutes. She will sleep ten more minutes; then she can no longer delay the inevitability of time.

Thank the forest that classes start late in Hemlock Falls to accommodate corpse duty and last night's hunters . . . *and* to accommodate the frequent parties.

Winnie's heart pinches thinking of Grayson Friday.

Then it pinches tighter thinking of Jay. She held his hand for what seemed a lifetime, thought it was really only half an hour in the end. Her shivering eventually roused him like a revenant in the forest, and together they returned to the party. She found the twins playing a game of catch-the-source—where you try to catch a Wiffle ball using only a Solo cup filled with booze—and Jay vanished into the crowds.

She didn't see him again. She hates how much she wishes she had.

Winnie rolls to her side and squints at the Wednesday bear on the back of her door. It's fuzzy without her glasses, like a creature trapped in the forest's mist. And as tired as she might be, she did manage to assemble a plan in the wee hours of her partying night. All the howls, all her failed attempts to burn bright as phoenix . . . She can't continue like this. She needs to know she isn't going mad.

"The cause above all else," she murmurs. "Loyalty through and through." She yanks off her sunflower covers, warm and bright and kind—more lies like the lights of downtown—and fumbles her glasses off her nightstand.

The Wednesday bear sharpens. And Winnie nods good morning. It's time to start her Sunday.

She has work to do.

9

Nightmare Masquerade: An annual festival hosted in each Lumi-
nary city around the world intended to display new local night-
mare discoveries, the latest technological advancements, and new
methodological developments. The weeklong event culminates in
an elaborate masquerade.

Winnie doesn't go straight to the Sunday estate for the required weekend training. Instead, she veers her bike north, pedaling onto a pier
that hugs the Little Lake. Fog drifts lazily over the water, and a light
drizzle mists her glasses.

She just wants one person to tell her she isn't crazy. That's it—only one.
Then she can feel normal again. No more questioning her own sanity, no
more grenade shrapnel in the heart.

As she rolls north, an enormous circus tent rises before her. Though
it's used for the Nightmare Masquerade, signs now promise a WEREWOLF
TESTING SITE COMING SOON.

Once upon a time, the Masquerade was just a single party hosted on the
Saturday estate. Now it's a veritable spidrin of a festival, its web spread
all over Hemlock Falls and lasting seven days. Here beside the pier is where
the Floating Carnival will unfurl, colorful and brilliant in a way the forest
never can be.

Before Dad left, the Floating Carnival was Winnie's favorite part of the Masquerade. The booths and the rides and the funnel cake. Now, though, she just sees a place where the Whisperer could spill a lot of blood.

But hey, at least then people might believe it's real!

She hates herself for thinking that.

Winnie leans her bike against a bench overlooking the waters, then makes her way toward the tent's main entrance. People zoom about with boxes and crates and folding tables. In and out of the tent they move, Monday worker ants going where their councilor, Theresa Monday, barks and orders.

Winnie does not want to interact with that high-powered, boardroom-worthy lady, so she ducks into the tent behind a man pushing a dolly. His boxes are labeled with various dire warnings: *Fragile! Toxic! Handle with care!*

Inside the tent, the clatter of voices, ripping tape, and groaning tables pummels against Winnie with all the ferocity of a harpy dive-bombing from the sky. She has to pause for a second beside a booth near the entrance to get her bearings.

ARCHIE'S FAMOUS FUNNEL CAKES, the sign reads, and Winnie realizes with a jolt of horror that they aren't just assembling a testing site—they're also assembling the Floating Carnival. Which . . . of course they are. Of *course* Dryden would use this chaos as an opportunity to get started on the only thing he really cares about.

As Winnie stands there, her breath suddenly frothy and teeth suddenly grinding, a rapid-fire *pop, pop, pop!* hits her ears. *Mario.* Just the man she wants to see.

She pushes away from the booth, weaves through more people and boxes until she finally reaches the scientist in charge of testing. "Mario," she greets.

He glances up from a tablet, a pink bubble swelling before his face. Recognition sets in. *Pop!* "What are you doing here?"

Winnie sniffs. "It's great to see you too this fine Sunday."

Mario at least has the decency to flush, his olive skin darkening toward mauve. "Sorry. It's just that only Mondays and Saturdays are supposed to be here." His brown eyes sink into frustrated slits at the name *Saturday*. It would seem Mario is about as pleased that the Masquerade continues as

Winnie is. Likely even less so, since he's the one having to cram in all this testing before the big event.

"I need to talk to you," Winnie says. "It's about . . . Grayson Friday."

Mario's bubble deflates mid-blow. "This is not a good time, Winnie. Or place."

"I know." She scoots closer. "But it's important. *Please.*"

He sighs, chest rising against his white lab coat. "Fine." He scowls. "This way." He doesn't wait to see if she follows (she does, of course) before swiveling toward the back of the tent. The navy-striped canvas opens onto the Little Lake. That's where the Ferris wheel will go.

Wind sweeps over them as they exit. Mario cuts left, to where two portable toilets glow blue. Winnie is relieved to *not* smell them as Mario leads her behind one.

He slides his tablet under one arm and pats at his lab coat pocket. One heartbeat later, a fresh pack of gum appears. "So what's up, Winnie? I don't have much time."

"I need to know what killed Grayson Friday." Grayson's face—blurry and unformed on a shadowy printout—comes to her mind . . . until it's Jay's face Winnie sees instead, with red-rimmed eyes and skin pale as moonlight. "It wasn't really the werewolf, was it?"

Mario doesn't respond. He just smacks his gum more loudly and bounces his weight from foot to foot.

"Well?" Winnie presses. "It's a yes-or-no question."

"Actually, it's an 'I don't know' question." Mario glares at her. "Do I think it was your Whisperer? Yeah, maybe. The, uh . . . *damage* to Grayson is similar to what we've seen that thing do before."

Your Whisperer. Winnie's stomach constricts.

"But," Mario finishes on a defeated sigh, "there were undeniable signs of a werewolf at the kill site too. Tufts of hair and bite marks on the body parts."

Her stomach constricts even more. "But did . . . did Jay actually see it? The werewolf, I mean." As much as Winnie wanted to ask Jay about it last night, she never worked up the courage. It felt too insensitive, too cold. *Hey, I know your heart is breaking, but can you tell me what you remember while I hold your hand?*

"Jay didn't see the werewolf," Mario says, "but he also didn't see the Whisperer. So if you want my honest opinion . . ."

Winnie holds her breath.

"All signs *do* point to Whisperer."

"Ah." Winnie's shoulders slump. She needed to hear that. Oh *god,* she needed to hear that.

"The problem is," Mario continues, "we are also dealing with a werewolf—and this town has a bad history with those." He waves absently toward downtown, where the Diana alarm was refashioned seventeen years ago to warn of daywalkers too. "So Whisperer or not, I still have to catch this *lupinotuum.*"

"Okay, but how long will that take?" Winnie wags her head. "Everyone is already complaining the testing is taking too long to set up—"

"Oh really?" Mario scowls. *Pop!* "I hadn't noticed."

"And people are dying because of a nightmare no one but me . . . and *you* believe in. Grayson Friday is dead. *I* almost died in the same way. Who else has to get hurt?"

Mario shrugs helplessly. "I don't know what you want me to say, Winnie. By all means, if you've got a solution, then give it to me. We've got Alpha scorps combing the forest all day. We've got sensors and cameras and more sensors lined up throughout the forest. *Nothing* is turning up. Not a Whisperer and not a werewolf either. It's like . . ." He pauses, eyebrows lifting as if what he's about to say makes no sense. He says it anyway: "It's like these nightmares only show up when you're around, Winnie. Or like you've got some special power that only lets you see them."

"Well, this power sucks then." As Winnie utters this—and as she crosses her arms over her chest, half sullen, half defensive—a little spark ignites in the back of her brain. She can't see it yet, but soon . . .

Soon it will take over. A bonfire on a cold spring night.

"If this new nightmare is out there, Winnie," Mario assures her, "it *will* show up eventually. We just have to be patient."

"Right. Because the Whisperer itself is so patient." Winnie's arms drop. "Well, thanks for talking to me, at least. Let me know if you learn anything, okay?"

"Of course," he replies. "You know I always do. And hey . . ." He fumbles at his pockets again, but this time, he retrieves a crumpled paper. "This has log-in info for testing results. It's available via the usual hunter website, if you want to track our progress."

Winnie glances at the page, creased from Mario's folding it. It shows the Monday scroll at the top, then numbered instructions for how to access the citywide werewolf results. *Updated daily,* it reads, *at midnight!*

"Thanks," Winnie murmurs, refolding the paper and shoving it into her pocket.

"No problem." *Pop!*

After a muttered goodbye, Winnie sets off to retrieve her bike. Surprisingly, her mission hasn't made her feel much better. Sure, she might not be going crazy, and that is one thousand percent a relief. But if finding the Whisperer hinges on first finding the werewolf, then that isn't a great development.

For one, it could take ages to catch the werewolf.

For two, there's a tiny, secret part of Winnie that is worried maybe the werewolf isn't even *bad*. She knows it makes zero sense; she knows it's anathema to what the Compendium teaches and what Luminaries believe about the relationship between nightmares and humans . . .

Yet her heart can't seem to let that little hunch go. It's almost like she identifies with the creature—like she *pities* him because she too has been blamed for something she never actually did. But while her punishment was to be cast out of the society, his will most certainly be death.

If only Winnie could remember the werewolf bite. If only she could recall what happened beneath those sledgehammer waves.

Cold wind sweeps off the Little Lake by the time Winnie kicks onto her bike again. She smells a coming rain.

10

That evening, as rain breaks over Hemlock Falls, Winnie boots up her family's computer in the living room. It's loud as an airplane on the runway—or what Winnie imagines an airplane might sound like given that she's never actually been on one.

It makes her think of something else that hums and whispers too.

Once the welcome screen appears, Winnie clicks open a browser and navigates to a website used only in Hemlock Falls. If anyone outside ever lands here, it will look like an innocent page for a florist that went out of business six years ago.

Shopping cart, the site says in the top corner, and with a few clicks and a few more taps at the keyboard, Winnie opens up the true site she's looking for. *Hunter Updates,* it declares at the top. No frills, just a black screen and text pale as vampira skin beneath the moon. To scroll down is to move backward in time, revealing all the nightmare locations reported by the clans each night. First the dates, then the hunters attending, then a rough map of the forest with different spots marked in different symbols.

There's a new addition, though, above all the kill coordinates. Now a bright red link declares *Monday Test Results.*

Winnie clicks it. A page appears, white background with basic black text.

HEMLOCK FALLS TESTING PORTAL
SUNDAY, APRIL 7

TEST RESULTS for PREVIOUS DAY:
Tests Administered: 17
Positive Results: 0

AVAILABLE TESTING LOCATIONS:
Monday hospital, BY APPOINTMENT ONLY
Sunday estate auditorium, COMING SOON
Floating Carnival, COMING SOON

DO YOUR CIVIC DUTY AND GET TESTED AS SOON AS A SITE IS
AVAILABLE NEAR YOU!

Well, it ain't fancy, but like the hunter site, it gets the job done.

Winnie hits the back button to return to the kill coordinates. As Aunt Rachel said yesterday at the funeral, more hunters means more nightmares slain . . . and that means more symbols upon the maps. *So* many symbols. Winnie has never seen anything like this, not even during her four years of exile when she used to obsessively check the hunter site just so she could feel connected.

She scrolls down until she reaches the map from Friday night—a map Jay must have turned in even as his heart was breaking.

She swallows at the thought of that. And she wishes, silly as it is, that she had been there to help him. His name is right there, second on the list after Grayson Friday, which now says *deceased* in parentheses.

Winnie's gaze drifts toward the landline phone on the desk's edge. She could call Jay. He gave her his number two weeks ago; she hasn't used it yet because she hasn't had any reason to.

And she definitely has no reason now that he is Lead Hunter. There's no way he has time to keep training her. Plus, last night on the roof—whatever the hell that was—might as well have never happened. Winnie is 100 percent certain she is sitting here thinking of Jay while he is *not* thinking of her.

She forces her attention back to the screen, dragging the mouse over every point indicated. A blue dot for hellions in the northwest, a green triangle for a banshee beside the southwestern shore. Red squares for manticore hatchlings, still reappearing every night beside the lake. When she clicks on each symbol, a window pops up detailing the kill site: what nightmare died, how many, and who did the slaying.

Jay's name pops up often. Grayson's too.

Winnie's teeth click slowly, her jaw slightly askew so her top right canine connects directly onto the bottom one. *Click, click, click.* The sound taps out in near-perfect unison with her clicks upon the mouse.

As she gets closer and closer to the top right of the map, she wonders if maybe they wouldn't have included Grayson's deadly encounter. Like out of respect for his family or something. But then her cursor reaches the open meadow known as Stone Hollow, where a black X awaits.

Winnie blinks at it. Why does she know this area? Why does she feel like she has seen this X before?

Then it hits: this is where the X on Dad's map is too. The secret map he hid for her at the Monday library.

Winnie's fingers freeze atop the mouse. Her heart seems to freeze too, and her glasses slide slowly down her nose. *It could be just coincidence,* her brain provides even as her heart booms out: *But what exactly are the odds?*

Good, she decides. The odds have to be good. There are so many hunters out each night, so many nightmares to kill . . .

Winnie clicks on the black X. *Werewolf,* the window reads. *4:33 A.M. Still at large.*

There's nothing else there. No other description, no hint that this is the spot where Grayson Friday went from vibrant and living, his green eyes taking in a world he wasn't afraid of, to ripped apart in a thousand little pieces.

No way it was the werewolf. That is the first thought Winnie has because it is the same thought she has had for almost two days now. The neural pathways are primed as a bobsled chute, and that particular idea is ready to glide, glide, glide. *No way it was the werewolf who killed Grayson.*

The second thought Winnie has, though, is about her dad. It takes a minute to assemble, its bobsled runners off to a slower start. But once it gets going, it's a *beast*. Like the giant rocket in Mario Kart, it just inciner-ates every other neural impulse in its path.

Bright, insistent, terrifying.

This is where Grayson died and this is where Dad's map leads. That means Mondays and Tuesdays will have found what Dad's map leads to. When a hunter dies, his body isn't left for corpse duty to find. There is a limit to how much death is part of life for the under-sixteen crowd in Hemlock Falls, and cleaning up one of your own parents most assuredly qualifies as *too far.* So when a hunter dies, Mondays come in to retrieve the body . . .

Or body parts, in this case.

Then Tuesdays come in to secure the kill site and get statements from any hunters who were there. Sometimes, if the nightmare is a nasty one, they'll rope off the spot for days—and set up extra Alpha patrols at night, just in case the spirit's mist creates the same monstrous creature in that area again.

In other words, if Dad's map leads to a physical item that Winnie is sup-posed to find, if it will take her to another clue in this scavenger hunt she abandoned, then that physical item is going to be discovered soon.

If it hasn't been already.

There might even be Tuesdays on the way to Winnie's house right now to arrest her. The Lambdas this time, who are in charge of tracking and disposing of Dianas.

Strangely, Winnie feels a cool sort of detachment grip her. Perhaps be-cause there is nothing she can do at this *exact* moment. It's almost night; the mist will rise soon, and if Tuesdays or Mondays found something at the kill site, wouldn't they have come for her by now? It has been a day and a half since Grayson died.

Winnie leans across the desk and snags the phone. When the dial tone hums out, her fingers do not dial Jay's number. Instead she scrolls the mouse back to the top of the page to where seven phone numbers glow in white pixels. Winnie chooses the one farthest to the right; gentle beeps fill the living room; her glasses slide down her nose again.

Then the phone is ringing and she's holding the receiver to her ear.

"Sunday clan," a voice chimes. "How may I direct your call?"

"Corpse duty," Winnie says, her voice a bit crackly, a bit rough. She clears her throat. "I need to talk to the person running tomorrow's corpse duty."

Nine days ago when Winnie first found Dad's secret messages in the birthday cards, she was angry. But more than that, she was scared. What if someone were to find the clues Dad left behind? What if her family was blamed *again* for colluding with a witch they hadn't known about?

Thus she decided she must clean up Dad's trail before anyone could discover it.

Luck favored her, for when Winnie traced the first secret message to the library, she found that Dad's hidden drawing was still intact. If anyone had found the image in the last four years, they hadn't understood what they were looking at. Winnie herself was barely able to solve the various codes and ciphers. It was only right after nearly dying on her third trial and then being told her family would likely be Luminaries again that she *finally* decoded what Dad's messages were trying to say.

I was framed.

At first, Winnie was too shocked to fully process that message. *I was framed.* Did that mean another Diana had framed him? Or did it mean a Luminary had? And why would anyone do that—for what purpose? How did Dad even *know*?

However, the more Winnie stewed over those questions, the more her fear of being caught by the Tuesday Lambdas transmuted into ire.

Incandescent, volcanic ire that suffused every drop of her being. Because if Dad was framed, then why did he run away? If he was *innocent,* then why did he leave behind a convoluted set of clues for his *twelve-year-old daughter* to follow?

Who does that? What innocent man abandons his wife to pick up the broken pieces of his family and then makes his child solve the crime he was allegedly framed for?

The longer the rage simmered and stewed, turning Winnie into a miniature Pompeii just waiting to blow, the more she realized that there was no reason at all to follow Dad's map into the forest. Now that she and her family were essentially Luminaries again, nothing in Winnie's life would change by proving his innocence. All she would do was prove he was a coward.

And that was why Winnie shoved the memories, the clues, and the fury, into a lockbox and stuffed it deep, deep into the pit of her intestines. It's why she threw away the key and scarcely glanced in that box's direction for a full nine days.

Because screw that guy. Screw him and whatever vehicle he rode out on four years ago. She doesn't need her dad. Her family has made a new life for themselves without him. And whatever he wanted her to find in the forest can stay hidden there for the rest of time.

Except now . . .

Now, that unknown *thing* might actually be found by someone. Now, the magmatic tide has turned against Winnie, and she can't just ignore the secret map from the library. There's too much at risk for her family again.

She will have to unlock the box marked *Dad* and let everything inside free.

Winnie just hopes she survives the eruption.

HEMLOCK FALLS TESTING PORTAL
MONDAY, APRIL 8

TEST RESULTS for PREVIOUS DAY:
Tests Administered: 19
Positive Results: 0

AVAILABLE TESTING LOCATIONS:
Monday hospital, BY APPOINTMENT ONLY
Sunday estate auditorium, UNDER AGE 18 ONLY
Floating Carnival, COMING SOON

DO YOUR CIVIC DUTY AND GET TESTED AS SOON AS A
SITE IS AVAILABLE NEAR YOU!

C H A P T E R

11

S unday corpse duty runs differently from Wednesday corpse duty, and it's jarring to Winnie at first. It's not merely the fact that the participants meet in a different place—at the *Sunday* estate instead of in the forest directly—but the person in charge is also scattered and inefficient.

Finn Sunday, fourteen and recently in charge of the operation, fumbles with a tablet that has all the nightmare corpse coordinates from the night before. No non bodies this time; Winnie is surprised how relieved she is over that fact. She never used to think about nons or worry over their deaths . . .

Which she now realizes makes her an unfeeling monster. Although it's not like she was born this way. She was *trained* to feel nothing over nons since the day she was born. Culture runs thicker than blood, and all that. Even now, Winnie can remember exactly how Chad Wednesday sounded on her first morning of corpse duty: *Death is a part of life,* he laughed at her. *Get used to it, Little Win-Win, or you won't last a week inside the forest.*

"Uh," Finn says, swiping at the tablet. The sun has barely begun its ascent; the map glowing on the screen lights his babyish face up like a ghost. "I guess we can start by the parking lot where this . . . uh, this sylphid is. And then there's a bunch of manticores by the shore . . . We'll loop over to get 'em. Oh wait, there's a droll arm over here too."

Winnie has to bite her tongue not to interfere.

Or to point out that Finn is mispronouncing the word "droll." *The "o" is long. Have you never paid attention in class before?* This is actually a silly question, because she is in class with him, thanks to her demotion to eighth grade at the Sunday estate, so she can say with great certainty he doesn't pay attention.

He is also friends with Winnie's cousin Marcus, and that fact automatically makes him unbearable.

Though Winnie has no desire to call attention to herself this morning (or ever), when Finn ends the huddle without giving instructions, she can't stay silent. After all, they've got three four-wheelers, and people need to know exactly where they're going. Worse, Finn has missed pointing out not two, but *three* corpses near the southwestern shore of the Big Lake, and if you leave a corpse in the forest, you're going to end up with a revenant.

That's just science.

So Winnie finally barks, "Oh my god, give me that." She snatches the tablet from him, and to his credit, he doesn't look upset so much as relieved—as do the three other Sundays, two Tuesdays, and three Thursdays with them.

"Elaine, take your crew to the northern side of the lake," Winnie declares. "Hector, you're staying on the western side. And then Finn, we're circling over to the east. You all have your coordinates?" Now it's Winnie's face that glows in the screen—as do Hector's and Elaine's, since they each have a tablet too.

It's fancy, and Winnie almost wonders why the Wednesdays don't use tablets too . . . until she gets her answer a few moments later. The instant the screen is off, she can see all the smears and streaks from dead nightmare guts. Gross.

And also peak Sunday to have tech that's great for a classroom but crap in the field.

"I'm driving," Winnie says as everyone heads for their four-wheelers. These, at least, are just like the Wednesday clan's.

It takes a solid fifteen minutes to get north past the Monday and Tuesday estates, and the full light of morning brightens around them, shifting the world from colorless night to fledgling spring green. It is well and truly dawn, the sun a promise lightening the eastern sky.

The four-wheeler bumps and bounces through the trees, a crude path Winnie has taken many times. Then the red sensors of the forest's edge appear; Winnie swerves around them . . . and the world transforms. Green erases. Birdsong silences.

Strangely, Winnie feels more at ease as soon as they're over that line. It is the opposite of the funeral; the forest settles her, welcomes her. As if within the dawn shadows, she no longer has to pretend to be someone she's not. The forest, after all, never pretends. *I am dangerous and I will eat you. Do you dare come inside?*

Winnie's fellow Luminaries rarely speak, not even when gathering the corpses, which takes a full hour. And where Winnie had expected to see signs of the Whisperer—especially after what happened with Grayson—she doesn't. All the nightmare remains they retrieve were clearly killed by Sunday hunters: one sylphid, three manticore hatchlings, and a hellion.

The most interesting thing they find is a droll arm, enormous and meaty and almost as large as Winnie's whole body.

Drolls: These humanoid nightmares can grow as large and as heavy as a tractor-trailer cab. Known for hoarding treasures, drolls are particularly drawn to shiny objects and anything gold or silver.

Actually, Winnie doesn't understand why they have to retrieve the arm. It isn't as if the single body part will reanimate as a revenant . . . will it? Winnie chews her lip as she imagines the possibilities. As her mind scrolls through the Compendium, a search engine hunting for some line or reference she might have missed.

When she can't think of anything, she makes a mental note to ask Mario when she drops off the arm . . . *Wait,* her brain snaps out. *You're not delivering these bodies. You're not here for actual corpse duty. Remember the map? Remember the volcanic box labeled "Dad"?*

Her breath hisses out. Somehow, even with this stupid tablet that is now grimy with nightmare viscera, her mind was sucked completely into the cold air against her cheeks. Into the mutilated corpses slumped across the four-wheeler's flatbed, smelling of earth and blood and rot.

She almost doesn't want to leave it all. Actually, she *definitely* doesn't want to leave it all to finish a task she should never have had to start in the first place.

"Okay," she says, once the droll arm is strapped down—they have to bungee-cord it because it doesn't want to lie nicely atop the other bodies. "You're driving now, Finn, and I'm leaving."

"What?" This is from Lucille Thursday, who looks appalled that Winnie would abandon them to Finn's poor leadership. Or maybe it's just horror that Winnie plans to strut off into the forest by herself.

Which is fair.

"I'm, uh, going that way." Winnie points vaguely southeast. "My house isn't far." This is a line she practiced last night in the mirror. It's not a lie—she *does* live in that direction . . . eventually—so it comes out with a decent heft of confidence behind it. Hopefully no one will question why she is going home from this location and not at least riding in the four-wheeler to the street.

But then Finn comes up with an explanation all on his own: "Oh, right. You and Jay Friday are hooking up, right?"

"*What?*" Winnie blurts this so loudly that Lucille and a boy named Elliot flinch. And her follow-up "*No!*" is even louder.

Which only causes everyone to exchange smirks. As if somehow her emphatic rejection has proven Finn right.

"Have fun," Finn says with a dramatic wink that earns a few laughs.

Winnie's eyes screw shut. She sucks in a long, crisp breath that stinks of dead things. "Yep," she makes herself reply—because this is better, isn't it? If they all think she's going over to the Friday estate to see Jay, then the town is way less likely to guess what she's *actually* about to do. Better to endure the snickering than have someone give her a second thought—or worse, tell a Sunday in charge that she stayed behind in the forest.

"Bye," Winnie forces out before veering away.

"Have fun, Girl Who Jumped!" Finn calls at her back. "Don't get bitten again!"

Don't get bitten again. Like it's all a grand joke. Like this jagged scar on Winnie's right arm is just a wee paper cut, and she really should be more careful when handling werewolves!

Culture runs thicker than blood. That's what Dad always used to say about the Luminaries. About the clans and how everyone conforms to their respective virtues even if it's not really who they are.

"They?" Winnie whispers to herself. "Shouldn't it be *we*?" She pushes into a jog. The rubber soles of her sneakers pound over pine needles and moss. Soft earth that feels as if it still clings to winter's last snow.

Silver maple. Black walnut. Balsam fir. Winnie rounds the trees, following a map imprinted on her brain. Clouds clot in overhead. Johnny Saturday *had* mentioned more rain on the way. Winnie hopes it doesn't hit while she's out here.

Soon, icy morning wind bites against Winnie as the space between trees widens. Stone Hollow waits ahead. She sees no one amid the natural monoliths, but it's so exposed, she lingers within the trees, half crouched atop the shadowy pine needle floor.

It's strange to see the wide meadow and stones. Clouds might darken the sky, suspended above like guards on a prison wall, and the spirit's magic might leach away most color, but it is still a thousand times brighter than the last time she was here, during her third trial. No ghost-deer sprint across the field. No slithering whispers fill the air. Winnie wonders if Emma's blood still smears the rock from twelve days ago.

She's glad she isn't near enough to find out.

Staying within the trees, Winnie circles the field. The X on her dad's map could lead to any spot within this field or the stream beside it, but it makes the most sense for her to start searching at the crescent-shaped stream. That is Grayson's kill site, so that is where someone else is most likely to stumble on Dad's next clue.

Winnie reaches the western side of the field. Orange tape drapes across the forest here like a toxic spidrin web, looped and stretched around white birch trees rising up from the cold earth.

Winnie stops moving. This is where Grayson died. This is where Jay found the body parts of his Lead Hunter. She drops to a squat beside the orange tape, letting her muscles relax and her breathing steady. If there is anyone here, they are quiet as a basilisk.

She adjusts her glasses several times, squinting over the terrain. There is little to see from this distance beyond the stream's silty, rocky shore, curving around like a crescent. That running water helped protect her during her third trial by sending ghost-deer leaping another way and drawing the Whisperer after them . . .

Winnie swallows. She navigates through the tape like a thief through security beams. Duck, bend, shimmy, crouch until she is through. And *now* she can clearly see what happened. Boot prints are stamped everywhere in the silty shore—likely from the Mondays and Tuesdays who cleared the scene. Maybe even from Jay. *Maybe* even from Grayson.

It's what Winnie glimpses when she peers backward, though, that makes her stomach revolt.

Blood. So much blood.

She's never seen anything like it. She has to clap a hand to her mouth to keep from crying out. The birch trees' white bark is streaked in line after line after smear after spray. Like someone came out here with a can of brownish-red paint and started flinging. A royally screwed-up version of Blue Man Group.

Distantly, Winnie supposes it might not be blood but just actual paint. Viscerally, though, she knows that is impossible. *This* is what remains of Grayson Friday. Not ashes in the lake, but blood on white trees.

Winnie's fingers turn to claws, digging into the skin around her mouth. She is having trouble breathing.

This could have been you, her brain reminds her. *This* should *have been you.* Then, fast on the heels of that thought comes another: *How the hell can anyone think a werewolf did this?* That thought is a bright buoy in a gush of horror saturating her brain.

The werewolf could not have caused this scene. Winnie doesn't have to be a Monday or a Tuesday trained in nightmare forensics to recognize that. The wide spray of blood wasn't from a body getting slashed to bits right *next* to the trees. Grayson was ripped apart in multiple places; his death happened all over this site. Limb by limb, organ by organ.

It's horrific. It's monstrous. And it makes no sense at all. Why, why, *why* would a nightmare do this to a person?

To judge a nightmare with human emotion, the Compendium states, *or to anthropomorphize them in any way is to fundamentally misunderstand their inner motivations and decision-making. They do not operate according to Maslow's pyramid of needs, but rather to an arrangement of needs that is entirely their own.*

Winnie swivels back toward the stream. The river and last night's rain have washed away any blood that might have marked the stones beside the shore. But the birch trees with their skeletal white can hide nothing.

Nor can the half-submerged log in the middle of the stream. Even at this distance, Winnie can see something happened to it. Or something happened *on* it.

She tromps in—no concern for the freezing water. *Splash, splash, splash.* The water quickly deepens. It kicks up to her knees by the time she reaches the log, where three bolts poke from the wood like a pincushion. Loosed by Jay or by Grayson, Winnie can't say. And it doesn't really matter. They were aiming *here*. Into the stream. Not across the stream. Not at the stream's edge. But right here at the heart of the running water.

No one may know why most land-based nightmares avoid running water, but the fact of the matter is that they do.

Not the Whisperer, though. Of course not the Whisperer.

A hurried scan and a hurried splash around the log reveal nothing more to be found. The water rises to Winnie's thighs. Cold, cold, cold and soaking up her jeans toward her abdomen.

There is no sign of anything left from Dad. There are no clearly tampered-with stones in the water, and no visibly dug-up holes upon either shore. Short of bringing a metal detector out here and roving over the area like a morbid treasure hunter, Winnie has no way of knowing if Dad's next clue was ever hiding in this stream—assuming it's even a thing she is meant to *find*. For all she really knows, he wrote a message in the silt four years ago and it's long gone.

She hopes that's the case. She wants to be done with this and his clues and all the memories that ever tied her to him.

Winnie is about to slosh back to shore so she can methodically search Stone Hollow next, when sunlight glints on a stretch of rapids nearby. *Except the sun isn't out.* Winnie eyes snap to the clouded sky; the low clouds are practically reaching for her now, ready to erupt.

Winnie charges to where a small pool gathers between two stones. Unnaturally placed stones, she realizes as she studies them—and as the water continues to flash and beam around the stones.

She glances around her; there's still no one, so she thrusts both hands into the pool. Her fingers dig into slimy detritus and silt gathered over substrate. Her dexterity vanishes by the second, her legs already icy and toes long lost to numbness.

But *something* was glinting, and that *something* might be what Dad wanted her to find.

Her fingers scrape a box, metal and cold. Unlike the stones around it, there's no algae to string across it or dead leaves to cling and coat. Not even silt has gathered here.

It's almost as if someone has recently handled it.

Water sloughs off Winnie as she rises, lifting the box into the stormy light. It's a simple silver tin like for storing cookies, and the longer she squints at it, the more she realizes it *has* most definitely been tampered with.

There are scratch marks around the edges, and it's dented. This used to be sealed and airtight. It isn't anymore.

Winnie's heart booms faster as she pries her frozen fingers under the lid and pulls, pulls . . . Then it is open and Winnie can see inside.

Except she doesn't know what she's staring at. Scrunched-up moss is tucked within, and pounded into the center is a spherical indentation. It reminds her of a nest, except the bird is missing and it's all soaking wet.

What the actual hell? she thinks. Then out loud, "What the actual hell?" Is this what Dad wanted her to find four years ago? Winnie is so confused, she has no space to be angry at him. Nor space to be relieved this hasn't been found by Mondays or Tuesdays yet. It's all just a giant, glowing question mark hovering above her head.

One thing *is* clear, though: Winnie can't leave this here and risk it being found now. Even if it wasn't left here by Dad, it's safer for her to assume it *was* until she figures out what the heck it is and what she ought to do with it. She returns the lid to the tin and spins around to retrace her steps to shore . . .

When her eyes meet someone standing there. She has no idea how long he has been watching her, no idea what he saw her do, but it's too late now to hide the cookie tin.

And judging by the stoop in his posture and the spark in his gray eyes, Jay is not pleased to see her.

12

W hat are you doing?" Jay calls as Winnie sloshes toward shore. His jaw is clenching and his fingers are flexing and fisting at his sides. Behind him, birch trees creak and sway. He is almost as pale as they are, and with his red buffalo flannel, he melts right into the stripes and splatters of blood.

Winnie has all of ten seconds to find an answer for his question, and those ten seconds fly by fast as a charging hellion. She reaches the shore; water pours off her; and vaguely, it occurs to her that her toes are numb and she is shivering.

The tin filled with moss is clutched against her chest. It too is freezing, and Jay's attention is very clearly locked upon it. "What are you doing?" he repeats. His gray eyes rise to meet hers—and his hands lift slightly too. "And why, Winnie, are you holding a dampener?"

Winnie blinks at him while her hastily assembled lie about corpse duty (that he would never have believed anyway) evaporates in a heartbeat. "A . . . what?"

"That." He points at the cookie tin. "A Diana dampener, Winnie. Why are you holding one?"

Winnie's gaze lurches down, her jaw slackening while gas and dust collapse into a very cohesive baby star inside her brain that says, *Oh yeah, this is without a doubt what Dad wanted me to find.* Diana dampeners are meant to hide sources from Luminary detection, and if Winnie had ever bothered to study the Dianas as enthusiastically as she studied nightmares, she would have remembered that way sooner.

Dampeners are always metal cases with moss inside, and if she looks more closely, she'll probably find a paper clip or an old key tucked into the moss—something metal that can occasionally discharge stolen spirit power without detonating the entire thing.

"Oh no," Winnie whispers at the tin. Then at Jay. "Oh no."

"Yeah," he agrees. "Jesus, Winnie, why do you have that?"

"I . . . don't know." This is definitely not true. She *definitely* knows why she has it, and the reason starts with the letter *D* and ends with *-ad*.

"Winnie." Jay walks toward her, a warning in the slant of his shoulders. "I want you to hand that to me, and then we're going to put it right back where you found it, okay?"

Winnie gulps. Then clutches the cookie tin . . . no, the *dampener* more tightly to her chest. "I can't give it to you, Jay."

He comes to a stop before her, a frown pinching onto his papery, exhausted brow. "Okay, then *you* return it. One way or another, it needs to get back into that river. The Tuesdays are almost here."

Winnie feels all the blood drain from her face. "What do you mean the Tuesdays are almost here?"

"Exactly what I said." His eyes briefly shutter. "Because of . . . well, because of the werewolf testing, today was the earliest they could get equipment together for site containment. So now it's Monday, and I have to guide them through everything I remember."

"Oh," Winnie breathes.

"So please, can we hurry up and put that back? Then the Tuesdays can find it on their routine sweep, and you can get the hell away from here before anyone other than me wonders how you found it in the first place."

Winnie swallows. Then glances into the trees. She has the illogical sensation that the blood on the birches is pulsing. Little hearts visible through a rib cage. If any Tuesdays approach, she cannot see them. Yet.

"Okay," she tells Jay, backing slowly away from him. "I'll leave before anyone finds me here."

"Good." His posture deflates, although only momentarily as he realizes she isn't returning the dampener. He locks up tight, shoulders wrenching toward his ears and gray eyes hardening to gunmetal.

Winnie keeps backing away.

"What are you doing?"

"I can't return this."

"You have to."

"I *can't.*" She wipes her wet face on her shoulder; it knocks her glasses askew. "Jay, I *can't,*" she repeats. "There's no source in it, okay? It's not dangerous. But I need whatever else it might tell me."

"Why?" He moves forward as if to follow . . . but he only makes it two steps before his head snaps sideways. His pupils dilate. His stance lowers. "Tuesdays," he says. "You need to go."

"Yes," Winnie agrees, and she pins the dampener under one arm so her other hand can be free.

Watching her adjust, Jay's face creases into an expression that is simultaneously horrified, furious, *and* resigned. "Shit," he mutters to himself, fingers flying to unbutton his flannel. "*Shit,* why do you always cause me so much trouble?" He stalks toward her, peeling his arms out of his sleeves.

And although Winnie would like to demand, *When have I* ever *caused you trouble, Jay Friday?,* she instead keeps her mouth shut. "Take this," he mutters, and he shoves the flannel at her. "Drape it over the dampener so no one else will see it."

Chill bumps rise along his pale arms as he waits for Winnie to take his shirt. And as much as she wants to point out that he will freeze in this weather or that she has a sweatshirt of her own she can remove, there really isn't any time. So she yanks the buffalo plaid from him—one more shirt of his to add to her collection at home—and murmurs, "Thank you."

She turns away, wrapping up the dampener as she aims for the birch trees.

"You owe me an explanation," Jay calls to her back. Winnie doesn't answer, and by the time she dives into the forest, she hears distant shouts from Alpha scorpions arriving on the scene.

It is only when she is halfway through the forest that the full weight of what Jay is about to do sinks over her. She was so caught up with the dampener, with the Tuesdays coming, with the water shedding off her that she didn't really process *why* he was standing on that shoreline.

He is about to relive everything he went through with Grayson on Friday night. He is about to work through all that hell, step by awful step, while Tuesdays poke and prod and press with questions that someone has to ask . . . and only Jay can answer.

Yet, despite that slice of pain coming down the pipeline for him, Jay still took the time to help her. He still gave her his flannel and let her leave before anyone could see.

Winnie doesn't know what it means, only that she owes him. Big time.

13

Clusterfuck: An occurrence not confined to the forest in which everything goes very badly all at once. See also: Winnie Wednesday.

Winnie didn't think it was possible to hate her dad any more than she already does. It's like he just can't help it, like he just *has* to constantly make her life as hard as possible. Running off four years ago as a Diana wasn't enough; he then had to make a scavenger hunt that led right to a Diana dampener.

But where's the source? Winnie's brain wants to know. A valid question. Probably the *most* valid question, along with: *Did Dad put this dampener in the stream or was it the person who supposedly framed him?*

As Winnie half sprints with frantic purpose through the forest, no Tuesdays pop up and shout, "GOTCHA!" But that doesn't mean they won't. It doesn't mean she is safe with this dampener wrapped in wet flannel.

Nothing in Winnie's body feels connected, frozen feet attached to frozen legs attached to a brain that is a ticking time bomb. If she can just cut the right wires, she can turn herself off . . . but it's like she keeps snipping the wrong ones. Now the countdown is moving faster. Soon she will explode.

When Winnie reaches the edge of the forest and the red sensors promise safety beyond, she finally lets her clumsy, stream-numb pace slow. Not because she *wants* to slow, but because she will reach the road soon—and at this hour, there will be people out.

In other words, she needs to play it cool. She is the epitome of normal, a model Wednesday, a loyal bear lumbering along at a completely respectable, unhurried pace toward home.

After all, a person who has nothing to hide will *act* like they have nothing to hide. They won't frantically sprint home, tear into their attic, dig out the birthday cards that could implicate their entire family as having colluded with a Diana, and then burn them in a trash can out back.

That is decidedly guilty behavior, and Winnie needs to behave like she is *not* guilty. The empty tin in the stream was just a container that once held cookies. It is not a Diana dampener that looks like someone recently pulled a source out of it.

Friday estate, her brain suggests as she steps gingerly around the stakes at the forest's edge. If she goes there, she could then walk home and reinforce the story that she was "hooking up with Jay."

God, how has it only been an hour since she left Finn and corpse duty? It feels like a lifetime, and she hopes Mom is still in bed so she can hide this dampener in peace before the day begins.

When at last Winnie reaches the gloomy Friday estate, part of her wants to tear into the mansion and wait for Jay to return. He was so calm, so steady back in the forest. He can give her a ride home *and* add an extra layer of authenticity to her tale.

But the Friday estate is not a welcoming place in the mornings. Or ever really, and it seems especially forbidding in the weak light of a cold A.M., with its burned-out tower and gruesome gargoyles lurking on the rooftop, with its chipped paint and sad attempt at landscaping.

It is a house built for grief, and now it is filled fresh with it.

So Winnie does not go to the mudroom door and she does not wait for Jay to come back from his brutal interrogation with the Tuesdays. Instead, she continues strolling at a painful snail's pace toward her neighborhood. Her jeans are dry enough now that there's at least no recognizing she was knee-deep in stream water. And by the time she gets to her house, ten minutes later, her heart has *finally* calmed its frantic beating.

Winnie slomps inside via the kitchen door and dumps all her corpse-duty clothes into the washing machine, grateful to hear no signs of Mom rousing out of bed yet. She removes most of her clothes, a ritual she has done after corpse duty for the past three years, and for a brief flicker of a moment, as Winnie scoops up detergent and the scent of powdery lavender washes away the stench of dead things, she considers the fact that Jay is going to want an explanation from her. Like, a full one that goes into *all* the Dad-shaped mess from the past two weeks.

And Winnie is going to have to give it to him. She can't lie; Jay will only see right through whatever tale she might try to spin. Plus, he helped her evade the Tuesdays. He *let* her leave with that cookie tin filled with wet moss, even though his Friday sparrow heart must have been shrieking, *Mayday, Mayday! This is not what you're supposed to do! Where is the integrity?* Hell, her own Wednesday bear heart has been screaming the same thing ever since she found Dad's birthday cards in the attic . . .

And it's not feeling too pleased right now about this *mother-effing dampener* either.

Winnie's stomach spins like the washing machine is about to. She hits start on Heavy Load; the appliance groans noisily to life. Then Winnie continues her slomping pace upstairs—this time, half naked—and into her bedroom. Mom is only just stirring in her room across the hall, so Winnie still has some privacy to finish what needs finishing.

Namely hiding this dampener.

She trades Jay's now-wet flannel for a grocery bag at the bottom of her backpack that held Friday's lunch, and after wrapping the dampener in it tightly—it smells like cold creek water and wet moss—she slides it far, far beneath her bed. All the way to the wall and behind her box of summer clothes.

Winnie now has time for a quick shower before training. Her teeth click while she waits for the water to warm up, and she assembles a running list of what she can safely claim she knows right now.

1) *I know someone put a dampener in the stream.*
2) *I know there was a source in it at one point.*
3) *I know Dad wanted me to find it. Probably.*
4) *I know it somehow connects to the possibility Dad was framed.*

That is the entirety of what Winnie knows for certain. Meanwhile, the list of what she doesn't know is longer.

1) *I don't know where the source is.*
2) *I don't know when it was removed. It looks really recent, but I can't be sure.*
3) *I don't know who put the dampener in the stream. Was it Dad or someone else?*
4) *I don't know why they put it in the stream.*
5) *I don't really know what a dampener is because I spent the last four years actively avoiding anything that had to do with Dianas.*
6) *I don't know what I'm going to tell Jay.*

The pipes in the house click and expand as the water warms them with aching slowness. Mom calls out from the hall, "Morning, kiddo!" And Winnie forces herself to shout back, "Morning!" Then the back of Winnie's brain resumes its shouting of the fake Compendium . . . although now it's got the real Compendium all jumbled in there too.

Clusterfuck: An occurrence not confined to the forest in which everything goes very badly all at once.

Were-creatures: When in their animal form, these nightmares are almost unkillable. However, like the non legends, they are hurt by silver—and, in some rare cases, by gold.

See also: Winnie Wednesday, birch trees, blood.

Meanwhile, the front of Winnie's brain runs back through her list of unknowns. Six things she can't answer right now—six things she doesn't even know *how* to answer and cannot deal with because right now, she needs to go through her day exactly like the model Luminary she has always strived to be.

The model Luminary she now *gets* to be because she passed her trials and finally undid all the mess Dad made . . . that maybe he *didn't* make because he was in fact framed, and the person who framed him is now walking around Hemlock Falls scot-free.

Winnie's heartbeat instantly ramps up again at that thought. It is one more thing for her Do Not Know list: *7) I don't know if Dad was actually framed.*

Once the shower is so hot it scalds like phoenix feathers, Winnie shoves inside. She scrubs off the grime of dead things. She thaws out the frost of dawn. And she imagines herself, over and over again, stepping out of this painful heat, pink-skinned and reborn. The ashes of what Dad did forgotten and left behind . . . At least until a boy, lost and lonely in the woods, inevitably comes to her for answers.

Winnie really doesn't know what she'll tell him.

14

Somehow, despite the eternity of Winnie's morning, it is still only Monday by the time she actually reaches school. And somehow, she has gotten even more famous since yesterday. Everyone is grinning at her or fist-bumping her or giving her the *what's up?* chin bounce they've all bestowed these past two weeks, but now they've added a new epithet: *Wolf Girl.*

"Hey, Wolf Girl," says a Sunday named Shaunielle.

"Aroo, Wolf Girl!" shouts Imran Saturday as he passes, while Astrid Söndag chants "Aroo, aroo!" beside him.

When dear cousin Marcus shoots finger guns at Winnie in the hallway and howls at her—*aroo! aroo!*—it is just too much. She corners him by a locker. "Why are people calling me Wolf Girl?"

To her mild satisfaction . . . and okay, slight shame, Marcus looks terrified at Winnie's entrapment. She withdraws several inches.

"It's the news," he explains. "They, uh, showed more footage from your trial. From when the wolf bit you by the Big Lake."

"Huh?" Winnie rears back. The wolf didn't bite her by the Big Lake.

"With the manticore," Marcus explains. "It's really cool watching how the wolf came right for you at the same time as the manticore. You really should be dead."

"Yes." Winnie lurches into his face once more. "I should be. And no, it is not *cool* watching that, Marcus. That is my actual life, thank you." Winnie releases him, and he scampers off like the goblin he is. Then she stomps toward homeroom while all around her people howl, *Aroo! Aroo!*

Weirdly, she doesn't feel like her heart might explode. Or like spiders are trapped beneath her skin. She's just . . . tired. So, so tired.

Because come on, people. *Wolf Girl*? That's the best you can do? The nightmare mutation didn't even pass into her with the bite, so if you're going to call her anything, "Not Wolf Girl" would actually make more sense.

At least Fatima gives Winnie a cheery grin as Winnie ducks into her desk at the front of the room. Two weeks ago, Winnie hated this spot because it made her way too easy a target. Now she hates it because she feels a very different sort of gaze beaming onto her.

But what's wild is that if you'd asked Winnie of two weeks ago which type of stare she'd prefer, she would have assumed the latter. Of *course*. Popularity and acclaim? Yes, please! I'll have that one in droves!

The tardy bell rings.

"I hope all of you are ready for a finger prick," Ms. Morgan declares, moving in front of Winnie's desk. She holds up her hand, where a Band-Aid gleams on her middle finger. "You'll be getting tested for werewolf contamination at the Sunday estate today." Her gaze flicks to Winnie.

Please, don't say anything about the new footage. Please, don't say anything about the new footage.

Thank the forest, Ms. Morgan doesn't say anything. "It's also that time of year where we all get to encourage the antiquated and—in my opinion—*toxic* tradition of selecting our Nightmare Court for the Masquerade." She retrieves a stack of papers from her desk. "If you all would be so kind as to write down three nominees from your peers—whomever you want, except *no*, Peter, you cannot nominate yourself, so don't try that again."

The room laughs. Winnie hopes he is squirming with shame behind her. She would look if it didn't mean potentially making eye contact with him.

A paper falls onto Winnie's desk as Ms. Morgan strolls by. It has three lines on it, and Winnie frowns. In the past, she was not allowed to vote. Now, she is and she knows she ought to be happy about it. This is exactly what she wanted. This is what normal Luminaries do on a normal Luminary day.

Somehow, she only feels more tired.

Winnie inhales through a yawn and quickly scrawls down the three names of the only people in this town she actually likes: Emma Wednesday, Bretta Wednesday, Fatima Wednesday. Then she folds it in half to drop in the makeshift ballot box (a.k.a. an old shoebox) on her way toward the door.

Except Ms. Morgan stops her before she can reach the hall. "You okay?"

"Yeah," Winnie tries—except it doesn't sound true at all. And as she eyes Ms. Morgan's skeptical face, it occurs to her that if *anyone* will get it, surely it's Ms. Morgan. After all, she is a non who grew up outside the Luminary world; her culture doesn't run thicker than blood.

So Winnie takes the honest plunge.

"Do you ever find it weird how people here . . . Well, terrible stuff happens to us, but no one ever acts like it?"

"Ah." Ms. Morgan sighs. Then fiddles with her Band-Aid. "I saw the footage last night too. And yes, Winnie, I *do* find it weird. But that doesn't make it wrong."

"Ma'am?" Winnie frowns.

"Growing up, my brother was an EMT near a nasty stretch of highway where people were always going too fast. He was a first responder at so many accidents. Bad ones where the drivers or their families or their dogs did not survive. And after every wreck like that, he and his partners would go gorge themselves at a twelve-dollar pizza buffet two exits down."

Winnie's stomach flips. "Oh god."

"Exactly." Ms. Morgan's lips press tight. "It sounds disgusting. And you know what else sounds disgusting? Corpse duty. My point is, Winnie, that I don't think most people here are in denial. The forest is violent and awful—and so is the rest of the world beyond Hemlock Falls. People die, sometimes in horrific ways, and the only way to really deal with that is to switch off your empathy switch and eat a lot of pizza."

Winnie bites her lip. On the one hand, she gets what Ms. Morgan is saying—she really does. She *knows* people have to compartmentalize, and she *knows* that until recently, she herself was good at doing so. But what Winnie can't figure out is why she has lost that ability. Why her thoughts spiral every day and she can't stand to hear another person howl in her direction.

Culture runs thicker than blood, she thinks, *except apparently for me.* Aloud though, she simply says, "Thanks, Ms. Morgan."

"Any time," the non teacher replies. "I'm always on your side, Winnie, and always here if you need me."

The first thing that happens when everyone reaches the Sunday estate for afternoon training is—as Ms. Morgan promised—the werewolf test. While a few students grumble in line outside the Sunday auditorium, most people are just glad to miss class and ready to get their pokes over with.

Since Winnie hitched a ride with her friends, she spends the majority of her time in line with Emma, Bretta, and Fatima. It's a nice reprieve after the morning that lasted a century; her brain can switch off and simply revel in Fatima's descriptions of her Masquerade Ball costume. (She is going as a siren, complete with glossy scales.)

Unfortunately, when they reach the double doors into the auditorium, Winnie gets separated from her friends. *So close,* she thinks as she watches them hurry toward tables and lab-coated Mondays bustling in front of the stage. Winnie wants to sprint after them, but Headmaster Gina is *right* there, her wheelchair locked in position by the doors while a walkie-talkie fuzzes every few minutes with a *Send in three more!* message.

Winnie doesn't need to excel in math to see that she is now stuck outside alone. Although her solitude doesn't last long before Casey and Peter sidle up beside her.

"Hey, Wolf Girl." Casey leans against a locker next to Winnie. The banner for the Sundays hangs silently above, its swan glaring down in barely masked hatred.

Or maybe that's just Winnie projecting.

"That was some badass footage from the forest," Casey says. "The werewolf *and* a manticore."

Compartmentalize, compartmentalize. Winnie inhales. Exhales. "Thanks," she grinds out.

"You got a date to the Masquerade yet?"

Winnie chokes.

"We do not," Peter inserts, leaning on Winnie's other side.

Do not punch them, Winnie. Compartmentalize. She inhales again—except now Peter's cologne sears up her nose. She starts coughing.

Rather than ask if she's okay, though, Casey just lifts his voice: "You could go with one of us," he suggests. "Or . . ." He flips his hair with a hand. "You could just go with *me*."

Winnie's eyes have teared up from the coughing. She yanks off her glasses, blurring both horrible boys into impressionist versions of themselves. If only she could now make them totally disappear.

Amazingly, Winnie of four years ago would have been flattered by such open Luminary approval. And pre-trial Winnie too, who wouldn't have known yet how jarring her return to the Luminaries would feel. After all, all these people were just following the rules on outcasts, right?

But now, no matter how far Winnie tips her head to the side and squints without her glasses on, she just can't seem to make herself feel anything other than disdain.

Do not punch him, Winnie. Do not punch him. Headmaster Gina is literally right there.

"No," a voice calls out, sharp as icicles. "Winnie will not go with you." Heels clack over wood, and suddenly Erica Thursday has arrived. She pins Casey with a thin-eyed stare—not quite a glare, but certainly not warm either.

Winnie pushes her glasses back on, and Erica's glorious avenging angel form crystallizes.

"Winnie will not go with you to the Masquerade, Casey. Nor you, Peter. And you"—Erica flings her dark gaze onto Wyatt Saturday, who is on Casey's other side and oblivious to this whole exchange—"come here. We're all going into the auditorium together."

Wyatt hops to attention as if Erica were a drill sergeant. Then, perfectly timed, the walkie-talkie in Gina's hand snaps on. *Send up three more!*

Winnie doesn't need to be told twice. She shoves off the lockers, falls into step beside Erica, while Wyatt hurries behind them. Winnie has never considered herself someone who needed rescuing, but she will *gladly* play Damsel in Distress if it means the Ice Queen will talk to her.

And talk to her Erica does, as their strides match cadence toward the front of the room. "They're assholes," Erica says, and that little almost smile Winnie saw her wear at the party now returns.

It's awesome.

"Thank you," Winnie says somewhat breathlessly. "You didn't have to do that."

A single shoulder shrugs. "As a councilor's daughter, I can't usually go around telling people what I think about them, but sometimes, if it's in service to someone else . . ." Her smile stretches another half inch.

And Winnie desperately racks her brain for something to talk about. Literally anything will do. They're only ten steps away from the front of the room; they will split up and this moment of almost kindness will pass. Then Winnie's eyes drop, and she spots something she hadn't noticed before.

"Oh my god, you found it!" Winnie grinds to a halt and claps her hands. "You found Jenna's locket!"

Erica also stops, and for a fraction of a second—just a tiny, almost imperceptible flash of time—her eyes widen. Her lips part. Then it's over. So fast, Winnie thinks she must have imagined it.

"Yeah." Erica reaches up to pat the gold locket resting against her collarbone. "I need to get it cleaned."

Winnie leans in, and sure enough, there's a brownish speck beside the moon. There's something familiar about that speck . . . although Winnie can't quite place why. Her own locket is completely clean.

"That's wild," Winnie says, drawing out her own chain. "They look identical. No wonder you thought I'd stolen it. My locket belonged to my grandmother on my dad's side apparently. How did Jenna get hers?"

Erica's lips purse and she rears back from Winnie's proximity.

Winnie's face heats up. She is clearly invading her *ex*–best friend's personal space—and her personal business. "Sorry," she mumbles, retreating as Erica tucks the locket into her blouse. "I don't mean to pry."

Erica bears a tight smile. No teeth. No crinkle in the eyes. And although she says, "You weren't," Winnie can tell it's a lie.

So she backs away a full step, screaming inwardly as she does. *Why did you mention Jenna? Why did you ruin this moment?* It's like Winnie has gotten so spoiled by all the popularity and attention from the rest of the Luminaries, she has forgotten that four years of antagonism still yawn between her and Erica.

And it's not merely those four years. Erica isn't the same person now that she was back then. Old Erica was all mischief and banter and devilish, sideways smiles—and gentle too, just like her dad. She always had her raven hair in a ponytail, and although she dressed with style, it was never so sharp-heeled or straight-edged as it is today.

Now she is Marcia 2.0, even if Winnie cannot fathom why.

"I'm glad you found the locket," Winnie makes herself say as she watches the wintery force field rise up around Erica again.

"Me too," Erica agrees. Then she bows her head and steps away to get her blood drawn.

Winnie's heart hurts watching her leave.

15

After Sunday training, Winnie spends a few hours with Fatima, Emma, and Bretta in Fatima's room at the Wednesday estate (it is still so weird that Winnie can walk in and out of the estate at will), and Winnie is able to *almost* finish a paper due for Ms. Morgan. She is also able to burn so brightly she *almost* stuns herself into forgetting that everything else in Hemlock Falls is going wrong.

Clusterfuck? What clusterfuck?

She lets herself ooh and aah over Fatima's designs for her Nightmare Masquerade gown: to complete the look for her siren costume, she has a sequin-lined hijab that will look *just* like flickering scales beneath the Saturday chandeliers.

The twins give Winnie a ride home in their dad's van, and when Winnie hauls her tired self inside the house—she has been up *so long* because somehow today is still Monday—she finds a plate of ham sandwiches on the kitchen table and a note from Mom.

Early shift at the Daughter tomorrow. Staying at Darian's tonight. Left the Volvo for you. Keys by the door. Then it finishes in all caps with two underlines: *LOVE YOU SO MUCH. YOU'RE MY FAVORITE DAUGHTER EVER.—MOM*

Winnie snags a sandwich before hurrying upstairs. The silence in the house is blessedly welcome, and she spends a full five minutes simply standing at the center of her room noshing away at her dinner.

There is a faint smell like rotting moss, but Winnie isn't ready to let her phoenix flames vanish. She would like to bask in the glow of Fatima's dress plans for a few moments longer, please.

Eventually, though, the sandwich is swallowed and there is no more avoiding the grocery bag hidden behind the box of summer clothes. Winnie's hands tremble as she crouches beside her bed and tows out the dampener. Bloodstained birch trees fill her mind—and smoky gray eyes too. Jay wasn't at Sunday training today; she doubts he'll ever come back again. Why would he, now that he's Lead Hunter?

Once the grocery bag is removed, Winnie wipes the tin down with a washcloth and then transports it to her desk. She has already cleared off all her sketchbooks, within which hide her drawing of Dad's map and the X that derailed her entire week . . . and possibly her entire future.

The birthday cards, meanwhile, are stowed in the attic where she first found them.

A flip of the switch on her desk lamp sends yellow light flooding over the cookie tin. It glitters just as it had in the stream thirteen hours ago, and Winnie's hands are still shaking as she once more wrestles off the lid. Then the moss is revealed, damp and imprinted with a deep circle.

That circle is where a source used to rest, and after digging around in the stinky, sloppy moss, she finds a fishhook.

"A vent," Winnie murmurs, "because it releases power." It just sits there, right next to where the source would have rested. It's rusted, but still sharp when Winnie plucks it out and taps it against her pointer finger. *How,* she wonders, *do you work?*

She will need to do some serious research on Dianas. Otherwise, Winnie is completely and totally clueless on how to proceed. There is no message here. No note from Dad that says, *Well done, Win-Ben! Here's why this dampener proves I was framed! LOVE YOU SO MUCH. YOU'RE MY FAVORITE DAUGHTER EVER.—DAD*

There is just a cookie tin, some sodden moss, and a fishhook. Winnie even studies all the dings and dents in the tin to see if *maybe* they align into some hidden message or a new map. But it all looks random. More like the effects of a stream always burbling over two unsteady stones.

Without her thinking, Winnie's hands reach for a sketchbook and open it to an empty page. She finds a pen from the cup beside the lamp. Like a pipeline converting crude oil into gasoline or corn into moonshine, she distills the raw, useless words that float around her mind into feelings scrawled across a page.

She intends to draw the dampener and the empty circle now filled with mysteries . . . but instead, she draws Jay. It just happens, completely uncontrolled by her muscles. The pipeline knows what it needs to do; it transforms and adjusts and creates the *actual* outcome Winnie needs right now.

Jay standing beside a stream, offering her his flannel, eyes sharp and ever so slightly hunted because the Tuesdays are near. Although, whether it's fear that Winnie will get caught or fear over what he is about to have to relive, Winnie cannot say.

Her chest hurts staring at him. It has been so many years since she drew Jay—and it was always such a challenge because he never stood still. He was a creature of movement, a wild animal who could never be caged. No matter how many times she tried to sketch him, she could never get the *life force* of him onto the paper. He always felt flat, two dimensional, absent.

Right now, though, as she stares at the subtle shading she used for his gray, gray, forever gray eyes, she feels almost as if he is gazing right back.

And she doesn't like it. Real Jay would never hold her eyes for this long.

Winnie closes the sketchbook and shoves it off the desk. One more illustration to add to her collection of nightmares.

It is nearing ten o'clock and Winnie is adding the final lines to her paper for Ms. Morgan when something taps at her bedroom window. Her first thought is that it must be that damnable crow that has built a nest on the roof, and she glares at the curtain hanging over the glass.

But then the tapping comes again, and Winnie realizes there is a vaguely human-shaped shadow outside her window where the roof is super slanted.

She almost falls out of her desk chair and *does* fall onto her bed after reeling across the rug. She rips back the curtain and finds Jay's ghostly face waiting on the other side of her window. He gives a weak wave, as if it's perfectly normal for him to be there right now.

"Oh my god," Winnie says once she has hefted the ancient glass high.

Cold, wet air sweeps in, and droplets from the latest drizzle hit Winnie's face. "What are you doing here?"

"I need to talk to you."

"No, I mean, *here*. On my roof and at my window. We have a front door."

"Your mom's light was off. I didn't want to wake her." What he doesn't add but that Winnie intuitively understands is *Or have her wonder why I'm here at this hour to talk to you.*

Winnie has to admit that both of these reasons are valid, and since the Volvo is parked on the curb, he has no way of knowing Mom isn't actually here. Which is why she informs him: "Mom isn't actually here."

"Oh." He flushes bright enough for her to spot in the weak yellow of her lamp. "Should I . . . go to the front door?"

"Don't be ridiculous." Winnie grabs his white V-neck by the collar and hauls him forcefully into her room. Her bed bounces; the box springs groan; water drips off Jay onto her bedspread; and Winnie stoutly avoids considering the fact that she and Jay are on her bed together.

"You're soaking wet," she scolds, scrabbling off the bed and onto the safety of the rug as fast as she can. Unfortunately, Jay has the same idea, and by the time she is upright he is upright too.

And now dripping onto her rug.

"It's raining," he says by way of explanation.

To which Winnie responds, "Oh really?" And pushes past him toward her closet. Two weeks ago, Winnie thought it weird to see Jay in her family's kitchen, the boy she used to knew transformed into a man.

Turns out having Jay in her bedroom is eighty-five thousand times weirder, not merely because his head nearly reaches her low, sloped ceiling, but because he is *in her freaking bedroom.* The last time he was here was over four years ago. He sat at her desk and worked on his math homework (gasp! he actually used to do assignments back then), while Winnie snuggled on her bed and read the Hunter's Abridged Nightmare Compendium and wondered how *anyone* found it useful when all the good stuff had been removed.

Now here they are again, each of them taller, while Winnie pretends she has not shifted back into overheating-furnace mode and Jay tries to make himself as small as possible and avoid more drippage onto the rug.

"Here," Winnie says once she finds the first flannel he lent her two weeks ago, the navy tartan recently washed and smelling like dryer sheets.

"Oh." Jay takes it. "Thanks." He drops it onto the bed, and before Winnie can process what is happening in front of her, much less intervene, he removes his wet T-shirt.

"Oh my god." She claps her hands over her glasses and frantically flings herself toward her bedroom door. But it's too late. She has now seen exactly what she *felt* on the motorcycle ride with Jay two weeks ago, and there is no erasing it from her brain. It's like staring into the sun: when you close your eyes, the memory of the light still sears. Replace "light" with "abs" and that is all Winnie can see right now as she digs her fingers under her lenses.

The image of Jay is permanently imprinted, with his waist (lean), shoulders (sculpted), and abs that did not used to be there.

"I meant," Winnie grits out, cracking open a single eye to glare at the Wednesday bear on the back of her door. "Put the flannel on over the shirt." The bear looks as horrified as she feels. Her glasses are also now smudged thanks to her panicked smashing of hands onto lenses.

"Oh," Jay replies, and Winnie can hear him now hesitating behind her. Then grabbing for his wet T-shirt as if to put it back on.

"No!" she barks. "It's too late now. Just finish what you were doing."

"O . . . kay." Floorboards creak and Winnie hears him once more drop the wet shirt to the floor and grab for the flannel on the bed.

"Um, all done," he says moments later, and Winnie sucks in a steeling breath. Eventually one's eyes recover from staring at direct sunlight. Therefore, her own eyes will recover too.

She isn't so sure about the bear's, though.

Winnie twirls around to face Jay, pointedly keeping her attention laser-locked on his face. His cheeks are flagged with red as he clears his throat, and Winnie tries not to notice how defined his Adam's apple is. It is an absolutely irrelevant feature upon his body, and in combination with the small glimpse of skin where he did not fully button up his shirt, there is nothing at all visible upon his person that Winnie hasn't seen before. Therefore, he is a boring sack of flesh and she can stop hyperventilating.

"We need to talk about what happened this morning," Jay says, as if it's not obvious that's why he has come here.

"Can it . . . wait until tomorrow?"

"No." Jay frowns at her. "It cannot."

Well, Winnie thinks, *it was worth trying. Can't blame a girl for that.*

The flush that had overtaken Jay's cheeks now fades. "Winnie, you found a Diana dampener in the forest. Right where Grayson and I were. I think I deserve an explanation, not to mention, I deserve to know what you're planning to do with it. It's in here right?" His nose crinkles, as if he can smell it.

And Winnie quite absurdly finds herself blushing as she wonders what other smells he might detect. She hopes that they are nice ones.

"Fine," she tells him. "Let's talk about what happened this morning. You sit there." She points to her bed. "And I will sit here." She moves to her desk chair. Once they are both seated, Jay looking extremely long and awkward next to the sunflowers of her bedspread, Winnie uses her shirt to wipe the smudges off her lenses as if what is about to follow doesn't terrify her. Her teeth click behind closed lips.

Honesty, honesty. It is what the Fridays value about all else. It is what Winnie *has* to give him, because he will spot any attempt otherwise.

It's also what he deserves after everything he did for her this morning.

Winnie's teeth click together twice more. She shoves her glasses back on. *Let's begin.*

16

Winnie doesn't know what to expect from sharing the story. At first, she only plans to give Jay the broad strokes. A quick pencil outline on the page that gives him enough contour to follow along, but that isn't filled in yet with any details.

A ridiculous aim in hindsight. And it isn't even questions from Jay that push Winnie deeper, make her share more and more and more . . . It is herself. It's that cursed volcano that surges upward whenever she thinks about Dad.

It erupts now. The miniature Pompeii that leaves nothing behind but scorched body parts and choking ash. She doesn't stay still for long. She gets hot. *So* hot she has to stretch her legs. She paces from side to side along the rug.

Until at last—and after a lot of snarled instances of *I hate him. No seriously, I hate him*—she has finished her tale. "And that is when you found me in the forest."

She stands before Jay, lamplight sliding over her and a draft blowing in from the window she must not have shut all the way. Weirdly, she is panting, and for half a moment, Winnie thinks Jay has fallen asleep. He has lain back on the bed, his eyes closed, and fresh fury sparks inside Winnie—an aftershock for the eruption that just obliterated her brain. But right as she drops to Jay's side, mattress bouncing, to smack him back awake, his eyes spring wide.

He pushes upright, face swimming close to hers. "You need to tell the Tuesdays, Winnie. Like, right now."

"What?" Winnie recoils. "*That* is your takeaway from everything I just said?"

"Yeah, obviously. Because right now, you're telling me you have proof there's a Diana in Hemlock Falls." Jay motions vaguely toward the forest. Or maybe toward downtown or maybe even toward the Tuesday estate. Somewhere that isn't *here* and isn't *safe*. "That's not a secret you can keep to yourself, Win."

Winnie's jaw unhinges. She gapes at Jay, trying to process what he is commanding her to do—and it is a command. He is a hard-edged version of himself that leaves no room for argument. This is a newly appointed Lead Hunter who already expects everyone to fall in line around him.

Part of Winnie knew he would say this. He wouldn't be a true Friday if he didn't insist she do the open, honest thing. But then he also protected her at the kill site; he *let* her walk away with that dampener before Tuesdays could find her.

She thought that counted for something.

"I can't do that, Jay. Do you realize what could happen if people found out my mom kept those birthday cards?"

"So . . . burn the cards."

"That won't help if Lambdas interrogate her. You know my family is incapable of telling a lie."

He winces. "Okay, but Winnie, do you *realize* what could happen if there's a Diana living here? That dampener was empty, which means there's a witch somewhere in Hemlock Falls walking around with a *live* source. And in case you don't remember from Intro to Dianas in third grade," he continues, "that means they can cast spells. Like, anywhere they want to on anyone they want to."

Winnie rolls her eyes. "I do remember," she mutters, even though she has actually forgotten almost everything she learned from Professor Nasreen. "But we don't know there's a Diana with a live source out there. Maybe the dampener held my *dad's* source, and he wasn't actually framed at all."

"And that's better how?" Jay opens his hands. "I don't think you want your dad out there with a live source either." He pulls in his legs to stand, but Winnie beats him to it, springing off the bed and stalking five steps toward the bear on her door. It glares in disapproval now.

Despite what Jay might believe about her, Winnie does understand the dangers of a loose Diana with a live source. It's just not as intense or immediate as the dangers to her family from the Tuesdays.

Jay wasn't there when the Lambdas descended on her house like harpies on a kill, dragging her *literally* out of bed and putting her in handcuffs.

Actual handcuffs.

Jay wasn't there when Jeremiah Tuesday shut Winnie in a holding cell for six hours all by herself and grilled her with endless questions. *Were there burn marks on your dad's fingers? Did you ever smell strange things in the house? Did he have any small wooden coins in his possession?*

And Jay wasn't there when Winnie got home to discover her dad was gone for good and no one in Hemlock Falls would speak to her again.

Clothes rustle behind her, but Winnie doesn't turn around to face Jay, still on the bed. So he speaks to her back: "You don't have to implicate yourself, Win. Or your mom. Just give me the dampener, and I'll say I found it on the hunt."

Winnie swallows. Her teeth want to chatter, but she resists—and second by second, tension builds in her jaw. Today has been such a long day. Almost as long as the day that ended in her jumping off a waterfall. Certainly as long as the day of her first trial, except this time there's no possible redemption waiting for her when the mist rises. Only possible damnation for her and Mom and Darian.

The last Diana caught in Hemlock Falls was Winnie's dad, so where will the Lambdas go if Jay hands them an empty dampener? Who will Jeremiah Tuesday blame? And what punishment will the Council dole out this time?

Winnie can't go through that again. She *can't.*

"No," Winnie says. Quiet at first, then louder as her eyes lock on the word *Loyalty* written beneath the bear. "No. You can't have the dampener, Jay."

More squeaking bedsprings. Then soft footsteps before body heat and bergamot close in on Winnie's back. He says her name quietly: "Winnie."

She tips her face sideways until she finds the edges of him.

"I get why you're afraid."

No. You really don't.

"But we have to take your dad at his word here and assume he was framed." Jay moves until he's right against Winnie's shoulder and she can more clearly see him. The lamp flickers gold into his eyes. "And if he was framed, then that means the real Diana has been evading detection for four years. We can't let someone like that run free all over Hemlock Falls."

A witch. A werewolf. A Whisperer. So many *W*'s to hit Hemlock Falls all at once and that have all, somehow, become Winnie's problem—the girl who still isn't even officially a Luminary. *It's like these nightmares only show up when you're around,* Mario said yesterday. *Or like you've got some special power that only lets* you *see them.*

"Jay." Now Winnie is the one to say his name quietly. She turns to face him. His eyes glitter golden as a droll's hoard in this light. "As much as I want Dad's clues to . . . to mean something, as much as I *want* that last message to be true so that I can say, once and for all, me and Mom and Darian were never wrong about what Dad was doing . . . I can't take that risk.

"Turning in the dampener will unleash fresh hell onto my family—*right* when we're getting back to normal. I know your integrity compels you to tell the Tuesdays, but my loyalty"—she waves to the bear—"compels me to protect my family."

A pause. A long breath expands in Jay's chest. Then departs again. "Crap," he mutters eventually, twisting away from the door. He stalks back to the bed. "Crap." He scrubs with both hands at his damp hair, an unusually expressive display for Jay. Unusually mobile and wound up. Winnie can practically see the deliberation warring inside him.

Until he rounds toward her, his hair shooting out at all angles. "Fine, Winnie. You win. For now. But we need to figure out what message your dad was trying to leave with that dampener, and we need to figure it out fast. Even if this witch hasn't done anything yet, it doesn't mean they won't. They removed that source for a reason, so what is it they're planning to do to Hemlock Falls? And who else are they going to hurt in the process?"

17

W e, Winnie thinks. That is what Jay just said: We *need to figure out what message your dad was trying to leave.* Not "you," not "I," but "*we.*"

And it is like two tectonic plates grinding together—one that's labeled *Four Years Ago* and one that's labeled *Tonight.* Two events that, from afar, might look the same. But once you're up close, you can see that the jagged, stony edges don't align. The earth is still shifting and moving and magma is still boiling within.

Four years ago, Winnie went to Jay. "Help me," she said, standing at his bedroom door in the Friday estate while he stared at her with bloodshot eyes on the other side. "I know my dad isn't a Diana. Jay, please help me."

"I can't." Those were the only words he said to her. *I. Can't.* Then he shut the door in her face, and Winnie was left alone. Erica had already said no too; the triangle was broken; Winnie was a hypotenuse cast adrift.

Now, here she and Jay stand in a different bedroom with different bodies and different histories, and one leg of the triangle is basically saying, *Let me help you. Now I can be here for you.* His eyes are still bloodshot, his expression still grim. But now Jay wants to be a *we* when four years ago he broke that *we* apart.

Winnie's fingers curl at her sides. She can feel the plates shifting inside her, trembling into an earthquake that will eventually rip her in two. She is afraid that if she doesn't hold this in, she is going to scream at Jay. And worse—so much worse—she is going to cry. Furious, magmatic tears of hurt and confusion and rage.

He must sense her emotional shift, because his posture grows wary. His jaw sets slightly to the side, as if he is bracing for a blow to come.

Winnie won't do it, though. She won't shout at him, and she won't cry. Instead, she will give him one chance: "You told me you had your own things going on," she forces out. "Two weeks ago, you said you didn't ditch me because of my dad, but instead because you had your own stuff to deal with. So Jay—" Her voice cracks slightly on his name. She swallows, grinds her teeth together, and tries again. "So Jay, if it wasn't my dad, then why did you ditch me four years ago? What was it you had going on?"

His body turns visibly cold. Like winter frost settling over a corpse in the forest, his skin pales toward death and his muscles freeze toward rigor mortis. Even his chest stops moving, no inhales or exhales to sustain his life.

He is the opposite of Winnie's violent heated rage, and Winnie almost wonders if she isn't watching him truly die before her.

Until at last his voice rasps out, so low she almost doesn't hear it: "I can't answer that question for you."

She knew this would be what he'd say, although god, she'd hoped otherwise. She knew he would evade her question because it seems to be all he *can* do. Her eyes close. Her nostrils flare. She will not cry where he can see her. "Then go, please." She steps aside from the door, eyes still wound shut. "Go, Jay. Because I did not need your help back then, and I do not need it now."

She hears him move. Feels the cold of him pass by like a ghost-deer. Her door opens. Her door shuts, and part of Winnie wants to chase after him because she *knows* she's being foolish to turn away the only person who knows the truth of everything.

Right now, though, she can't do it. She needs to be alone.

Jay's retreating footsteps hammer, stairs groan (third from the bottom is the loudest of all), and only when she hears the front door shut—not a slam, but not gentle either—does Winnie finally let herself erupt.

Just tears at first, then hiccups, then full-on sobs as she collapses onto her bed that now annoyingly smells like Jay. First she cries for that twelve-year-old girl whose best friend rejected her; then she cries for the twelve-year-old girl who lost her dad; then she cries for the sixteen-year-old girl who almost died by a monster no one believes in and who now has a dampener under her bed slowly rotting and stinking up the room.

Lastly, though, Winnie cries for Grayson Friday. A guy she never knew and never will know because he is just fish food in an aquarium. Blood splattered on white trees.

Outside, rain falls.

HEMLOCK FALLS TESTING PORTAL

TUESDAY, APRIL 9

TEST RESULTS for PREVIOUS DAY:

Tests Administered: 478

Positive Results: 0

AVAILABLE TESTING LOCATIONS:

Monday hospital, BY APPOINTMENT ONLY

Sunday estate auditorium, UNDER AGE 18 ONLY

Floating Carnival, COMING SOON

DO YOUR CIVIC DUTY AND GET TESTED AS SOON AS A SITE IS AVAILABLE NEAR YOU!

18

Winnie awakens Tuesday morning with a sob-hangover. Her head hurts, her sinuses are stuffed full, and her eyes are so puffy she can barely get them open. Outside, cardinals sing and a tufted titmouse on Winnie's windowsill calls, *Peter, Peter, Peter!*

Peter, Winnie thinks, should really effing answer so she can go back to sleep.

After kicking off her covers, Winnie yanks her glasses from her nightstand and staggers for the hall—where she runs directly into her Wednesday bear because her fingers aren't fast enough with the doorknob.

It glowers with deep disdain as she fumbles past. *Tsk, tsk, tsk, you really should hand over that dampener to the Tuesdays.*

Winnie glowers right back. She has a plan now, thank you. The benefit of her late-night eruption was that, once the tectonic plates calmed and her tears finally stopped flowing, she was left with a large, empty crater. Suddenly, there was all sorts of space for logic to seep in.

Winnie fell asleep with a new plan floating right there at the top of her brain.

After a quick splash of water on her face in the bathroom, Winnie's feet carry her to the hall's end, where the door into the attic awaits, its rectangular frame fixed into the ceiling and a rope dangling down.

Winnie pulls. The door creaks wide, revealing shadows and a scent like old insulation and mothballs. She spares a quick peek out a nearby window, but Mom has not staged a surprise return. Winnie quickly lowers the ladder and heads into the darkness.

Wink. The attic light turns on with the plucking of a string. Then there are the boxes Winnie found just over two weeks ago. She zooms for the one she needs, and with none of the care she exhibited the first time she came here, she digs past old photos until she finds the stack of cards left from Dad. She has opened each of hers, but Darian's remain untouched.

She withdraws the four unopened cards and lifts them up. They look just like the ones Dad sent to her: red, square envelopes with *For my son Darian* written in Dad's distinctive print that always has the dot for the *i* not quite over its intended mark.

It's time to open these cards. Past time, probably, but Winnie hasn't had the heart to face what might be inside them—nor the heart to bash open the same Dad-shaped lockboxes hidden inside Darian. And while yes, she *could* open these cards without ever telling Darian about them . . .

It feels wrong. An invasion of privacy. The theft of a gift that, admittedly, Darian probably doesn't want, but that belongs to him all the same.

Winnie inhales, feeling her lungs press against her ribs. Then she exhales, closing the shoebox and returning it to its spot in the larger box. As she is rearranging things to look exactly as she found them, she spies one photograph that has fluttered free from the rest: it's of Winnie and Darian as kids, on one of their rare trips to visit Grandma Harriet. They're at a gas station two states over, Harriet with her arms around her grandkids' shoulders.

She has thick auburn hair like Dad's and Winnie's, except with gray that is only just starting to shoot through. She's smiling, but there's something uncomfortable about the expression. Like she isn't quite sure she's doing this whole *pose with your family* thing right. Dad always said that although Harriet wasn't a bad mom, she wasn't a particularly present one either. It was like she never got the hang of motherhood, and then she had even less interest in getting the hang of grandmotherhood later on.

When Dad left Winnie's life, so did Grandma Harriet. It was never something Winnie dwelled on. It just was. The woman she awkwardly visited once a year became the woman she never visited at all.

For a moment, Winnie wonders if maybe this was where Dad went four years ago. Back to his mom, back to the life he had before, back to the house he grew up in six hours away.

She banishes the idea as soon as it strikes, then she shoves the photograph back into its box—and Harriet back into her lockbox of pointless memories.

In moments, Winnie has descended the ladder. *THWACK.* The door slams into place, and she hurries down the hall. Yet rather than go into her room, she pushes into Mom's. The lights are off. The curtains are closed. There is a smell like Mom's shampoo coupled with a staleness that reveals how little she is actually in here. The bed is made—if crudely—and the pillows are lined crookedly against the pine headboard.

It was a long-standing argument between her and Dad: Mom saw no point in making a bed you were going to mess up again the following evening. Dad, meanwhile, made the bed very precisely every single morning. Perfect corners. Fluffed pillows. A ruler-straight line for the duvet.

Ever since Dad left, Mom has attempted to make it too. Winnie has never understood why, and even now, watching dust motes flicker through the shadows, she doesn't understand. Did Mom just change her stance on bed neatness, or is she clinging to some old way that can never be again?

But what if it can *be again?* asks a part of Winnie's brain that she is too afraid to look at. *What if Dad really is only six hours away and can come home again?*

She snaps her head sideways. She will not indulge those thoughts. She will *not* let them rise any higher. They are basilisks who will turn her eyes to stone if she stares too closely at them.

With loping steps, Winnie reaches Mom's bedside table and yanks the phone off its charging stand. Then, cards safely clasped in one hand, phone in the other, Winnie steals back into her bedroom. She shoves the cards deep into a sketchbook at the bottom of a deskside stack and finally punches in Darian's number. He does not answer.

This isn't surprising. He probably thinks it's Mom, and as much as Winnie knows he loves their mother, she *does* tend to call him a lot. (And in Mom's defense, Darian has been her only friend for a really long time.) So Winnie calls again. Then a third time. And finally, on the fourth attempt, Darian picks up. "Oh my *god,* Mom."

"Not Mom," Winnie says. "It's me. What are you doing right now?"

"Oh. Win." A sound like scraping fabric fills the receiver, as if Darian is pinning the phone between his shoulder and jaw. "I'm helping get the werewolf test site set up at the pier. This is almost as complicated as the Masquerade preparation. You would not believe how many boxes have to be unloaded—*Sandra!* That is not where that goes!"

For several seconds, Darian is distracted ordering Sandra about (which must be *extremely* satisfying given how Sandra treated him for so many years before he replaced her as Dryden's assistant). Then the fabric scrapes again and Darian returns.

"What do you need, Win? I'm kind of busy here. The scale of this is just bananas. You would not believe how many microscopes we needed. And Dryden is insisting we make it all look *fun* so as not to detract from the Floating Carnival. As if werewolf testing is *fun*—"

"Right," Winnie cuts in before Darian's rant can really hit its stride. "I need to see you. Is there a moment we can meet? Just us two."

"You can come over tonight. I'm making a risotto—*no, Sandra. No.* What don't you understand about 'keeping the arrow on the boxes pointed up'?"

"Will Andrew be there?"

"Of course."

"I said *just us two,* Darian. As in, *just us alone.*"

"Oh." For the first time since picking up the phone, Darian seems to still on the other end. Winnie can feel his whole attention latch on to her. "What's going on, Winnie?"

"I'll explain in person."

"Okay." There's a wariness now. "How about I take you to school tomorrow morning. Will that work? Just us, no Andrew."

"Yeah, that would be great."

"Cool." Instantly, Darian is back to distracted, and Winnie hears a loud *rip!* as if packing tape is coming off a box. "I'll see you tomorrow, then. Love you. Talk later."

The line goes dead.

Since Winnie won't see Darian today, she leaves the birthday cards hidden away in her room before emerging into the day. Her plan has multiple pieces, and it's time to check off the next part.

Of course, thanks to the Volvo, Winnie travels so fast, she overestimates the time she will need to cross town before school and arrives at the Monday history library five minutes before they open. She huddles in the hallway outside, apparently the only overeager Luminary hoping to get in at 8:00 A.M. on a Tuesday morning. As soon as Winnie spots the librarian unlocking the door, she blazes inside.

"Morning!" she says with a weak smile. *Don't mind me. I am just a dork here to study.* The librarian waves tiredly, and Winnie's blaze continues uninterrupted toward the row of shelves dedicated to Diana books—and in particular, the shelf with books on sources. It is the same spot where Dad's secret map is still hidden.

When Winnie reaches the row in question, however, she discovers someone already standing there. He is backlit from the window twenty feet behind him—the overhead fluorescent lights haven't been switched on in this part of the library yet—but Winnie has no problem recognizing his lean frame given that he was slouched in her bedroom nine hours ago.

She skids to a halt before him. "What are you doing here?" she blurts. Then, at a lower whisper-shout: "And *how*?"

"I have a key." Jay lifts a lanyard, where sure enough a white keycard dangles. "All Lead Hunters get them."

"Oh." There is a lot to parse in this one sentence—the reminder that Jay is Lead Hunter now (*Youngest in Hemlock Falls! You must be so proud!*), that Grayson had to die for him to become that Lead Hunter, and the startling new revelation that he has a keycard *and* has used it to access the library before it opens.

All so he could come *here*, no less, right where Winnie told him that her dad's map would be.

She approaches Jay warily. He wears his usual uniform, though his jeans are darker today. New, maybe, and this time, the white V-neck beneath his navy flannel is not soaking wet. Bergamot and lime drift her way.

As does the faint scent of chlorine, and when she glances behind Jay, she sees a package of bleach wipes. "What are those for?" Winnie asks, even though the answer is obvious.

Jay grimaces. "I removed the map, Winnie." He stuffs a used wipe into his pocket, the wipe mostly dried and now stained with black ink. "At least your dad used washable markers, so it was easy."

"No, no, Jay." Winnie scoots forward to the shelves where the map was, pushing in front of Jay to do so. *The Awakening of the Spirit by Source, Signs of Sources, Soil Composition for Optimal Sources*—all of Theodosia Monday's titles wink out at Winnie, a mockery of the secret message that hid behind them.

Dad really wasn't subtle about where his map would lead.

Although Winnie does suppose this makes researching the subject much easier. No need for electronic catalogues or input from a librarian.

She snatches two titles from the shelf and confirms that, yes, her dad's crude drawing has been completely erased. She backs away a step, the two books clutched to her chest. She is so shocked, she doesn't even have the space to feel rage right now.

"Why?" She whirls about to face Jay. He looks slightly sheepish—although only *slightly*. Mostly, he looks hard and serious. "Why did you do this?" As she speaks, her voice still lowered to basilisk level, the fluorescent light finally snaps on overhead.

Glaring light sears down.

Winnie flinches. Jay does not.

"I did this," he replies, "because anyone could have found that map, Winnie. It is literally only sheer good luck that no one has yet."

"And anyone could have seen you wiping it away!"

"That's why I came here before the library opens. So no one would notice me. And now no one will notice your map either. You're welcome." He snags the package of wipes and turns as if to leave.

"I'm welcome?" Winnie darts around him so she can block his way. "I told you I didn't need your help, Jay, so you decide the alternative is to actively impede me? Thanks, but I think I preferred your absence over the last four years to this."

"Impede you?" Jay's eyes flash. "Winnie, I just covered your ass because apparently you're dying to get caught."

"I'm *what* now?" Her jaw drops. "You erased my primary piece of evidence, Jay, should I ever have to explain myself to the Tuesday Lambdas!"

"Oh, come on." He dips toward her, his voice lowering. "Should you ever have to explain yourself to the Tuesdays, Win, then that map is not going to protect you. Also, I'm not completely useless, okay? I did take a photo of it with my phone." To demonstrate this, he withdraws his cell and swipes it open to reveal a somewhat blurry but instantly recognizable picture of the map.

Winnie gives it only a cursory glance before she locks her glare on Jay again. "They'll say it's a fake. That I made that in Photoshop."

"And they can also just as easily accuse you of drawing the map, Winnie. The fact is"—closer, closer he leans until their noses are only inches apart and his eyes are very, *very* gray—"if the Tuesdays catch you with a *dampener,* then no evidence of any kind is going to protect you. At least now, with the map gone, no one will accidentally stumble onto it."

Winnie swallows. The urge to adjust her glasses or yell something childish at Jay's entirely too-near face—something like *I know you are but what am I!*—burns inside her chest. She refrains. Particularly because there's a tickling at the back of her skull . . . A swirl of gas and dust that is spinning so fast it will collapse very soon . . .

Then there it is.

Kaboom. A star is born; the first in a new constellation.

Winnie grabs for Jay's phone. The screen has only just winked off, and after a frazzled "Open it back up, please, open it back up," Jay indeed opens it back up.

The map brightens before Winnie's eyes, exactly as she remembers it. Exactly as she drew it on a piece of paper still hiding inside her bedroom.

However, she got *one thing very wrong.* She hadn't noticed it before because she was so flustered, so rushed with Erica arriving on the scene—plus, with the fluorescent lights on as they are now, shadows land differently on the bookcase. On Jay's phone, though, the map is cast in natural sunlight and much easier to see.

"One," Winnie says, pointing to the big X that she already visited in the forest, where the locket led to a dampener and where Grayson died. "Two." She slides her fingers sideways to the very edge of the map, where a second, teensy tiny X awaits.

"Well, shit," Jay murmurs beside her.

"Well, shit," Winnie agrees. "There's another place in the forest I have to go."

20

I can't get into the forest," Winnie says once she and Jay are outside of the library. They walk with long strides toward the parking lot, Jay's hands in his pockets and Winnie clutching a book entitled *Understanding Sources: A Brief History and Guide.*

Brisk, sunny air gusts against them.

"Unless I do another corpse duty," Winnie continues, "I can't avoid the Tuesdays like you do, Jay. I don't know where all the sensors are, so there's no way I can get to that second X."

"I guess that means . . ." Jay slows to a stop before the parking lot's curb. The Volvo is another thirty feet away. Jay's bike—which Winnie *really* should have noticed when she got here—is parked twenty feet more beyond that.

"Means what?" Winnie doesn't like the half frown now gathering over Jay's eyes.

"I guess that means you need my help."

"Ah." Winnie feels her own frown forming, but rather than a surge of geologic heat to light up her veins or even grief for that girl of four years ago, she feels only . . .

Empty.

Resigned.

She does need Jay's help, because there is no way she can get into the forest without detection unless she has him to lead the way. On top of that, loath as she is to admit it, he *was* right to erase that stupid map.

He was also right to check out this book on sources (by Theodosia Monday, of course) instead of letting Winnie do it. It is far less incriminating for him to show an interest in Dianas. Winnie, though? *Now that's weird,* they'll think. *Why is that girl whose dad was a witch now reading about witches?*

"Yes," Winnie says as a fresh burst of morning wind sweeps over her. It knocks hair in her face and rattles through the ivy now turning green on the building. "I need your help, Jay. Please." She offers this with no emotion, no inflection. She is tired, and she cannot deal with any kind of gloating.

He doesn't gloat, though. He simply nods, hands still in his pockets, and squints vaguely toward downtown. After several silent seconds, he offers: "Best time to go will be in the hour before the mist rises tonight. The Alphas leave the forest then, but the Tuesday-night hunters won't be on shift yet."

"Okay." Winnie's teeth click as she tries to remember if Mom has work tonight. "Where do I meet you?"

"I'll pick you up at eight."

"Okay," she says again—and apparently that acknowledgment is the end of their conversation, since Jay nods once at Winnie, a wordless goodbye, and then strides off the curb into the parking lot.

He is already past the Volvo before it occurs to Winnie that maybe she should have thanked him. That maybe she should *still* thank him, lifting her voice over the morning birdsong and breeze.

She doesn't, though, and Jay never looks back.

21

The rest of Tuesday passes at the tedious slog of fly larvae growing in a vampira corpse—except the larvae are more interesting. Which is why, during Luminary history with Professor Samuel, Winnie starts drawing actual fly larvae in the margins of her notes.

Chrysomya megacephala. They're so squirmy, so pale. Able to smell a dead body from ten miles away, they're usually the first fly species to arrive on a dead thing. And while most people don't care about them at all, according to the Compendium they can teach you a lot about the forest.

Forensic entomology of forest cadavers provides a reliable means of assessing when a nightmare or human died. Although various arthropod species will eventually grow into adults on a human corpse, they will never make it past the first larval stage on a nightmare. Studies of dead maggots have revealed magic in their systems; it is believed that the concentration of such magic is deadly, much like a Diana who steals too much power from the spirit—

"Winnie Wednesday, answer the question."

Winnie's head whips up; her pencil stills against her notebook where she just finished sketching the pointed tail of a third-stage *Chrysomya megacephala* maggot. She finds Professor Samuel staring at her from behind his auto-tinting glasses that have decided today was the day for staying creepily shaded. He loves tormenting her with questions he knows she can't answer; she loves imagining what it would be like if *he* encountered a basilisk in the forest and *his* glasses turned instantly to stone like hers had.

"Uh," she answers honestly, and Marcus sniggers a few desks away.

"Who founded the Nightmare Masquerade?" Samuel barks, and he swipes his hand toward the whiteboard, his laser pointer homing in on a single name.

Gianna Sabato.

Okay, that name is actually familiar to Winnie. She might give zero craps about the history of the Luminaries—it's too abstract, too *old*—but she does know a few key basics.

Like how Gianna was the first Saturday in Hemlock Falls and famous for marrying a prince from some tiny nation in the Mediterranean, which is basically the most on-brand thing a Saturday could ever do. In fact, Winnie is pretty sure 90 percent of Dryden's general nastiness is because he knows he can never live up to his great-great-great-grandmother. The other 10 percent is just bitter old man.

Winnie did not know, however, until this exact moment that Gianna had also founded the Nightmare Masquerade, and she wishes she could go back in time and have a word. *Excuse me, but can you please draft a document that says, "Do not hold Masquerade if entire town is in danger"?*

Winnie of course says none of these things aloud. She simply recites the name on the whiteboard and slumps into her seat. Her face is warm, partly from embarrassment, mostly from annoyance. When Professor Samuel pushes his glasses up his nose in a move that Winnie knows she herself is prone to making, her annoyance only swells wider.

The Venn diagram circles for herself and Samuel should have absolutely zero overlap, thank you.

"And," Samuel continues, dragging his shaded gaze over the classroom, "can anyone else here tell me what events comprised the original Masquerade?"

Marcus's hand shoots up.

Because of course it does.

"It was just a fancy ball with masks and stuff. It wasn't until the 1950s that Augustus Saturday added the Floating Carnival and the famed Ferris wheel."

Winnie half expects him to turn around and stick out his tongue at her. She's almost sad when he doesn't.

Samuel returns to the board and pops off the cap of a black marker. Professor Il-Hwa loves to get colorful with her notations—especially when she's drawing nightmare anatomical diagrams—but not Samuel. Black markers always, and the *thin* kind so it's hard to read from the back of the room.

"Each clan opens their estate during the Masquerade, allowing everyone to enter for tours and parties of their own. One party for each night of the week." His marker squeaks as he adds another name to the board. "And this tradition was introduced in the 1970s by Tessa Tuesday, who—after visiting the World's Fair in Osaka—wanted to establish something similar here. She was the first to invite foreign Luminaries, and that is why each Luminary outpost around the world now hosts their own variation of the Masquerade. Ours, however, is the largest." He smirks here, as if this fact somehow makes Hemlock Falls better than the other Luminaries outposts.

As far as Winnie can tell, it's just more people for the Whisperer to kill . . . or the werewolf. Or hell, maybe even a Diana. *Pick your nightmare! Spin the wheel! Get ripped apart as a forest meal!*

Oh god. Winnie is really losing it.

It's funny because the Winnie of two weeks ago wouldn't have been allowed to participate in the Masquerade, and she would have passed all the setup on her bike, frustrated and furious that yet again, she was outside looking in. Then during the week of the parties, she would have holed up in her house and pretended it didn't bother her that literally *everyone else* in Hemlock Falls was out celebrating the return of spring.

It's also funny because the Winnie of two weeks ago had no idea that a nightmare like the Whisperer could exist or that it might rip apart innocent hunters like Grayson Friday. That Winnie had *no idea* a werewolf would get blamed for it all—and actually bite her along the way.

She also had no idea her dad might never have been guilty four years ago.

Too bad Winnie doesn't feel like laughing.

When the bell finally rings to release the history prisoners into the hall, Professor Samuel calls, "Winnie?"

Her face crumples. Her insides too. She was so close to the exit. *So close.*

"Yes, sir?" she asks when she trudges up to the whiteboard, where he now erases with Karate Kid enthusiasm, waxing on and off until the board is nearly clean. All while Winnie gets to watch because there is no second eraser for her to grab and assist him with.

"I want a paper," he says when he is *finally* finished. He missed a spot near the bottom. Winnie doesn't point it out. "On the history of the Wednesday Masquerade party. Five pages, single-spaced. You can start at the school library, though I *encourage* you to go more widely."

Meaning he *expects* her to go more widely.

"Wait," Winnie says as the actual meaning of Samuel's words connects in her brain. "I have to write a paper?"

"Five pages, single-spaced."

"What about the rest of the class? Are they writing one too?"

"No." He smiles; his glasses shadow even more. "The rest of the class listens during my lecture."

"I listen!"

"While drawing worms?"

"*Chrysomya megacephala,*" she counters. "And yes. I can draw and listen at the same time."

"Excellent. Then everything I taught today should give you a good head start." He spins toward his desk, a gust of mothballs and old wool wafting off him. Winnie has to fight the urge to grab a marker and start scribbling all over his stupid whiteboard. He wants worms? She'll show him worms.

"Five pages?" she grits out when he sidles onto the yoga ball he uses instead of a desk chair. "Single-spaced?"

"Precisely."

"And when is it due?"

His eyes flick up to meet hers, two dark spots behind his glasses. He bares a smile so smug it could give Marcus a run for his money. "Tomorrow will suffice. After all, you said you were listening, so it should be no trouble for you to get it done."

Winnie is positively fuming during nightmare anatomy. It's like ever since she decided three days ago that she was *done* putting up with people's crap and she was going to embrace her low-grade fame . . . the forest has decided to lift its middle finger and laugh.

Pick your nightmare! Spin the wheel! You sure taste good as a forest meal!

She makes herself pay attention to Professor Il-Hwa—not because she thinks Il-Hwa will do anything to her like Samuel did, but because it's at least a fun distraction. Possibly even *the* thing she missed more than anything else when her family got kicked out of the Luminaries.

Well, that and being treated like a worthwhile human.

During a breakout session to dissect a harpy eyeball (*powerful eyesight, although they cannot swivel their eyeballs within the sockets*), Winnie is forced to partner with Casey and Peter. They spend the entire time rehashing Grayson's "memorial" party without once mentioning Grayson—as well as confirming *twice* that Winnie really is sure she doesn't want to go with them to the Masquerade ball—while Winnie spends the entire time doing the work they don't want to do.

She makes eye contact with Erica twice. The second time, Erica actually gives her a smile.

When the bell rings marking the end of class, Winnie is all prepared to bolt for the locker room, then bolt around the obstacle course before she has to encounter Marcus. Except the twins and Fatima move into her path. Well, Emma crutches into her path, rather.

"Hey, you okay?" This is from Fatima, who smooths her rose-pink hijab while she asks.

"Um . . ." Winnie blinks. There are so many things that have gone wrong lately, she's not sure where she can begin. *Just choose a word that starts with W, my friend! Whisperer, werewolf, witch—I've gotta catch 'em all just like a Pokémon!*

"I'm fine," Winnie lies instead. Then, because it doesn't sound even a little bit convincing and her three friends are now exchanging glances of skepticism, Winnie amends, "I mean, I'm not fine. Professor Samuel just assigned me a five-page paper—*single-spaced*—due tomorrow on the history of the Wednesday clan's Nightmare Masquerade party."

Bretta's jaw drops so hard her curls bounce. "Are you *serious*? Due tomorrow?"

Winnie groans out a "*Yesssss.* I have twenty-four hours."

"What a dick," Emma provides, looking as outraged as Winnie feels. She is squeezing her crutches with a violent ferocity Winnie appreciates.

"Why?" Fatima demands.

As Winnie explains what happened, she and the trio head into the hall. They're all going to be late, and Winnie's plans of avoiding Marcus are fading fast. It's nice to vent, though, and it occurs to Winnie as they all shuffle past lockers, the banners of each clan peering down at them with warning over their impending tardiness, that she needs to do this more often.

She needs to remember *she isn't actually alone.*

She's so used to solitude, so used to thinking of her life in terms of two triangles—her, Mom, Darian, and then her, Erica, Jay—that she's forgotten there's now a new shape in her geometry. A lovely little square that she can absolutely depend upon.

Bretta, Emma, and Fatima have more than proven they care about her. Emma especially, by forgiving Winnie for not finding her fast enough on the third trial, as if that mistake were no more than a late arrival at Joe Squared.

"Well," Bretta declares when they reach Professor Svenia's classroom— where the three of them will now study third-year history, "let's meet at the library after school."

"Sunday library?" Fatima asks, even as Winnie is struggling to keep up. "Or Monday?"

"Sunday," Emma says, referring to the teaching library behind the Sunday estate. "We've got that lab write-up due for anatomy, so we can help our poor beleaguered buddy here"—she makes a face that can only be described as *haunted revenant rising from the dead*—"write her paper while she helps *us* with all her Compendium smarts."

Winnie actually thinks she might cry. Her chest is swelling so fast, it's like a balloon is expanding inside her rib cage—and it's the exact opposite of the grinding tectonic plates she felt last night while staring at her ex–best friend.

Yes, she lost a Friday four years ago, and a Thursday too . . . but she has now gained three loyal Wednesday bears. She needs to stop forgetting that.

"Thank you," Winnie says, embarrassingly choked up.

The three other corners of her square all notice. They beam and nudge her. Emma even offers an awkward sideways hug, crutches held tight in one hand. "See you after school!" she whispers before hurrying into class with way more weight on her left leg than she's supposed to be using.

The bell rings.

Winnie is officially late to Coach Rosa's class, and she will definitely have to talk to Marcus.

But she doesn't even care. If he wants to mess with her, she will just flash on her phoenix flames as a distraction, then run away before he can speak to her again.

Winnie's plan works quite effectively. At the first sight of Marcus on the training course, she breaks into a flat-out sprint, and soon, she is so far ahead of the class that there is no way his obnoxious self—or anyone else's—will ever catch up to her.

"*Meu Deus,*" Coach Rosa says as Winnie comes barreling over the finish line of the obstacle course, mud up to her knees and sweat pouring off her face. Her heart thunders in her chest. "Did you snort phoenix powder or something?"

Something like that.

Coach Rosa gapes at the stopwatch in her hand. "That is twice as fast as you have ever done it before."

"Can . . . I . . . leave . . . early then?" Winnie pants. She might have pushed it a little too hard. She feels borderline puke-y.

"Absolutely." Coach Rosa gives an impressed laugh. "Enjoy the showers while the locker room is empty."

Winnie does not enjoy the showers, but rather rinses off as fast as she can, changes back into her "civilian" clothes, and scoots out of the echoing expanse of the locker room before anyone can catch her there. Then she makes her way across campus to the Sunday library.

It is a strange building that doesn't fit with the aesthetic of the rest of the estate: instead of the standard red bricks and wooden roof, there are white stones and a domed top. Two columns frame the front double doors, and it feels more like Winnie is stepping into a Roman palace than a library meant for students. There are even a few cypress trees reaching for the sky.

Winnie used to love this building. In fact, other than the Monday library and the old museum, this was her favorite building in Hemlock Falls, and as she steps inside, an almost painful wave of nostalgia razes over her.

Nothing has changed here; for a few moments, she can pretend she hasn't changed either.

The door crashes shut behind Winnie. "Hello?" a voice calls. "Ms. Thursday, is that you with my coffee?"

Winnie hurries forward. Skylights filter in natural light to illuminate curved bookcases. Shelves stream past and colorful spines flash like melusine scales beneath the sun.

"Ms. Thursday?"

"Uh, no, ma'am." Winnie pushes into the central area to find the Sunday librarian standing at her round desk. And *oh my god.* This is not the librarian Winnie remembers. This woman is a walking advertisement for color. Never has Winnie seen so many shades in one place. It's like if a tropical fish exploded on top of a bird of paradise while an entire paint store rained down.

And it's not just color, but texture and dimension too. The woman's knit sweater has little tufts and balls all over it, while her overalls are assembled from strips of different fabric, like velvet and burlap and denim. As she steps around the desk to greet Winnie, Winnie catches sight of boots that are lime-green snakeskin. Then there are her thick-framed glasses with raised yellow polka dots, and her wide headband flashes with magenta sequins and orange lace. Her pale cheeks are dabbed with rouge that is *very* bright, and her lips and eyelids are even brighter with matching orange smears. The only part of her that lacks color is her hair, but it's so shiny and white it almost reflects all the color right back at you.

Winnie literally has to squint to focus on this woman.

"Oh, you're that girl on the TV," the woman says. She is extremely tiny, and her voice is like a squeaking field mouse. "I'm Professor Teddy Funday."

"Fun . . . day?"

"Oh yes." The woman laughs, a wee twitter of sound. "I belong to three different clans—can you believe it? But saying, 'Oh, I'm Professor Teddy Sunday Monday Saturday,' is just *such* a mouthful, don't you think? I tried Sunmonsaturday too, as well as Satmonsunday, but it just didn't have the right ring."

But Funday most certainly does. In fact, there is not a single word to better describe this woman. It's so appropriate, Winnie is left wondering why she has never heard of her—or *seen* her. Admittedly, Winnie hasn't been allowed at the most popular Luminary haunts in four years, but a gal doesn't miss a woman like this. She is like one of the cockatrice subspecies only found in the Pakistani forest, and there is no escaping all that plumage.

"Are you here for any particular reason, dear?" Professor Funday asks. "Or just to look around?"

Winnie swallows. She really *doesn't* want help. Yes, she has a paper to write for Professor Samuel, but it has been four years since she was allowed inside this library. She kind of wants to savor that alone.

However, before Winnie can answer *I'm just here to browse,* Professor Funday claps her hands and says, "Oh, my! What a lovely necklace! Does it stand for something?"

"Ma'am?" Winnie claps a hand over her locket. "Stand for . . . something?"

"Yes! You know—like how ancient Luminaries used to use the crescent moon and stars as a way to send messages. The number of stars and the arrangement of the moon meant different things. Is that what your necklace is for? A secret message?"

Winnie feels as if the breath has been punched right out of her. Her mouth sags open. Her brain clunks to a grinding slog. *Send messages. Arrangement of moon and stars.* Could that be why Dad left the necklace in the attic? Was he trying to say something more than what Winnie figured out with his map?

It seems unlikely he would have known such a specialized corner of Luminary history. Not to mention, this locket belonged to Grandma Harriet first.

But it also feels like way too big a coincidence to completely ignore.

"Moon and stars," Winnie blurts. Then she flushes and swallows. "I mean, what you just said about the moon and stars. Do you have any books on that?"

Funday blinks behind her own glasses, her eyelids briefly lowering like two orange garage doors. She scratches at her chin. Foundation smears onto her fingers. "We certainly don't *here*—that's quite a niche topic. But I can dig up some titles if you'd like and see if the Monday library has them?"

Winnie nods eagerly. "That would be so helpful. Thank you!"

"Of course!" Professor Funday beams. "You know, you remind me of myself at your age, Ms. Wednesday, and the pursuit of knowledge is always a virtuous one!" She bustles past, a staggering blur of color and dimension. "I will find you in the basement once I have those titles for you! Oh, and do be warned: the basement is positively *freezing*."

23

It truly is freezing in the basement, yet this is a small price to pay to for the peace and quiet of it all. Unlike the library's upper floor, the basement is a long rectangle with gray stone walls and floor-to-ceiling shelves, as well as rows of gleaming tables and cubbyhole desks where computers await. Wooden chairs are arranged between the tables, and occasional leather armchairs rest at stately angles in a few odd corners.

It's how Winnie imagines a secret speakeasy might look, except instead of alcohol, the proprietors are gathering books.

There are no windows down here; everything is lit by amber wall sconces and little desk lamps; and since Winnie is currently the only person around, none of those lamps are on, leaving the whole space dim.

And silent.

Blessedly silent.

Jay wasn't wrong on Saturday night when he said parties weren't Winnie's scene. Libraries and books will forever be more her speed, no matter how cold it might get down here.

Winnie ducks into the closest cubbyhole, a stone nook that sinks into the wall with a desk and a computer. She drops her backpack onto the scratched surface of the desk. *Flip,* goes the lamp's switch. *Beam,* goes the light—and *ow.* It sends her shadow straight across the room, huge and menacing.

Before Winnie can settle in to start reviewing her admittedly scant notes from Samuel's class, Funday arrives to tell her that "there are no books on that ancient messaging system in Hemlock Falls. But do not fret, my dear, for there is one in Italy, and I have already requested the Lunedìs send the title to the Monday history library here! So you need not travel all the way to Italy to fetch it."

Funday also gives Winnie a fond pat on the shoulder. "Perhaps you too will change clans one day, once you have absorbed all the lessons the Wednesdays can provide. I haven't tried them yet, but who knows? When I feel my work here is done, maybe I will next become a bear." She opens her arms, bangles clacking, and then, with a quick shiver and mumble about *frostbite,* she meanders once more upstairs.

Change clans. Winnie didn't even know you could do that, and she wonders which clan Funday was actually born into. What a kooky, fascinating lady. Someday, when Winnie is *not* stuck writing a paper for the grumpiest Sunday who ever lived, she will actually ask Funday about her past.

Winnie has only just finished pulling out her class notes from Samuel and then grabbing extra chairs for her cubbyhole when Bretta comes skipping down the stairs. Fatima is right behind. "Emma is taking the elevator," Bretta explains, plopping down next to Winnie. Fatima drops to Winnie's other side. "You got here fast."

"Yeah, I did *not* want to deal with Marcus."

Fatima and Bretta both roll their eyes. Kind Emma, who is now arriving from her elevator ride, coos, "Aw, but he means well."

"No," Winnie replies. "He really doesn't."

As Emma hops the final few steps toward the cubbyhole, Bretta asks, "Have you gotten started yet?"

"No. And thanks for helping me." Winnie smiles at her friends, and they—of course—smile back. "Should we do your lab work first? I already finished in class, if you want to see."

"Dang." Fatima gives a low whistle. "I didn't think *anyone* finished in class. Impressive."

"Nah." Winnie flushes and withdraws her notebook. "I already know most of it."

"Compendium smarts," Emma says with a nod. "I told you guys she had 'em."

Winnie's flush deepens—but it's a happy one. "Here. Take a look if you want."

"Ooooh. We do want." Bretta takes the notebook, her fingers grabbing like little crab claws. "This is excellent, Winnie. Thank you."

Emma, meanwhile, says, "I'll help you, Winnie. I wrote a paper about the Wednesday Masquerade right after we moved here, so I know exactly where to start."

Where they start is at the Sunday Encyclopedia. It's divided into twenty-six volumes, with one book for each letter of the alphabet spaced out across three tables in the basement. Each tome has nice thick paper that students can't easily damage, and the separation into multiple volumes means multiple people can use it at the same time.

Winnie goes for the letter *M* (for *Masquerade*), Emma goes to *W* (for *Wednesday Clan*). Then they settle at a table nearby, so Emma won't have to keep hobbling all the way back and forth to the cubbyhole.

"Sometimes the entries reference other books to check out," Emma says, flipping through the *W*'s. "I remember finding a whole bunch of stuff on the first Wednesday party . . ." She trails off.

Winnie, who is thumbing through her own volume, glances up—and finds that Emma's face has turned sickly. Alarmed, Winnie shifts toward her . . . only to catch sight of what Emma is staring at.

It's the entry for *Werewolf.*

Below the name is a drawing of a werewolf that's horribly inaccurate. The canines are too small, the fur too thin, the shoulders too narrow. It's like the opposite of Red Riding Hood: *My, what small eyes you have.* There's even a full moon sketched above it, even though real werewolves have no connection to cycles of the moon. They rise when the forest wants them to; they kill when the forest commands.

For half a moment, Winnie is struck by how these illustrations never live up to reality. The werewolf's real size and power. The kelpie's watery glisten. The vampira's vicious claws . . .

And the fantasy of being a Luminary again.

That hasn't lived up at all—not merely because a pen can't capture reality, but because Winnie herself can't. She is too small, too boring, too one-dimensional to be a proper lantern shining against the night.

She forces her thoughts back to Emma, who looks to be spiraling just as hard as Winnie is. "You okay?" she asks her friend.

Emma swallows. "Yeah, I'm fine. I just . . ." She scratches absently at her injured leg, eyes almost vacant, almost hazy. Like she is existing in a very different time, a very different place.

And Winnie knows exactly where Emma is—and she in turn rubs at her scarred forearm. "How much do you remember from the night of our trial, Emma?"

"Some." Emma's eyes twitch. Her pupils shrink. "The harpy . . . I think it had me, and then the wolf showed up howling. I . . ." She shakes her head. Her eyes shift back into focus. "It's all so fuzzy after that, but then I remember you getting it off me and screaming at it. It didn't bite at me, did it?"

Winnie shakes her head. "No."

"It just bit at you, then." Emma's eyes drop to Winnie's covered arm. She has seen the scars only once before, when Winnie was in the hospital. Her frown deepens. "I'm sorry."

"Sorry?" Winnie blinks. "For what?"

"For Saturday night. At the party." She leans over the table, over the Encyclopedia and the wolf's snarling face, to lay a hand on Winnie's. "We shouldn't have said what we said to you. About the scars and getting bitten and . . . and the howling. It was really insensitive. Especially since that monster is still out there."

"Oh," Winnie breathes. She hadn't been expecting a conversation like this—not ever and not from anyone. Instead of making her feel better about everything, though, it only makes her feel worse. There's still a piece of her that's missing. A werewolf-shaped hole that she can't seem to fill, no matter how hard she tries to remember.

A few days after Winnie got home from the hospital, she towed out her Xeroxed Compendium, and stared at the entry on were-creatures. She hoped it would jog something loose. Unlock this unintentional compartment in which she has stuffed all her memories.

The wolf bit her. When? Where? *Why?*

But the copied pages of the were-creature entry had no more answers for her than this encyclopedia does. No more answers for her than Emma does. There is no gas or dust here to form a star; there is only dark matter.

"Thanks," Winnie murmurs to Emma—and she means it. She *does* appreciate the apology.

She just wishes she could have some memories to go with it.

C H A P T E R

24

fter two hours at the Sunday library—and with a finished paper to show for it (thanks, Emma!)—Winnie drives straight home. At one point, she gets into third gear, and *whoa*. She is so fast! A veritable unicorn galloping through the forest!

Winnie rolls to a stop beside the curb and shoves outside into the cool afternoon, where she discovers Mom in the midst of some hard-to-ignore handiwork: a long strip of green fabric with the Wednesday bear now dangles from the family's front porch in all its ferocious, rampant glory. Curled in Latin script underneath is the word *FIDES.*

Loyalty.

The flag billows in the afternoon breeze, staked into a newly installed flagpole holder while Mom stands on the porch beneath it, tightening a screw with a drill as orange as pumpkin.

Rmmmmm, the drill declares, followed by the *ck-ck-ck-ck* of a screw that has reached its end. Mom is totally oblivious to Winnie's arrival until Winnie calls out, "Mom?"

She whips around, orange drill in hand and cheeks flushed. "My favorite daughter!" She opens her arms to the flag. "What do you think?" She doesn't wait for an answer before hopping down the porch steps to join Winnie on the sidewalk.

There, the two of them study the flag together: Mom with her head tilted like a hellion hearing potential prey, and Winnie with her jaw agog because it's a *really big flag.*

"Huh," Mom says. The delighted joy she'd first donned upon spotting Winnie now shifts to something embarrassed. "Do you think it's too much?"

"Uh," Winnie says, afraid honesty is not the best policy here, but also afraid that any lie she attempts will be spotted in an instant. "It's . . . big."

"But is it *too* big?" Mom taps the drill against her chin. "I've had it in the attic for forever and decided it was time to pull out the old thing."

At the word "attic," Winnie's insides lock up. *Attic* is where all the cards from Dad were until this morning. And *attic* is where Mom originally hid them instead of turning them over to the Council as she should have done.

Yet nothing in Mom's current demeanor indicates that she has checked on whether the cards are still intact, and since Winnie would like to keep it that way, she is about to get wholeheartedly behind this ginormous flag.

"Is there such a thing as too big?" Winnie asks, tapping her chin much like Mom is doing with the drill. "I mean, loyalty can't be too big, can it, Mom?"

A contemplative pause from Mom. Then a nod. "No. You're right, Winnebago. Loyalty *can't* be too big, and I want the Council to see that no matter what they decide, we are still Wednesdays." She aims her drill toward the sky as she declares this, reminding Winnie of Dryden with his starter gun before the annual Hemlock Falls Fun Run—which Winnie now knows from her paper was *actually* introduced by Anthony Wednesday in 1984 for the Nightmare Masquerade.

"We are still Wednesdays," Winnie repeats, hoping she sounds just as enthusiastic as Mom does. "Have you, uh . . . had any news on that front?"

Mom deflates slightly—though only slightly as she lowers the drill and sets off toward the back of the house. Winnie follows. "I have *not* had any news, but I'm having dinner with Rachel tonight, so . . . I'm hopeful."

"And that prompted you to pull out the bear?"

"It prompted me to pull out the bear."

Mom and Winnie both aim for the shed, which has its door hanging wide. "I suspect," Mom says as she returns the drill to a box of tools with her initials, *FW,* stamped in the side (a gift from her handy father, who taught her everything she knows about maintaining the house), "that we will get good news at tomorrow night's clan dinner. I just have a feeling."

Winnie doesn't point out that Mom frequently *just has a feeling,* and it frequently turns out to be *just indigestion.* In this instance, she might actually be right. Surely the Council can't drag this out much longer. Then again, knowing Dryden . . . and knowing Erica's mom Marcia . . .

Mom seems to sense something isn't quite right with Winnie as they walk toward the kitchen door. "How about we make your favorite dinner?"

Winnie's breath catches with salivary excitement. "Macaroni and cheese? The real kind?"

"The kind in a box is real too," Mom says with a grin. "But yes, the *real* kind from scratch."

"But I thought you had dinner plans tonight."

"I do, but it doesn't mean I can't cook for you before I go. And I'll even put on *extra* cheddar and those bacon bits you like."

And Winnie finds her breath is catching again, except this time, it's more choked up, more pained. Dad left; Mom stayed. And not just *remained-in-the-area* stayed, but supported and loved and made non-box macaroni and cheese whenever she thought her daughter was down.

No one else but Darian did that.

No one else.

Winnie grabs the back door's knob—unlocked because her family never locks their doors—and turns a slightly serious, slightly uncomfortable face on Mom. "Thanks, Mom. That sounds awesome right about now."

"Of course." Mom flushes. "Anything for my Winnebago. Now open the door please, before that crow on the roof poops on us."

While Mom heads off to the grocery store, Winnie locks her bedroom door and retrieves the dampener. Much as she did yesterday, she disassembles it on her desk—the moss is drier, but still slimy. And still stinky. This time, though, rather than study the rotting contents alone, she retrieves Theodosia Monday's book and adds it to the mix.

Understanding Sources: A Brief History and Guide. "Show me what you've got, Theodosia." Winnie opens to the first page. The spine offers the satisfying crack of a book that has rarely been opened before. The pages are pristine, the print minuscule.

Brief this book is not. And the reading is excruciatingly slow thanks to a million new terms Winnie has never seen before—many of them in Latin, most of them for spells.

Effūsiō: A spell that can be cast outside the forest using power stored in a source.

Silva: A spell that can only be cast within the forest, relying on immediately absorbed spirit power.

Mundanus: A spell cast to accomplish small tasks, such as lighting fires or muffling sight. These require little magic and are the first spells Dianas learn.

Incubo: A spell modeled after a nightmare. For example, a banshee incubo mimics the grief and paralysis caused by a banshee. Such spells require power taken directly from the corresponding nightmare.

Sagitta aurea: These spells are used to kill or maim a target. Just as the Dianas are named for the Roman goddess of the hunt, these spells are modeled after Diana's preferred weapon of golden arrows.

It is, to Winnie's dismay (and a rather large dose of magmatic heat), interesting to read. *Really* interesting. If not for Dad ruining her family's lives, she might have checked this book out years ago and added it to her brain-bank of forest knowledge. Though it's also a challenge not to think back to her time on the Tuesday estate. To Jeremiah Tuesday with his red hair and redder mustache, asking questions that now have some context.

Were there burn marks on your dad's fingers? Winnie now knows the blisters left behind from spell-casting have a distinctive pucker around the edges.

Did you ever smell strange things in the house? Apparently magic stolen from the spirit has a chemical, unnatural smell when it is expelled via spells.

Did he have any small wooden coins in his possession? Dianas believe (without empirical evidence) that rowan wood protects against nightmares.

There's even a whole section in Theodosia's books devoted to the hierarchy of Dianas, which Winnie never realized was so complex . . . or so pretentious. As with the spells, it's a lot of Latin terminology that would no doubt be easier for *everyone* if it were just modernized. At least they now call the Dianas who specialize in hunting nightmares "hounds" instead of the Latin word "*canēs*." Or call the elected witches in leadership "crows" instead of "*cornīcēs*"?

Although—to be fair—at least Dianas aren't separated into fourteen branches like the Luminaries. They are one, diffuse beast with thorny tendrils rooted into any spirit corner the Tuesday Lambdas aren't looking. Not to mention, the Diana order split off from the Luminaries during the Roman Empire, shortly after the society formed, so maybe all the Latin *does* make sense in the end.

Mom eventually gets home, and Winnie hears the clanking of pots and clacking of utensils. A mixer whirs. The fridge door repeatedly thumps. It is a nice sound made by a nice mom whose excitement over being a Luminary again has transformed her as much as being in the forest transforms Winnie—except that this is long-term. *This* has restored Mom's color, and if all goes well tomorrow, then that color will be permanent.

While the macaroni and cheese gets assembled downstairs, Winnie reads and reads and reads, and she learns four important things that seem relevant to her dampener.

First: the moss inside is a peat moss, which is best used for sources made from metal because the acidity of the moss neutralizes the alkalinity of the oxidized metal. The peat moss also *reeks,* and Winnie is going to have to throw this away soon.

Second: the tin itself is stainless steel, which is both the best for hiding sources from Luminary detection (because steel isn't very conductive) and the most effective at containing power.

A lot of power.

Third: the size of the fishhook—large—and the arrangement of the "vent" in the top left corner also suggests that the source this dampener once held was strong. Like, really strong. It needed frequent venting to prevent the absorbed power from detonating within and blowing a giant crater into the forest.

Fourth: the running water this dampener was in should have nullified the source's power. This particular fact, found on page 123, really throws Winnie, since it turns out that just as running water deters a nightmare, the best way to *remove* a source's power over time is to leave it in a stream.

Either someone put the source in the water four years ago to nullify it—
and Dad figured that out . . .

Or else Dad put it there himself.

Either way, this is good news, right? If the source is powerless, then a
Diana can't be running amok about to kill everyone with an *effusio* spell.
As for why the source itself is missing from the dampener . . . that remains
an open question, and Winnie has to pause her reading on page 147 when
Mom hollers, "I'm leaving! I've set a timer on the oven! *Make good choices!*"

Winnie scrabbles to her bedroom door and unlocks it just in time to
shout back, "Thank you, Mom!"

"Loveyoubye!" The front door shuts; the house rattles.

And Winnie ducks back into her room to put away the dampener and
the book before her dinner goes *bzzzzzz!* in the oven. Jay will be here soon;
they will return once more to the forest—this time in pursuit of a second X.

Illogical as it is, Winnie can't wait.

25

True to his word, Jay arrives for Winnie at eight in Mathilda. Since Mom is out for dinner, Winnie ducks out the front door with no fear of nosy questions. She wears her training gear, just as Jay suggested, although underneath her black joggers and hoodie, she has also donned purple jogging shorts and a white tank top. These are her backup plan in case she doesn't get home before Mom does.

I was just out for an evening jog, see?

Jay is deep in his head the instant Winnie plops into the Wagoneer's front seat. And his head, meanwhile, seems to be deep in the forest. Other than offering Winnie a thermos of fresh coffee—which Winnie does not accept because it is *way* too late in the day for caffeine—Jay says nothing on the drive back to the Friday estate.

In fact, Winnie counts on one hand how many sentences he utters between her entering the Wagoneer and him parking them just outside the Friday garage. First: *Coffee?* Second: *Watch your step.* This is in reference to a divot of mud beside the garage. Third: *Wait.* Because he is tipping back another swig of coffee before depositing the thermos on the stoop beside the garage. And fourth: *Okay, let's go.*

Admittedly, Winnie also says next to nothing save for some targeted replies: *It's way too late for coffee, I see the mud, Okay, I'll wait,* and then a yawn so fierce it almost knocks her over because she ate too much macaroni and cheese and now she really just wants a nap. She wonders once or twice if maybe she should talk to Jay about what she read in *Understanding Sources: A Brief History and Guide*—namely that the stream likely nullified the missing source . . .

But there will be time for that later. For now, Jay is quiet and Winnie wants quiet too.

When they reach the edge of the forest, they both utter slightly more—though only slightly. They have traced along their usual path into the trees, except this time, they are not going to their training spot with the fallen sugar maple and red pine.

"Are you ready?" Jay asks.

"Yes," Winnie answers. Her dinner is not fully digested, but it will have to do.

"We've got to move fast," he continues. "There's only one hour before the patrol shift changes and the mist rises. Plus, there are a lot of new sensors between here and that X on the map, so we'll need to stay as close together as we can." He rolls his shoulders, and there is a bounce to his movements like a racer about to shoot off from the starting line. He too wears all black and his hood is pulled over his head.

"Okay." Winnie sucks in a bracing breath. Then adjusts her glasses, which now have a neoprene strap attached in the back because she learned her lesson about glasses in the forest: too easy to lose, too easy to break.

But also, invaluable when facing a basilisk.

Thanks, she wants to tell Jay, but just like at the library, the word never comes. She can't seem to force it when there is still this big looming question mark stuck between them.

Winnie might now be standing on the tectonic plate labeled *Tonight* in which he will help her, but it doesn't negate the one labeled *Four Years Ago* in which he wouldn't. The plates still crunch and grind and burn so hot they could melt her all over again.

Jay quickly tests a small flashlight—*wink, wink*—before depositing it into a pocket. "Let's go," he orders. Then he sets off into the trees, and Winnie darts after him. He moves fast—so fast—which Winnie is accustomed to from their training sessions together . . .

But this is next level. This is "straight to maximum sustainable pace" without any sort of warm-up. Winnie's lungs and heart are happy for all of forty-five seconds before they start to rebel. *Girl, you can't just steal all our blood for your muscles yet! We need time to acclimate!* There is no time to acclimate. There is no time to slow down. And her stomach is the least happy of all. *Why did you fill me with bacon bits? Please, can we stop now? Please, I do not like all this bouncing.*

Winnie forces herself to focus on Jay's back—on mimicking his movements around trees and over roots, through ditches and up mounds. The terrain of the forest is never even; Winnie's ankles and feet, despite the intense two weeks of training with Jay, are still woefully weak against it.

Soon, though, her heart and lungs have warmed up enough and her stomach has adjusted. Oxygen gets where it needs to be in her organs; her breathing steadies; she finally starts to feel alive again—and *oh,* how she missed it. No clusterfuck, no light. Only darkness, darkness, darkness.

Existence is so much simpler in the forest. Especially with Jay beside her.

It's strange to think, but sometimes Winnie cannot separate the two: Jay and the forest. Where the hazy hemlocks and pines end, Jay seems to begin. And tonight, where the hazy hemlocks and pines end, Winnie begins too.

She loses all track of time once her body settles into the rhythm of Jay's body. He moves with such grace that if she does not focus directly on him, she will lose him in a heartbeat.

She never notices any sensors or cameras or Tuesdays, but she can tell from Jay's sudden sharp turns or abrupt stops that they must be skirting close. She strains to see what he sees, to hear what he hears, but he has so much more experience in the forest, not to mention proper Luminary training.

Winnie wants that too. She wants to duck and dive and hop and hurdle without ever losing her bearings or her feet. She wants to fade and melt and blend so deeply into the gray of the forest, she forgets who she is.

Jay circles them around Stone Hollow; Winnie imagines she can see orange tape rattling far across the meadow. She can't, though, not really. Already, light is draining fast—which means time is draining fast too. The sun has almost escaped beyond the horizon.

At the top of Stone Hollow, Jay swerves north, following an empty streambed that trails sharply downward into a stagnant pool filled with dead leaves and detritus. The water glitters black, rippling as Jay and then Winnie sprint around it before charging up a fresh hill. Here, on the northern edges of the forest, the altitude rises more sharply. Not mountains by any stretch, but certainly proper hills with crude ridges and plenty of boulders.

Winnie has collected so many nons over the years who came here for good climbing . . . then never made it out again. *Death is a part of life. Get used to it, Little Win-Win, or you won't last a week inside the forest.*

Winnie swallows past a knot in her throat. For all that Chad Wednesday shamed her four years ago, she isn't any better. After all, she and Bretta made fun of Marcus only two weeks ago for getting sick at the sight of a dead non.

It doesn't feel good to remember that.

And it feels even worse when Winnie makes herself actually *think* about that non corpse she and Bretta collected. He was a halfer—no torso, no feet. Just a pair of legs in shredded jeans. And while the Luminaries of Hemlock Falls might think a werewolf did it, Winnie knows it was the Whisperer.

She hopes the guy didn't know what hit him. She hopes he didn't feel any pain.

And she hopes his family isn't out there wondering where he disappeared to.

The trees become sparser, less secondary growth and more sprawling canopy. It means Winnie can spot the extra sensors herself now—as well as two of Lizzy's cameras, crudely assembled but seemingly active with blinking red lights that say, *I see you.*

Jay is forced to move more slowly, occasionally clambering up rock faces before leaning back to help Winnie. He is panting, she is panting, and they never speak. Not even when she loses her footing on one ridge and takes a brutal tumble ten feet down.

Even then, Jay merely helps her stand, then gives her a stern once-over in the gathering shadows, and they resume their forward charge. Until finally, finally—when Winnie's lungs and heart and stomach are once more raising the banner of revolt—they reach the second X on Dad's map.

It is in a pocket of damp lowland surrounded by elms just earning their first buds of spring. The sun is completely set now, and with the hills rising up on all sides like walls, there is little light to trickle in. It's not yet dark enough for Jay's flashlight, but it will be soon.

Strangely, a square pit sits in the middle of the lowland. Ten feet by ten feet, no more than five feet deep, it looks as if the spirit used a cookie cutter to pluck granite right out of the earth.

Winnie approaches the edge of one of the granite sides of the pit and peers in. It's like a rough-hewn pool that got abandoned mid-construction and then filled up with last year's fallen leaves. At the center, rainwater has gathered in a murky puddle the size of a bathtub.

Oh yes, this *has* to be where the little X on the map was leading.

"Come on," Jay murmurs, and after an easy leap down the edge into the hole, he reaches up to help Winnie descend. She isn't entirely sure why she would need his assistance—the pit isn't that deep . . .

But looking down at him, his hood fallen back and his cheeks flushed with exertion, a faint glow of sweat across his brow, Winnie finds that her brain has deposited itself somewhere outside of her body so her body is now acting without proper supervision.

Which is perhaps why she lets him grab her waist and ease her gently down. Lets his hands linger on her hips as if he needs to steady her when they both know she is absolutely solid on this mostly flat ground.

Then he releases her as if whatever just happened between them was totally normal and probably never happened at all. Just like when they held hands on top of the old museum.

Winnie swallows. Jay coughs, and they both stride for the puddle and take up sentry on either side. Winnie gazes toward the southern and eastern walls of granite, he to the north and the west. They each take a full circle before finding each other's faces again.

"Well," Winnie begins quietly. "I have no idea what to look for."

Jay grunts, a sound that is part agreement and part laugh. "We should've brought a shovel."

"Agreed. It couldn't have slowed us any more than I did."

Jay's lips pinch. "You're not as bad as you think you are."

"But I'm not as good as you."

"No one is as good as me."

Winnie blinks. This is such a startlingly arrogant thing to say, yet nothing in Jay's demeanor is braggadocious. If anything, he just murmured the statement with all the absentminded detachment of a comment on the weather. He certainly doesn't notice how the words might be perceived to a casual listener.

Youngest Lead Hunter in Hemlock Falls! You must be so proud!

Pride is definitely not what Jay feels. Instead, he is all focused competence and meticulous control. With careful movements, he fans away from Winnie, kicking up last year's leaves and beaming his small flashlight over the ground. Winnie wants to imitate him and help, but she is actually worried she might disrupt whatever primed hunter skills he currently wields.

So she turns her attention to the strange assemblage of walls that make up this granite pit. Mist must collect here when it rises, hot and choking like the worst hot tub ever. It grows darker by the second, Winnie's eyes adjusting in time to twilight.

Her dad was here at some point. Right here, either before he fled or after. He *had* to have come here, just as he *had* to have gone to that stream beside Stone Hollow. For once the Pompeii rage of the previous days doesn't rise in Winnie as she considers this. Instead, she just feels . . . confused.

A breeze rustles through elm trees. A crow caws in the distance. It makes Winnie think of the *cornīcēs* who lead the Dianas. Who are they? Where do they live? And *how* do they become theses "crows in charge," or for that matter, how do they become Dianas? Winnie still has half of Theodosia Monday's book to read, and traitorous as it feels, she can't wait to get back to it.

A splash sounds behind her. She whirls around, to find Jay pushing into the puddle, his sleeves rolled up to his elbows and flashlight chomped in his teeth. He wades to the middle—it reaches his mid-calves—then bends over and shoves his hands in.

Winnie watches him, unsure what he's looking for and afraid to break the silence they've maintained for most of their journey. Her teeth click together. It is getting cold fast, and she wishes she'd worn a watch. The mist must be rising soon.

She watches Jay dig around for several seconds as one particular passage from Theodosia's book rises to the surface of her brain, just like these loosened leaves and silt rise around Jay's feet.

Much as animal evolution frequently diverges from a single ances-

tral species into unrecognizably different beasts—e.g., the cichlids of Lake Victoria—the Dianas and the Luminaries are two societies rooted in a common ancestor yet totally unrecognizable.

However, both carnivores and herbivores are essential for healthy ecosystems, and this author posits that so too are our disparate organizations. The question then becomes: Which society is the predator? And which society is the prey?

After what feels like an eternity of sunlight vanishing and cold creeping in, Jay finally straightens and returns the flashlight to his pocket. "Nothing," he says, his haggard face tight with frustration. Water sloughs off his hands and arms. He yanks his hood back. "I thought maybe there was another dampener in here, but I'm not finding anything under all this muck."

"Maybe someone already found whatever it was Dad wanted me to find."

Jay's face winds up tighter. "Maybe. But this isn't a place hunters come often." He waves around. "Most of the nightmares rise closer to the Big Lake, and especially on the western side. That's why we park over there, you know?"

Winnie did *not* know this is why the parking area is to the west, and she hastily files that information away for later consideration. Then she offers Jay her hand. He doesn't need it.

He takes it anyway.

His fingers are freezing and slightly damp, and she has a weird urge to clutch his hands and rub them like Mom used to do for her when she was a little girl. Jay's boots squelch and filthy water splatters onto Winnie's legs. Then he is out and they release each other. Again.

Winnie pushes her glasses up her nose. "So this is a dead end?"

"Looks that way." Jay squints down at his watch, beaming the flashlight onto the old face. "Whatever your dad wanted you to find, I'm not seeing it."

"Me neither." Winnie kicks ineffectually at a lump of leaves; the first sparks of rage are flickering along the back of her neck and she doesn't want to indulge them. "Why can't he just give me an address, you know? Like, why couldn't the X on the map just lead me to the real Diana's house?"

Jay shrugs a shoulder. "Maybe because no one would believe you if you showed up shouting, *Witch!* You need proof, Win, and . . . well, I assume that's where all these clues are meant to go. Plus," Jay adds, sliding his hands into his jogger pockets, "if this Diana is as dangerous as they seem, then writing you a letter is way too risky. Instead, your dad made all these steps to follow to keep you from getting caught—and even doing that was probably a risk for him."

"A risk for *him*?" Winnie repeats. "The guy that might be innocent but still ran off and abandoned his family? *He* was at risk?"

"I'm not defending him, Winnie—"

"You sure about that?"

"—I just get why he might have done what he did to protect you." Jay pins Winnie with an uncompromising stare. "I also think that understanding his headspace will make it easier to follow his clues. He's trying to lead you to proof so you can actually catch the real Diana. That means something here is important. I just . . . have no idea what." His shoulders shrug, hands still in his pockets.

Then he withdraws them and taps at his watch. "We need to go. The mist will rise soon."

Winnie clenches her molars and swallows back the urge to snarl and snap at him like one of those aquatic wyrms in the Mexican forest. Jay is not the enemy, and now is not the time for a fight.

She scans the granite pit once more. What are they missing? What is *she* missing? "Can I have the flashlight?"

Jay rifles it out. It's warm, and their fingers briefly touch. Winnie winks it on and beams it over the pit's walls. This is such a distinctive place—one she has somehow never seen before in all her years of corpse duty.

Up, down, side to side. Winnie drags the shaft of light over grooved stone that must have stood here for millions of years. Long before the trees, long after the threes. Long before the spirit, and perhaps long after it too.

Theodosia Monday mentioned that no one *really* knows what happens when a spirit dies. Dianas claim it will mean safety across the world; Luminaries believe it will mean a global ecosystem collapse. That latter option is what has always been taught to Luminaries, and it makes perfect sense to Winnie's science mind. Ecosystems are just that: *systems*. To remove one piece from a system means every other component no longer functions as it evolved to do . . .

But what if the Dianas learn explanations that make just as much sense to them? What if they also have evolutionary and ecological examples that point to why the spirits should be eliminated? There's no way to test it empirically, no experiment to run that would clearly say, *Oh yes, this is what happens when a spirit dies.*

Which is why, even centuries after the two societies split apart, their enmity still remains.

"Stop," Jay says, a scalpel through Winnie's thoughts. "Swing the light back this way." He guides her wrist, and the flashlight finds a stretch of stone. "There."

He stalks away from Winnie, circles the edge of the puddle, and reaches the wall—where yes, a long strip of shadow is now illuminated.

Winnie's lungs hitch. "That's not natural." It was impossible to see in the darkness, but Jay's hunter eyes caught what Winnie's did not. She scoots to his side and light gleams over streaks and smears.

It looks very familiar, and Winnie knows right away why: something died here. Some*one* died here.

And they died exactly as Grayson had.

Before Winnie can say anything—not that she knows what to say anyway—she catches sight of the unmistakable sign that she and Jay are in trouble. White fog curls around her feet.

The night's mist has begun to rise.

26

J ay spots the mist at the same moment as Winnie. His head shakes—an incredulous movement while he glances uselessly at his watch. Whatever hour is shown there doesn't matter. The mist is the final arbiter of their actions, and the mist is here.

Now.

Jay seems to come to the same conclusion, since he suddenly twists away and moves fast as an arrow for the nearest granite wall. Winnie staggers after him, the mist expanding around her. It is balmy, a welcoming embrace collecting in this low pocket like a steam room. *Let me clean you, let me warm you, let me wash away all your cares.*

She flings herself at the wall where Jay now stretches down to help her out. His grip is strong. "We . . . can't stay still," he grunts as Winnie digs her feet into the granite. "We have to move."

You think? Winnie wants to snap at him. Instead, she clambers onto higher ground and searches for their best escape. Mist tentacles over her arms toward her face. *Let me clean you, let me taste you—*

Jay scoops beneath Winnie's arms and hauls her to her feet. "Come on, Winnie. Follow me."

Winnie tries to obey, but where Jay immediately shoots off, his uncanny hunter senses taking hold, she feels only panic. They weren't supposed to be here when the nightmares rose. They were supposed to be safely away and far from any monsters or Whisperers or death.

Pure Heart, her dream had illogically called it. *Trust the Pure Heart.* She imagines she can hear the Whisperer now, coming for her in the trees. That unnatural rustling like a record player scratching backward on the wrong side of vinyl. Her own hunter instincts aren't rising—the ones that she and Jay have honed and honed and honed within these trees.

Was it fun jumping off the falls?

Aroo-aroo!

Wolf Girl, that footage looked so cool.

"Winnie." Jay's arms come around her. "We have to keep moving."

Winnie knows this is true. The Compendium is very clear about this, and its words are already scrolling in her brain. *Since there is no predicting the location of a nightmare's arrival, the hunter must keep moving. Otherwise, one could apparate exactly where the hunter stands.*

The mist is all the way to Winnie's waist now, and it's quickly getting hotter. A pot to boil lobsters alive. Soon air will come squealing out of her carapace and she'll wonder why the chef didn't just kill her and be done with it. After all, the Whisperer is on its way and no one survives its supernova embrace.

That's what the blood meant, right? That granite pit was a feeding ground.

"Come on." Jay's arms tighten around Winnie's shoulders. "Winnie, *move.*" He shoves her into a walk, and as much as her feet desperately want to stay rooted in place . . . they walk.

And the walking is good. Mist cloys and claws. It encases her and steals her sight, sears her exposed hands and face. Fire, flames, magma that used to roil within but now come from without.

Though initially thick and hot, the mist quickly fades into a more typical post-rain fog.

"Keep breathing," Jay whispers to her. "Keep moving."

"Yes," Winnie replies, though the word is quickly eaten by the mist. It sees an access point; it charges into her mouth, her throat. *Keep moving, keep moving. Don't cough, don't cough.*

Somehow, she doesn't cough. Or stop moving. And, as the mist slowly falls away, it carries with it the panic and the terror and Winnie's certainty that the Whisperer must be *right* there. The mist really did clean her and warm her and wash away what she did not need.

And at last, her own hunter senses awaken. Her vision sharpens behind her glasses; her heartbeat steadies; and the mist slowly crawls back down to the forest floor.

Jay grinds to a halt, stopping Winnie beside him. She does not speak; he does not speak; and with near-silent movements, they both crouch low to the earth. Thirty paces away is a nightmare. It has yet to turn its snuffing face upward and notice the hunters nearby—hunters without weapons, without backup or alarm lanyards, with *nothing* but each other and a very, very long way to go.

Then the creature lifts its head, and Winnie gets a full glimpse of exactly what it is and what it can do to them.

Sadhuzag: A rare but massive stag with seventy-four antler prongs and razor-sharp hooves. Though not flesh eaters, they will kill any who enter their territory, including other nightmares. As of this writing, the sadhuzag has only ever risen in the Italian and Swedish forests.

And apparently, the American forest too. Under normal circumstances, such as from the safety of a classroom or even corpse duty, Winnie would be overjoyed by this fact. Even now, a little spark in the back of her brain is like, *Oh my god, I can't wait to tell Mario.* The survival component of her brain, however, is gauging whether or not they can outrun that thing. Its tawny legs are almost as long as Winnie is tall, and those antlers . . .

They must reach six feet off its head and span eight feet wide. Each prong glints with a pearlescent sheen—as if they are so sharp, light does not know how to land upon them.

How the creature can even lift its neck with so much weight is unfathomable to Winnie, but then again, it doesn't really matter *how* the sadhuzag keeps its head upright so much as that it does.

Still, Winnie's mind can't resist adding a footnote to the printed Compendium in her closet: *The weight of antlers does not limit the sadhuzag's movement, but the sheer girth of the seventy-four prongs must. It will not fit in tight spaces.*

As if a Compendium footnote unfurls in Jay's brain too, he nudges Winnie and points sideways. A quick squint into the shadows—it is fully night now—reveals a thick copse of trees. More trees means less space for those antlers.

One, Jay mouths, lifting a single finger. His skin glows pale, but the black-clad rest of him blends away.

Winnie checks her glasses: the neoprene strap is tight.

Two. Another finger, and she readies her muscles to rise.

Three. No finger this time. Jay simply springs to his feet and launches straight north.

Winnie does too. Or rather, she *tries* to, but she's half as fast and twice as loud. Jay is somehow already five paces away before Winnie has fully stood and taken her first step. A stick snaps and dead leaves she would *swear* weren't there ten seconds ago now rip and rattle. She doesn't need to look at the sadhuzag to know it has spotted her.

She looks at it anyway, a slow-motion swivel of her head as her arms pump and her knees rise and she abandons all attempt at quiet . . .

Oh yes. It saw her, it *sees* her, and its head tips with a vicious, barking bellow to fill the forest. So loud, it shakes straight into Winnie's skeleton. It pounds her eardrums and expands inside her skull, this vibrating howl that says, *You are not where you belong.*

The Compendium definitely never mentioned that sound.

Nor did it describe how much the ground would quake with each of the sadhuzag's now stamping hooves. Winnie's own footfalls turn unsteady, and despite her pushing, pushing, *pushing* to catch up with Jay, it is as if the sadhuzag's movements recalibrate the earth beneath her. Her feet don't land like they should; she can't gain any rebound to kick her knees high.

Hoofbeats thunder closer. The rocky and rising terrain is no challenge for the sadhuzag, and branches thrash and break as if its antlers slice through all in the beast's path.

Nope, nope, *nope.* Winnie is not going to outrun it, and now Jay—who has reached the cluster of elm trees ahead—is swiveling back and realizing the same thing.

"DUCK!" he roars, and Winnie somehow actually obeys.

She dives straight down onto the ground.

Antlers slice above her, and a smell like ancient fury crushes over her. *Razor hooves,* her mind provides, and Winnie rolls sideways. Silver cuts through the edge of her vision. The earth rips and shreds.

Then the sadhuzag is past and Winnie is trying to scrabble to her feet again. Ahead, Jay is shouting and waving his hands. "Come here, you dip-shit! I'm right here! Come and get me!"

Dipshit, Winnie wants to inform him, is really no way to address this majestic nightmare and she is profoundly annoyed on the nightmare's be-half. She is also quite relieved those hooves did not make impact because holy crap, they have literally ruined the earth. Like someone took a sword to the soil and just started slashing.

Winnie has two thoughts while the beast stampedes away and Jay van-ishes behind the enormity of the wild, deadly antlers.

1) She and Jay are now separated.
2) Bad things happen when she is alone in the forest.

It's like these nightmares only show up when you're around, Winnie. Or like you've got some special power that only lets you *see them.*

Sure enough, a slight wind kicks against her, carrying with it a smell like burning plastic. No whispers—yet—but then the sadhuzag's hooves and bellows dominate all sound.

Not again, she thinks. *Not again.* She kicks into a sprint after Jay, after a nightmare she's pretty sure Jay couldn't take down even with a weapon—at least not by himself. That thing is the size of Hummer, and the cluster of trees remain the only option to escape it. Let the Whisperer deal with the sadhuzag. Let her and Jay simply get away.

The wind churns faster. Winnie pushes herself harder. The sadhuzag is a vague, enormous shadow in the darkness, and she occasionally glimpses a figure rolling and diving and running and sliding.

"*Jay!*" she tries to shriek at him, knowing it will draw the wrath of the sadhuzag onto her again. "*Jay! To the trees! Back to the trees!*" That's all Winnie says—all she *can* say, really, because yes, the nightmare stag with seventy-four antler prongs is now veering around to gallop across the un-even terrain at her.

Its eyes glow like headlights, and just like a car, Winnie can tell it's ap-proaching fast because those lights are getting bigger.

Winnie hurtles toward the copse of trees that she prays offers safety. She also prays that the Compendium is right: *Though not flesh eaters, they will kill any who enter their territory, including other nightmares.* Otherwise, with the way she's moving, she could step on a basilisk or into a spidrin web without realizing before it's too late.

The thicker clot of elm trees looms ahead, a wall of darkness now lit up by glowing green from a nightmare that wants Winnie and Jay *off its land.* Winnie wishes she could scream at it, *Gladly! We will* gladly *leave if you would just let us go!*

Her breath comes in punctuated gasps. Her hairs once more prick upward—and there's that stench again, like a plastic spatula forgotten on the stove. Oh yes, the Whisperer is coming. The wind isn't wild enough yet to herald its imminent arrival, but it is most certainly on the way.

The line of elm trees is so close. Winnie spies a rowan tree too.

Some Dianas will craft small coins from rowan wood that has been harvested in a spirit forest, believing such amulets can protect against nightmares.

Please let it protect Winnie, please let it protect Jay. She dares not look behind to see where he is. The sadhuzag's breaths are rasping so near, its hoof falls vibrating in her ribs, in her lungs.

"DROP!" Jay commands from behind her.

Winnie doesn't drop. She propels herself straight forward, right between the rowan and an elm.

Heat slices across her calf. Then antlers connect with tree trunks and Winnie connects with the ground. She rolls. Wood crunches, and chips spray wide. The ground shakes; the sadhuzag bellows; then somehow Jay is beside Winnie and dragging her onto her feet.

Pain sears up from her calf. One of the antlers got her. But there's no time to look at it or deal with it or even really *feel* the sharp burn rising through her. There is only time to let Jay tug her deeper into the trees.

The sadhuzag roars again behind them. Then it crashes against the trunks, seventy-four prongs that will soon enough knock an elm and a rowan to the ground. Jay and Winnie will not be here when that happens.

Meanwhile, at the heart of a granite pit lined with leaves, a creature made of wormholes and broken carburetors shivers into being. It smells prey nearby, fresh and young and tempting. But even more appealing is the other, purer smell beside it. So close, so powerful. Not yet ready for feasting . . .

But soon.

CHAPTER

27

"Where are we?" Winnie pants as she and Jay finally slow to a run . . . a jog . . . a walk. "I don't . . . recognize any of this."

"We're almost out of the forest." Jay's cheeks are flushed—dark banners of color in this shadowy night. It's the only sign of exertion he wears; he isn't even breathing heavily.

Winnie, meanwhile, is on the verge of collapse. She's angry about it too. Angry her legs are shaking and her arms feel weak. Angry that the sweat on her body is already cooling into something frozen. She hates that Jay still moves with the natural ease of a hunter, while she just wants water and a minute or two to catch her breath.

Also, her leg hurts.

It *really* hurts.

She doesn't stop, of course. If she could manage the pure hellfire that was her third trial—if she could survive the Whisperer and jump off the waterfall—then this is nothing.

"The boundary stakes are ahead," Jay explains. His voice is barely audible over Winnie's panting. "We're going to leave the forest there and circle home outside."

"Circle . . . home." Winnie's eyes briefly shut. If they are on the northern edge of the forest, then circling outside will take hours. Mom must already be back at the house by now, and though Winnie was smart enough to turn off her bedroom light and shove pillows under the covers, she doesn't relish the thought of sneaking in at 3:00 A.M. with a gaping wound on the back of her leg.

Sorry about the blood all over the rug, Mom. Paper cut from my home-work! You know how it is.

Winnie squashes her worries. There is nothing she can do except keep moving. One foot. Then the other. Even if it hurts.

In minutes, they reach the red stakes that mark the forest boundary. Jay circles them around the sensors so no Tuesdays will come this way in search of nightmares. The shift in the air is instantly palpable: the night warms and the stars brighten. There are faint hints of color here too, and the breeze, when it caresses Winnie's face, doesn't smell of carrion.

They reach a crude trail between the trees that could be from animals— natural ones—or could be from Luminaries who regularly check that boundary stakes remain intact. Either way, Winnie is grateful for the eas-ier terrain of cleared underbrush and packed earth.

She and Jay have not made it far, though, when a light flashes ahead.

Jay stops, towing Winnie to a halt beside him. Her calf throbs; she wills herself to ignore it.

The light flashes again, and this time, a sound like a chirping bird rises into the night—pained, pathetic, and almost too shrill to fully hear. *Will-o'-wisp*, Winnie thinks, stunned by two thoughts colliding in her brain simultaneously. One, that she has never seen a will-o'-wisp alive before . . .

And two, that a will-o'-wisp is currently outside the forest bounds.

Will-o'-wisp: Like large hummingbirds, these nightmares are plumed all over in silvery flames instead of feathers. When the flames die out, will-o'-wisps are revealed to be nothing more than hollow skeletons. The Com-pendium's definition digs through Winnie's brain, surprisingly coherent despite the pain rising in her leg.

"It's outside the bounds," Jay whispers beside her, and there's a tautness coiling through him as his hunter persona re-calcifies in his veins. "We need to do something."

Winnie nods. This is why the Luminaries exist: to keep the monsters *inside* the forest where their bloodthirsty ways cannot harm humans.

And will-o'-wisps would definitely harm humans.

They hunt by drawing prey to their nest, where hundreds will attack at once with syringe-like beaks. Hunters should avoid any lights that flash with

*a rhythmic quality; some subspecies of will-o'-wisp can also use their flames
to hypnotize.*

The pathetic chirp comes again, and Jay tenses harder beside Winnie.
"Come on." He sets off toward it, and Winnie limps after. Her calf shrieks;
her nostrils flare and she stomps against the pain.

They round a shadowy oak tree and reach the creature. It flickers with
a pale, smokeless fire that is weaker than a phone on its lowest brightness
setting. Winnie is spellbound as she creeps closer—although not because
the creature has hypnotized her with its flames, but because her scientist's
mind is utterly enthralled.

As is the human part of her too, for this will-o'-wisp is not hunting. This
will-o'-wisp is dying.

Winnie gapes down at it, a sharp sadness burrowing into her heart. She
has seen these nightmares countless times on corpse duty. She *knows* what
this hollow skeleton looks like on a diagram, and she can draw every indi-
vidual bone in its tiny wings and even tinier feet. Yet as is always the case,
the Compendium illustration of a will-o'-wisp has failed to capture even a
fraction of its true beauty.

"Look away," Jay commands. Then he lifts his leg, power rising through
him. He's going to stomp it to death.

"No." Winnie shoves him, a startled movement that is weakened by a
surge of pain in her calf. But a frantic attempt is all she needs to throw Jay
off course. To keep his boot from slamming down and crushing the last of
this nightmare's life from its fragile body. "What are you doing, Jay?"

"What are you doing?" he counters, and the will-o'-wisp briefly flares
anew, a kiss of silvery flame into the night.

"You can't just kill it like that!"

"I can, and I need to." He stares at her with horrified eyes. *"We* need to,
Winnie, because that is what hunters do."

Winnie gnaws her lip. Jay is right. Of course he's right. It's one of the
first things a Luminary learns: *Any nightmares outside the forest boundary
must be killed on sight.* Yet the thought of killing this insubstantial, glittering creature . . .

Winnie sinks to the earth beside it. Ancient leaves from last year's au-
tumn crunch beneath her knees. The pain in her calf prods deeper; she can
feel her heartbeat directly in her muscles now. "Can we help it?" she asks,

leaning closer to the will-o'-wisp. "If we bring it back into the forest, can we help it? Won't the dawn mist heal it?"

"Are you serious right now?" Jay drops to a much more fluid crouch beside Winnie. The will-o'-wisp flares. It is a cold fire that stretches outward, reaching like an infant for its mother.

It hurts Winnie's heart to see.

"If this nightmare lives long enough for the mist to heal it at dawn, Winnie, do you know what it will do tomorrow night? It will hunt us down and kill us. Because that is what nightmares do. That's the only thing nightmares *can* do."

Something about the way Jay says this gives Winnie pause. It makes her lift her eyes from the dying will-o'-wisp and fasten them on the Friday before her. Jay's cheeks are flushed to gray in this darkness; his hair is flecked with pine needles; and his midnight eyes hold an urgency that says, *Trust me, I know exactly what I am talking about.*

"Winnie," he murmurs, and he lifts his hands—almost pleading. Though whether he is pleading with her to agree that nightmares are irredeemable or whether he is begging her to argue that they are not, Winnie can't say. "There's nothing we can do for this will-o'-wisp. It won't survive until the dawn mist, and even if it did, there's no guarantee the mist will stitch it back together again. All we can do is end its suffering as quickly as possible. Trust me, Winnie. Please."

Her teeth click softly together. She knows Jay is right; she knows this is how the forest operates. It can break almost anything—including your heart.

"Okay," she says after several seconds, and when Jay offers a hand to help her rise, she takes it. His fingers are cold. So are Winnie's.

The pain in her calf roars anew once she is on her feet. Still, she forces herself to gaze down at the dying will-o'-wisp. And she forces herself to hold its hollow eye sockets and murmur, "I'm sorry you're hurt, little one. And I'm so sorry I couldn't save you."

Jay swallows audibly at those words, and there is no denying the pain on his hunter face when he once more lifts his boot—faint moonlight glinting on the leather—then stamps the nightmare away.

Bones crack. Silver light fades.

And Winnie turns around to yank off her glasses. She scrubs at eyes that suddenly sting.

It is when she moves to replace her lenses that she spies another light. Twenty paces to the right—just as silvery, but so much brighter. Then another flares on her left. Then another straight ahead, until tens of them are sparkling through the trees around her.

An entire nest of will-o'-wisps, all right there, watching as one of their own dies.

Winnie lifts her arms, bracing for an attack. But the will-o'-wisps never move, never take flight off the branches they perch upon. They simply glitter and flare as Jay's boot crunches down a second time. Then a third.

By the time Jay twists around to join Winnie and resume his march beside her, all the lights have disappeared. It was a display for only Winnie to see. A display she should probably report to the Tuesday hunters . . .

But one she knows she never will.

The rest of the journey is an aching, hobbling affair in which Winnie tries to ignore the pain in her leg and just *move*. She leans on Jay and jogs as much as she can, and when that becomes too miserable, she walks.

Until at last Winnie can't walk anymore. She *needs* to stop, she *needs* to look at her leg, and she *needs* just a few seconds to process what happened—first with the sadhuzag, then with the will-o'-wisps.

"Please," she finds herself saying as she staggers to a nearby beech tree and drops onto a gnarled root. Her glasses are filthy. Sweat pours off her brow.

Jay drops to the earth in front of her. "Leave it," he tells her quietly, catching her hands before she can try to pull apart the slashed cotton of her joggers and examine the damage.

"It . . . hurts."

"Because the sural nerve got hit," he replies, and Winnie hates how much her traitorous body responds to him saying the words *sural nerve* or that she then imagines him studying an anatomy book. *Pain is making you ridiculous.*

Jay tips forward until his shadowy head blocks her view of her leg. Somehow, although he smells of sweat and forest, the scent of bergamot and lime still wavers through. Winnie is overcome with the urge to curl forward and rest her head on top of his. Take a nap that way or maybe wail her stress and confusion into the trees.

Instead, she squeezes her teeth together and closes her eyes. A good plan, since two seconds later Jay's fingers move into the cut and pain like a thousand phoenix burns erupts inside her brain. *Way* more pain than a simple slash should be causing—even in the sural nerve.

"I think there's poison in the wound."

"Venom," she corrects automatically. "Poison is ingested." Her teeth grind and grind and *grind*.

Jay's head lifts and Winnie cracks open one eye. A smudge on her glasses blurs over the left half of his face. Despite the distortion, it is impossible to miss the hard fury that has settled over his features.

Except where Winnie expects him to unload on her, he instead seethes: "I'm sorry, Win. I should have been better prepared. My watch must need winding." He raises his arm, although she can't see the glass face in this light. "I got the time all wrong."

"Jay," Winnie says softly, "we're here on *my* behalf, which makes all of this *my* fault."

"I'm a hunte—" He breaks off, a grimace tightening his eyes. Then he amends, "I'm Lead Hunter. I should know better than this, Win. I'll go to the Friday estate and get a four-wheeler. Then I'll come back for you." He shoves to his feet, stealing the bergamot and lime and blocking out what little light the sky provides. "It'll take me about an hour. Maybe a little more."

"An *hour*?" Winnie shakes her head, clutching at the rough bark of the beech. She tries to stand. Pain screams through her, and she topples right back down. On attempt number two, however, the muscle holds and she stands before Jay. "I can go with you. I can do this. A four-wheeler will draw attention, and an hour . . ." Her voice wavers. "I can't wait an hour."

"You can't run, either. Winnie. It's probably eight miles back to the estate. I can get there fastest by myself and then return—"

"No." Her voice rips out, louder than she intends and edged with a shrill panic she wasn't expecting. "I don't want to be left here alone." She can't believe she is uttering this aloud, she can't believe she even *feels* this way. So much for being a tough Wednesday hunter with the forest in her blood.

A sadhuzag that shouldn't be in the American forest almost got her, and now a venom it shouldn't have is coursing inside her veins.

And what about the will-o'-wisps? Maybe Winnie got it all wrong—maybe they weren't peaceful observers outside the forest. Maybe they're stalking Jay and Winnie right now . . .

Thanks, Dad, she thinks vaguely, a maniacal laughter echoing at the back of her brain. *Yet again, you screw up everything.*

"Please Jay," she says more softly. "Please, don't . . . leave me alone."

"I won't, Winnie," he murmurs back, sliding his arm behind her and letting her lean against him. "I'll never leave you alone."

But you already did, she thinks as they ease into a walk . . . and then a limping jog. *And I wish I could understand why.*

Winnie's thoughts leap like the ghost-deer across her brain as she stumbles onward, clutching onto Jay for dear life.

A will-o'-wisp crushed beneath a boot.

A sadhuzag with eyes that glow.

A leaf-lined hole made of granite and stained with blood.

Then of course, the Whisperer.

It lurks beneath everything else, a wordless static like those microwaves left over from the big bang that make radios go crackly. There's a name for that . . . *cosmic microwave background*. It was discovered in the 1960s after scientists kept picking up feedback on their radios.

Why does Winnie know that? Why is she even thinking about it right now?

Occasionally noises rise from the forest. Snarls or a plaintive howl. Once, Winnie hears a familiar, heartbreaking sob that instantly loosens the lock on her compartment labeled *Dad*. It is a banshee, just like the dead one that allowed Winnie to pass her first trial.

Jay hears the banshee too; he tugs Winnie into a jog, then a run until the sound of its grief can no longer cocoon them in sorrow. Winnie was sad to hear it, but she is sadder to hear it go.

And she is saddest of all thinking about the will-o'-wisp she should never have wanted to save. *Why can't you be a proper Luminary anymore, Winnie? Why can't you be a bear?*

Jay checks his watch often, the old glass face glinting in the near dark. He has rewound it so even if the time is wrong, he can at least gauge their speed. And it's not as if the actual time matters now anyway. The answer is: late. And the anticipated reaction from Mom if she notices Winnie is gone is: terror and fury.

Best not to think about that part of the evening. Focus instead on all the other leaping, racing thoughts.

Whisperer: This nightmare is a new creature native to the American forest. No one believes it is real except for Winnie Winona Wednesday, despite ample evidence that the monster exists. See also: burning plastic, cosmic microwave background.

"Did you . . . hear it?" she asks. "Back at the granite pit, did you smell it?"

"The stag?" Jay adjusts his grip against Winnie. His fingers dig into her side, and she is deeply vexed that in the back of her brain, a silly little part of her hopes he likes what he feels. "It was hard to miss—hey, hey, Winnie, are you okay?" He pauses his forward stride to peer into her face.

But Winnie only wags her head. Of course she isn't okay. It's why they have to keep moving. It's why they can't just stand here as they do right now with Jay cupping her jaw and studying her while she clutches at his hoodie and strains to stay upright.

"The . . . Whisperer," she says, pushing at Jay to keep walking. He doesn't move. "Did you hear it at the granite pit?"

Jay's brows cinch. "No, Win. I didn't hear—or see—anything but the stag."

"Sadhuzag," she corrects. "That was a sadhuzag. Though I've never read of one . . . with . . . venom." She shoves against Jay, a pathetic movement meant to propel him forward.

He still doesn't obey. Instead, as her attempt to push him turns into a near collapse against his chest, he gathers her to him in an awkward, unwieldy embrace. *What is happening to me?*

"Talk to me," he says, voice sharp. "What else did you see? Hey, Winnie. Hey." He snaps his fingers in her face. "Talk to me."

So she does. "It was coming, Jay. I could hear it coming. And I could smell it too. The burning plastic. It always smells like burning plastic. Like . . ." She swallows down a throat gone rusty. "Like a key chain dropped into a toaster. Like . . . a . . . like . . ." She can't conjure another example, so instead she asks, "You really . . . didn't smell anything?"

He grunts, a sound that might be a *no* or might just as easily be a symptom of his exertion. Either way, it vibrates inside Winnie, sidling into her abdomen and up to the base of her skull. The same place the Whisperer always seems to find.

At that thought—half coherent, half amorphous—the nonsensical phrase from her dream emerges once more like a lantern in the light. *Pure Heart. Trust the Pure Heart.* She has no idea what it means or why she has thought it twice tonight, but it is the splash of cold she needs.

Water to the face. Lightning in a storm.

The pain, the haziness briefly scatter.

"Was it there on Friday night?" She lifts her head so she can stare at Jay's jawline. "When Grayson died . . . was it there, Jay?"

His hold on her tightens. Before it was a steadying embrace. Now it is a vise grip. "No," he rasps. "I didn't see anything like the Whisperer."

"It has to have been there, though." Winnie shakes her head against him. "I saw the blood. I saw the arrows on the log in the stream—Jay, it *was* there. It killed Grayson—"

"Winnie, it didn't." Jay's voice lashes out, harder than she expects from him. Harder than she can ever remember hearing before. Then the vise grip releases, and when he pulls away, there is no missing the hurt in his eyes. The gray irises glow almost as the sadhuzag's had. "It *was* the werewolf," he tells her. "I promise you, it was the werewolf that killed Grayson. Just like that will-o'-wisp and that sadhuzag, killing is all that a werewolf lives for. Nightmares . . . they can't help it, Winnie. It's what the spirit created them to do."

No, she wants to argue. *Not all of them live to kill, Jay.* She might have been sensitive to his grief on Saturday night at the party, but now she just needs to know what he really saw. *Blood streaked on birch trees. Blood staining a granite hole.*

The answers to all of her questions—they're so close. Hovering little keys to a hundred little padlocks for the compartment Jay keeps bolted up inside him.

But Winnie's brain can't fight the venom in her blood. Her body can't fight the venom rushing to her heart. So the only word that comes from her mouth is a soft "Oh," before she falls once more against Jay's chest.

She feels him scoop his arms beneath her and lift her, and she feels her own arms slide around his neck. "Hang on, Winnie," Jay murmurs, and he starts to run. She bounces like a sack of bones. Like the skeleton that hangs in Professor Il-Hwa's lab at the Sunday estate.

Oh dear, she thinks, bouncing and bouncing and bouncing, *this is not a good development.*

Jay can't maintain a constant run, so he alternates jogging and walking. Steady, relentless. "Hang on," he repeats often. "Please, Winnie, hang on."

"Good . . . thing," she summons at one point, "you didn't leave me behind. This venom is . . . strong."

Jay doesn't answer. Only huffs, a sound that reveals how labored his breaths are, how parched his throat. Until at last, the forest around them looks familiar. They are at the Friday estate.

"Hospital?" Winnie murmurs, her head resting on the groove between Jay's head and his shoulder. He is damp with sweat; her sweat has frozen to ice against her skin. A sharp contrast to the fire that burns inside her leg—a conflagration spreading through her body.

This venom really might reach her heart.

The Friday estate rises before them, backlit by stars, as Jay hauls Winnie onto the training grounds. His gait has weakened, and he isn't jogging anymore. He must have carried her almost two miles. His arms have to be wrecked, not to mention his back muscles and thighs. Winnie is not a small human, and for all his height, Jay is not a huge one.

"Winnie," Jay replies, "I can take you to the hospital, but then there will be questions. A lot of questions." He pauses to suck in breath. Ahead, the Friday estate swims closer, looking more like a fairy's castle than a haunted house. The burned tower is invisible from here, and the chipping paint glows pure and fresh. The overgrown hedges blend together into seemingly tamed rows, and all the ancient windows glisten and gleam as if magic happens within.

Winnie can almost imagine how beautiful this place was before it fell into disrepair.

"Or," Jay continues, "I can treat you here. You have to trust me, though."

Winnie digs her head into his neck, nodding. Her eyes loll shut. Her glasses press against her face. "Yes," she murmurs. "I . . . trust you." Jay might have hurt her and he might have too many secrets inside for her to ever draw free, but at his core, Jay will always be a Friday.

Integrity in all. Honesty to the end.

Jay carries Winnie through a back door on the estate and into a subterranean area not so different from the Wednesday clan's Armory. Except that where the Armory also includes all the training facilities, this area is only a locker room and an old pool that hasn't been updated since it was built in the 1920s. Right now, the pool sits empty and drained.

It looks a lot like the granite pit in the forest. Smoother, yes, and brighter . . . but just as stale. Just as forgotten. And perhaps too, just as filled with nightmares.

Jays steps grow shorter and more shambling by the second. Or maybe that's Winnie's grasp on reality. The world is spinning, and her lungs are aching in much the same way her calf first was.

Once past the pool, Jay carries Winnie into a short hall, and at the first door on the left, he shoves them both inside. He kicks the door shut behind him, briefly blanketing them in total darkness before he shifts Winnie in his arms and flips a switch with one hand. Two bulbs of three wink on in an overhead light.

Winnie's vision wavers, but she takes in dark paneled walls and darker floors. A dinged-up but sturdy desk, a lone chair askew, its cane seat sagging.

Jay carries Winnie to a couch on the right. It is the only new piece of furniture in the room, its cushions a simple gray cotton trimmed with white—and a weirdly homey touch to a windowless room that is otherwise all haggard functionality.

Jay eases Winnie down with muscles that shake from exhaustion. She feels cold and bare as soon as he releases her. Pain courses through her anew, forcing her to close her eyes and once more grind her teeth against it. Jay moves quickly around the small space, gathering things Winnie can't see because her glasses slid off her nose when he deposited her, and everything is a poorly lit blur.

Soon, Jay returns, kneeling before her and lifting her head upright. "Hey, Win." He leans in close so she can see him.

His eyes are lambent gray.

"I need you to drink this, okay?" He holds a small vial with the cap already removed. "Just one sip. No more. Can you do that? Or should I get a dropper—we must have one here . . ." He turns his head as if to find one, but Winnie stops him with a hand.

"I can do it." She *can* do it, because she does not want to suffer the indignity of drinking some unknown liquid from an dropper as if she is fledgling harpy eating regurgitated human feet. "What is it?"

"Drink it first," Jay murmurs, and his thumb lightly traces her cheek. "Then I'll explain."

"You better not be poisoning me." Winnie tries for a pained smile. "I'm already . . . messed up enough as it is." With Jay still holding the vial, Winnie guides his grip to her mouth until her lips hit the glass. She smells nothing, tastes nothing . . .

Then the liquid hits her tongue, cool and thick and strangely sweet.

One sip, she takes only one sip, then Jay withdraws the vial and she quickly swallows. The liquid slides down her throat, instantly easing a rasp she hadn't noticed was there. Her esophagus, her chest, her stomach—she feels the liquid reach each part of her, and the cooling sensation spreads and soothes. It is amazing; like eating your favorite ice cream on a boiling hot day, if the ice cream could also erase every ache and agony inside your body.

And inside your brain.

Her thoughts calm, one by one. Each Compendium entry, each memory of Dad that won't stay locked away, and each fear—over Mom catching her, over dying from a stupid injury she should never have gotten, over Tuesdays realizing she has communicated with her dad and arresting her family, over the Whisperer finally catching up to her and ripping her to shreds so she is one more offering for the spirit at the bottom of the Big Lake . . .

It all drifts away. Even that obnoxious voice that says, *Clusterfuck: see Winnie Wednesday* disappears, and all that is left is Jay's face, urgent and near, and his hand against her cheek.

"Melusine blood," she murmurs softly. Her eyes drift shut. A song like Jenna used to sing winds into her brain, beautiful and haunting and so familiar. She heard that song under the waterfall. Impossible, she knows, to have heard it there . . . and yet she did. It's the only thing she really remembers from those crushing waves, and she wonders if maybe she has been here before. As if this has happened to her before, and now all that's missing . . .

Then there it is: Jay's arms wrap around her to keep her warm.

Winnie falls asleep.

HEMLOCK FALLS TESTING PORTAL
WEDNESDAY, APRIL 10

TEST RESULTS for PREVIOUS DAY:
Tests Administered: 1381
Positive Results: 0

AVAILABLE TESTING LOCATIONS:
Monday hospital, BY APPOINTMENT ONLY
Sunday estate auditorium, UNDER AGE 18 ONLY
Floating Carnival, ALL AGES WELCOME

DO YOUR CIVIC DUTY AND GET TESTED AS SOON AS A
SITE IS AVAILABLE NEAR YOU!

29

W innie awakens in Jay's bedroom.

In Jay's bed, to be precise. It smells strongly of bergamot and lime, which Winnie is beginning to suspect must be the scent of his shampoo. Or maybe it's the scent of pheromones that ooze out of his pores and drive everyone in Hemlock Falls wild—or at least everyone under the age of eighteen.

Winnie giggles at this thought as she takes in his bedroom with blurry, un-lens-corrected eyes. It's so much like she remembers from four years ago: the high ceilings, the tall window draped in a navy curtain, the closet to her right with the knob that won't latch so it always hangs open two inches.

Now there's also a bass guitar by the foot of the bed and an upright bass beside it. A dresser stands by the closet, simple and modern and bright—and totally at odds with the Gothic-mansion heaviness of the room. Then there is the bed upon which Winnie now sprawls: same four-poster twin, but no more X-Men bedspread. There's just a simple navy duvet with white pinstripes.

There's also a new nightstand by the bed with a lamp and two photos. One is a framed image of Jay's mom, pregnant and beaming and completely unaware of the death that is coming for her when she finally delivers him. Then, leaning against that photo is an unframed picture of Jay, Erica, and Winnie.

Winnie snatches the second photo to her, its edges dusty. She remembers the day Jay's aunt took this photo—it was on Winnie's twelfth birthday and only a few weeks before Dad ruined everything. She, Jay, and Erica met for birthday pie at the Revenant's Daughter and then had a movie marathon in the faded but still grand living room of the Friday estate.

It was the best birthday ever—they watched *every live-action X-Men movie in existence* and gorged on frozen pizza. In the photo, you can see the crusts left behind that Erica would never eat on a plate on the coffee table. Then Jay, Erica, and Winnie are all seated on the couch behind, the girls sharing a blanket while Jay has draped himself over the armrest like some rich lady's ermine stole.

They're all grinning, although Erica is also blinking and the flash from Lizzy's camera is making Jay's eyes glow.

Winnie can't believe Jay has kept this photograph—or that he has it right here, where he can see it every morning when he wakes up.

She also has no idea what it *means.*

She returns the photo so she can study the very live, much older boy now lying on the floor. He has a pillow under his head and one arm draped over his stomach. It looks extremely uncomfortable, although Jay must not mind since he is completely comatose.

Winnie can't resist. She slides out from under the covers and creeps toward him. Hazily, she notices that the bottom half of her right jogger leg has been cut off, and a bandage is wrapped around her calf—which is now free of pain. If anything, her calf feels stronger than it has in weeks. Her whole body does, and her crouch beside Jay's head is graceful, smooth, silent. Her hair falls forward, but it doesn't reach him as she bends closer, closer. Her right pointer finger unfurls. "Boop—argh!"

Jay catches her wrist before she can make contact. His eyes snap wide, the gray irises almost swallowed entirely by throbbing black pupils. "Did you not learn your lesson last time?" His voice is low as if to keep from waking his aunt down the hall. There is also a ragged quality to it, since he was asleep only moments ago.

Or maybe . . . maybe it's something else that makes it ragged. Something Winnie doesn't recognize or want to examine too closely. At least not right now, when she feels *so, so* good.

"Never startle a nightmare, Winnie."

"But you're not a nightmare." She grins at him.

"And *you're* high." He releases her wrist to boop *her* on the nose. Then his lips twitch into an almost grin of his own.

"Melusine blood," Winnie squeals. "I knew it. How on earth did you get melusine blood?"

He pushes onto his elbows. "Wouldn't you like to know."

"Yes," she replies. "That is literally why I asked."

"And I will explain after the effects of this"—he nods his head toward her face—"have worn off."

"I'm not high," she insists as he pushes all the way into sitting. It brings their faces close. "I feel amazing, Jay. Like . . . like I could run all the way around the forest again. *Twice.* Like I could go face that sadhuzag's seventy-four prongs—"

"Is that how many there were?"

"—and slash it with *my* seventy-four prongs." She demonstrates this by head butting Jay in the chest.

"Oh my god," he says, laughing now. "You are so very, very high."

"I know you are, but what am I?"

Another laugh, and a shake of his head. "I hope your mom isn't home when I get you there."

"Mom." Winnie blinks. Then sinks onto her haunches. "She must be so worried. Oh crap, Jay, we need to get home and let her know where I am and that I'm safe and that the venom didn't get me—venom *which,* by the way, is not mentioned in the Compendium, meaning we discovered a new species of sadhuzag last night. Do you think they'll let me name it? Winnie's Sadhuzag. Ooh, or just *The Winnie.* Much better to have a nightmare named after me than a coffee . . ." Winnie trails off. Then cringes. "Maybe I *am* high."

"Can I see your leg?" Jay motions to her calf, and Winnie obliges by shifting her position from kneeling into sitting. She drapes her leg over Jay's lap and in the dim light of morning through his curtain, he removes the bandage. When at last the skin is exposed, other than some dried blood, there is nothing to see. All that remains from the antler wound is a faint, faint, *almost invisible* line. More like she scratched herself too hard than a nightmare swiped her and injected her with venom.

"Whoa," Winnie breathes.

"Whoa indeed," Jay murmurs. He pokes gently at the line, glancing at Winnie's face as he does so. "Any pain or numbness?"

She shakes her head. "It feels good as new." As she says this, a memory prickles in the back of her skull. The sense that she has felt this way previously . . . that this isn't *actually* her first time healing quickly and feeling invincible.

She chews her lip. "Have we done this before?"

His eyebrows rise questioningly. "Done what before? Sat so close together that if my aunt walks in here right now she's going to think we are, ah . . ."

He doesn't finish that sentence, and he doesn't need to. Yet rather than yank in her leg and scuttle away, Winnie only laughs. Then claps her hands. "It does look bad, doesn't it, Jay? Especially since"—she slants toward him, her voice dropping low—"everyone already thinks we're dating."

He doesn't look impressed by this secret, suggesting he was already quite aware of the gossip. "I think it's time we get you home and into your own bed, Winnie Wednesday. Without your mom noticing." He pushes to his feet with the languid ease of a wild animal, then offers both his hands down to her.

Winnie takes them and lets him haul her up. "That doesn't bother you? That people think I'm your girlfriend?"

"No." He pulls away and sidles to his nightstand, where he snags her glasses. The neoprene cord still dangles off them. "Why would it bother me?"

"Well, it bothers *me*."

"Ah." His grip tightens on the glasses. "Because dating me would be such a terrible thing?"

"Yes. I mean, *no*." Winnie's forehead scrunches. Then she shakes her head and snatches the glasses from him. "I mean, *yes*. It would be."

His nostrils flare. "And why is that?"

"Because . . ." Now Winnie's lips pucker to one side. Jay isn't reacting like she thought he would, and for some reason, it appears she has hurt his feelings. "Well, because you don't like me."

"Of course I like you, Winnie."

"Not like *that*." Winnie yanks the neoprene cord off her glasses, then deposits the lenses onto her face. Jay's face crystallizes before her, surprisingly refreshed given everything he had to do for her last night.

He also looks surprisingly serious, and Winnie has the sudden sense she has stepped into dangerous territory. Like a non meandering into the forest after dark.

Her heart starts pounding. "You don't like me like *that*, Jay, do you? Not like everyone thinks?"

"Or maybe," he counters, "it's *you* who doesn't like me like that, which is not like everyone thinks."

Winnie's eyes thin behind her lenses. The effects of the melusine blood must be muddling her brain, because she can't seem to parse what Jay just said. There were too many negatives that might have ultimately turned into a positive . . . ? Maybe?

And the longer she squints at Jay, the less she seems to see.

He, however, just continues staring back at Winnie, his gray eyes cool in the dim, curtained light. "Winnie."

She has to swallow before she can choke out, "Yes?" Her heart is *really* pounding now.

"If I kissed you right now, you wouldn't like that, right?"

Her breath snags in her lungs. Her eyes bulge to bursting. And against her greatest wish, she summons a ready-made image of her and Jay kissing in the forest, kissing in the old museum stairwell, kissing on a cold rooftop . . .

"No?" she blurts. Then louder, "*No?*" Except for some reason, both times she insists this, the words come out like questions. So she tries again: "No? No, I wouldn't like it if you kissed me?"

She's only making it worse. In fact, if she didn't know better, she would also think she's trying to lie right now—which she isn't. Because of course she doesn't want to kiss Jay. At least, not right now. Not like this.

Which is like what? her brain helpfully asks. *What would you prefer?*

She has no answer for that question—and the answer doesn't ultimately matter, because Jay takes Winnie at her word. "I guess it's a good thing then," he says, "that I have no plans to kiss you."

"Oh," Winnie breathes. "Right." She watches as he twists away to pad toward his bedroom door, no signs of stiffness in his muscles after a night spent on the floor. The door opens. The door closes.

And only then does Winnie move again. She flings herself onto his bed, burrows under the still-warm covers, and wills the magic of a melusine to sparkle once more inside her veins.

The magic obeys.

In fact, it's as if the brief burst of not-kissed adrenaline somehow spikes the melusine power to greater heights, and by the time Jay drives Winnie to her house thirty minutes later, she has become a font of nonstop talking. She can't seem to help it. She has fourteen thousand things happening in her brain, and she needs to express them all. Right now. Simultaneously.

It honestly feels amazing. All that awkwardness with Jay might as well have never happened. She has banished it from her brain and will never think of it again!

"Which reminds me," Winnie says as Jay turns Mathilda onto her street, "where did you get a whole vial of melusine blood? Or was it Grayson's? Where did *he* get it?"

Jay, who has not uttered a single word since they got into the Wagoneer, gives Winnie a tired side-eye. His lips part to answer. The blinker tick-tick-ticks . . .

"Oh!" Winnie cries. "We're almost to my house!" That means she is almost out of time to get ready. In a burst of speed that makes all her muscles feel alive and elated, she yanks off her seat belt and starts shimmying out of her pants.

Jay hits the brakes. His side-eye has turned into a fully horrified gape. "What is happening right now? Please put your clothes back on."

"No, no, no. You know you love it." Winnie shimmies and shakes and shimmies some more until her joggers—now missing half a leg—are down to her ankles and her purple running shorts are on full display. "If it's cool with you, I'll just get out here, okay?" She slides the joggers over her feet. Then shoves them onto Jay's lap. "And you can dispose of these, thank you. Except! Oh wait. Silly me." She scrabbles to him and rummages around in the joggers, searching for her pocket. *Where is it, where is it . . .*

The pants, of course, are still resting atop Jay's lap, and he is very slowly, very stiffly putting the Wagoneer into park. They are in the middle of the road. He closes his eyes as Winnie continues rummaging. "May I help you with that, Winnie?"

"Nope!" She finally finds the pocket she needs—and more importantly the neoprene cord for her glasses. She yanks it free and dangles it in front of his face. "Got what I came for! We can meet later and figure out what to do next. *Boop!*" She taps his nose, offering her widest, smiliest grin, before scrabbling back over the seat and out of the Wagoneer.

This time, she actually does shout "Thank you!" behind her before slamming shut the door and kicking into a jog. So much spring in her step! And no pain at all! Do melusine just swim around in a constant state of ecstasy? If so, she wants to become one. Like immediately.

Jay rumbles alongside her for several seconds before finally revving the engine and hurrying on, leaving behind a noxious cloud that would make a forest wyrm proud. Soon Winnie reaches her family's back door and shoves inside. She has worked up a slight pant.

Mom is at the kitchen counter in her robe and nursing a cup of coffee. Her cheeks bunch up at the sight of Winnie. "Were you out running? I thought you were still in your room."

"Early *Chrysomya megacephala* catches the corpse!" Winnie declares, pointing a finger toward the ceiling.

"I don't know what that means." Steam rises off Mom's coffee, coiling in front of her face. "But whatever you're on, I would like some."

"Melusine blood." Winnie gives her a big wink. "And I can't share it."

Mom laughs, assuming of course that Winnie is joking. And Winnie laughs too because the joke is that it's not a joke! She is so hilarious!

"I'm going to shower," she cries before twisting toward the living room.

"Wait." Mom takes two steps after her. "Darian called a few minutes ago. He says he can't give you a ride this morning. He's, uh, really sorry. Um . . ." Her face screws sideways as if she's trying to remember what else her son might have said. "He . . . will try to catch you tonight at clan dinner." Mom nods. "Yes, that was all of it. Now"—she gestures with her cup toward Winnie—"do you need *me* to give you a ride to school?"

"Nope," Winnie says, relieved to find she isn't upset at all over Darian's failure to meet her—or worried about what that might mean in her pursuit of Dad-related clues. Everything will work out just fine! "I will take the bike, Mother, and arrive speedily at my destination."

"Okay." Mom frowns. "That . . . sounds like a good idea, *Daughter*. Jeez," she adds under her breath, twisting away to refill her coffee. "I need to get back into running."

Winnie doesn't answer. Just chuckles to herself and sets off with an arm-swinging march across the living room, upstairs, and finally into her bedroom. Time for a shower! Time for school! Today is going to be so awesome! Nothing at all can bring her down!

C H A P T E R

30

Winnie feels like a piece of crap. Not just any piece of crap either, but the old kind you find on the side of the road, left by a dog and its irresponsible owner.

There's no pain in her leg—that is totally gone, since the melusine blood really did heal her up entirely—but the comedown. The *comedown*. Why didn't Jay warn her it would be this bad? And why would anyone ever *want* to illegally drop this stuff if this is the eventual aftermath?

Never again. Winnie doesn't care if she's legit dying next time. Never again.

Thank goodness she didn't have corpse duty this morning—though she's not entirely sure how she'll ever get enough sleep tonight to survive it tomorrow. At least the twins have their mom's van today and give Winnie a ride from school to the Sunday estate, so she doesn't have to pedal herself all the way over there. Or home again at the end of the day.

Unfortunately, they also give rides home to Fatima, Katie, and Xavier. All Winnie can manage is to slump in the back seat and massage her temples until at last she's able to topple from the confined minivan filled with laughter and teasing and excitement over the Masquerade.

They also joke three separate times about Winnie and Jay K-I-S-S-I-N-G.

Winnie's face heats up at what is definitely *not* her first imagery of K-I-S-S-I-N-G Jay. God, she acted *so absolutely stupidly* with him this morning.

The booping! The tussling! The jokes about them dating! He must think her a fool.

Or worse, he must think she's in love with him.

"See you at clan dinner!" Bretta calls after Winnie drags her revenant body out of the van, and then her bike from the trunk. Bretta leans out the open window. "Do you want us to bring you an outfit?"

Winnie makes herself look back and roll her eyes. "I do have clothes, Bretta Wednesday, thank you very much. And I promise they're not all bad."

"Are you sure—" Bretta begins, but Emma silences her with a hiss. Then a shouted "Great! We'll see you soon!"

Too soon, as far as Winnie is concerned. Not because she doesn't want to see Emma or Bretta or Fatima, but because she just wants sleep. And painkillers. And more sleep. The thought of navigating clan dinner in her current state sounds like a cruel combination of both physical and emotional torture, as well as some psychological and spiritual torture thrown in too. And hell, there's some probably existential torture in the mix as well. That's a thing, right?

The enormous black bear on the front porch flaps at Winnie as she leans the bike against the porch. *Tonight is the big night,* he seems to say. *Loyalty, loyalty, loyalty—you ready for it?*

No. Not really, if Winnie is being honest. If not for the fact that her family will probably be welcomed back into the Luminaries officially and that Mom has talked about nothing else for days, Winnie would totally skip . . .

After downing two Tylenol, Winnie makes herself a cup of Earl Grey. As much as she would prefer sleep, time is short. She needs to think. A lot happened last night, and she hasn't had a single chance to sit with everything she did—and didn't—discover at that granite pit in the forest.

When the tea is finally ready, the scent of bergamot fills her kitchen. Not quite like Jay, but close enough to make her think of him, to remember how he stood here only two weeks ago when everything had been so different between them . . . and yet, exactly the same.

Winnie trudges upstairs. Mom isn't home, but Winnie still locks her bedroom door before settling at her desk and gathering her supplies: a piece of sketch paper, a pen. Then she starts to write. Write *and* draw, because sometimes it's the only way to make sense of things.

Clusterfuck, she slopes out at the top of the page, imitating the serif font of the Compendium. Then beside it, and with the meticulous care needed to add each little serif stroke, she adds, *An occurrence not confined to the forest in which everything goes very badly all at once. See also: Winnie Wednesday, Were-creatures, Whisperer, and Witches.* At the end of the definition, Winnie adds a little crescent moon and three stars, like the one on her locket.

Which reminds her: she needs to go to the library and see when that book on secret messages that Professor Funday requested will arrive. She still has no idea how Dad might have known about old Luminary tricks with moons and stars, and it seems even less likely that Grandma Harriet (the original owner of the locket) would have known either . . .

But still, Winnie should pursue every avenue of investigation, no matter how implausible it might be. Plus, it's not like she has to deal with the secret message idea *now,* since there's no way the book will have arrived from Italy yet. Best of all, if she waits a few days before checking in at the Monday history library, maybe her embarrassment over how she acted with *Jay Freaking Friday* (K-I-S-S-I-N-G!) will have subsided and she can bring him along too.

Below Winnie's new written definition for "clusterfuck," she scribbles down a list that she first began mentally two days ago.

What I know:

1) I know someone put a dampener in the stream.
2) I know there used to be a source in the dampener. Probably.
3) I know Dad wanted me to find it. Probably.
4) I know it somehow connects to the possibility Dad was framed.
5) I know there was a second X on the map that led me to a weird hole in the forest with blood on granite walls.

Here, Winnie's pen pauses. Because a tiny light bulb has just switched on above her head. A mere Christmas light, really, like the ones that drape and circle downtown, but still—a memory that didn't exist a moment ago.

She shoves from her desk and hurries to her closet. She has to fling aside some dirty shirts, including the latest flannel from Jay, but soon Winnie finds a lime-green three-ring binder that says in very straightforward handwriting, Nightmare Compendium, the Complete International Edition. Winnie wanted to draw a moon pattern on the front, like the one on the actual Compendium, but at age twelve, she lacked the confidence.

She squats on the floor beside her closet, not even bothering to rise and heft the Compendium to her desk. It's heavy; she is accustomed to this goblin-like crouch. Plus, she is soon so lost in the pages, her body becomes a forgotten vessel. A mere tool that allows her brain to do what needs doing.

With the practiced ease of someone who has handled these pages more than any other book in the house—or really, in the world—Winnie opens the binder. The pages within are worn, their edges curled until what was once only three inches thick is now closer to four. They're also crammed full of Winnie's sketches and notes, little scraps from school notebooks or sometimes thicker sheets from her sketch pad.

She thumbs to the *S*'s.

And the faint scent of rotting moss tickles her nose from beneath the bed.

Sadhuzag, she finds. A drawing of a stag appears before her. She can tell right away that the artist was lazy and did not include all seventy-four antler prongs. She can also tell right away that—like the illustration of the werewolf in the Sunday Encyclopedia—the artist has captured none of the sadhuzag's actual menace.

What follows is a short entry, given that sadhuzags aren't common nightmares globally. But at the end of the definition is the reference Winnie was searching for: it's a citation for the Addendum.

Winnie flips to the back of her Compendium, to where more Xeroxed pages wait behind a divider with a torn red tab. Again in very simple lettering, Winnie had written, *Addendum to the Nightmare Compendium: New Research, New Theories.*

Her legs burn from holding her crude squat. The light bulb in the closet flickers a warning that its sixty watts will soon die. She even gets a paper cut on a page discussing ghost-raccoon research in countries where raccoons aren't native.

Then Winnie finds it: the tiny addition to the sadhuzag. *Some evidence suggests the sadhuzag is drawn to residual magic, such as areas where Diana spells have been cast. Further research is needed.*

And that's it. That one sentence has everything Winnie needs.

Because that *has* to be the connection. A spell was cast in a granite crater in the forest, and that's why the mist created a sadhuzag there.

Winnie drops the Compendium's binder with a thud worthy of a droll's
footstep and half falls, half crawls back to her desk. All those spells described by Theodosia Monday—*mundanus, silva, effūsiō*—could any of
them have left enough magical residue to attract a sadhuzag?

Winnie returns to her desk and cracks open *Understanding Sources* to
find out. It takes a few moments to find the pages that describe the various
spells . . . and then a few more moments to realize Theodora's list won't
be terribly helpful. It's all so vague, so simplistic. There's no way to possibly guess which of these many, *many* options would leave enough residual
magic to attract a sadhuzag.

If only Winnie could get her hands on a book of spells. Theodosia refers
to such volumes often, describing how Luminaries have managed to nab
these rare, heavily guarded tomes throughout history. In fact, it became
such a problem for the Dianas—the Luminary spies stealing their written
spells—that they stopped scribing their spells onto paper a century ago
and instead shifted to an oral tradition.

Still, there *are* books out there.

And god, if only Winnie had one right now. Not merely to solve her mys-
tery and follow Dad's clues . . . but because *the knowledge* that such a book
would contain! It would be like dissecting a manticore hatchling in nightmare anatomy, but better. She'd be getting an up-close look at the inner
workings of her sworn enemy—an enemy that is just as human as she is.

Winnie grabs her pen once more. Draw, draw, think, think. The ideas
are all right there, so close. Raw crude oil ready to be refined. Coal ready to
be compressed into a diamond.

Sources. Spells. Sadhuzag. No more *W*'s for her list, but *S*'s instead.
"What," Winnie mutters, "do I know?" She adds a sixth item to her list:
Sadhuzags are attracted to spell sites.

Below that, Winnie draws the granite walls of the perfectly square pit.
She has never been good at landscapes, but this place had a life of its own.
Residual power, she thinks, sketching her view as she watched Jay kick
up detritus from stagnant rainwater. *Residual power from what? Residual
power from when?*

Her pen rolls over the paper, feeling almost as good as that night on her second trial when she cut down vampira and her heart sang with the hunt. Almost as good as the melusine blood in her veins.

When at last she finishes her sketch, she stares at the blood streaks. Here, captured in black-and-white, it really does look identical to the birch trees. Is that mere coincidence, or could it mean that the Whisperer is also attracted to residual Diana magic?

Winnie slides the paper aside and grabs a fresh sheet.

What I Don't Know:

1) *I don't know where the dampener's source is.*
2) *I don't know when it was removed or who removed it.*
3) *I don't know who put the dampener in the stream. Was it Dad or someone else?*
4) *I don't know why they put it in the stream→Though I do know that water neutralizes power.*
5) *I don't know what residual power drew the sadhuzag to the second X→though I can assume it was a Diana spell.*
6) *Does the Whisperer connect to it all? Or is it total coincidence that it once killed there and that I sensed it last night?*

Winnie looks at her two lists. They are at least the same length now, and surely Winnie can shorten that *Do Not Know* list with a bit of hard thinking.

Her glasses have slid down her nose. They perch just above her nostrils, the lenses warping her list and distorting her drawings until the granite hole almost looks as if the Whisperer hovers within.

Somehow that second spot on the map is where everything connects. Where the *W*'s and the *S*'s overlap. *Sources, spells, sadhuzag. Whisperer, witches, werewolf.*

She pushes her glasses back up. Her teeth click steadily, while the tea she made sits at the edge of her desk, untouched and oversteeped, growing cooler by the second like a body left in the forest for tomorrow's corpse duty to retrieve.

Winnie draws a three-circle Venn diagram. In one circle, she writes

Source. In another, she writes *Sadhuzag.* In the final, she writes *Dad.* Then, in the very middle of it all, where all three circles overlap, she writes her own name: *Winnie.*

Except no. That doesn't work.

She strikes through it and starts anew. She trades out *Spell* for *Source.* Tries *Witches* instead of *Dad.* Then tries *Whisperer* instead of *Sadhuzag* . . . And oh, it looks much better now. The diamond is so close to forming from all this coal.

Winnie shifts her focus to the areas where circles overlap: *Spell* and *Witches* overlap to form *Source. Spell* and *Whisperer* overlap to form *Sadhuzag*—although that's a tenuous connection at best. Sure, they both appeared on Tuesday night and are both connected to the granite hole . . .

But correlation does not prove causation and all that. Plus, how do witches and Whisperer overlap? In the end, Winnie can't find an answer, so she scribbles a question mark in that particular area. And then she shades in the very center of the diagram, where all three circles meet to form her own name.

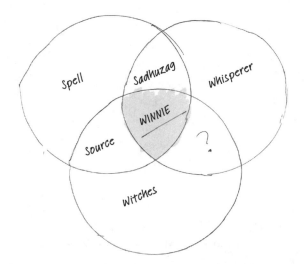

She stares at her sketch, time bleeding past. Her hangover from the melusine blood still throbs, but it's a dull pinprick now. She rubs at her forehead. Her teeth click in a slow, reliable drumbeat that matches her heart. Her fingers casually fill in circles from her discarded Venn diagrams. She adds stems. She adds leaves. She creates three-petaled trillium flowers like Dad would have loved long ago . . .

Then she removes her glasses and cleans them. When she puts them back on again, the answer sharpens along with her vision.

Just like that, Winnie sees where her latest Venn diagram went wrong.

She strikes through *Winnie* in the center of the circles, then *Whisperer* on the right circle. Because of course, *she* isn't the one that connects everything—*she* isn't the one that started this clusterfuck and keeps it churning and churning like water over the Big Lake's falls. It's the other way around. Winnie is just another *W*, another piece of the puzzle, another person who has to jump to stay alive . . .

But if she puts herself where the Whisperer was, then *ah*, she sees it now. In seconds, she draws a new, clean diagram and fills it in with her final conclusions.

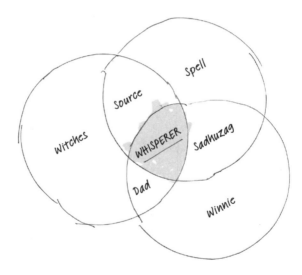

It looks like nothing she would ever have guessed or ever seen without her pen to guide her. Because what if the Whisperer isn't merely attracted to the same area as the sadhuzag because of residual power? What if it isn't just *connected* to sources and witches . . .

What if, instead, the Whisperer *is* a spell? What if it was something made by the Dianas to haunt Winnie every time she steps into the forest?

And what if the Whisperer is exactly what Dad wanted Winnie to find all along?

CHAPTER

31

It makes so much sense Winnie can't believe she didn't think of this sooner. It's like a missing semicolon in a line of failed code. She was missing *one little detail* that would let the program finally run. Now she's got it, and everything makes sense.

The Whisperer was never a nightmare.

It was . . . it *is* a Diana spell.

And that's why Winnie and Mario could find no record of a creature like it in the Nightmare Compendium. That's why the Whisperer doesn't vanish with other nightmares after the dawn mist rises. Heck, it might even explain why the Whisperer goes through the forest each night hunting anything in its path . . .

There was a spell like that, wasn't there?

Winnie finds her answer almost instantly. *Understanding Sources* is open right beside her elbow, the list of spells glaring up at her. *Famēs,* she reads halfway down the page. *These spells are self-feeding and sustain themselves in the forest.*

Holy crap. It really is right there, staring up at her in stark black-and-white.

Pure Heart, she thinks. *Trust the Pure Heart.* Now she knows why she dreamed that phrase on Sunday night. Her subconscious already had the answer, even if she was too slow to pick it up. The heart of the Venn diagram, the pistil of the flower, the piece upon which everything else in Winnie's chaotic life hinges . . .

Is the Whisperer.

It is a spell. It is a *famēs*.

Winnie needs to tell someone. Like, right away, no time to waste. This one piece of information—this one word, "*famēs*"—could change all the calculations for Hemlock Falls. If the Whisperer really is a Diana spell, then while everyone is waiting around for the Mondays or Tuesdays to catch a werewolf, an actual self-feeding spell is out there killing Luminaries.

A spell cast by a witch who might have framed Winnie's dad four years ago.

Winnie leans back in her chair, tongue sliding over her teeth. Her eyes find bits of adhesive stuck to the wall—remnant tape from when her nightmare sketches filled this stretch of beige. She ripped the drawings down after her second trial, when she first encountered the Whisperer directly. The night when it shredded an entire vampira horde, and *no one* would believe that Winnie had seen it.

If she couldn't make Aunt Rachel or the Council believe her then, how will she possibly make anyone believe her now? Especially since, other than her Venn diagram, she has no proof. No direct connection between the Whisperer and the Dianas—at least not one that's obvious and easy to point to.

Sure, she can probably get away with telling Mario about the Whisperer and its potential connection to *famēs* spells, but she can't give him a detailed explanation of *how* she came to that conclusion. It's still too risky for her family.

She also can't sit here and do nothing, though.

After cramming her new lists and new diagrams deep into the bowels of her sketchbooks, Winnie digs out a Post-it note.

The paper is so crumpled, so handled, its fibers have softened into something resembling cloth. The ten numbers on it are faded to near oblivion.

Of course Jay would include his area code on here. As if Winnie wouldn't know it already—as if not everyone in Hemlock Falls has exactly the same one.

She studies his handwriting by the warm light of her desk lamp. It is much like she remembers it: very tiny. As if he's always conserving, always holding back. Each number is a perfect little pen scratch, no bigger than it needs to be.

She snags her tea off the table, cold and inky. It looks borderline toxic. She hurries downstairs; Mom will be home soon, and she'd rather make this call alone.

After dumping the teabag, then rinsing out the cup for later use (it's not gross, Darian, since it's just going to hold more tea), she snags the phone off the receiver in the kitchen and plugs in Jay's number.

The beeps fill the kitchen. Her fingers are shaking and her heart is hammering so hard—though if that hammering is because of the new Whisperer connection exploding in her brain or because it has been four years since she called Jay Friday, Winnie can't say.

She puts the phone to her ear, listening as the rings begin. Then continue. Then eventually stop. Her breath is held. Has he answered or is it just—

Voicemail. "Leave a message," says Jay in his gruffest tones. Then the beep comes.

Winnie doesn't leave a message. Her heart still thunders. For some reason, she is cold. And now she's downright pissy too, because Jay knows her house number. She *knows* he knows it, and she would bet all thirty-four dollars and twelve cents in her old piggy bank that he saw the caller ID and opted not to answer.

And god, how typically Jay to take the time to record a voicemail welcome message, but then to half-ass the execution. *Yes, I will give you my phone number, but then I'll write it so small you have to hurt your eyes to read it.*

Yes, I will play in a band and bare my soul through song, but the instant I'm onstage performing, I will shut down and stare at the floor.

Yes, I will train with you in the forest and even joke with you like old times, but the instant you want answers about the past, I will retreat and reject you.

Winnie slams the phone onto its stand and stomps back upstairs. Once in her room, she curls onto her bed and tows her sunflower covers up to her chin. She doesn't need Jay's help to find a way forward here. She is a Big Girl and a Wednesday hunter, so she can 100 percent figure out how to protect Hemlock Falls from a Diana . . . while also protecting her family from Hemlock Falls.

She doesn't actually conjure any solutions, though. At least not before her eyes drift shut, her exhaustion from the night before finally catching up to her.

Pure Heart. Trust the Pure Heart.

Winnie awakens an indeterminate amount of time to her mom banging at the door. "Winnie? Are you in there? We need to go."

Crap, Winnie thinks, wiping drool off her cheek. Then aloud, "Crap. I'm coming, I'm coming!" So much for looking great for the twins. She almost hopes Bretta does bring her something, because her haphazard flail around a room lit only by sunset through the curtains is turning into an even bigger nightmare than the sadhuzag.

Mom cracks the door open right as Winnie is yanking off her jeans from school. Her Save the Whales hoodie hangs off the back of her desk chair. Mom's eyes widen at the sight of it. "Don't wear that."

Winnie sighs. "I'm *not.*"

"Then . . ." Mom gives her a wary once-over. "What *are* you wearing?"

"Erm." Now Winnie is the one to fling a once-over at Mom, who wears a very respectable green blouse with long fluttery sleeves and a pair of dark skinny jeans that Winnie thinks might be new. Mom also has on smart leather boots with actual heels that Winnie knows are *definitely* new.

"Thanks for taking me shopping with you." Winnie glowers. "All I have clean are my black jeans and that black turtleneck—"

"That is about three sizes too small," Mom finishes for her, her face crumpling. "Oh Winnie, you need to get better about doing laundry."

"And you need to get better about inviting me to . . . to wherever you bought that." She gestures at Mom's ensemble, heat sliding onto her face because why didn't she set an alarm? As much as she doesn't want to go hobnob with Wednesdays right now, she also doesn't want to look terrible doing it. Especially since, for once, Mom looks really sharp—and Darian most certainly will too.

"Lucky for you," Mom replies, dipping out of the room, "I bought some extra items. Maybe something will fit you!"

Winnie hopes so. She also hopes it doesn't look too . . . well, mommish. She tugs on her black jeans, and by the time they're squeezed over her mid-section and zipped up, Mom is back with two tops to choose from: a simple blue sweater and a red floral blouse. They are both *very* mommish, but Winnie is also *very* desperate. She snags the blue sweater and hauls it on. It is fitted and V-neck and hugs a bit more tightly to her body than she likes, but . . .

It's clean! And new. It will have to do. As for shoes, well . . .

"Oh, not your Converse," Mom begs as she watches Winnie scoop them off the floor.

"They're all I've got," Winnie mutters. "Unless you prefer combat boots?"

Mom shudders. "We're going shopping next week." She twists back toward the hall.

"Yes, please," Winnie calls after her, still wondering when Mom went shopping *this* week. Or for that matter, where she got the money to afford those fancy boots. She must be feeling really confident about getting back into the Luminaries—and on top of that, getting a more stable job with the Wednesdays.

Winnie wonders what kind of job that might be. Before Mom was Lead Hunter, she worked as a networker contact point, communicating con-stantly with all the Wednesday networkers (like the twins' parents), who live in the non world to ensure Luminaries keep getting all the supplies they need to exist as a society . . . like the clothes at Falls' Finest downtown or the coffee beans for Joe Squared.

Winnie never actually saw Mom do that job, of course; it was before she was born. Throughout Winnie's childhood, Mom was Lead Hunter. Pe-riod. Handling all the duties and work and weight that such a job entailed.

Just like Jay has to do now.

Winnie rubs at her eyes. Then realizes she should probably put on makeup . . . then realizes she doesn't have time, so she just snags her glasses off the nightstand and bolts for her bedroom door. Mom is already at the bottom of the stairs, tapping her foot and muttering, "Come on, Winnie. This is only the most important night of our lives."

"I'm here." Winnie stomps dramatically down the steps, giving partic-ular *oomph* to the third stair from the bottom. It groans as much as she wishes her vocal cords would. "And I'm ready. Is Darian meeting us there?"

"Indeed he is." Mom beams at her, her posture abruptly straightening. Her face shedding years and stress before Winnie's very eyes. She holds Winnie's leather jacket and offers it to her—a not-so-subtle message that her whole ensemble will look better if she just covers the darn thing up.

"Thank you, my most favorite daughter." Mom slings an arm around Winnie once the jacket is on. "Darian and I owe you everything. You're my loyal, loyal, fierce-hearted little bear."

Winnie's throat tightens. She thinks of the four birthday cards for Darian now in her pocket, of the moss slowly rotting beneath her bed in a dampener no one but Jay Friday knows about, and of the Venn diagrams that all point to a Diana spell currently ravaging Hemlock Falls . . .

She's loyal all right.

Just not in the way Mom probably wants her to be.

CHAPTER

32

Light pours off the Wednesday estate, brighter than the sunset still hugging the sky. Voices pour out too, along with laughter and clinking glasses and a low-grade thrill, as if a live wire thrums inside the brick walls.

A second live wire thrums next to Winnie. Mom is raw, exposed, and she moves with the strident steps of a hunter about to face the forest. Though she hasn't said it, Winnie knows Mom is terrified.

Terrified it might not actually happen tonight. That all the lunches with the Luminaries, all the clan dinners and promises from Aunt Rachel, all her loyalty and flag-bearing and her Wolf Girl daughter will not be enough to counteract what happened four years ago. That tonight will *not* be The Night and tomorrow she'll be back to picking up shifts at whatever store or restaurant will have her—and probably returning those leather boots if it's not too late.

"It's going to be fine, Mom." Winnie has nothing on which to base this assertion, but she pumps her voice full of confidence and briefly nudges her mom's shoulder as they approach the open Wednesday front doors. "They wouldn't want us here if it weren't going to be fine."

"Hmmm" is all mom offers in reply, and Winnie's posture deflates. She wishes Darian were here; she wishes she could off-load this job of propping up Mom to someone else. She knows it's cruel and unfair of her—Mom spent four years as a solo parent in a town that tried to crush her. But Winnie has so much to deal with right now. The three circles from her Venn diagram bounce around in her skull like Ping-Pong balls flung onto a table where the Whisperer is the net.

Pick your nightmare, spin the wheel! Or you'll end up a Diana meal!

It doesn't help that Winnie needs to talk to Darian about Dad's birthday cards. Does it seem cruel to ruin Darian's night? *The* night that could shape up to be the best for him and their family in four years? Without a doubt. But Winnie also can't wait much longer. There's just way too much at stake.

He owes you anyway, says a little part of her she doesn't like. *He wouldn't be here tonight if not for all you've done.*

Aunt Rachel is the first to greet Mom and Winnie when they walk in the front door. "No Darian?" Rachel has to lift her voice to be heard over all the conversation. The main hall is *packed,* and to Winnie's shock, extra tables have been set up near the dining room doors.

"Spillover," Rachel explains when she notices Winnie's gape. "Some networkers have come in just for tonight."

Somehow, Mom's live wire spews even more electricity. She tenses up so much, Winnie half expects her hair to stand on end. But this time, it's Rachel who nudges: "It's going to be great, Frannie. Trust me on this. It's going to be great. Now, come on. Let's get you a drink."

Mom doesn't relax, although she does turn dark, grateful eyes onto Rachel. Mom has forgotten to remove her driving glasses, so she hastily slides them off now, patting absently at the purse that hangs on her hip. She flashes Winnie a tight smile—part apology, as if she is ashamed she can't quite keep it together, and part dismissal, because Rachel clearly has this all in hand now. "Let's sit together," Mom murmurs to Winnie. "And keep an eye out for Darian."

Winnie nods, as the live wire stops pummeling her. Yet while Mom moves away to find a drink, Rachel lingers. "You ready for corpse duty in the morning?"

Winnie tries not to wince. She is most assuredly not ready. "Right," she says. "I'll be there." *And putting up with your horrible son the entire time.*

Rachel smiles, though it's strained. She isn't a live wire like Mom, but there's obviously something on her mind. She shifts from foot to foot. Her arms cross over her chest. Then uncross. Then she finally sighs.

"Look, now that Jay Friday is a Lead Hunter, I know he doesn't have time to train you. That means you're not getting in the work you need to hone your skills, and, uh . . ." She pats at her slacks' pockets until she finds a folded paper. She offers it to Winnie. "This is the Wednesday training schedule. I expect to see you at some of the meetups, okay? Assuming you still want to hunt."

Rachel says that last bit almost jokingly—*assuming you still want to hunt*—and Winnie forces herself to laugh. It's a sound that's part punch of air, part giggle because of *course* she wants to hunt. Of *course* she wants to train. That is literally the only thing she has ever wanted for the last four years. Every moment for over *fourteen hundred* days she has spent focused on that one goal: becoming a hunter, restoring her family's name.

And yet . . .

Winnie swallows. Her throat is itchy, and though she grips the folded training schedule, she makes no move to open it. The Ping-Pong balls bounce inside her skull. None of them are labeled *Hunter*.

As if Rachel can see these thoughts playing out on Winnie's face— which good god, Winnie hopes she cannot—her expression softens. It's a flash of sympathy that stirs a memory in Winnie's brain. A time when she saw those same slanting brows, those same sideways-pursing lips. Except then, Rachel was standing on Winnie's front porch when she said, *I'm sorry, Win. You have no idea how sorry I am, but I have to follow the rules. I can't talk to you anymore.* Then she walked away and stayed away for four eternal years.

Now, Rachel says, "There's no rush, okay? I mean that." She rests a hand on Winnie's biceps. It's awkward, but the sentiment in her grip is genuine. "Why don't you pick one session a week to train, and we'll start there. We can ease you in slowly because really, Winnie"—her grip tightens—"there really is no rush. Safety and comfort are the priority."

Are they though? Winnie thinks as she watches Rachel turn away and melt into the crowd. Unlike Winnie or Mom or Darian, Rachel is an adept liar. Like, top-notch, lie-to-your-face-without-missing-a-beat liar. She lied after Winnie's trial, first to Winnie and then to everyone else. And then she lied during the second and third trials too.

She knew Winnie didn't kill that banshee; she knows it still today; and for some reason that thought makes a question rise in Winnie's mind: If Aunt Rachel lies so easily about the banshee, then what else is she hiding? What else does she know?

And . . . does any of it have to do with Winnie's dad?

CHAPTER

33

Winnie has no time to study her Rachel-shaped questions before the twins find her. Bretta, dressed in a floral-print baby doll dress, gives Winnie a once-over. "It's not terrible," she admits grudgingly, a wave directed at Winnie's outfit. "But that sweater is a little—"

"Mommish." Winnie's spine sags. "I *know*, okay? I took a nap and overslept. This was the best I could do." She waves helplessly at the blah outfit that her amazing leather jacket can't quite elevate.

"And it's fine," Emma inserts, glaring at her sister. She is dressed in fitted black jeans and a pink button-up, her crutches wrapped in black scarves. "Winnie looks just *fine*, and we'd better go sit down or we'll end up at the *kids'* table."

Everyone collectively shudders at this. The kids' table, as suggested by the name, is where the under-twelve crowd sit, and it is the actual worst. Even when you're under twelve. It's the farthest corner from the main table, where Fatima's mom, Leila, sits with special guests. It's also the farthest from the fireplace, so in winter it gets really cold. Like, *really* cold.

Maybe there's a lesson in there. Or maybe the Luminary adults just really don't want to deal with their children.

Fortunately, there is no problem finding a table, even with Emma moving slower on her crutches, because of course Leila has invited Winnie's family to join her tonight—and she even extends that welcome to Emma and Bretta. "As Fatima's friends," she explains, ever the beneficent head of the Wednesday clan. Tonight, Leila wears a stunning violet gown with a black blazer overtop, and her hijab is a mauve that Winnie would never have thought to match with violet but that most definitely works.

Clearly this is where Fatima's design sense comes from.

Winnie sits next to Darian—who must have arrived while Winnie was chatting with her friends. When he spies Winnie, he leans over to give her a sideways hug. He wears an outfit similar to what he wore at clan dinner two weeks ago—a sweater and khakis—except tonight he lacks the polish. He's rumpled. He's tired. His normally olive skin is sallow and pale.

On Darian's left sits Andrew, who for once looks like the more put-together half of their partnership. No scrubs or textbook-studying sweats for Andrew tonight. He wears an ice-blue button-up that sets off the warm tones of his dark brown skin. And when he smiles at Winnie, his brown eyes are bright. There is no misreading the expression on his face; he is always so open, so real. *I am so excited for you and Darian. This is going to be amazing.*

Winnie can't help but smile back.

Fatima sits on Winnie's left, dressed with the same easy, understated elegance as her mom, where the quality of the fabric speaks louder than any cut or pattern ever will. Her wide-leg pants are a silvery gray, her red turtleneck tucked in without wrinkle. Her hijab is a complementary shade of brown that matches her heeled boots.

Okay. Winnie looks hands-down the worst at this table. Even Aunt Rachel, who also sits with them, looks more polished.

Maybe Winnie *will* take Mom up on that shopping offer.

Assuming tonight goes well.

Leila stands at the table and tinks a knife against an empty champagne flute. The room falls silent. Eerily, uncomfortably silent. The sort of silence that only the mist can bring, where sound is muffled and danger could be hiding anywhere.

"As you all know, we have come together tonight for a very special clan dinner."

Cheers rise up here from several quarters of the room; Mom flushes, and Darian grins tiredly. Winnie spies his hand clasped in Andrew's—and she spies Andrew giving it a squeeze.

Strangely, Winnie wishes someone were holding *her* hand. She wishes someone would give *her* a squeeze that says everything Andrew's hand and eyes now say: *I'm here for you, always here for you, and I could not be more proud.*

She wonders if Mom thinks of Dad every time she sees Darian and Andrew supporting each other. And she wonders how Mom doesn't break down crying when she does . . . Then she feels shame for not supporting Mom more. For four years, Mom has done all she can to keep their family going. Now, tonight, she can maybe finally breathe again.

Please, Winnie prays. *Please, please, please.*

"Francesca, Darian, and Winnie," Leila continues, "have toiled for so long under their punishment as outcasts. But . . ." She pauses here for effect, her eyebrows rising and a sly smile towing at her lips. "No longer. You are officially Luminaries again. The Council voted this morning to let you back in—"

She doesn't get a chance to finish before the entire room becomes a stun grenade of noise. It's deafening, it's *physical.* A slam of cheers and whistles and applause from hundreds of Wednesdays who somehow seem happier than Winnie or her family are at this development.

It really is like the last four years never happened.

Winnie grabs for a glass of ice water in front of her empty plate. The condensation coats her hand. The ice inside vibrates from all the noise. She wants to take a sip because her throat is suddenly swollen . . . but she can't seem to lift it.

The Wednesday bear on her plate laughs at her, no longer a ferocious beast standing rampant, but a bear dancing for the Nightmare Masquerade. Winnie knows what's coming. Like the shudder of a mama manticore's steps before the beast's arrival, she just *knows* what is about to hit her . . .

And there it is. *Aroo!*

Later, she will learn Marcus started it because of course he did. But in that moment, there's no real sensing who utters the first howl or who utters the second. There are just the sounds of an excited crowd, and then there is an entire room of howling.

Winnie is going to be sick.

She releases her glass, palm wet, and grabs at the table's edge to push away. She meets Fatima's eyes, and her friend already seems to know exactly how

Winnie feels. It is so vastly different from how she and the twins reacted at the party on Saturday night, and a little corner of Winnie's heart warms knowing that her friends really *did* learn from that encounter. That Emma's apology in the library yesterday was genuine.

Most of Winnie, however, is consumed by the howling. It rattles in her skeleton. It pokes inside her ears and scuttles under her skin.

Aroo! Aroo!

She shoves away from the table. Fatima rises beside her, while on her other side, Darian reaches for her. Winnie brushes away his hand. "I'm fine," she shouts, "I'm fine." She won't ruin this moment for him. Or for Mom, who is looking at her with a terrified face that only a mom can wear when she knows her child isn't well.

"I'm fine," Winnie repeats for her. "I just need some fresh air." She doesn't know if Mom or Darian or anyone else can hear her, but as she hurries from the table toward the nearest door into the garden, only Fatima joins her. And one of Fatima's arms slides behind Winnie while the other braces against Winnie's elbow.

Amazingly, Winnie realizes she needs that support. That without it, she might fall over as easily as Emma without her crutches.

As if the thought of Emma summons her, the twins soon fall into step beside Winnie, Emma moving with surprising, if unbalanced, speed. They reach the garden door. Bretta scoots ahead to open it. Then cold, clear air crashes against Winnie. She gulps it in.

Howls chase from behind.

Fatima guides Winnie past the burbling bear fountain surrounded by potted flowers, off the brick patio, and into the perfect rows of organized garden. A cement bench waits beside the rosebushes, the branches recently pruned in preparation for spring. They look like sadhuzag antlers. Like seventy-four prongs of danger and venom and death.

Fatima and Bretta help Winnie sit while Emma leans her crutches against the nearest bush and joins her on the bench. "You okay?" Emma asks softly. These are the first words spoken since they all fled the dining room. The howls are gone now; there is only the general buzz of dinner being served and conversation rumbling; Winnie still feels sick though.

"I hope I didn't ruin it." She tugs off her glasses and leans onto her knees. Her head hangs down. She stares at shadowy gravel. "For my mom and my brother, I mean."

"You didn't," Fatima assures her. She drops to a crouch before Winnie. It makes Winnie feel like a kid being coddled by her mother . . . and she doesn't actually hate it. "We can say you got food poisoning."

"Before the meal was served?" Bretta settles onto the bench too, except that with Emma and Winnie on there, only one butt cheek will fit. "How about we instead just tell everyone to piss off."

Winnie snorts—*Classic Bretta*—and glances toward the estate. It looks like a jack-o'-lantern, the lights on the ground floor forming its smile while the two lights on the top, where Fatima lives, form its eyes.

It makes Winnie think of the lying lights of downtown. It makes her think of her third trial and how it all began right here. All Winnie has to do is walk northeast from this exact spot and she will reach the forest, where the mist will soon rise.

"I have an idea," Emma murmurs. "What if we get of out here? Bretta and I have the van again." She leans onto Winnie's shoulder and rests her head there. Normally Winnie hates physical touch—*especially* when she's upset—but right now, she can't deny it's nice. Emma smells like lilacs. The night air smells like woodsmoke.

"Ooooh." Fatima rises to standing in an impressive display of quad strength. "Where to?"

"Joe Squared?" Bretta suggests. "It's open mic night. We can hide in the back where no one will see us."

Winnie can't imagine the Wednesday twins or Fatima *ever* hiding. Even in the forest, they must shine like the lanterns they are.

"And," Bretta adds, elbowing Winnie, "I'll even get you a small *Winnie*, if you want. I hear they're half off on Wednesdays."

Winnie laughs at that—a full release of air and a smile that she can't contain. Because her square of friends have just banished the howls of the night more effectively than any dawn mist can. "I've got a tab," Winnie says as she slides her glasses back on. "So we can actually all get whatever we want—the fancier, the better, since Mario Monday is paying."

Emma squeals and grabs for her crutches. "Oooh, this going to be fun."

"Yeah," Winnie answers, and to her surprise, she actually thinks it might be.

34

Winnie manages to endure the heat and eyes of the Wednesday dining room long enough to tell Mom and Darian, "I'm leaving with Fatima and the twins."

Mom looks alarmed. Darian looks confused. Only Andrew seems to get it. "She needs some air," he says, reiterating what Winnie already told them—all while his expression says, *Hey, I'll deal with this. You get out of here while you can.*

Winnie tries to do precisely that. She even makes it out of the dining room, past the spillover tables, and to the front door—which is open and letting in cold night—before Darian calls out to her. Her friends pause. "You go on." Winnie waves them toward the parking lot just visible through burgeoning spring trees. "I'll catch up in a second."

They obey, and moments later, Darian joins Winnie on the estate's front steps. "You said you had something you needed to talk to me about." He is panting slightly. "Is it this? Is it . . . whatever just happened?" He gestures ineffectually behind him, to where dinner clatters on, unaffected by Wolf Girl's departure.

Winnie chews her lip, unsure what to say. Darian's cheeks are flushed and his glasses slightly crooked. His sweater has a loose thread near the collar, and Winnie is 99 percent sure that if she pulls it, his entire soul will unravel.

Nonetheless, he is also the brightest, shiniest version of himself that

Winnie has seen in four years. *Maybe he can become a councilor again,*
Winnie realizes, and she can't believe she hadn't considered that sooner—
that maybe Darian can once again work up the ranks and try to replace
Leila one day. The rule that prohibited him only applied to outcasts. Not
outcasts who have had their punishment nullified . . .

Winnie knows right then and there that she can't ruin this for her
brother. She can't tell him about the birthday cards currently stuffed in her
pocket; she can't risk his happiness for a wild-goose chase that might ultimately lead her nowhere. Just as only *she* could be the one to enter the trials
and face the nightmares, now *she* must be the one to follow Dad's clues, to
steady these Ping-Pong balls in her head and crack open the full meaning
of her Venn diagram . . .

For Darian, the lights of downtown aren't swamp fires—they're real
fairies, they're *everything* he has ever wanted, and now he can have them
back again.

So although Winnie is a terrible liar, she makes herself paste on a smile.
She makes herself say, "Yeah. I just really hate all the attention." True. "And
I was hoping you might have some advice for me." Not quite true, but also
not a total fabrication.

"Aw, Win." Darian's face crumples, and he pulls her to him for a hug
worthy of a true Wednesday bear. "I'm sorry. I should have noticed how
you felt sooner. I should have been there for you these last two weeks. It's a
lot." He is talking into her hair, and there's a ferocity in his arms that takes
Winnie back four years, to one of the many nights they'd spent crying over
Dad and what he did to them.

Darian isn't crying now though, and to her surprise, neither is Winnie.
Just as she felt better being with Emma, Bretta, and Fatima in the garden,
she feels better now too. Like she is a swelling balloon floating up into the
night.

She will open Darian's birthday cards later; she will get the clues she
needs; and he will never have to learn that messages from Dad existed.
Is it a breach of his privacy? Maybe. Probably. But better that than a total
obliteration of the joy he feels tonight.

Darian breaks their hug first. After all, their family doesn't do physical
touch except in the most extreme of circumstances. His glasses now have

smears on them—as do Winnie's, made from eyelids pressed against poly-carbonate. He smiles. She smiles back, and this time it isn't forced.

"Have fun with your friends," he tells her, and a more familiar family awkwardness takes hold. He pats her shoulder. "Mom, Andrew, and I will hold down the fort tonight. Tomorrow, though, let's catch up for real, okay?"

"Sure," Winnie replies, even though they both know it won't happen. After all, the werewolf testing sites won't run themselves, and the Night-mare Masquerade can't self-assemble. "Let's talk tomorrow, Darian."

It is a packed house at Joe Squared. Much like the night Winnie snuck in and saw the Forgotten perform, the tables have been cleared away. Strands of Christmas lights twine around columns and support beams, setting the whole shop aglow.

An elderly fiddler pours out his heart on the low stage, his bow flying back and forth across the strings in a warm, rousing song that leaps and dances around the shop's exposed brick surfaces. One person is particu-larly enraptured by the show, standing at the foot of the stage. Her brace-lets clank and her orange sweater glows like a construction cone.

Professor Funday. Either the fiddler is her partner or she really wants him to be.

It is absolutely adorable.

True to Bretta's promise, the twins and Fatima *do* find a quiet corner, near the back door, and once a chair has been acquired for Emma, Bretta thrusts a pointed finger toward the ceiling. "Smoothies," she declares. "What do you want, Winnie?"

"Strawberry and banana," Winnie answers, ducking her head as a smat-tering of nearby Luminaries glance their way. It's shadowy; hopefully they won't recognize her; she wishes she had her trusty old hoodie on. It might be ragged and unfashionable, but it's also as effective as the mist at swal-lowing her whole and erasing her into the dawn. "Oh, and don't forget my tab, Bretta. Let's all feast on Mario's dime."

As Bretta and Fatima march off to acquire sustenance, the fiddler ends his performance. Winnie and Emma clap along with the rest of the shop. Professor Funday claps and cheers loudest of all. She even shouts, "*Encore! Encore!*"

The man does not give an encore.

A half hour slides by this way, smooth as the blended strawberries and bananas that soon become Winnie's dinner. Music and laughter and coffee-scented warmth curl around her, and it is *exactly* what she needed. No one ever notices the Wolf Girl tucked beside the back door—no one except Jo, who gives her a conspiratorial wink and then sneaks her a free blueberry muffin.

Two more performers take to the stage: a shy tween on her banjo that Winnie vaguely remembers from the ill-fated corpse duty on Monday morning (everyone cheers a *ton* for her), and then a middle-aged sister duo who sing a cappella in Italian.

Winnie catches few familiar words, like *incubi* for nightmares and *foresta* for the forest.

When the sisters finish, the gap between performers stretches long. Twice, Jo steps to the mic to ask *if the next performer is here? All it says on the list is Thursday?* Conversation buzzes while everyone waits. Bees in a hive. Manticores in a nest. Voices that hum and build while smoothies blend and coffee grinds.

The combination of it all sounds like the Whisperer. *Feels* like the Whisperer, minus that hair-raising scent of burning plastic.

Fatima and Bretta discuss the Nightmare Masquerade; Emma scrolls on her phone; and Winnie lets herself sink against the brick wall behind her. The Ping-Pong balls are back, although they've settled into a gentle float. They bob and bounce, dropped atop the pond that is her mind.

Spells. Sources. Sadhuzags. Winnie. Witches. Whisperer. Whisperer. Whisperer.

How can Winnie prove the Whisperer is a Diana spell? A *famēs* that's sustaining itself by eating all in its path? She's close, she's *so* close. But it's like hopping across a river via rocks: she has made it most of the way, over riffles and rapids and pools, only to realize the final rock is *way* too far from shore. That although she can *see* the other side, there is no way in hell she will ever be able to jump that far.

Winnie just prays the answers are tucked in Darian's birthday cards—or maybe, just *maybe* in the title Professor Funday sent for from Italy.

Otherwise, Winnie is all out of options, all out of luck. She is trapped in the river while the current rises around her and the water claws her down. She will be forced to choose between the safety of her family . . .

Or the safety of Hemlock Falls.

Spells. Sources. Sadhuzags. Winnie. Witches. Whisperer. Whisperer. Whisperer.

A wind creeps in from the open back door. It smells of dead leaves and lost memories—and also fried food from the Revenant's Daughter. Winnie's stomach grumbles; the smoothie and muffin weren't enough supper.

The wind kicks a bit harder, and this time, she thinks she hears crying.

Instantly, her spine tenses. Her eyes snap wide. *Banshee.* A burst of adrenaline stabs her heart.

But then she hears the sound again, and she knows of *course* it isn't a banshee. It's just a person in the alley, all alone and very sad.

Dead leaves and lost memories.

The mic squeals with feedback from the stage. "Um, I guess our Thursday performer didn't make it, so we'll move on to the next. Unless . . ." Jo peers hopefully through her glasses at the crowd. "Alrighty, I don't see our Thursday, so in that case, let's welcome our next guests to the stage. They need no introduction, as they've graced this shop many times before."

The sniffling comes again, this time laced with a whimper. It's just a sliver of sound as the crowd *erupts* with excitement because they all know who is coming. Even Winnie has guessed, thanks to Bretta's and Fatima's sudden bouncing and Emma's sudden scream.

The Forgotten! The Forgotten!

Winnie finds she is almost as excited as they are. There is a piece of her that is still caught up in the performance from two weeks ago at the twins' birthday party. The night when she was forced to face feelings she had buried almost as deeply as her fury at her Dad. Feelings that keep punching into her chest like a droll fist, and that, no matter how hard she tries, she just can't seem to burn to ash. *Fish food in an aquarium.*

But there is also someone in the alley who needs her. They have a banshee bearing down and no werewolf there to save them.

Winnie sneaks away from her friends and emerges into the night. A waxing crescent moon shines overhead, briefly stealing Winnie's sight after the shadows of the coffee shop. She smells french fries and burgers. She hears Archie shouting orders that most nights Mom would be picking up.

Winnie adjusts her glasses and frowns around her. She can't see anyone. Just the usual dumpster and a stack of pallets from recent deliveries.

Then Winnie spots Erica, tucked into a shadow with her back ramrod straight against the wall. She has a hand over her mouth, and it's clear she is hoping Winnie won't notice her. She also has a guitar case leaning against her: a red guitar case that used to belong to her sister.

Erica's eyes shutter. She knows she has been caught. She isn't going to try to run. Instead she will face the inevitable hunter now striding her way.

Winnie stops with five paces between them. The night is truly cold now; it twines into her leather jacket. "E," she says by way of greeting.

"Winnie," Erica replies.

"You . . . didn't perform."

"No."

"I didn't know you played guitar."

"Yes." Erica sets her jaw, a defiance hardening in her eyes as if she is just *raring* for a fight and Winnie showed up at the perfect moment for one. Winnie remembers that look—it is a look Erica's mother Marcia employs to great effect on the Council.

Winnie also remembers how to deal with it: she cracks a joke. "And here I thought all those Band-Aids on your fingers made you a Diana."

Erica's eyes widen. Then she lifts her fingers, as if she has forgotten that yes, they are regularly covered in Band-Aids—as her thumb is right now.

Winnie moves to the wall and leans against it. This wall is much colder than the one inside. The bricks exhale ice. "Have you been taking lessons?"

"Um, sort of," Erica answers, and Winnie watches as the fight leaks out of her. *Drip, drip, drain.* "I . . . found some YouTube channels. But . . ." Pause. Swallow. "I'm not very good. Not like, you know . . ."

"Like Jenna."

"Yeah." She sucks in a breath. Her hands lower. "Like Jenna."

Inside, the crowd is going absolutely wild. Full-on party-at-the-old-museum wild. It pours out of the coffee shop's back door, a soda erupting beyond its measly can. For several moments, there is no space to speak in the alleyway.

Then L.A. Saturday, the lead singer, comes on the mic. "This is for everyone we've lost. Grayson, you're never forgotten."

Somehow the crowd gets *even louder*. It barrels into Winnie, a tornado's wind. A werewolf shoving her out of a manticore's way. She sways sideways, bricks catching her until the roar subsides and the bass line begins, more sensation than actual sound. It hums low in Winnie's belly, and the crowd falls silent. Too silent, the memory of their eruption still hanging in the air. Little echoes that hover like butterflies around Winnie and Erica in the alleyway.

And for half a second—a tiny flicker of an *almost* moment—Winnie thinks she might get it. The darkness, the darkness, the light.

Only when the guitar joins in and then L.A. starts singing—a song Winnie has heard before—do she and Erica speak again. And it is like the old museum all over again, when Winnie met Erica in front of Grayson's photograph: tightly leashed sadness crosses her face.

Until Erica abruptly turns to Winnie and declares: "I *did* know Grayson Friday."

Winnie blinks. Then blinks again, her lashes falling in time to Jay's bass line. "Because . . . he invited you to that party for Jenna?" Winnie is straining to remember what else Erica said on Saturday night.

But Erica shakes her head. "No. Because he was the one who found Jenna on the night she died."

"Oh." Winnie's head rears back. *"Oh."*

"Yeah." Erica scowls down at her Band-Aid, and the leashed sadness gives way to something frothy, something mad. "He was on his trial like she was. He found her, tried to revive her, and . . . well, you know the rest."

No. Winnie *doesn't* know the rest because this was right after Dad left, and Erica was no longer her friend. All Winnie knows about Jenna's death was that it happened during her second hunter trial, when she was meant to survive a night in the forest all alone. And she knows that it was ugly. *Real* ugly with her body mutilated by vampira and everyone wondering why she was on the trial in the first place.

As if following the same thoughts, Erica says, "She never wanted to be a hunter." Erica is picking at her Band-Aid now, peeling up the edge and then pressing it back down. Her words fog slightly as she speaks; the night has grown colder. "I have played it over and over and *over* again: she didn't want to be a hunter, so why did she do the trials?"

Winnie knows Erica doesn't expect an answer, but she can't help but attempt one anyway: "I don't know. She wanted to leave Hemlock Falls, and it never made any sense to me either."

"No." Erica sniffs. "It didn't." Then she smiles, a cruel thing that stretches her lips like she's a changeling who has never imitated a human before. It's made all the more unnatural because she isn't smiling *at* Winnie but almost *beyond* her, at some ghost hovering just out of sight.

And suddenly Winnie knows what she needs to say. A split-second decision, a choice to jump right off the falls. "I heard her, you know. When I was under the waterfall." Winnie isn't sure why she adds the *you know.* Because of course Erica doesn't *know.* That's why Winnie is telling her. "It's the only thing I remember, E. Right before everything went black, I heard her singing. And it was . . ." Winnie bounces one shoulder. "It was beautiful. Even now, her music moves people. Maybe it even saves."

"Ah." Erica lifts a fist to her mouth as if trying to hold in tears. When she does finally speak again, her voice is totally steady: "Thank you for telling me that."

Winnie wants to answer—she wants to say, *Thank you for talking to me right now.* But she doesn't get a chance. The Forgotten have finished their first song, and now are sidestepping into a new one.

"You should get back in there." Erica has to shout now because the crowd is yet again losing it.

"Nah," Winnie replies, except that when she meets Erica's eyes again, the anger and inhumanity are gone. There is a look in them that she remembers from Saturday night. A look she remembers from childhood. It's mischievous and it's teasing. A *dare.*

Winnie has no idea what it means, coming as it is right now.

What she does know, however, is that this moment between them is over. The realness, the rawness, the brief trust flavored with fried grease—that has ended. Erica isn't a full-on ice queen, but she's also no longer crushed by a banshee. She no longer needs Winnie to save her.

Erica swoops up the guitar case, while inside Joe Squared, the screams and claps of the adoring crowd settle into rapturous silence. Erica dabs at her eyes; it smears her mascara.

"You should *really* get back in there," she repeats. "I think you're going to want to hear them tonight. There's one song in particular . . ." She pauses, pretending to chew on her words in a way that is part of the mis-chief, part of the game. "Well, you'll have to let me know what you think when you hear it."

Winnie doesn't get a chance to answer before Erica twirls on her two-inch heels and strides away. Her footsteps are lost to the music, her posture straight despite the weight of the guitar case no doubt pulling her to one side.

Erica has never been one to bend. Certainly never one to break.

Then Erica exits the alley, a fairy flickering off into the swamp fires. One more light lost in the cold night.

I t is not merely Winnie's curiosity that drives her back into Joe Squared. *You'll have to let me know what you think when you hear it.* It's the music too, the pump and boom of each bouncing note.

This is a song Winnie has heard twice before. First, when she saw the Forgotten perform at Joe Squared two and a half weeks ago, then again at the twins' birthday party a few days later. It was before she was a Luminary again. Before Jay was Lead Hunter and Grayson Friday was dead.

Winnie's glasses fog as soon as she steps inside and rejoins the twins and Fatima. The coffee shop has become a sauna of body heat and sound. And it's like some infectious virus has taken hold—a nightmare mutation that jolts from one person to the next. Winnie feels it in her spine, her chest cavity, along the base of her skull. The hairs on her arms stand up, a rippling sensation as energy swells into the rafters.

And *now,* Winnie discovers she actually gets it. She actually *feels* it, the light, the fire, the shadows running away.

The Luminaries really are lanterns burning bright and alive, because what other choice is there? The forest is right there. It takes their families and friends and futures, but it cannot take this too.

It can't. And neither can the Dianas, neither can the Whisperer. This moment is *theirs,* and right now, they are all alive.

The song closes and the Forgotten slide into the next. At some point, Winnie finds herself dancing. No one howls at her, no one calls her "Wolf

Girl." There is only listening and dancing and smiling against the darkness that swallows the rest of the world.

And Jay—Jay transforms up on that stage. The pallor of his skin flushes into the warmth of a living boy. Like L.A. and Trevor too, he has become a beacon guiding everyone in this room out of the mist and back into the light. *We are the Forgotten, but we will never forget.*

Winnie has no idea how many songs pump through the coffee shop. She has no idea how much time passes with her and Bretta banging against each other or Emma hopping around on crutches or Fatima locking arms and shouting at the fairy lights *"More, more, more!"* every time one song ends and another begins. Jo and her husband dance too, behind the counter where coffee brews and nightmares can't reach.

And Winnie knows that *this* is what Grandpa Frank was really talking about. Her life might be a clusterfuck, there might be a monster out there who has killed and will kill again, who might be a Diana spell at the heart of her Venn diagram or might just turn out to be a nightmare living at the heart of the forest . . .

And there might also be a Diana who has ruined her family's life and could easily ruin it all again . . .

But for now, Winnie can dance and compartmentalize. Eat the pizza and burn so bright. Because there is always time for the pain tomorrow.

36

The Forgotten are winding down. It's clear they are getting tired. L.A. is on her fifth bottle of water, and she's pausing more and more often to gulp it back. Both Trevor and Jay have peeled off layers—Trevor with his coveralls pulled down to his waist and Jay with his flannel mysteriously vanished somewhere in the crowd. Sweat glistens on all three, and it is a testament to their hunter fitness that they are still moving with so much spring and passion after what has been at least forty-five minutes of intense performing.

As the last beats of a song echo away, L.A. says softly, "This next song is our last. It's called 'Backlit.'" Then, to Winnie's shock, she puts the mic into a stand and steps aside . . .

So Jay can walk up to it.

Everyone loses it. Emma, Fatima, Bretta, Katie. Wyatt, Astrid, Shaunielle, Xavier. Literally every person Winnie's eyes find in the darkness is clapping and jumping and screaming. Clearly this is a song the entirety of Hemlock Falls knows . . . but one that Winnie herself has never heard before.

Like *this* is the secret Jay always keeps tucked away, and she is the last to find out.

There's one song in particular, Erica said. *You'll have to let me know what you think when you hear it.*

Trevor kicks off a low, electric beat—more restless throb than actual percussion—and L.A. leans into the harmony mic that Trevor typically uses. Then comes Jay's bass line, a slow thrum that pulses over Trevor's beat before both Trevor and L.A. lean into the harmony mic and hum.

It is one of the most haunting sounds Winnie has ever heard in her life. She stops moving, though her friends swing and sway around her, Bretta with her eyes closed and Emma with a look of intense concentration—a look not so different from the one Jay must wear.

Winnie can't see his face from here, pushed as she is to the back of the shop, but his whole body is a taut bowstring until he finally looses his voice.

He does not sound like Winnie expects. The boy she once knew never sang beyond the occasional "Happy Birthday." The Disney songs were left to Erica and Winnie while he rolled his eyes and acted like he was above it.

Yet here he is, his voice low and gruff and, even now, tucked deep inside. As if yes, he will bare *some* secrets, but only a tantalizing hint. The rest must remain forever trapped away.

Winnie is so stunned by Jay's singing—actual *singing*—that she loses track of the song. It takes her a full verse before the words finally settle in.

> *The more I forget you, the deeper you sink in*
> *Fangs at the neck and red paint on a lost cabin*
> *Ten dollars to kiss, a bet I can never win*
> *Snow on your lips*
> *It's feast or it's full famine.*

The chorus picks up, and now Trevor and L.A. sing along with Jay—no longer ghostly humming, but with a harmony that hovers over and below.

> *I miss you more now*
> *Now that it's been so long*

Winnie's heart is thumping harder and harder by the second. She feels sick. Not like she did at the Wednesday estate, where eyes and howls clashed against her, inescapable and hungry . . . but sick in a way that makes her whole body numb. Like she is a revenant. Like she is a ghost.

Then comes the second verse, and it is too much.

To kiss across shadows into a bright fever
The dawn mist rises inside me like a wildfire
With heat on your skin I spin until I can't see us
I find no relief, inside I'm still a hopeless curse.

Jay's voice cracks on that last word, as L.A. and Trevor move in for another chorus. Somehow, it doesn't ruin the song. If anything, the vocal quaver enhances it. As if the hopeless curse is real and he truly will never find relief.

And Winnie feels that pain as if it were her own. The whole coffee shop does. He is the siren, and they are captured by his song.

And Winnie now understands why Erica flashed that mischievous grin before she departed. She knew darn well that this song was about Winnie.

Exhibit A: The cabin is where the old WTF triangle used to meet, though it's really just a garden shed on the edge of the Thursday estate where one afternoon Winnie and Jay drew a vampira in red paint on the wall—then he pretended to bite her with his "fangs" until they were both laughing so hard they were crying on the cabin floor.

Exhibit B: The ten-dollar bet happened on a snowy night right before Winnie's world ended. Erica bet that Jay and Winnie wouldn't kiss for ten dollars . . . so Winnie and Jay totally kissed for ten dollars.

It was only a pop kiss, but Winnie *still* remembers how warm Jay's lips were when all around them the night was cold.

And Jay apparently remembers it too.

At some point, Winnie leaves Joe Squared. She isn't upset, although she knows she has every right to be. Instead, she is determined. Everything has been stripped away—everything she thought she knew about her, about Jay, about what they shared four years ago. It's a photograph that has hung crooked for too long, yet now has been arranged upright again.

The chorus builds and builds, chasing after Winnie. *I miss you more now. Now that it's been so long.* It's like the sadhuzag is behind her, or even the Whisperer, hunting her down without reprieve.

She has to deal with this.

She deserves an answer.

It takes her under a minute to find Mathilda parked outside. The ancient Wagoneer is an elephant in a herd of sleek gazelle, and Winnie perches on the back bumper to wait. Cold air snakes against her, carrying with it the final strains of the night's show.

There's one song in particular. You'll have to let me know what you think when you hear it.

How very like Erica. The *old* Erica. The one who thought it was funny to bet ten dollars and watch her best friends awkwardly touch lips while snow fell around them. That Erica laughed and clapped with trickster joy, her scarlet-red mittens slapping together in a downy *thwap!* Winnie will never forget the sound of.

She bets Erica is laughing now too, wherever she is.

And Winnie also bets she herself will never forget this rapturous applause currently unspooling in Joe Squared. The Forgotten have finished their show. "Backlit" was their last song.

Three weeks ago, Bretta mentioned that Jay never stayed after a show. At the time, Winnie replied, *He doesn't perform for attention.* Winnie was wrong, though. Or at least, attention avoidance is only part of the reason why he never hangs around when the performance is done. The main reason, she now understands, is that Jay is tapped dry. He is a lantern with no fuel left, shattered and empty.

He will need to hide back inside himself to refuel, regrow, restore.

Winnie zips up her leather jacket. She was hot in Joe Squared from all the bodies and the dancing, but now her sweat has dried and the cold of early spring has latched on to her like *Chrysomya megacephala* on dead flesh.

She swings her legs against Mathilda's filthy bumper. Her teeth click together in a staccato double beat. Her friends are probably wondering where she went.

Winnie pushes off the bumper. She stuffs her hands in her pockets. Maybe this was a bad idea. Maybe she should go back—there's still time. She can sneak into the crowd and pretend she never came out here. Pretend she never called Jay's phone hours ago. Never woke up on his bedroom floor this morning. Never felt all those things she felt four years ago . . .

She doesn't flee, though, and soon enough, Jay is within sight, striding between parked cars. He steps off the curb and aims Winnie's way.

He spots her, but other than a momentary stutter in his steps, he offers no reaction. No tensing, no retreat, no real emotion. He just keeps moving forward with the same silent determination she felt when she came out here.

His flannel is draped over one shoulder, and sweat from the show gleams on his skin as he passes from one streetlight to the next. Until at last he has reached Mathilda.

I miss you more now.

Now that it's been so long.

Jay meets Winnie's eyes, a slight arch lifting one eyebrow. He doesn't speak, and she doesn't either. Not yet, anyway. She waits for him to get to Mathilda. To open the trunk and slide his bass guitar inside, then his amp. And lastly, to hoist the shirt off his shoulder and fling that in too.

Then he turns to face Winnie head-on. His eyes are intense in that way only he can do—but they're startled too. Like he is the ghost-deer who just saw his death arrive clad in faded jeans and ratty sneakers.

Except that he is also the hunter. Winnie can see it in the way his muscles are coiling inward, until he practically vibrates with the potential energy of an attack that she is both afraid might come at any moment . . . and also kind of hoping will.

Never startle a nightmare, she thinks.

The cold and shadows of downtown press against her. She doesn't move, and neither does Jay. His gray eyes look ashen in the moonlight.

"You wrote that song about me," Winnie says by way of introduction. No small talk. Just rip off the Band-Aid.

Jay nods.

"Does that mean you used to like me? Four years ago?"

Another nod. Then, to her surprise, he adds, "Yes." It is an unequivocal response. A sharp line drawn in the sand, a smear of bright blood on pallid birch trees.

Winnie tugs off her glasses. She is near enough to Jay that he doesn't haze away completely. He simply softens and smudges from a moon-sharp line drawing to an impressionist painting.

It is easier to hold his gaze this way.

"And do you like me now?" she asks.

"Yes," he repeats, although this time he doesn't nod. There is only the word to hang in the air between them. *Yes.* It is too heavy to be carried away by the wind. *Yes.* It is too uncompromising, too one-dimensional, too simple to be misinterpreted.

Yes, I used to like you.

Yes, I like you now.

Neither Winnie nor Jay moves. Neither speaks. Stars and galaxies form and collapse while they stand there, only three paces apart. Chills gather on Jay's bare arms as the night wind, scented with detritus and petrichor, bites against him. Winnie's arms meanwhile hang limp and useless at her sides, her glasses still clasped in one hand.

Until at last they both move—simultaneously. Two watches synchronized eleven years ago on a carpool ride to the Sunday estate. But two watches who must, for now, go their separate ways.

Because there is a second question still tangling between them. One they both know that Jay will never answer because its nightmare fangs have sunk in too deeply to ever fully let go.

Jay grabs the Wagoneer's door to shut it. Winnie backs away three steps. The door slams. She turns away. And the weight of the *yes* finally collapses. Dead leaves from a silver maple, whisked off into the night while sharp teeth snap and chase from behind.

When Winnie gets home, she is in a daze. She found her friends; they gave her a ride home; and through some unspoken agreement, no one asked her where she disappeared to or why it took her ten minutes to find them at the Wednesday family van.

Mom isn't home yet, thank the spirit, because all Winnie wants to do is sit at her desk with her pen and think about what just happened.

Yes.

After all her revelations tonight—the S's and the W's and the Pure Heart of her Venn diagram, the wolf howls and her square of friends and her shining lantern in the coffee shop—it has all been capped off by a single, monosyllabic word of affirmation.

Yes.

While she waits for the kettle to boil so she can make a cup of tea, she remembers Jay in her kitchen. Jay in her bedroom. Young Jay, old Jay, a thousand iterations she loved from the first day she met him.

The kettle whistles. Winnie steeps her chamomile in a tall, ancient mug with Pikachu on the side. The heat warms her hand; the steam warms her nose. She shuffles upstairs, shuts herself in her bedroom, and sinks down at her desk.

It's like she never left four hours ago.

A sip of tea, and Winnie withdraws Darian's birthday cards from her pocket. Jay's *yes* will have to wait in favor of a new one: the *yes* that comes when you've run out of reasons to procrastinate. When a task must be done, and now is the time for doing it. On the one hand, it *still* feels wrong to open up something that wasn't sent to her . . .

But on the other hand, Winnie's Venn diagrams need more information, and that information might live inside these envelopes that Mom has collected each year from the family mailbox.

After spreading the cards on her desk, Winnie stares for several minutes. Four red squares. Four potential clues from Dad. Her knee bounces. Her fingers tap.

Then she takes a steeling sip of tea and, with fingers warm from the mug, she tears into each envelope. *Rrriiiippp,* goes the paper. *Rrrrrriiiippp, rrrrriiiippp, rrrriiiippp.*

She slides out the cards and lays them before her. Her chest feels tight as she studies them. Her teeth click softly behind her closed lips. They are identical to the plain white postcards Dad sent her on her own birthday, yet Dad wrote significantly less for Darian—so little, in fact, that there is nowhere for any secret message to hide.

Happy Birthday, Son. Love you.

Below these straightforward assertions is a drawing. Simple, clean lines from a man trained in landscape architecture. From *the* man who bought Winnie her first sketchbook, her first graphite drawing pencil. The man who first showed her how you can capture the essence of a place without actually drawing everything you see.

But where Dad always stuck to flowers, to trees, to gardens stretched before him, Winnie found she preferred sketching people . . . and then nightmares. The rules he taught her still applied to people and nightmares, though, and essence ultimately mattered more than accuracy.

A pen distilling crude thoughts into feelings across a page.

Right now, the essence is very clear: Dad has drawn a family of four with their arms around each other. No faces, only the vague outline of hair and shoulders and arms and torsos. A dad, a mom, a brother, a sister. Everyone but the mom wears glasses, and though they lack specific features, there is no missing the ease in their postures, the comfort in their togetherness.

And that is when it happens. A bright, hungry feeling that glitters like siren scales. That feels like the rising sun after the dawn mist has fled. It is warm and buoyant as it scrapes with gentle claws inside Winnie's rib cage.

Hope.

Desperate hope that things can go back to what they were. That these four figures Dad drew can exist again, exactly as they are in the illustration, where expressions don't matter because the essence says everything: *We love each other and always will.*

But it's an impossible hope—not merely improbable, but truly *impossible.* Because even if Winnie can somehow finish solving Dad's clues, what will that do for her? She doesn't know where he is; she doesn't know if Mom or Darian will want him back; and four years have passed with struggle and pain, with rage and grief and hate. None of that can be undone.

She hates hope. She *hates* it. She thought she had killed it four years ago when it was clear there would never be any fairness for her family, never be any justice. She *hates* that instead of eradicating that hope, she has actually only hidden it away all this time in her secret lockbox.

It was always there, just waiting for a moment like this to overwhelm her.

Winnie feels heat on her cheeks. She swipes a tear aside and flips the postcard over. Just like her own birthday cards, the next three cards are exact replicas of the first. *Happy Birthday, Son. Love you.* The only change is that in each illustration, Winnie gets a little taller. Darian a little more fleshed out. It is surprisingly accurate, and not for the first time, Winnie wonders how Dad got these cards in the family mailbox.

And why Mom didn't turn them over to the Council.

Winnie yanks off her glasses to dig more forcefully at her eyes. "No," she whispers to the questions rising in her brain. *What if you can have him back? What if you can be that family again?* "No, no, no."

It doesn't matter how many times she says it. The hope has returned, and this time, it will not be shoved away. Because the truth is that it was never fear that propelled her to follow her father's clues. It was never a desire to avoid getting in trouble again with the Tuesdays. And it was *never* a need to protect Hemlock Falls from some Diana who might have framed Dad.

It was always pitiful, pathetic hope. *What if you can have him back? What if you can be that family again?*

Winnie shoves away from her desk. These cards have no answers for her, they offer nothing useful for her Venn diagram. She's glad she never showed them to Darian.

And now she wishes she'd never shown them to herself.

It is almost an hour later—and after two cups of tea—that Winnie's brain finally feels settled enough to attempt sleep. She has corpse duty in the morning; she can't miss that, even if it means facing Marcus.

It is as she is curling under her covers in her pj's that she notices something she should have noticed the instant she stepped into her room: the *absence* of any smell. There should be a smell . . .

But there isn't one.

Her heart surges into her throat. She drops down flat against the floor, where sure enough the box of summer clothes under her bed has been shoved aside to reveal nothing else there. The plastic bag is gone, the dampener is gone. There is nothing *at all* beneath her bed beyond dust bunnies, recently disturbed and scattered about.

Winnie scrabbles back to her desk, to the sketchbook where she kept all her notes, all her ideas, all her *clues* about Dad and his secret scavenger hunt . . . But it's empty. Of course it's empty—she could sense that as soon as she lifted it and found the weight too feathery. Pages have been ripped out. No map, no Venn diagrams, no scrawled-down messages from the birthday cards Dad sent to Winnie, no maps taken from the library.

Winnie's first thought is that Mom must have found everything. Winnie's second thought is that this makes no sense because Mom was with Winnie at dinner, and if she *had* found something, she would have confronted Winnie directly—not searched through her room and stolen everything.

Winnie's third thought—frantic and skittery and propelling her to her feet—is that maybe Tuesday Lambdas were in here. That they discovered some of Dad's clues and followed them straight under her bed.

But this also makes no sense. The Lambdas would have swarmed Winnie at clan dinner or at Joe Squared. They would never have snuck in, swiped key information, and then snuck back out again.

Winnie's vision is crossing as she stumbles toward her bedroom door. Her heart is pounding as hard as it did the night the Whisperer chased her. The Wednesday bear gapes at her as she pushes into the hall. Her bare feet slap on uneven wooden floors, sluggish to start . . . then practically sprinting by the time she reaches the attic hatch. She yanks it down, the ladder unfolding too slow.

Up, up, she climbs. *Yank,* goes the light switch. *Flash,* goes the bulb. Winnie doesn't even care if Mom comes home and sees the light on. She doesn't care if she gets caught. Someone was in the house, someone was in her room, and that person knew exactly what to look for when they got here. *Exactly* what to take.

Winnie finds the old box filled with photographs. She rifles through, passing picture after picture of a family that hasn't been hers in years, despite what Darian's cards might have shown. No nuclear family happily intact, no Grandma Harriet to visit every summer. Winnie gets all the way to the bottom of the box without hitting a single one of the red envelopes that hold the birthday cards Dad sent to her.

Her hands are shaking as she returns everything the way she found it. Her fingers are numb, her toes and face and brain. There's even a ringing in her ears, like her Pompeii finally detonated and oh, Winnie! You were standing *much* too close!

Winnie does not return to her bedroom right away. Instead, she walks past it to pause at the top of the stairs and gaze down at the front door that her family never locks. The one Jay scolded her about only three weeks ago—a long-running exchange between them that began even when they were children.

Why don't you ever lock your front door? he would ask.

Why do you always lock yours? she would counter. *No one is going to break into the Friday estate.*

You don't know that. There are bad people, even in the Luminaries.

Yes, Winnie thinks as she finally returns to her bedroom. As one plodding step after the other carries her into a room where someone unknown recently invaded.

Although they aren't unknown any longer. Not *entirely,* at least. For there's only one someone that makes any sense. A circle on her Venn diagram, a *W* on her ever-growing list of problems: a witch who is loose in Hemlock Falls.

A witch with a source in their possession and who might have created the Whisperer.

C H A P T E R

37

There is one thing, at least, that the Diana didn't find: the photograph on Jay's phone of the map in the library. It is presumably still saved, and without that photograph, the witch can't know about the second little X.

Although, this fact isn't much help for Winnie. Not at this precise moment while she stands ineffectually at the center of her room, the ceiling light illuminating her like the Joe Squared stage light. Her mouth is dry. Her heart is somehow thudding harder . . . yet also *slower,* like it has been shoved beneath a pile of cinder blocks and left to fend for itself.

Danger, her brain suggests. *You might be in danger.* Without another thought, Winnie strips out of her pj's, shoves on her clothes from before—trading her Converse for combat boots this time—then grabs her school bag and shoves Darian's birthday cards inside. Maybe, just maybe they have some secret meaning. Either way, she isn't about to stay here to mull it all over or leave them behind for the Diana to find if they come back again.

There is only one place Winnie knows to flee to, both for her own general safety *and* to ensure the map photograph is protected. Admittedly, the Friday estate is the last place on earth she wants to go, and Jay is the last person she wants to talk to—*yes, yes, yes*—but she sees no other option. She can hardly go to Darian right now and say, *Hey, I know you're tipsy on champagne and triumph, but d'you think we could talk about how Dad was framed?*

And Dad was definitely framed.

If there's one thing Winnie can now say without a doubt—can now move into her *What I Know* column—it is that Dad was most definitely, unequivocally framed. She might have no idea where his clues ultimately lead, she might have no idea why he ran off four years ago instead of staying, she might *hate* how much hope burns inside her that she'll see him again . . .

But the man was innocent. He was not a Diana, he was never a Diana, and someone in Hemlock Falls got away with not only ruining his life, but ruining all his family's lives too.

Her family's lives. *Her* life.

It is a strange thought—that there is a single person to blame for everything that Winnie, Mom, and Darian have endured for the past four years . . . and that that person is not Dad.

Yet there it is: a key-shaped truth meant for a lockbox she never knew existed. One that has been crammed inside her organs somewhere between her stomach and her spleen. And now, as Winnie leaves her house by the way she came in (the unlocked front door), the lockbox is opening wide.

It is a fury she has never felt before. It is not explosive. It is not choking with its dust and ash. And it is nothing like the pent-up rage she has nursed for her father these last agonizing years. Instead this rage is as sharp as vampira claws. It's as focused as a shot of adrenaline straight to her heart.

Someone fucked over her family.

They fucked over her life, Mom's life, Darian's life, and Dad's life too.

Worst of all, they have been coasting totally free for these last four years while Winnie, Mom, and Darian have had to scrape and grovel and *endure,* and while Dad has been god knows where in the world beyond.

All this time, a Diana has been walking around Hemlock Falls laughing at what they got away with.

And what they got away with might very well include the Whisperer.

Winnie finds the family bike leaning against the front porch. Mom must have used it today and never returned it to the shed. (*Why put it up, if I'm only going to use it tomorrow?*) Winnie hops on and with muscles powered by cold fury, she kicks off into the night.

Once, when Winnie and Erica were eleven, they watched *The Empire Strikes Back*. They'd seen it before, of course, but this was the first time it really hit Winnie that Luke was abandoning his training too soon.

Like sure—Darth Vader was horrible and he had Han Solo as a hostage, yada yada. But Yoda also made it very clear that leaving the training was a bad way to go. *If it were me*, Winnie told Erica, *I would keep training until I knew I was strong enough to defeat Vader. After all, Han Solo is frozen. He can wait.*

Except if you wait, Erica pointed out, *you won't care about winning anymore. Your Jedi heart will be able to forgive, and then Vader will forever go free.*

Well, then that's even better, Winnie replied. *I will be above revenge and anger. Sounds like a great way to live.*

No, actually. Winnie can see very clearly now that it *doesn't* sound great. That forgiveness is the way of failure. That *justice* is what actually matters in the end.

She already lost the training part—the Dagobah system and the Yoda guide were taken away from her by a ten-year outcast sentence. As such, Winnie has had no chance to learn how to fight for the light side of the Force. Instead, there has only been one failure after another, one misstep after another.

All because of a Diana.

Literally, *all* of it: Dad disappearing, her family becoming outcasts, four years of misery and training on her own, and then a Whisperer chasing her off a waterfall. Every one of those Ping-Pong balls can be traced back to a *W* for *Witch*. A *D* for *Diana*. Even Winnie's stupid, ridiculous hope circles right over to this Diana.

Winnie boils in her leather jacket. Sweat slides down her back, where her pack is pressed against her. She checks constantly to see if anyone follows, but the night is empty. She pedals from one streetlight to the next until there are no more and she is racing onto a gravel driveway she can see somewhat clearly thanks to the crescent moon beaming overhead.

No clouds mar the sky.

The Friday estate glooms before her, settled as a crypt unopened for years. Winnie knows people are home. It's eleven thirty. Lizzy is no doubt asleep, and maybe Jay is too.

Not for much longer, though.

Winnie tries the doorknob on the mudroom that leads into the kitchen. It's locked, as she knew it would be, but a slight lean with her arm, a slight *shove* with her shoulder, and she can get the latch bolt out of the strike plate. The door pitches wide, still locked but now useless.

So much for keeping bad Luminaries outside.

With long strides, Winnies crosses the ancient entrance area into the kitchen. Her legs vibrate and wobble from the bike ride; it feels as if she is still pedaling as she runs across the amber tiles into the hallway beyond. Vaulted ceilings echo her footfalls back to her.

She reaches the stairs that lead to the estate's living quarters and races up. Jay carried her this way two nights ago; she had no idea it was happening. She barely notices now.

On the third landing, Winnie slows. Then halts when she spies light pouring out from Lizzy's lab. The doors are wide open. It startles Winnie because *why* is Lizzy up at this hour—and in her lab no less? She is the opposite of a night owl.

No light comes from Jay's door, but Winnie strides there anyway. She knocks. Her breath sucks in . . .

But nothing happens. No sounds, no stirrings, no response.

She knocks again. Her heart beating faster. "Jay?" she murmurs against the door. Then louder, "Jay? Are you in here?" She nudges the door, and its hinges carry it open with no resistance.

The room is empty, yet it's also thick with a residual staleness that can only come from hours of uncirculated air.

Winnie crosses inside, gaze scouring like a hunter's. Jay hasn't come home yet. He must have left Joe Squared and gone . . . somewhere. Not hunting because he missed the meetup time for that. And not here to sleep like a normal human.

So . . . partying. That is sort of the only other possibility.

A fresh flare of anger rises inside Winnie at that realization. She knows it isn't fair—Jay can't have known she would come here to check that a Diana hasn't stolen his phone. He can't possibly have *predicted* that she would come to him again and say, *Jay, please help me.*

But she is angry all the same.

Footsteps thump behind Winnie. She whirls around, heart surging into her throat. But where she hopes-hopes-*hopes* to find Jay striding into his room, it's only Aunt Lizzy.

"Winnie." Lizzy blinks at her, clearly as startled to find Winnie as Winnie is to find her. She wears her pj's—loose shorts and a heather-gray T-shirt. Her blond hair is a fallen version of the usual braid she keeps crowned upon her head. "I, uh . . . thought you were Jay."

"I thought you were Jay too." Winnie frowns, her righteous rage briefly dulling. "Do you know where he is right now?"

Lizzy glances behind Winnie at the empty bed. Then gives a quick scan of the stale room before shrugging. "Guess he went out for the night. He does that, you know?"

"No, I don't know," Winnie says, even though she obviously does. For some reason, she needs to hear Lizzy say it. She needs to have Lizzy *acknowledge* it.

And Lizzy does at least have the decency to look sheepish as she explains, "Oh, sure, you know. He's always out partying at the old museum or hanging with those older Fridays, but what are you gonna do?"

"There's a lot you could do," Winnie responds. "Like, not let Jay leave the house."

"Oh yeah?" Lizzy sniffs. "You know a lot about teen boys, then, Winnie?"

"I know letting Jay drink and smoke his life away isn't good parenting."

"And I'm not his parent." Lizzy plants her hands on her hips, a glare taking hold of her gray eyes. "I'm just the aunt trying really hard to make him happy. He's seventeen, Winnie, and Lead Hunter. If he wants to party, then he can party."

"He skips school too."

"I'm well aware." Now Lizzy is full-on pissed. Her shoulders puff up. "Did you come here tonight to yell at me?"

No, of course not. That's what Winnie *should* say. Instead, she says nothing and simply glares right back.

Lizzy shakes her head. "It's so easy to criticize when you aren't here, isn't it? And you *haven't* been here, Winnie Wednesday. You've spent four years walking around, furious that Jay wasn't at your beck and call, but it's not like you've been around at his. So stop being such a hypocrite, and try looking at your own choices for once."

Winnie's jaw unhinges. She is so stunned, she actually cannot breathe. Her backpack slides off her shoulders . . . then hits the floor by her feet.

And Lizzy isn't done yet. In fact, she's only just getting started. "*You* try locking the doors and windows, Winnie. Jay always finds a way out. *You* try pleading with him that school actually matters. He always promises to do better. And *you* try getting him to see a therapist because his bad dreams never stop. By all means"—Lizzy opens her arms wide—"have at it because I have run out of cards to play here. At the end of the day, Jay is Lead Hunter. If he can go face the nightmares of the forest, then he can decide how he wants to live his life.

"Now, if you're done lecturing me," Lizzy finishes, "I'm going into my lab to wait on Mario."

And that's it. That's the end of the conversation before Lizzy stomps away.

Winnie lets the Friday councilor leave. Her jaw still hangs open, a host of arguments jammed bumper-to-bumper inside her throat. Because this night just keeps getting better. One clusterfuck after another. One person after another who doesn't want to help her.

For half a fragile moment, while the music played at Joe Squared and Winnie's friends danced around her, Winnie thought she was going to be okay. That she was going to be a lantern after all.

But now the light is gone and there is only darkness, darkness, darkness. *Furious* darkness at the hypocrisy of it all. At how hard she fought for these four years only to discover her Luminary prize was an illusion.

Winnie is so angry, she is trembling. Her muscles feel like they belong to someone else; her teeth start chattering with the ferocity of a staple gun.

She turns in to Jay's room to search for pen and paper. She will leave him a *strongly worded* note because what else can she do? He isn't here; she isn't waiting. But her eyes catch on the photograph beside his bed—the one with her and Erica and Jay. It makes her think of the drawings in Darian's birthday cards. Of how Dad managed to capture the essence of her and Darian growing up.

This photograph has essence too, of a different boy named Jay and a different girl named Winnie. But while it is obvious why Winnie has changed so much, why, why, *why* has Jay?

As she stares at those young, hopeful kids only weeks away from watching their worlds end, it hits Winnie: the words Lizzy barked before she stalked away. *I'm going to my lab to wait on Mario.*

At eleven thirty on a Wednesday night, Mario Monday is coming here? And they are meeting in Lizzy's lab ?

Winnie's whole body goes cold at that realization. A blast of AC after walking through a sweltering day. She lurches out of the bedroom. "Mario?" she shouts down the hall. Lizzy has only just reached her lab door. Light floods over her. "Why is Mario coming here?"

Lizzy pauses.

"Why?" Winnie repeats, her voice almost frantic now. Somehow, she knows what Lizzy is going to say even if the gas and dust haven't quite become a star yet. "Why is Mario coming here in the middle of the night?"

"Because," Lizzy answers coolly, "the Wednesday hunters have finally hit the werewolf. Your aunt, actually, with six bolts to the abdomen. Now all they have to do is to track it down and land the final blow."

Later, Winnie will be impressed she manages to follow Lizzy into the lab without collapsing. A heavy, compressive sensation has fallen over her, like one of those weighted vests they make you wear during X-rays.

The Wednesday hunters have finally hit the werewolf.

Lizzy leads Winnie to her wall of computers. The lights beam down overly bright, garish even, at this hour. The lab used to be a living room, the aging sofas and tables replaced by tables and mismatched shelves, all littered with books and papers and beakers and Bunsen burners.

Winnie fixes her glasses with fingers that don't feel like her own. Her joints are locking up, while beside her, Lizzy swipes open a touchscreen computer. A grid of four squares reveals sites throughout the forest.

Under normal circumstances, Winnie would be thrilled to watch these screens slide by: the forest is *alive* right now, the nightmares awake and prowling—even if the quality is grainy at best. Each square glitches and winks every few seconds, the cameras doing their best to fulfill their duty. There is only so long they can resist the supernatural energy of the forest.

"My tech won't last the night," Lizzy says, as if following Winnie's line of thinking. She flicks aside grid after grid of video, like a bored singleton on a dating app. She knows what she's looking for, but it's all Winnie can do to keep up with the various nightmares flying by.

Manticore hatchlings, white and scuttling. A hellion, half-eaten, sprawled beside a stagnant pond. Winnie misses the bottom two squares before they're gone.

Next comes an empty slice of Stone Hollow; then a shoreline of the Big Lake; a shot of the overlook beside the falls; a view of the granite ridges in the north.

Throughout all of this, Lizzy chatters away—about how she might swap out night vision for heat detection in two of the cameras. About how the cameras by the Big Lake are always the first to go. About how everyone told her to take her cameras and piss off *until* this werewolf came along, and now they can't get enough of her inventions, unreliable or not.

Not once does Lizzy ask why Winnie is at the estate—or why Winnie was looking for Jay. She is too caught up in the thrill of being part of tonight's hunt.

A hunt that is for the werewolf.

As Lizzy continues her descriptions of camera advances against the spirit's energetic fields, Winnie nods and nods. She is one of those figurines that bobble on a car's front dash, and a weird buzzing grips her brain, right in the back where that gas and the dust have been accumulating for days.

Now, they're spinning really fast—like collapse-into-a-star fast. Collapse into *lots* of stars fast, so that soon, all she will see is a bright, obvious constellation she should have detected weeks ago.

Then Lizzy finds the screen she wants. "Bingo," she says, aiming finger guns toward the ceiling. "Here it is."

Here he *is,* Winnie silently corrects, and sure enough, the werewolf slumps across the screen. *Northeastern stream 11:41PM.* He's in bad shape, moving with aching slowness. His head hangs low, and streaks stain his white fur. In seconds, he is out of frame.

Lizzy reaches for a radio receiver at the edge of her desk.

And Winnie's hand moves of its own accord.

It is an extraordinary sensation to watch her body move without any conscious impulse from her brain. As if the constellation has finally formed, but there's too much chaos in there, it can't cut through all the noise.

She thinks again of the cosmic microwave background. How it makes everything buzz and buzz and buzz.

Right now, the big bang is drowning out everything. In spite of it, Winnie's arm muscles still manage to act. Her hand still manages to clamp on to Lizzy's wrist.

"Huh?" Lizzy snaps her attention to Winnie, and for the first time since discovering Winnie in Jay's room, she seems to realize it is *really bizarre* to have a sixteen-year-old in her lab at this hour.

The buzzing in Winnie's brain is louder. Yet like her arm, her diaphragm seems to have developed a mind of its own. Her vocal cords and mouth too, forming a word that she has yet to fully understand. "Wait."

Lizzy squares toward Winnie. "Huh?" She pushes to her feet. "Hey, Winnie—hey, Winnie, what's wrong? Are you okay?"

No. Winnie is definitely not okay. Because something about seeing the werewolf on the screen, white and hurt and with blood gushing out of him—it is acting like a trigger to her memories.

The memory that Winnie has been trying to reach for days.

38

She is trapped underwater.

She is going to die.

Hypothermia or drowning—she doesn't know which will come for her first, only that she is too tired to fight it.

She can hear Jenna singing, and blearily, she wonders if this is how Jenna died. She wonders if this is where it happened.

Then pain in her forearm punches into her awareness, two bright sparks like iron rods jammed into her flesh. Her eyes spring wide, and there he is. The werewolf. Blood trails above him from where Winnie stabbed a wooden stake into his neck.

He has come to finish me off, she thinks, hoping it doesn't hurt. Hoping he can just be quick about it.

Werewolves, like their non counterparts, attack by going for the jugular. If faced with one, protect your throat.

Winnie doesn't protect her throat. She instead lets the wolf pull her along, up, up and toward the shore. It is strange behavior—diving into turbulent water simply to retrieve prey . . . but she also can't pin down those thoughts long enough to truly process what they mean.

Death certainly is taking its sweet time.

It is only once she is on the shore—Jenna's song somehow louder now and soft—that it occurs to Winnie she *isn't* dead. She isn't drowning. She isn't even cold anymore. She is warm and safe, and the song surrounding her is pure.

She also thinks she sees scales sparkling in the wild, foaming waves nearby. *Melusine,* she thinks. *A melusine is healing me.* The Compendium never mentioned they could heal a human. And it certainly never mentioned that they *would* heal a human.

Winnie's last thought before sleep settles over her is *You either trust the forest or you don't.* And she almost thinks she hears Jay right beside her, whispering those words anew. *You either trust the forest or you don't, Winnie. You have to choose.*

39

Clusterfuck: When everything you thought you knew gets flipped upside down and the world starts collapsing around you. See also: werewolf, Winnie Wednesday, Jay Friday.

Winnie!" someone shouts at her. "Winnie, are you okay? Hey, Winnie, *Winnie*." They are shaking her, and she is no longer underwater. She's not even in the water.

Bergamot and lime. Winnie smells bergamot and lime, and she is so glad to know that Jay is beside her . . . except when she opens her eyes, she realizes it's only Lizzy because *of course,* they probably buy a family pack of soap. And *of course,* Winnie is still in the lab . . .

And of course, Jay is the werewolf.

Those words repeat on a loop in her brain. A simple sentence that Winnie can diagram easily upon a whiteboard, thanks to Ms. Morgan's tutelage. *Subject, predicate, article, predicate nominative.*

Jay is the werewolf.

Jay. Is. The. Werewolf.

How many times has he told her? All the answers have been there— right in front of her, backlit upon the stage. *Never startle a nightmare,* he said three weeks ago—and then again this morning as a joke. And yesterday, he defended Winnie's dad: *I just get why he might have done what he did to protect you.* And of course, the lyrics of the song: *I find no relief, inside I'm still a hopeless curse.*

Winnie very arrogantly assumed he referred to her and his Angsty Feelings . . . but no. The lyrics were literal; the curse was completely real; and all these years, Jay clearly believed—in that honest, Friday heart of his— that he was protecting Winnie by staying away from her. He said as much last night with the will-o'-wisp, didn't he? *It will hunt us down and kill us. Because that is what nightmares do. That's the only thing nightmares* can *do.*

Jay must have believed he was out there slaughtering people in the forest—and he must still believe he was the one who killed Grayson six nights ago. Which means he must not remember what happens when he's in his wolf form.

At that thought, a new memory unravels. One from Mario's office, of a Post-it on his enormous Compendium that read, *No sentience in wolf form?* It was one of many Post-its shoved onto the page for were-creatures.

Mario knows, Winnie realizes. All this time, Mario has known exactly who the werewolf was, yet somehow he kept it a secret throughout Winnie's nosing around. He distracted her with wagers for Joe Squared coffee when she thought the halfer was killed by a werewolf. And he bamboozled her with his constant *pop-pop!* of pink bubblegum when she asked about that Post-it note in the Compendium.

But in the end, Mario had been right: that halfer didn't die by a werewolf any more than Grayson did.

"Winnie," Lizzy repeats, and this time, she bends down to stare at Winnie's face. It would seem Winnie is doubled over. Her glasses have fallen off and now lie on the floor beside her combat boots. "Hey, Winnie, are you okay?"

"Yes," Winnie squeezes out, even though it's a blatant, bald-faced lie. Because Jay (subject) is (predicate) the (article) werewolf (predicate nominative).

Winnie grabs her glasses from the floor; they weigh approximately a million pounds, and somehow her head weighs even more as she tries to lift it. The blood that had reached her head now plummets toward her toes. Her vision briefly crosses, a roar throbs in her ears.

Lizzy is ogling her in open fear, her face almost as pale as her nephew's. *Almost as pale as the werewolf.* "What just happened to you?"

"Blood sugar," Winnie says, a weak lie that Lizzy doesn't buy for a second—but that she also can't contradict because Winnie is now turning away and walking toward the exit.

Lizzy tries to follow, but Winnie lifts a hand. "Tell Mario hi."

Maybe it's because this is such an innocuous thing to say, such a *normal* everyday request to make in the middle of what is clearly not a normal night, but Lizzy actually does stop following. She even murmurs, "Ohh-kay," and Winnie doesn't have to look behind her to know the woman is frowning.

Then Winnie is out of the lab, out of the light.

Part of her wants to wait right there in the hall so she can confront Mario—so she can get answers about Jay and demand that he protect Jay from afar while she goes after her friend. But there's no time for that. Not when Jay has six bolts embedded in his abdomen.

Six bolts shot by Winnie's own aunt.

She starts running. First to Jay's room to get her backpack, then downstairs to the ground floor. The stiffness in her muscles retreats with each step, the Tin Man getting a much-needed squirt of oil. The buzzing fades too, a familiar, reliable Compendium rising up to replace it instead.

Werewolf, were-creatures: Human by day and monster by night, these rare daywalkers blend in easily and are unrecognizable from other humans in their daytime form.

So true.

Winnie never had any idea just how true.

And of course, now her brain adds the notes from Mario's years of observation: *Unaffected by sunlight. Bites—nontransmissible. No sentience in wolf form?*

She doesn't return to the kitchen, but instead aims down a long hall that will eventually reach more steps. And once again, she thinks about how Jay carried her this way last night.

This time, however, she also considers if she might have to carry him.

In seconds, Winnie has reached the hunters' locker rooms. The Fridays might be the smallest, least funded of all the clans, but Lizzy doesn't let her hunters go out unprotected. She funnels all clan dues into their gear and into their safety.

So surely Winnie can find *something* that will get her through a night alone in the forest. Her first stop is at Grayson's office. The door is unlocked and when she finds the light switch, the shadows flee. For half a second, while her eyes adjust, she squints through her glasses and tries to orient herself. She was here only last night—where did Jay get that melusine blood?

Desk. She charges toward it and yanks open a single drawer. An innocuous white binder stares up at her, the words *Friday Schedule* written in unfamiliar handwriting. She yanks it out. Then another binder, then a notebook, until finally she comes upon a simple metal tin, not so different from the dampener. When she opens it, she finds five vials within.

Her Compendium resumes its detailed narration inside her brain, like a tour guide describing each item as she plucks it up and shoves it into her backpack.

These small black stones are gastroliths from a harpy's gizzard and produce sparks on impact with a hard surface.

This green liquid is spidrin venom. The acid can eat through most animal or nightmare flesh, but the reaction produces a deadly fog that must not be inhaled.

This gray powder is ground phoenix feather—a stimulant that can also replace gunpowder. Or explode your heart.

This clear liquid is melusine blood. When poured on a wound, it can heal external injuries. When ingested, it is an effective antidote against venoms and poison. Causes a horrible hangover.

Lastly, Winnie removes a red glass vial with no label. When she holds it to the light, it appears empty. She puts it in her backpack anyway. Just in case.

She is now a veritable pharmacy of nightmare contraband, and she has no lingering questions about why Jay has all this stuff in his possession. She suspects she also knows how he got it.

You either trust the forest or you don't. Those were the words he said to Winnie before her second trial. Those were the words she *lived* by when the Whisperer hunted her and the only path forward was straight down . . .

You either trust the forest or you don't.

It was the truth at the heart of everything—the answer she wasn't ready to see. Integrity in all. Honesty to the end. He wasn't just saying, *Trust the forest.* He was saying, *Trust me.* And she should have. All this time, she *should* have, because he was the one who saved her.

Every time. Every trial.

He lured away the Whisperer on that first night.

He told her where to hide on the second.

And he knocked her from a manticore's path, then rescued her from hypothermia and drowning on the third. Even that melusine she now knows must have healed her under the waterfall—she would bet it was only there thanks to Jay.

As Winnie twists back to the open drawer to return the empty tin, she sees something she didn't notice when she was yanking out everything: a framed photograph of Grayson Friday. In it, he is younger and happier, his lips smushed against a girl's forehead while she laughs. And all Winnie can think for several stunned moments is how amazing it is that so much motion can be captured by a static image.

So much emotion too, conveyed in the dark, crinkled eyes of a girl Winnie hasn't seen in almost four years.

The next thing Winnie thinks is: *Holy crap, that is Jenna Thursday.*

And oh boy, was Winnie wrong to ever think Erica looked like her sister. Sure, Erica has tried to imitate Jenna with the makeup and the long hair and the clothes that look *just so,* but Jenna had a such different energy.

Erica, when she used to smile, was all goofy gleam and mischief. She was filled to bursting with jokes and games and wagers. *Ten bucks to kiss Jay.* Jenna meanwhile wore innocence in her dark eyes and sweetness in her smile. She might have sung songs that could break you, but the songs always put you back together by the end.

The third thing Winnie thinks is: *Holy crap, Jenna and Grayson used to date.* Grayson didn't just find Jenna's dead body on the night of her second trial—and he didn't just throw a party for her after she died. They were together. And like, *happily* together.

These are the faces of two sixteen-year-olds who are very much in love.

The last thing Winnie notices is the locket hanging around Grayson's neck. Not Jenna's neck, but *Grayson's* neck. It is gold with a moon and two stars . . .

And a fleck of something staining it. Identical to the locket Erica wore on Monday.

It's as if the light in the office has snapped on all over again. Winnie knows exactly who was in her bedroom and in her attic. They are someone who would know her family's doors were always unlocked and they would certainly know their way around the house. They would also know that Winnie wasn't currently home because they had just seen her at Joe Squared.

But that circle on the Venn diagram will have to be dealt with later, because right now there is different ex–best friend who needs her.

Winnie shuts the drawer. It clangs loud as a gong in the hollowed-out basement of the Friday estate. Then she seizes her backpack and abandons the office filled with secrets.

She flips off the light on her way out.

40

It is just after midnight by the time Winnie leaves the Friday estate. She wears black body armor that protects her chest and abdomen. On her head, she has a simple helmet. Not because it will protect her—though it *will*—but because it will hide her identity when she traipses through the forest on a Wednesday night. She needs any hunters who spy her to assume she's one of them, and above all, she can't have Aunt Rachel spotting her auburn hair and thinking, *Hmmm, that sure looks like my niece!*

Unfortunately, the face shield won't slide over Winnie's glasses, so her face is exposed. Still, at a distance, she doesn't think anyone will recognize her.

Also unfortunately, she couldn't find a neoprene cord for her glasses, so she just has to pray the helmet will hold them in place.

In her backpack now strapped tightly to her back, Winnie has her nightmare contraband and a tiny first aid kit. Strapped to each of her thighs is a serrated hunting knife—the only weapons she could access. Everything else was locked up, and Winnie didn't want to waste time searching for a key.

No, she might not have much protection against the forest, but she still has way more than she had on any of her trials.

She follows the route Jay always leads her on into the forest. At the boundary between spirit domain and outside—a line sharp as the *yes* that hung between Jay and Winnie two hours ago—the temperature drops ten degrees. A scent like old leaves and mist coils into Winnie's nose. The moon, a bright slash in the sky, turns hazy. It's as if a bloom filter has dropped over everything.

It has been six days since the last time Winnie and Jay trained together—and though they only ever trained during daylight hours, she manages to navigate the trails solo. Maybe because the mist has already come and gone or maybe because she knows exactly why she is here and what she has to do . . . Either way, she feels ready. She feels competent.

Her hearing sharpens, her weak eyesight improves, and her muscles fire with a focused control she only ever feels inside these trees.

This is the forest. This is the spirit's domain . . . but it is also the Luminaries' domain. And though Winnie's route to becoming a hunter might not have been straight or entirely truthful, she was still deemed ready enough to face the nightmares. She is still technically a Wednesday hunter, and tonight, she actually feels like one.

By the time Winnie reaches the training spot with the fallen sugar maple and red pine, the urge to run aches in her legs. But speed means noise and noise means death, so she keeps her pace creeping. Forward, forward, always listening, always scanning the horizon, the branches, the grayscale darkness of the forest.

She travels at least a mile in this fashion without encountering a single nightmare, a single hunter. Yet as she approaches Stone Hollow, a sound like ancient bicycle brakes hits her ears. It's unnatural and somehow laced with laughter. Winnie holds her breath and slows to a stop. More shrieks layer in.

Harpy: While these nightmares look vaguely human, the lower halves of their bodies are fully avian with claws instead of feet. Vulture-like wings extend from their shoulder blades.

Winnie scoots forward. The fastest route to the northeastern stream, where Lizzy's camera captured the werewolf, would be straight through Stone Hollow. It is also the most exposed, and walking into harpy territory is a guaranteed death sentence. One harpy, okay. Maybe Winnie could handle that. But a whole group of them?

Harpies have powerful eyesight, although they cannot swivel their eyeballs within the sockets. They must rotate their heads to see peripherally.

Winnie reaches the open meadow's edge. Stone pillars rise up, dark sentries observing the harpies as they swoop and dive. Six harpies in all—a *huge* number that even a host of hunters would likely leave be.

It's going to cost Winnie a few minutes, but she will definitely need to circle around. She unstraps the hunting knife from her left thigh, just in case, and sets off west. Toward the stream where Grayson died. Toward the X on the map and the home of a dampener that set off a cascade of cluster-fuckery in a mere three days.

Except, of course, Winnie knows now she can't blame her dad for every-thing. She can't even blame the Diana who framed him. Not when so very many of Winnie's troubles have ultimately been caused by her own unwill-ingness to open her eyes and see what was *really* going on around her.

Winnie reaches the stream where Grayson died. The orange tape is no lon-ger strung across the birch trees; the blood, though, is still there, streaked and smeared upon white bark. The trees are glowing pylons at this hour. The blood looks tarry and black.

Winnie resheathes the hunting knife to her thigh before continuing onward. She does not step into the stream, but instead tracks northward alongside its gentle flow. And although theoretically the running water should help keep land-bound nightmares away, it occurs to Winnie as she stalks along the shoreline that running water hasn't stopped Jay. He went directly into the river while in his wolf form to save Winnie.

Although, she realizes, *it's possible he also paid for that.* Maybe it caused him unbearable pain; maybe it is one more thing she owes him for, one more sacrifice he made to keep her alive.

In another half mile, Winnie will reach Lizzy's camera. The one that captured Jay as he passed. She prays no other cameras have spotted him. She prays no hunters have yet tracked him down.

The good thing is that the forest kills most radio signals. Even if Lizzy sees Jay on one of her screens, communicating that to Aunt Rachel or any-one else will take time. She'll radio to a contact in the hunters' parking area, who will send a typed message to Rachel—but that message might take a minute or an hour to actually reach the small pager on Rachel's hip. If it even gets there at all.

Of course, if Rachel and her hunters are good enough, they'll never need Lizzy's help to track the werewolf. Six bolts in the abdomen. *Six bolts in the abdomen.* It will take a miracle for Jay to survive that.

Winnie hopes she can be that miracle.

She pushes herself faster. Her eyes scan left, right. She shifts her bag once more onto her back. Tightens the straps for good measure. Then checks that her hunting knives are still within easy reach.

The terrain changes, no longer silt shore but rocky bank. The stream's channel narrows and deepens. The current picks up speed, its burble growing to a churn. It is right as Winnie pushes through the draping tendrils of a willow so she can circle around that she hears a sound she prayed she would not hear tonight.

Whispers.

At once, she drops low and ducks back into the willow's dangling branches. Then she holds her breath and waits. Where is the Whisperer? Which direction is it moving? Or was that sound just a trick of the wind?

No. There it is again. Louder, closer . . . If Winnie is going to get away, she's going to have to sprint at full speed. Her adrenaline spikes. Her whole body feels like it shrinks down to half its usual size. Except . . .

There's something else within the whispers. Soft, padded beats like footsteps. *People,* Winnie realizes, and the longer she listens—breath still seized tight inside her lungs—the more she notices other details.

The absence of the burning plastic smell.

The absence of a charge to pluck and pull at her skin.

Then three figures emerge on the shoreline beyond the willow tree, and Winnie's breath loosens.

It isn't the Whisperer at all. It's just four people *whispering.*

Hunters, Winnie decides, squinting in the darkness to watch their black armor—almost identical to her own—slink past. Three smaller figures and a tall, broader one. Winnie can't make out defining features, though, or which Wednesday hunters they might be. The shadows of the night smear their faces like a hand dragged through fresh pencil. It gives them strange heads that aren't human, aren't helmet.

Then a flame flares, quick and tiny like a lighter being toggled into life. It vanishes almost as soon as it appears, and in that moment, Winnie sees the strangest thing—something incomprehensibly *weird* in an entire forest where nothing is normal.

For the humans before her don't look human. Three of the figures have charcoal-colored heads shaped like dogs, with sharp snouts and sharper ears. The fourth figure is avian, their charcoal-colored skull rounded while a golden beak protrudes.

This is all Winnie sees before the four figures and the flare of light all disappear. Completely, instantly—it's all just gone. Even the algae-slick boulders that line the stream vanish from Winnie's sight, leaving only clotted darkness and the ceaseless burble of a stream through the night.

Then comes burning plastic, acrid and unforgiving. It spears up Winnie's nostrils, and her breath locks up tight again. Her adrenaline spikes anew, so hard this time, it feels like she got stabbed directly with a syringe of it into her heart.

Because with that scent comes understanding: these are Dianas and they just cast a spell that hid them from view. Three hounds and a crow, here in the forest. Here in Hemlock Falls. And using magic right next to Winnie.

The small flame was a mundanus *spell,* says Winnie's newly acquired Diana knowledge, diagnosing what she sees just like her ever-present Compendium. *So was the erasure of the witches. Both were* mundanus *spells—easy to cast and requiring little power.*

Winnie forces herself to exhale. Her breaths are so shallow, she's afraid she might pass out. And although her thighs scream at her for holding this crouch too long, she doesn't move.

The hounds and the crow remain hidden by magic for several moments, and their whispers fade beneath the *mundanus* hiding spell. Winnie squints and strains for anything to hear, anything to *see*. But she gets nothing.

Nothing except the certainty that there are four Dianas *right here* in the forest. It was never one Diana who framed Dad. It was four—or more?—and now they are standing *right in front* of Winnie.

Her glasses slide down her nose. She is too afraid to adjust them. The burn in her thighs slides down into her calves like lava flow, and up into her lower back too. She just grits her teeth and ignores it.

Soon enough, the shadowy spell that hid the Dianas dissolves. It's like watching rain destroy a sandcastle: the unnatural darkness grows pocked and porous, boulders appearing and bits of stream. Then come armored limbs and hound ears, combat boots and a crow's glittery beak, until eventually all four figures stand once more upon the shore.

The largest *canis* appears to be keeping guard now, several paces away from the group with a single hand aloft as if about to start a lecture. The stance reminds her of Professor Samuel at the whiteboard.

The other two hounds are crouched beside the water as if studying something.

And the fourth figure—the only *cornīx*—stands with a ramrod authority beside the bent-backed hounds.

The *cornīx* speaks, a whispery sound that oozes out of its mask like air from a shredded tire. A kneeling hound answers with the same whisper, and the second kneeling hound does too—and with a sickening sort of lurch, Winnie realizes they're speaking. Not just in another language, but in another form of communication entirely.

That was not mentioned in Theodosia's book.

And if Winnie had any doubts before that the Whisperer was a Diana-made spell, she doesn't have them now. She presses a hand over her mouth to stifle her breathing. Maybe if she strains hard enough she can figure out what they're saying. She's a smart girl. There are rhythms and rules to all languages . . . right?

Wrong. She listens and listens, the night trudging past, but there is no familiar beat to latch on to here, no intuitive translation her brain can discern. There are only the whispers, alien and unsettling, seething out of each mask to fill the sky.

A wind picks up too, laced with a stench like singed arm hairs—a stench that might be a new spell from these Dianas or might just as easily be the Whisperer on its way. For all Winnie knows, they have summoned it.

For all she knows, they can *control* it.

At that thought, Winnie's hand over her mouth turns to a claw. Her fingernails dig into her cheek. Because even though she guessed the Whisperer was a *famēs* spell, she hadn't taken the next logical leap and considered that the Dianas could command it too.

And if they can order it about like some soldier, then that means

Grayson's death was no hunger spell turned murderous. Nor was it a merely a hunger spell that chased Winnie off the waterfall. It was a direct order from a Diana.

Winnie's jaw aches now. She has a sudden, grinding urge to *bite* at these people. She wants to attack with her hunting knives and get payback for every person these Dianas have killed, every family they have destroyed.

Luke was right to go after Vader when he did. Training would have changed nothing.

No. Winnie's nostrils flare. She makes herself inhale a full, real breath. *No.* Luke went to rescue Han; Winnie is here to rescue Jay. She can't lose sight of that mission, no matter who or what stands before her.

Especially since one of the hounds is now rising, and for a fraction of a moment, a fresh flame ignites in the forest.

There are the masks, stark and illuminated, covering witches who look wholly inhuman. The charcoal shade of each mask is a perfect match for the shadows of the forest; it contrasts with the whites of their open eyes.

And the one who has lit the fire has dark, almost russet-colored irises.

The fire winks out again, but not before Winnie sees what she needed to see: blood on the rocks and a single, dragging paw print.

It is Jay's blood, of course, and these Dianas must be tracking him. Just like Winnie is. Just like the Wednesday hunters are too.

Later, she will wonder *why* the Dianas would hunt Jay. Certainly, there are the *incubo* spells, taken from nightmares of the forest, but what even *is* the magic of a werewolf? And why would they want to take that power from Jay?

Later, Winnie will also discover that her Venn diagram has grown, each circle morphing and stretching like the Whisperer across her page, swallowing up everything in its path and melting away the lines she thought kept each *S* and *W* separated.

But right now, as she sits within these willow branches and desperately tries to keep from giving herself away, all she can think is *They are going after Jay, they are going after Jay, they are going after Jay . . .*

I need to get there first.

She has no idea how she'll move ahead of the Dianas. She has no idea what in her pathetic bag of contraband she can possibly use against them. But she also knows she has to try.

The hound who lit the flame is now being scolded by the other Dianas, a cacophony of snarls and hisses that Winnie doesn't need to understand to recognize. Light in the forest is deadly; how dare the hound make a flame without hiding it?

The crow is the angriest of all. A spitting snarl slides from their golden beak. Amazingly, though, where Winnie expects the scolded hound to back down or wilt against the others, their spine only straightens. Their shoulders—thin, but strong—only lift high. They point in the direction Winnie just came from. Then, as if *they* are the one in charge and not the crow, they set off directly toward the willow tree.

Winnie has barely enough time to dip sideways behind the willow's trunk before the hound is there, sweeping into the branches and stepping over the exact spot Winnie just abandoned.

Winnie is, yet again, not breathing.

And as illogical as it is, she has a desperate urge to close her eyes—as if by erasing the Dianas from her sight, she will in turn erase herself from theirs. All this hound must do is look left and they will see Winnie, right there pressed against the bark.

But they do not look, and soon they have marched farther downstream—while the three other Dianas now stomp furiously after. The two remaining hounds keep their snouts high, as if they have sniffed their quarry and now give pursuit. The *cornix* follows last, their beak roving from side to side. Their eyes glittering like a real crow's. All that's missing are wings and they will fly into the night.

In seconds, the Dianas are gone.

41

Winnie sips in careful breaths. Her heart is almost as loud as the stream beside her. The Dianas are totally out of sight now, having trekked south—which Winnie knows is the wrong direction, because she never found any signs of Jay on her journey that way. No blood on the earth, no paw prints dragging by, no white tufts of fur in the trees.

Winnie's chest loosens with relief. Jay's tracks must have gotten muddled right here, and now the Dianas are aiming the wrong way. *Or,* a new idea prods, *that hound intentionally led the other Dianas astray.*

Winnie thinks of the photograph in Grayson's desk. Of the locket with a small stain on it and all the items stolen from her room . . . And of dark, russet eyes.

She pushes back into a quiet clip, this time staying within the trees, where the terrain is smoother and no slippery boulders clog up the way.

It is darker here, the forest's canopy obliterating moonlight and dulling the world to cold emptiness. Vague shadows indicate where trees await, where scrub and stones and new saplings lurk like monsters ready to drag Winnie down with one misplaced boot. Noises echo in the distance—shrill cries that might be harpies, might be vampira, might be any other assortment of nasty creatures going bump in the night. *Pick your nightmare, spin the wheel.*

Winnie loses all sense of time or distance. There is only moving cautiously forward, listening and scanning and listening and scanning. *Dianas in Hemlock Falls. Dianas in the forest. Dianas hunting Jay.*

Eventually, Winnie spies a red light blinking in the dark: Lizzy's camera.

She knows it is aimed away from the stream, so after a brief pause to verify that she is still alone, Winnie tiptoes sideways and circles behind the camera. Once she reaches it, she hits the record button; the red light dies.

Hopefully, Winnie thinks, *Lizzy will assume her tech has failed her.* She detaches the camera from its tripod—it fits easily into her left hand—and fumbles with buttons until she finds a flash.

It is a risk to use it here. A really, really big risk, which is precisely why those Dianas got so pissed at the hound who cast the *mundanus* spell of flame. Turning on a light and then remaining in one place to use said light . . .

It could get ugly real fast. Winnie needs to be ready for it.

As soon as the light sprays outward, white and briefly disorienting, Winnie uses her free hand to unstrap a hunting knife from her leg. Then she aims the flash around and searches for signs of werewolf.

She spots the blood right away, in a spray pattern across stones. The trees are evergreen. Pines and firs and hemlocks with needles that rarely fall upon a granite substrate.

One black stain goes toward the stream—the way Winnie just came from and where the Dianas now aim. Another stain drags and drips west into the forest. That was the way Jay appeared to be going on the camera, so it is the way Winnie will go too.

She snaps off the camera's flash and sets off into the trees.

Winnie is being followed.

A presence curls around her, brushing along the back of her neck every few seconds and tickling into her helmet. It is the sensation of being watched by eyes she cannot see. Yet every time she pauses to crouch low and search, she finds nothing and no one.

She has stowed the camera in her backpack, but the hunting knife she keeps clutched tight in her right hand. The Compendium meanwhile shuffles through a list of nightmares that stalk their prey.

Arassas, banshee, basilisk, changeling, dryad. Every letter has a stalker associated. In fact, the list is like those handkerchiefs magicians use: once Winnie starts pulling, the names of nightmares just keep coming and coming until there is no way she can possibly guess what it is she's up against without more information.

But to stop for reconnaissance is to lose precious time as Jay bleeds out somewhere and Dianas and Wednesdays search for him.

Salamander, urus, vampira, velue, were-creature, wyrm.

Then again, not stopping means potentially losing her own life.

Winnie grinds to a halt. She cannot tell if her stalker stops, but she *can* be certain it makes absolutely no noise either way . . . which is actually a clue. She discards banshee, urus, velue—and tens of other names from her magician's spool of handkerchiefs. They all rely on sound to lure or disorient their prey.

She also discards vampira, because although they are silent when hunting, she has the very pointed impulse that there is only *one* creature watching her. She trusts that impulse, even if she doesn't understand where it comes from.

Then it happens: she sees a slight glisten through a gap in the trees. It looks wet, it looks pale, and she knows right away what she's up against.

No, she mouths on an exhale, sliding her backpack in front of her. *No, no, no.* She still holds her knife, which makes opening the bag's zipper too rough, too loud. But there's little point in being quiet now. She is cornered and she needs to act. *Fast.*

Because the changeling is on the move. It has abandoned its silence and is charging this way. Underbrush shakes and a crude, choking sound comes from its throat.

Changeling: These daywalkers can perfectly mimic any human they see, though claws give them away.

Winnie's fingers find the vial she wants right as the changeling emerges from cover, a slimy and unformed blob currently in its larval form.

The larval form of a changeling requires human blood to first begin human mimicry and develop claws.

This is, yet again, a nightmare that the Compendium has failed to fully capture. The drawing might show the main anatomy and the overall bipedal shape, but no illustration can contain the wriggling movement of its limbs. The unformed, malleable nature of its featureless face.

It is a piece of clay waiting to taste Winnie's blood, waiting to become her. And she cannot kill it with just a blade—the flesh will simply move around the knife like dough around a mixing spoon.

The changeling lunges at Winnie, skull stretched long as if it wants to scream but lacks the mouth. All it has are the two slits at the center of its head where that choking breath punches out.

It smells like dead things.

And it looks like *Chrysomya megacephala* maggots in their third stage.

The changeling slams into Winnie and she drops her backpack, no vial retrieved. Then she thrusts up her hunting knife in a pointless attack born from instinct, not logic. The knife enters the monster's abdomen, where the white flesh simply absorbs it. The changeling's full weight is atop Winnie now, and the nostril slits—coughing and gagging and coughing—widen to reveal teeth.

It is going to bite her in the face.

Winnie digs the knife in deeper and hikes up her left hip. It is a move she has practiced with Jay in recent weeks, and the instinct is a good one. She tips the changeling sideways. Its nose-mouth and fangs careen past her to land on the dirt.

The choking noise tangles louder. So close to Winnie's ear. It is the sound a person makes before they vomit.

Winnie flips the changeling, reorienting herself atop it—which is somehow worse than being below it. The visceral horror of *straddling* this nightmare is like a thousand fingernails dragged down her spine.

Gorge rises in her esophagus. She coughs out the same sound as the monster.

The unnatural, unformed shape of a changeling has been known to elicit nausea in some hunters.

Winnie shoves the knife deeper. It most definitely causes no pain to the nightmare—because it has no *freaking organs* and because its Maslow pyramid is basically just one need: taste human flesh and become human.

But Winnie is able to thrust so hard and so thoroughly that she stabs through to the other side and digs the knife into the cold earth. It won't hold the changeling long, but it is momentarily trapped.

Winnie dives off the nightmare, grappling for her backpack.

She manages only a single step before the changeling's wormlike arm slings around her ankle. It yanks. Winnie falls, thudding onto her stomach. Her glasses fly off her face. The front of her helmet hits the ground; her nose crunches.

And that is when she feels the changeling bite her—though "bite" doesn't even *begin* to describe the sensation of its teeth on her calf. It is like a hundred syringes poking her all at once, except the sensation of the syringes almost immediately vanishes. *Changeling saliva possesses a numbing agent that keeps prey alive during feeding though unable to move or feel pain.*

In approximately one minute, if the changeling doesn't release Winnie, that numbing agent will reach her brain. She kicks at the creature's head with her free foot, but the changeling's teeth are stuck in. All she does is drag the creature along with her while briefly collapsing its skull inward with her boot.

The head instantly re-forms. More of Winnie's blood flows into its nose-mouth. And already, Winnie can see the monster starting to change.

It is growing auburn hair.

She kicks again, harder and more frantically, rolling and writhing as numbness creeps up her leg. She just needs her backpack, she just needs her backpack.

Then she spots something glittering nearby: a vial of nightmare contraband. Her vision is obscured, the darkness near complete within the trees, but it looks vaguely square-shaped. It's not the vial she wants, but it is better than having her blood slurped out by a changeling.

Changeling saliva also possesses an anticoagulant to thin the blood for easier consumption. Once bitten, a human victim can be drained entirely within minutes.

Winnie snatches up the vial, rips off the cork, and slings the contents at the changeling.

Green liquid arcs out.

It hits the nightmare, a splash of spidrin venom in a long spray down its back—a back that is quickly becoming as pink as Winnie's human flesh. The acid hisses, some sinking into the changeling, some rising as fog into the night.

A splatter hits Winnie's calf too. She can't feel it, though, because of the numbing agent. She kicks again at the changeling, and this time she loosens the nightmare's hold on her calf. Its teeth release. It chokes and flails. And Winnie scrabbles away from it on hands and knees. She can't breathe this air, she can't breathe this air, she needs to get away before the evaporating acid hits her lungs.

Winnie tears her glasses off the earth, then her backpack, then she half drags, half sprints into the trees.

She glances back only once to find a body, naked and identical to her own, stretched prone across the forest floor. There's a hole all the way through its back from which green fog spews.

Winnie runs.

Winnie is limping now. Not from pain, but from numbness. There will be pain eventually, when the effects of the changeling saliva fade. And while she could try a drop of melusine blood to nullify and heal her right away, she's afraid that will render her foolish. That she will heal . . . and then skip around the forest, trying to befriend every hunter or nightmare—or worse, every Diana.

She can't risk that.

Winnie does, however, at least pause long enough to don her glasses—filthy and warped again—and bind up her changeling wound. The anticoagulant from the bite means her bleeding won't stanch quickly and the wound won't scab easily. Plus, the line of spidrin venom on her skin is developing blisters.

Much as sharks can sense blood in the water from miles away or vultures can smell carrion, most nightmares are drawn to open wounds.

Winnie stops at a granite ridge to remove her socks and wrap them around the bloodied fang marks. Then she cuts off a strip of bandage from her meager first aid kit and winds that around the socks. It's not great, but the blood really is so slippery, so profuse, that she needs as much cotton as she can to compress the bite and absorb the flow.

Lastly, Winnie covers the standard bandage in a thicker, plastic bandage made just for Luminaries that will contain the smell of blood.

It looks like she is wearing an inner tube around her leg, and it takes her a few awkward steps to get used to the weight, the shape, and the continued numbness in her calf muscle. But the human brain is truly a masterpiece of evolutionary engineering, and within two steps, new neural pathways are forming. Within ten steps, her brain has fully adapted to this new arrangement. And within twenty, she is moving forward with exactly the same quiet purpose as before.

She must be getting close to Jay. Surely, surely he is somewhere nearby.

His tracks become easier to follow the farther she hikes. Partly because there is more of his blood to mark the earth. But mostly because his prints leave deeper indentations with every step, his claws dragging lines across the dirt as if he can scarcely lift his legs anymore.

Winnie is too afraid to even consider what that might mean—or what she might find when she finally catches up to him.

Eventually, she reaches a trickle of water slurping by. More rill than proper stream, it is even weaker, even more pathetic than the rainwater stream that surrounded the hemlock Winnie hid in for her second trial. A place Jay showed her . . .

A place that looks a lot like *this* almost island, where a red cedar stands shadowy and towering against the night.

Heat bowls over Winnie—shamed heat, furious heat. Because in all her fixation on surviving that second trial, Winnie never wondered why Jay even *knew* about that island east of the lake. Not once did she question why a skilled hunter like Jay might need a safe haven surrounded by running water where nightmares do not tread . . .

A trained Luminary has no need to hide, but a boy hoping to survive the night?

I had my own stuff going on.

Understatement of the century. While Winnie fumed and hurt, Jay was just trying to make it through each night alive, trying to fight off a curse that grew and festered inside him.

Her glasses fog slightly, her body an inferno from the fighting, the creeping, the *shame* at everything she never bothered to see in her best friend. All Winnie has focused on for four years has been how her dad got caught as a Diana, how her family became outcasts, and how she was going to make it okay again with the hunter trials. That was *all* she existed for—a single-minded fixation that she ate, slept, and dreamed of for four eternal years.

She blamed Jay for ditching her, she blamed Erica for abandoning her, but not once did Winnie turn around and flip that mirror onto herself. *So stop being such a hypocrite,* Lizzy said back in Jay's bedroom, *and try looking at your own choices for once.*

Winnie thinks of Jay's drawer of contraband now crammed inside her backpack. She thinks of the photograph with Jenna completely in love. Two ex–best friends with their own stuff going on. *I find no relief, inside I'm still a hopeless curse.*

Winnie shoots forward. Five paces. Ten. Sixteen. Then she is to the trunk's base and her neck is flexing backward so she can squint into the cedar's branches. But if there's anyone up there, she can't see them.

A rasping breath slides through the night. Gurgling and weak and coming from the ground nearby. Winnie lurches around the tree . . . and there he is. The wolf. The boy she has always loved.

He is fully nightmare now, his enormous lupine body curled into a ball against the darkened tree. He glows like a full moon, the blood smears on his abdomen like clouds wisping by.

Winnie kneels beside him. He does not move.

Three arrow bolts protrude from his belly. There might be more, but Winnie can't see them with his body clenched up like this. And all she can think is he should be dead right now, and he *will* be dead soon if she doesn't do something. They both will be dead because it's only a matter of time before those witches circle back or Aunt Rachel finally catches up to him or nightmares scent his blood.

Winnie tugs off her helmet and drops it to the earth. One of the wolf's eyes opens; the iris is silvery gray, the pupil dilated and lost. If there is recognition in his gaze, Winnie doesn't see it. If there is any *human* in his gaze, she doesn't see it. No more than she could the night of her third trial when he tumbled her to the ground and she staked him in the neck.

All she finds is resignation. *You have caught me. Kill me quickly please.*

For several seconds Winnie's resolve falters. Maybe she has this wrong. Maybe this is a nightmare drawing twisted sideways on her sketchpad.

Maybe Jay *isn't* the werewolf and this is nobody she knows, so now she will heal someone that will ultimately kill her in the end—

No.

Winnie snaps her head to the side. Because even if all of that is true, if there is one thing she has learned in this forest, it's that not every nightmare is evil. Not every nightmare deserves to die.

Nightmares like the will-o'-wisp. Nightmares like the ghost-deer. And nightmares like this wolf who may or may not be the boy Winnie grew up with—they all deserve a chance to keep on living. And just as this werewolf saved her beneath those crashing, frozen waves, she will save him before the night can steal him away.

"Hey," she whispers, dipping her face toward his long white snout. "It's me. It's Winnie, and I'm here to help you."

Still no recognition, but at least the wolf doesn't retreat as Winnie rests her forehead against his. He is cold to the touch, his breaths so quiet now she can no longer hear them.

Far in the distance, a harpy laughs.

The wolf opens his other eye, and for a brief flicker of time—a liminal beat between pulsing aortic valves—Winnie thinks that maybe, *maybe* the wolf finally understands who she is. Just as she finally understands him.

Then his eyes shut, closing off the nightmare, the boy, the life of him, and Winnie knows she needs to move. She retreats, cold air sweeping between them as she flips her backpack around to her front. "Jay," she murmurs, digging out the vial of melusine blood. The liquid is so clear, so viscous, it looks empty in this darkness. "I need you to drink this."

No response, no reaction, so Winnie copies what he did to her two nights ago. She uncorks the vial with her teeth and then presses the glass to his mouth—a wolf mouth with fangs that shimmer beneath the moon.

A single drop slides between the left canine and first premolar. *Just one sip,* Winnie thinks—that was all he gave to her, so she stops as soon as she thinks it has poured in. Then she presses his lips closed and . . .

She waits, breath held until she sees his enormous throat work as if swallowing. Then she waits a few beats longer for the magic to take effect. The wolf's eyes trail open, his pupils find her face, and the gray irises briefly brighten as if lit by stars from within.

Then, before Winnie can stop him or make any movement at all, the wolf snaps out and takes the vial from her grasp. The entire thing vanishes into his mouth. Glass crunches and grinds.

Seconds later, he has eaten the entire thing.

And yet nothing happens after that. It's like a watched pot that never boils—the wound doesn't seem to heal no matter how long Winnie stares at it. There's movement in the wolf's body. His muscles ripple. His legs straighten. But the arrows remain lodged in his abdomen, and when he tries to rise . . .

He collapses right away.

One of the bolts snaps. And all six dig in deeper—Winnie can see them now. Each one that the Wednesdays lodged into him. Blood seeps and slithers onto the forest floor. Jay's eyes loll shut again. His broken breaths puff with fog.

And Winnie doesn't know what to do. The melusine blood was supposed to work. He was *supposed* to heal from a single sip. A whole vial? He should be sprinting away from her at top speed.

Winnie yanks open her backpack again. What does she have left? What can she possibly use? All she still possesses are harpy gastroliths and ground phoenix feather. While sure, the phoenix feather can act as a stimulant, there's also a pretty high risk of *exploding someone's heart* with it. Plus, what good is a stimulant if you're still bleeding to death and everything in the forest wants to kill you?

And as for the gastroliths, fiery explosions definitely won't help anyone.

There is still that other vial, though, her brain reminds her, and Winnie claws it into the light. The red glass looks black in this darkness and just as empty as it did in Grayson's office. She could open it. She could risk removing the cork and see if there's anything inside.

She is about to do that—to pop off the cork and pray there isn't a deadly gas within that kills them both instantly—when a voice cuts across the tiny island like a guillotine:

"Winnie."

Winnie knows who it is right away, just as she knows the sound of a compound bow being drawn. She swallows once. Then she gently sets the vial to the ground, pushes to her feet, and turns to face her aunt.

43

Rachel stands at the edge of the island, her boots in the rill while water trickles around them. It is too shallow to even cover the leather; a mere reflection of moonlight to crystallize the rock.

"Winnie," Rachel repeats. Her compound bow is aimed directly at her niece's head. "Step aside and let me deal with the wolf."

"No."

"You don't have any leverage here."

I have all the leverage actually, Winnie thinks as she wets her lips and searches for some clear exit she can sprint toward with a weakened wolf . . . But there's nothing. Rachel can easily outrun them—or easily shoot them down.

Although she won't. At least not the shooting part.

Probably.

Winnie decides to test her theory, fastening her gaze on Rachel. "If you want to shoot the wolf, you have to shoot me first."

"I don't want to shoot either of you," Rachel snaps. "But if Jay is the were-wolf, then he needs to be dealt with."

Jay. Aunt Rachel just said *Jay.* Winnie feels all the blood leave her body. It is the opposite of an adrenaline spike. This is death calmly taking hold. This is a head rolling off the guillotine into a basket. "Jay?" She struggles to get his name out. "Why . . . did you call him that?"

"Because that's who it is, isn't it?" Rachel releases her draw and snaps down the bow. Her arrow, however, stays noticeably nocked. "Why else would you be out here, Winnie? Who else would you want to protect?"

"Lots of people." This isn't a lie, but Winnie's voice trembles all the same.

And Rachel scowls. "I don't want to kill Jay. I don't want to kill *anyone*, but if I don't bring in that werewolf, then someone else will. The whole town has been alerted that we shot it. Tuesday scorpions are on their way here right now."

Somehow, Winnie dies a little bit more. "Oh," she tries to say, but only a sigh escapes, wintery as the forest always is. Because scorpions will be a lot harder to fight off than Aunt Rachel—and more inclined to shoot Winnie and Jay simultaneously. "Please . . ." Winnie pushes at her crooked glasses. "The werewolf won't hurt anyone. Just let him go, Aunt Rachel. Please, just let us both go."

"I can't do that." Rachel advances a step toward Winnie. Her sweaty face glistens like the changeling's. Fallen hair from her ponytail clings to her face. "I shot him, and now I'm going to deliver him to the proper authorities. Which means you are going to step aside."

Winnie doesn't move, and Rachel claims another four steps until she is close enough for Winnie to spot a tear in the abdomen of her armor. To notice dirt smeared on her cheek and a cut across her chin.

"How exactly do you think this will end, Winnie? If I know who the werewolf is, and I've seen you protecting him . . ." Rachel's nose wrinkles, although not with disgust so much as heartbreak. "You're ruining everything your family just got returned to them. For what?"

Yes, Winnie thinks, her eyes closing. The night disappearing. *For what?* "For loyalty," she whispers, and something hot tickles down her spine. The bear flag on her family's porch flaps and waves across her mind. "For loyalty," she repeats, opening her eyes. "For the cause. Because if we don't care about each other—if that isn't the ultimate point of all of this . . ." Winnie waves around her, at the forest, at the night, at all the monsters coming this way. "Then there is nothing left but *darkness,* and there won't ever be any light. There won't ever be a reason to keep fighting."

It's a pretty speech, and maybe under different circumstances, it would have had an impact. But as it stands, the instant Winnie utters *fighting,* the wolf wheezes loudly, pitifully, behind her.

And the standoff ends.

As Winnie whirls about to check if Jay still lives, Rachel uses the distraction to charge in. They both grab for the wolf in synchrony. Rachel grabs his back legs and Winnie drops beside his head.

Then she and her aunt stare at each other, separated only by a nightmare who never asked to be one.

It is uncanny how much Rachel looks like Winnie's mom in that moment. There is a weight that tows at her brow, a heavy sadness in her dark eyes, and there is something about the moonlight eking down that sets off silver in her hair.

The cut on Rachel's chin oozes blood.

"Don't do this," Rachel murmurs. "Walk away, Winnie, and no one ever needs to know you were here."

"No." Winnie rests a hand on the wolf's brow. His fur is frozen to the touch; soon he will be one more body that needs retrieving on tomorrow's corpse duty. His eyes are closed. His bloodied torso is barely moving.

"If you let me take him," Rachel presses, "I can get him to the hospital. We can keep him alive."

"What?" Winnie sputters a laugh that echoes over the island. "Take a *nightmare* to the Monday hospital? So they can what—heal him? And then give him to the Tuesdays for execution?"

Rachel's lips compress. "Would you rather the wolf keep executing Luminaries?"

"He hasn't, though. He hasn't killed anyone." Winnie's head shakes. "He hasn't even *hurt* anyone, Aunt Rachel. He has only ever helped."

"He bit you—"

"To save me from drowning. And he saved Emma too, from a harpy." Winnie pulls Jay's body to her, a rough movement that tips Rachel off-balance. Brings her dark, familiar eyes closer. "And who knows how many other lives he has saved? He is one of us. He's a Lead Hunter, just like you, and he is my best friend. Please don't let this be his end."

Rachel huffs a hard breath from her nose, expression completely unchanged. "Winnie, I don't have a choice. We're the cause above all else— the *Luminary* cause—and we are loyalty through and through. No one has to find out you were here, but to let this wolf walk free is to kill people." Now she is the one who yanks Jay closer, tipping Winnie off-balance. "And to keep arguing," Rachel adds, her face so near that Winnie sees every creasing line, "is to kill him too."

She's right. Winnie knows her aunt is right. Jay is already a ghost; soon he will disappear entirely. He needs healing—real, complete healing that she can't give him. But if she releases him, if she agrees to Rachel's terms . . .

Well, Jay might last the night, but he won't last another day. All she has to do is look at what happened to her family for simply *housing* a man they never knew was a Diana. What will the Luminaries do—what will the scorpions and the Council *do* to a boy who is a nightmare?

"What if," Winnie tries in one last attempt to salvage this night of her relentless wrongs, "I can prove Jay didn't hurt anyone? What if I can prove the Whisperer did it all?"

"Winnie." Rachel says this with an unexpected tenderness, and her face finally softens. As if she has heard this argument before. As if she knows it's ultimately futile, and Winnie will only end this night in pain. As if she really, truly doesn't want to hurt her only niece.

And Winnie can't help but wonder if maybe Mom made a similar plea four years ago. *What if I can prove my husband wasn't a Diana?*

For several breaths, Winnie watches her aunt. There are thin lines around Rachel's irises. Contacts like Winnie refuses to wear—and like Mom has never needed. It's an unexpected weakness, a chink in the armor for a Lead Hunter who hasn't wavered in four years and who has always put loyalty and the cause above everything else.

Or has she? After all, Rachel lied for Winnie after Winnie's first trial, pretending she believed that Winnie had killed a banshee. Then she kept on lying afterward, keeping the banshee secret from all the Wednesdays, from all the Luminaries. Now she has offered to lie yet again: *Walk away. No one has to find out you were here.*

But Winnie knows all too well how lies only breed more lies, and secrets only fester into wounds. There have been enough of both of those over the last four years.

That's when it occurs to Winnie that maybe *this* is where all the darkness comes from. It's not that people compartmentalize the loss, the pain, the violence, it's not that people eat all the pizza . . . It's that they eat all the pizza and pretend it's because they're hungry. They compartmentalize and then pretend the lockbox inside them doesn't exist.

Maybe, just maybe, Rachel has a whole buffet of problems all padlocked and hidden too. Contacts for eyes that can't see 20/20. Chinks in armor that protect a weak, human heart. So maybe, just maybe, Winnie needs to step outside herself once more tonight, outside this island filled with fragile moonlight folding down, and *look* at what is really going on around her.

Winnie releases Jay and rises clumsily to her feet. The forest wavers beyond her dirty glasses; her blood pulses in her ears; and Rachel's face telescopes upward, following her niece's ascent.

She is like a squire waiting to be knighted.

"Please," Winnie murmurs to her aunt. She brings her hands together as if to clasp them . . . but then lets them fall limp to her sides. "*Please* let the wolf go and let me prove that he's innocent. For *me,* Aunt Rachel. For our family. Just let us both walk away from here."

Rachel's eyes shutter. Her breath slides out, foggy and loud. A heartbeat passes. Two. The blood in Winnie's ears throbs louder. It sounds like the waterfall at the Big Lake. It sounds like the white noise rattling from an ancient furnace . . .

Oh no, Winnie thinks, and at the same moment, Rachel's eyes snap wide. Winnie twists toward the island's edge, to where the rill might hold back nightmares, but it won't hold back people.

Then there they are: three of the Dianas stalk from the trees.

Two hounds have their hands up, and Winnie watches in a horrified slow motion as something solid and golden flies through the air directly toward her. *Sagitta aurea,* she thinks, right before two magicked arrows collide with her rib cage.

Except the golden arrows never make impact.

Because Aunt Rachel leaps in the way.

One. The first bolt of light chunks through Rachel's shoulder, puncturing all the way through until a glowing tip punches out of Rachel's back.

Two. The second hits Rachel's stomach, a cruel repeat of what she did to Jay.

Then Aunt Rachel's limp body hits Winnie and they both crash to the ground.

44

Winnie is trapped beneath her aunt, Rachel's torso draped over her like a horrifying weighted blanket. Rachel doesn't move, although her body is still warm. Scalding, in fact, as if the *sagitta aurea* spell heated her from the inside out.

A sandpapery squawk fills the air.

It is laughter. The two hounds are *laughing,* and just as their words distorted into whispers, their laughs now distort into this callous scrape of vocal cords.

It's the masks, Winnie realizes—a fuzzy thought inside a brain that can't quite grab hold of reality because her aunt is sprawled atop her and the night seems much too dark. *The masks change their voices.*

Winnie tries to rise. To see if Rachel can be healed, saved, protected . . . but all it takes is one look at her aunt's face for Winnie to know there is nothing she can do. There is no color in Rachel's skin, no movement in her now-bloodied chest.

There is no life.

The two hounds stride this way, their whispers rising toward the moon like wasps shaken from their nest. *Why did I waste the melusine blood?* Winnie thinks, a pointless thought with no useful answer. *Why did I waste it on a boy I couldn't save?* Because Jay is lost too. He too has no color, no movement, no life.

The hissing laughter of the hounds rises. Their dark shapes tromp closer, thirty feet away at most and moving with the languid ease of predators who have their prey cornered. The third Diana, the leader, hangs back. Their masked head swivels from side to side like a real crow's.

Cornīcēs: These elected witches maintain roles of leadership within Diana society. To be eligible, one must have both skill and experience.

Static builds in the air, and Winnie doesn't need the noxious smell in her nose to realize the crow is preparing a spell—all while the hounds keep laughing. Winnie twists her body toward Jay, a movement that removes the last of Rachel's dead weight. That suddenly frees up muscles Winnie knows she needs to use.

She cannot save Rachel. She cannot save Jay. The only person she can still save tonight is herself. In fact, if she gets up now and runs, she might be able to escape without pursuit. It's what a real black bear would do: bellow and charge just for show, then run far away in the end.

But then, Winnie has never been a very good Wednesday bear, has she? Her loyalty has always been in the wrong place, and lately, her cause hasn't aligned with anyone else's. So if these Dianas are going to attack her and expect her to flee, then they are in for quite a surprise.

Especially since they aren't the only ones with nightmare powers at their command.

Winnie scoops up her backpack and fumbles out the harpy gastroliths. They bounce and tink within the glass, though she can't hear them. All she hears are the approaching whispers, laughing and laughing like hyenas brought back from the grave.

Distantly, she notices a heat gathering at the base of her collarbone. It is a bee buzzing in a hurricane as she fishes out the vial of ground phoenix feather. The hounds are only fifteen feet away.

Winnie jerks the cork off the phoenix feather, then chucks the vial at the hounds. She doesn't hear it land, doesn't hear it shatter. There are only the hounds rasping and hissing—and the crow rasping and hissing too.

Winnie does, however, see one of the hounds flinch as if the vial has hit them.

Both hounds pause, their arms still lifted but their posture now tense with surprise. With their masks, they look like two dogs who have just heard their master calling. And for a fraction of a moment, their whispers quiet. The pain on Winnie's sternum recedes.

She opens the harpy gastroliths, a weak movement with thumbs that don't seem to work properly. Then she slings the vial right at the largest hound, who is well over six feet tall.

It hits them. The glass doesn't shatter either, but it doesn't need to.

The smaller hound emits a buzzing laugh, as if to say, *Is that all you have for us, little girl?*

And Winnie laughs right back, a choke of sound as guttural and raw as the changeling when it tackled her. "Enjoy," she croaks at them before she lurches around to her aunt's body and flings herself down.

Harpy gastroliths: These small black stones from a harpy's gizzard produce sparks on impact with a hard surface. When exposed to air, they will gradually heat up before exploding.

Light and noise overtake the island as the gastroliths detonate inside their glass. The phoenix dust ignites. A conflagration erupts, and the world burns. Around the hounds, on the hounds, and anywhere the powdered feather landed.

Winnie hugs her aunt tight; Rachel's body is as cold and unfeeling as the forest. Heat beats against Winnie's back—as do full-throated screams that not even the masks can distort. After several moments, Winnie risks a glance behind her. Her glasses protect her eyes from the heat as she watches the hounds run and twirl like a juggler's flaming batons. Too graceful to be dying. Too brilliant and fiery to be anything but beautiful.

That is going to draw some nightmares. And Winnie is glad for it. Let the crow fight the forest. Let them die by the same pain they inflicted on Winnie's aunt.

As if in answer to that thought, Rachel stirs beneath Winnie.

It is such a slight movement and so brief that Winnie thinks it might just be a tremor of the earth. A trick played on her by a forest that laughs as the hounds did. She peels herself upward and gapes down.

The orange light from the flames casts Rachel in a warm, almost healthy glow. As if she has only just met Winnie in the front hall of the Wednesday estate and said, *Oh hey, don't forget about corpse duty tomorrow.*

Winnie gropes for Rachel's neck. Maybe there's a pulse, maybe she can still save her—

A burning punches against the top of Winnie's chest. So hot, so violent, she thinks she has been shot. That a bullet now tunnels into her and she too will die, alongside Jay, alongside Rachel, alongside the hounds lost in flame.

But then come the whispers. Inside her skull, as if they have commandeered her brain, and inside her arteries, as if they've hijacked each ventricle in her heart. Even her muscles feel swallowed up by the whispering.

Meanwhile the pain in her collarbone is so intense, yet so local. It is a hot poker plucked from this wildfire and stabbed into her chest, and the bee from the hurricane has now become a full-blown nest of murder hornets.

Winnie tries to turn around to face the crow she knows must prowl this way. She cannot. She tries to dip forward and protect Rachel from the attack that must be coming. She cannot. And when at last the crow strides through the fire as if there are no flames, as if this witch feels no heat and breathes no smoke . . .

Winnie cannot even lift her gaze to face the crow. Her whole body is locked in place by magic. And all she can see is the way light flashes and sprays on armored legs. Then come spoken words, pitched high enough to trip over the flames still raging, the whispers still throbbing, the pain still so intense at the top of her sternum: "You, Winnie Wednesday, are just like your father. And right now, that means you're in my way."

It is an older woman's voice. Mature and commanding. *Just like my father?* Winnie wants to demand. *What do you mean? What did you do to him?*

The whispers increase, and with them the heat on Winnie's chest becomes all-consuming. As if she is the one doused in phoenix feather and burning alive by the spark of a gastrolith. This time, though, Winnie has just enough logical space in her brain to think, *Oh, that isn't a bullet at all. It's just my locket.*

And then she thinks, with a detached sort of horror, *Is it trying to kill me too?*

The whispers feast and claw inside Winnie's skull. The locket scalds; her eyes stream with tears because they cannot blink and this island burns like an inferno. The melting-plastic smell sears her nose, and there's a charge on her skin that scuttles over her as if the Whisperer is on its way. But it isn't the Whisperer, is it? Not this time. It's just a Diana with a lot of power who wants, for some inexplicable reason, to find a werewolf.

Winnie watches as the crow steps past her to reach Jay. The woman squats, offering Winnie her first up-close view of the whorls and lines that stamp the crow mask like real feathers. The gold beak glows orange—although now that Winnie considers it, in a fuzzy connection of ideas at the back of her brain, shouldn't the crow have a black beak? Does the golden shade perhaps mean something?

The crow slides her hands under Jay's lupine shoulders, and with shocking strength given her tiny frame, she drags Jay away bit by bit. One foot. Two, three . . .

All the while, the whispers of a holding spell still course through Winnie's body.

The crow's movements soon become labored and clumsy. A thick strand of silvery hair slides free, dangling out behind the mask like a long gray feather.

I'm sorry, Winnie thinks at Jay, sliding inch by inch away. At Aunt Rachel. At the forest. *I'm sorry.* She should never have followed Dad's map. She should never have dragged Jay into her mess. And most of all, she should have seen what *Jay's* mess was all those years ago.

What if, when Winnie was twelve, she had actually looked at her best friend and instead of saying *Help me* she had said, *Please, let me help you.* And what if when Rachel had told her four years ago, *I'm sorry, I have to follow the rules,* Winnie had said, *No, I don't think you actually do.*

But Winnie never did any of that, and now it is all too late. This locket will roast a hole through her chest, and then the flames will eat her—all while this crow drags Jay farther and farther away. A boy who was never actually out of reach like Winnie thought he was.

At that thought, the heat in her locket seems to cool. A brief recession of that focused, scoring burn—and light flickers at the edge of Winnie's vision. Several flashes all at once, like paparazzi arriving on the scene.

Then tens of will-o'-wisps flare so bright Winnie has no choice but to close her eyes against their silvery flames. Despite the spell, despite the unrelenting whispers that hold her trapped in place, her eyelids snap shut.

And in that moment, the locket completely cools. The whispers fade from her muscles, her heart, her veins. *Some nightmares,* she thinks, *deserve to live.*

The crow screams.

Winnie is able to move now. Her muscles are stiff from the magic, from the crouch, but what she lacks in grace, she makes up for in fury. She tackles the crow, who glows white from the will-o'-wisps all around.

The crow drops Jay, and Winnie slams her to the ground with all the force of the bear she really is. But where Winnie expects spells and whispers as defense, she instead gets a knee to the groin, then a deft flip onto her back.

This Diana is well trained.

But so is Winnie.

Winnie punches sideways, knocking the woman's elbow outward and collapsing her body onto Winnie's chest. Then she uses her own knee to weave through the woman's legs and flip *her* this time.

They land at the rill that surrounds the island. The merest trickle of water that Winnie stomped through, then Rachel stomped through too. Water splashes, a spray of cold in this orange dome of heat.

Winnie wastes no time: she grabs for the crow's mask. If she can just get it off, if she can just *see* who is underneath this horrifying, inhuman thing. Her fingers close around a beak.

And it's like touching a source—or at least it's like what she was warned that touching a source might feel like. Power *booms!* outward. It barrels into Winnie like a freight train. Like a cargo jet. Like the sadhuzag amped up on phoenix powder.

Winnie flies off the crow. Literally, her body launches backward through the air and only stops when her back and skull crack against the red cedar. Her breath kicks out of her. Her vision shadows into nothing. Distantly, she feels her skeleton and muscles crumple beneath her, totally detached from the signals in her brain that scream, *Keep fighting! Keep fighting!*

She can't keep fighting. She can't move. All she can do is collapse at the base of a cedar still dyed by Jay's blood and watch the crow approach, backlit by flame.

The woman's mask is broken, leaving only her mouth and jaw hidden. She is a half-human, half-bird monster. Pale flesh with a sharp beak to poke down. Without her glasses, Winnie can't fasten onto any distinctive features. Even if she did still have her lenses, she can barely hold her eyes open anyway. The world buckles and twists, from heat and whispers and a blow to the brain that really needs a doctor's attention.

Winnie isn't going to get a doctor's attention. No Andrew in scrubs to hold her hand like he did after the werewolf bite. No Mom and Darian to show up beside her hospital bed saying, *Oh, thank god you made it!*

The crow approaches, and Winnie notes with hazy satisfaction that the woman is limping. Badly. Her boot hits something. It kicks a small object Winnie's way.

And in the flames, the object glows red as a pure heart, throbbing and alive.

It is the unmarked vial from Jay's desk. It is the last item in Winnie's arsenal and the one item that her forever-scrolling Compendium could not explain. But she either trusts the forest or she doesn't. She either trusts her best friend or she doesn't.

Winnie clasps the red vial in one hand and wiggles out the cork. It falls sluggishly to the ground while the crow bows over Winnie. Her gray hair is long, most of it fallen from a bun she'd worn beneath her mask.

"What is this?" the crow asks, her voice fully human now. She plucks the vial easily from Winnie's grasp and peers within. Her beak almost reaches the red mouth.

Winnie tries to stand, but all the crow does is thrust a hand against Winnie's chest . . . and Winnie topples right back against the tree. Her eyes sink shut. The fire is finally dying, its phoenix-feather fuel burned to nothing, but there is a new sound to crackle over the night—like a broken carburetor trapped inside a vending machine. The Whisperer has finally arrived at the beckoning of its Diana master.

It's like these nightmares only show up when you're around, Winnie. Or like you've got some special power that only lets you *see them.*

Not a special power after all. Just Winnie's name on a very unfortunate Venn diagram. If only she *were* the one at the heart of it all instead of the Whisperer, then maybe there would still be something that she could do. Some undiscovered use for her not-so-special power.

"Oh," the crow murmurs, a sound thick with surprise.

And Winnie lugs her eyes open, just in time to see white spewing out of the red vial like a fairy-tale genie from a lamp. It is a thick fog that rises into the night, soon shrouding the crow's face from view and masking everything in Winnie's blurred range of sight.

With it comes that balmy warmth Winnie has learned to recognize.

Impossible. Never, in all of her research and study, in all the editions of the Compendium she has combed, in all the footnotes and scribbles she has added to her own Xeroxed copy, has she ever heard of anything like this.

The forest mist.

Inside a vial.

In seconds, the crow is obscured—and the pressure of her body against Winnie recedes, as if she stands.

Winnie throws out her hand to grab at the crow's chest, fingers clasping onto anything with purchase. "No," Winnie says, yanking at the woman's armor. "No." She wants to see the woman's face, she wants to *see* the person who ruined her life and ruined her dad's—

But the crow withdraws as effortlessly as a siren through waves, and soon she is out of sight once more. The last thing Winnie hears before the mist steals sound along with sight is a snarl like a wolf's. A snap like vicious fangs. Then that vanishes as well, and all Winnie knows is the mist.

Spirit mist is both the origin of and end of the nightmares each night, her Compendium provides. *Often, nightmares mortally wounded at dawn will return fully healed the next evening, suggesting the mist is capable of both creation and restoration.* That healing ability was why Winnie hoped she could help the will-o'-wisp last night.

And it must also be why Jay has it stored inside a red vial. This must be the only way to heal him. To create him, to restore him.

Since there is no predicting the location of a nightmare's arrival, her inner Compendium continues, *the hunter must keep moving. Otherwise, one could apparate exactly where the hunter stands.*

Unfortunately, Winnie cannot move even if she wants to. Her muscles are still limp from touching that mask, and her brain seems to heave and yaw like a ship on stormy seas. But the seas are made of mist, and the monsters of the deep are vampira.

Nonsense, she tells herself. *You're thinking nonsense.* She needs to pull herself together. She needs to wrangle her thoughts under control and then her body too. The rill around the island won't stop nightmares if they apparate on this side of it. And the fire from the phoenix feather must be totally snuffed out by the mist . . .

Winnie thinks she hears more snarling. It is not lupine, but a coughing, choking hack. As if the changeling has come here. Like maybe the mist has healed all of its wounds too.

Winnie can't stay here.

She *can't* stay here.

At that thought, a light winks to her right. Then, a split second later, a second winks to her left, bright as a shooting star. And another light comes a heartbeat after that; then a fourth beams into existence mere inches from Winnie's face.

Will-o'-wisp: Like large hummingbirds, these nightmares are plumed all over in silvery flames instead of feathers. When the flames die out, will-o'-wisps are revealed to be nothing more than hollow skeletons.

The will-o'-wisp flares again before Winnie's eyes, forcing her to wince and recoil against the red cedar. She has the distinct sense that it is scolding her. That it is saying, *Get up, you foolish human, before we decide to eat you.*

"Yep," she groans at it, mist slithering into her throat—so hot, *why* is it always so hot? Then, with another groan, she heaves in her legs and digs her fingers into tree bark. She pushes, she pulls, she gulps in misty air, until at last she is standing and her muscles, though weak, feel as if they're totally her own again.

And all around her, she sees the mist. It is receding slowly, reluctantly. An impossible mist from an impossible red vial. Soon, it will dissipate completely.

The flames are also gone now, only damp ash left behind and two faint mounds on the earth to mark what used to be hounds.

But that's it. That is all Winnie sees. There is no changeling to feast on her, no crow to bewitch her, no werewolf once more alive and fighting.

And there is no Aunt Rachel either. The body is simply gone, as if the mist devoured her. As if the forest claimed her . . . Or as if a nightmare within did.

In that moment, Winnie realizes a nightmare *did* get Rachel, just as it got Winnie two weeks ago, and suddenly Winnie finds she is laughing. A high-pitched, wild laugh that wheezes out toward the sky. Because she would bet all that money in her old piggy bank that she knows where Rachel is and she knows who took her there.

She is at a spot beneath a waterfall where a melusine sings and heals anyone who might come near her—or at least a melusine who heals when her werewolf cousin asks her to. Tomorrow, Rachel will awaken in a hospital with fang marks on her arm and a sparkle in her blood.

Light gutters and gleams twenty feet away, as if the will-o'-wisps beckon. As if they want to lead Winnie into the forest to her doom. But you either trust the forest or you don't, and so far, trust has worked out pretty well for Winnie Winona Wednesday.

"Lead the way," she calls to the creatures in a voice made of eternal night. And the will-o'-wisps obey, because not all humans deserve to die.

And some might even be worth saving.

HEMLOCK FALLS TESTING PORTAL
THURSDAY, APRIL 11

TEST RESULTS for PREVIOUS DAY:
Tests Administered: 2734
Positive Results: 0

AVAILABLE TESTING LOCATIONS:
Monday hospital, BY APPOINTMENT ONLY
Sunday estate auditorium, UNDER AGE 18 ONLY
Floating Carnival, ALL AGES WELCOME

DO YOUR CIVIC DUTY AND GET TESTED AS SOON AS A
SITE IS AVAILABLE NEAR YOU!

46

When the Tuesday Alphas arrive at the location sent to them by the Wednesday Lead Hunter, they do not find a slain werewolf. Instead, they find two bodies roasted beyond recognition with hound masks melted against their faces.

Though no one actually says it, the Alphas are all thinking the same thing: *This night just got* way *more interesting.* After all, this was what their clan was originally formed to do: to fight an enemy that didn't vanish when the mist did. *Strength of body and heart,* their motto says. *We hold the line.*

Now they have something to actually hold the line against. There are two dead Dianas in the middle of the forest. Two dead enemies in Hemlock Falls. And that means *war* in Hemlock Falls.

Jeremiah Tuesday is going to be so happy.

Two Alphas make a halfhearted attempt to track the werewolf—which clearly came here at some point, since there are six bloodied arrows on the charred earth and tufts of white fur all over—but they only find human footprints in the area. Yes, there is *one* set of bare feet mixed in there that appears to have gone west, and later Isaac Tuesday will think, *Hmmm, could that have been the wolf turned human again?* But right now, he and everyone else is too excited by evidence of Dianas to really focus on much else.

And that excitement is only enhanced by the knowledge that in less than an hour, the Tuesday Lambdas will show up here, take over the crime scene, and force the Alphas to leave since this is technically *their* jurisdiction— and don't they just love to flaunt that in everybody's faces? Then all the details about this site will go hush-hush, and none of these twelve Alphas who actually discovered the dead Dianas will ever get any of the details.

Or any of the credit.

It's why Isaac Tuesday snaps a few photos of the bodies with his phone. A big no-no, of course, but it's not like he'll ever show it to anyone other than his girlfriend. And maybe his sister. Okay, and his dad too, who will probably want to show it to Isaac's stepmom.

But that's it. No one else will ever see how these masks have melted into grotesque versions of a dog's head, as if the forest spat out a new monster just for tonight. The edges of their magical sources are visible where the snouts used to be, and it brings to mind something Isaac studied years ago, during his brief stint with Lambda training before he decided it was too much homework without a worthwhile salary increase.

Dianas will put their sources directly into their masks, he learned, *which not only gives them constant access to the power in their source, but also modulates their voices into unrecognizable snarls.*

As Isaac considers whether maybe he should have just stuck with the Lambda program so now *he* could be the jerk swooping in to claim jurisdiction, it occurs to him that the witches under these melted masks could be people he actually knows.

It makes his stomach curdle for the first time tonight. Not enough of a curdle to make him pull out his phone and delete the snapped photos, of course, but enough to make him wish for the warmth of his bed and the bright, twinkling lights of downtown.

Isaac doesn't dwell on that curdle for long. It's probably just hunger anyway.

Good thing he bought that pizza to eat at the end of his shift.

47

The will-o'-wisps float just ahead of Winnie for miles, always at the margins of her vision, always swooping and shimmering and seeming to have no logical aim. Winnie follows and follows because she doesn't know what else to do. Straight through the changeling's domain—although all that remains of it now are bloodstains on the ground and bits of auburn hair—then straight across the stream.

Where the running water does nothing to deter them.

Eventually, after hours of trudging along, the will-o'-wisps lead Winnie to the southwestern edge of the forest. No nightmares get her along the way. No Tuesday scorpions or Wednesday hunters either.

And no crow with half a mask and gray hair streaming down.

Strangely, despite the fact that the will-o'-wisps can easily fly past the red-staked boundaries of the forest—as Winnie has seen them do before—they remain inside the trees and watch Winnie leave.

She files that detail away for later analysis. For when the night is done and she is safe in her room with the trusty Compendium open upon her closet floor.

Will-o'-wisps showed no interest in exiting the forest for prey, however did exit to witness death of a fellow will-o'-wisp.

Also, showed enough sentience to help a human.

The sun is rising by the time Winnie stumbles out of the trees and finds herself just south of the Tuesday estate, where uniformed soldiers scuttle and crawl at breakneck speed between the different bunker-like buildings. Without her glasses, the whole place looks like an ant mound riled up by a rainstorm.

Winnie supposes it's only a matter of time before some of those Tuesdays end up at her house. She has no idea what she's going to say when they do, but like the will-o'-wisps' movement patterns, it isn't something to worry about right now.

Winnie turns away from the Tuesday estate and aims south. As she plods onward, so tired she can barely keep her head up, she peels off the armor she took from the Friday estate. By the time she reaches the Monday grounds, where for the first time this year no morning frost whitens the grass, Winnie is stripped down to the same outfit she wore to Joe Squared all those hours ago.

A very *dirty* version of that outfit, anyway.

With a silent apology to Lizzy's budget, she tosses all the armor into the first trash can she sees. And when she squints at her reflection in the hospital's main glass sliding doors, she is relieved to see she doesn't actually look as broken or breathless as she feels. Sure, the bandaging around her calf looks wonky, but it's not terribly obvious.

The door slides open. Yet where Winnie thinks she is the one to have triggered the opening, she almost instantly sees she is not. Someone is coming out.

Someone she so desperately wanted to see.

Like her, Jay wears what he wore at Joe Squared last night—and like her, he looks worn and shattered. His skin is deathly pale, and his posture is as fragile as Winnie's. All it will take is one sharp gust from the morning breeze, and they will both collapse onto the pavement.

Jay draws up short at the sight of Winnie. His gray eyes flash with golden sunrise. The hospital doors hiss shut behind him.

Then he stares at Winnie while Winnie stares at him.

It is like their moment outside Joe Squared all over again, except the *yes* between them has multiplied from a single word of confirmation into four years' worth of secrets. A thousand swamp fires. A thousand lies all set free into the spring morning.

And the clockwork gears that synchronized them as children, that still bind them as young adults—rather than order them to turn away from each other, this time compel them to draw near.

Closer, closer, until they are only two feet apart and studying each other like they've never met before.

Winnie supposes they haven't. Not really. Not *fully*.

Why didn't you tell me? she thinks at him. A breeze slides over her. It rattles through pruned, flowerless hydrangeas nearby. *Why didn't you tell me?* She isn't sure when the words leave her brain by way of her mouth, but they emerge like a forest dawn, cold and ethereal: "Why didn't you tell me?"

Jay responds like a nightmare within: "I was afraid I would hurt you."

Winnie almost laughs at that. No, she *does* laugh—a weird, shrill huff. "That's impossible." She shakes her head. "You have never hurt me, Jay Friday. At least not when you were a wolf." She doesn't add that he hurt her as a human, because he knows that. And of course, she knows he wasn't entirely to blame.

"What do you remember?" she asks. Then she adds, "From last night," because she's almost certain he can't remember his other nights in the forest—a fact Mario probably knows more about.

"Not much," Jay admits. "Just the . . . end. When the mist came. But I know you were there, Winnie. I know you came for me. And I . . ." He pauses. Swallows. "I know I wouldn't be standing right now, if not for you."

That is all they need to say. The only *yes* that still needed to fall between them before they could move in synchrony again. Winnie moves to Jay, Jay moves to Winnie, and then they are squeezing each other so tightly that they briefly morph into one.

It is no longer where the hazy hemlocks and pines end that Jay seems to begin, nor is it where the hazy hemlocks and pines end that Winnie begins. It is simply with each other, two best friends who don't really fit with the rest of Hemlock Falls. Whose culture doesn't run thicker than blood, but whose friendship and history do.

Winnie has no idea how long they hold each other like that. She just knows it is too short. That even though she is so tired she could fall asleep right now, her muscles have found fresh energy to hold and hold and hold.

She wants to ask Jay how his wounds have healed—if it was the mist in the vial and how such a thing is possible. She wants to ask how he got out of the forest when hunters and Tuesdays prowled. But then a voice calls out, cracking with prepubescence, "Winnie? Are you here for my mom?"

And the moment is over. Marcus has arrived.

Winnie and Jay draw apart, and in a distant part of Winnie's brain where actual thought is still happening, she considers how much her cousin looks like Darian did on the night Dad disappeared. Marcus even has similar plaid pajamas—green and red flannel with wooden buttons.

There's also a similar terror in his eyes, as if he can't believe he's at the hospital before he even woke up for corpse duty, and surely he will wake up from this bad dream momentarily?

Marcus looks at Jay. "I heard you brought her in."

"Yeah," Jay replies. A sigh settles over him, as if he is shedding the young man from a few moments ago and slipping into his Lead Hunter's coat. The nascent sunrise warms his cheeks to pink. "She's going to be all right, Marcus."

Marcus starts crying at those words. Without realizing what she does, Winnie moves to him and pulls him in for a hug. A fierce, *Hey, the nightmares can't get you now* hug. Because in the end, Marcus is just a kid. One who vomits at the sight of dead things, who is trying *really hard* to accept that death is a part of life in Hemlock Falls, and who right now just wants his mom to be okay.

And although Winnie hates that she can see anything of herself in her cousin, she also knows what it feels like to wake up and wonder why one of your parents isn't coming home.

"Room two thirteen," Jay says, and when Winnie pulls away from Marcus, she finds a tension has crept into Jay's shoulders, into his jaw. *Vigilance,* she realizes, *because nightmares don't mix well with humans.* He doesn't want to venture back into the hospital with Winnie and Marcus; he has evaded swarms of Alphas thus far, but it's best not to press his day-walking luck.

So Winnie nods at him. "I'll find you later," she murmurs, shifting her weight so she can follow Marcus as he shuffles like a revenant toward the hospital doors. But where she expects to see a matching nod from Jay, she instead finds he is staring at her.

Just staring, still as the boy she sketched onto paper three nights ago.

The winds change. From south to north, they shift. Or maybe it's just that they intensify, like the forest is giving a final okay. A physical nudge at Jay's back that says, *I release you for the moment, human. Do not waste this time.*

So Jay doesn't. He closes the space between himself and Winnie, cups her face with gentle, callused hands, and kisses her.

It's just a kiss on her forehead. A brief pressure of his lips against her skin, but it's more than enough. A gesture that is too heavy to be carried away by the wind. That is too uncompromising, too three-dimensional, too simple to be misinterpreted.

Yes, I used to like you.

Yes, I like you now.

Then he withdraws, and Winnie lets him go. She already said she would find him later, and this moment between them—this kiss across shadows into a bright fever—was his answering promise that he would hold her to it.

Winnie and Marcus find Rachel on the second floor, hooked up to a beeping machine and a dangling sack of IV fluids. She is wide awake and unsettlingly alert, her dark eyes as bright as if she just woke up from a full night's rest. She has no bruises, no dirt streaks, and even the cut that Winnie noticed in the night is gone.

Which Winnie supposes shouldn't surprise her. Melusine blood can heal a mortal wound, so the direct magic of a melusine must heal even more. Winnie might not remember every detail from her time beneath the waterfall's waves, but that haunting music will never leave her—nor that mischievous flicker of scales and silvery light.

So although cables and tubes sling off Rachel, they are clearly just precautionary. As if even the Mondays are puzzled as to why Jay brought her in here. No bandages bind her chest that was ruined a few hours ago, and Winnie can't help but notice there are no bite marks on Rachel's bare arms.

Rachel has just enough time to sit up before Marcus has flung himself across the room and into her arms. They embrace with all the ferocity of Wednesday bears, and Winnie doesn't miss the tears building in Rachel's eyes. Like this was all she wanted at this moment. Like after a night of hell and forest claws, all she needed to make the world right was a hug from her son.

There is so much essence in this moment.

Winnie thinks of the sketches Dad made for Darian.

When at last Marcus pulls free, he beams at Rachel with a face Winnie knows well because she wore it a thousand times growing up. *I want to be just like you, Mom. I want to eat the pizza and stop feeling like a kid who's scared of the night.*

Rachel gives an embarrassed scrub at Marcus's hair, and wipes her eyes. Then she finally twists Winnie's way. And it's like watching Jay all over again, like he and Rachel have some Lead Hunter manual that says, *Step one: Lock up all emotions. Step two: Take control of the situation.*

"Hey, kid," Rachel says as Winnie cautiously approaches the hospital bed. *What does Rachel remember?* Winnie's brain pounds in time to her steps. *What is she going to tell, and to whom?*

Her answer comes in seconds: "Good thing Jay was on the hunt with me tonight," Rachel murmurs, and there's a soft lethalness to her voice—a warning that Winnie has heard before. "And it's a good thing," Rachel continues, eyebrows arching, "that you and your family were nowhere near me when those Dianas jumped us."

Ah, Winnie thinks as Marcus squawks, "Dianas? You got jumped by Dianas?" But Rachel ignores her son, opting instead to hold Winnie's gaze for the duration of several mechanical beeps.

There is no ignoring the implication in that stare. *Here,* Rachel's eyes seem to say. *I am giving you this easy, precooked lie. Now microwave it for thirty seconds, and we'll all be good to go.*

It is the same look Winnie saw after her third trial, when Rachel came to her bedroom and admitted she'd known all about the banshee head. This time, though, the secret isn't that her niece failed the first trial. And the lie isn't just a simple cover-up to keep her niece a Wednesday hunter.

This secret is about a werewolf the whole town fears. This lie is about a boy Winnie begged her to save.

"When I talk to Jeremiah Tuesday," Rachel finishes, "I'll make sure he knows to leave you, your mom, and Darian alone." Then she cuts her gaze away, a hard punctuation mark to end their conversation, and she pulls her son back in for another bear hug.

"Okay," Winnie murmurs, because what else can she say? She is suddenly the very uncomfortable third wheel in a touching family tableau. Plus, for right now, everything *is* okay. Somehow, everyone Winnie cared about survived the night.

And somehow, for *right now,* there are no Dianas trying to kill her. No nightmares trying to feast on her. No Tuesdays wanting to interrogate her or even Luminaries howling to ask, *Was it fun to jump?*

It won't last, because of course it won't last. Winnie has at least seventy-three new questions for her running list of *What I Don't Know*—starting with *If Dad was framed, then where is he?* And followed by *Does Rachel know anything about what happened to him?* But her vocal cords can't form words any longer, even if she wanted them to. Her bones have given up their fight, and her muscles just desperately want to sleep.

So Winnie nods at her aunt—who nods more solemnly back. Then she rounds about to scuffle into the hall. Her combat boots shed a trail of dirt behind her. The beeps of an unnecessary machine chase after.

48

By the time Winnie steps outside, back into the brisk morning, she feels as if she is the one with melusine magic inside her. It is illogical, really. All the knots in the tangled chain that is her life just got *so* much more tangled.

Two dead Dianas in the forest.

The unequivocal knowledge that the Whisperer is a Diana spell and not a nightmare.

A crow who swept off into the mist like a real crow.

And of course, the fact that Aunt Rachel now knows what Jay is. Even if Rachel is an A+ liar, she is still one more swamp fire to add to the lying lights of downtown. And what if Rachel ever changes her mind about keeping this particular secret? *Then* what will Winnie have to do?

Yet for all these enormous knots in Winnie's life, none feel particularly pressing at this moment. Because after four years of hating herself, hating her friends, hating her life, Winnie finally knows she had the whole thing wrong. And for all that she blamed herself in the forest, it's not as if she has to keep making the same mistakes moving forward.

She spent so many days and months and years believing that no one would help her—because no one *had*. Now, though, not only does she have new friends who will always be there when she needs them . . .

She has old friends whom she, Winnie, can support in turn. The lock-boxes are open; Winnie knows the biggest secrets Jay—and Erica too—had stuffed inside. And that's why Winnie feels like a new person as she exits the hospital via glass sliding doors. Not even the sound of their whispery hiss behind her can make her skin crawl or drag her back into the forest. Back into the flames and the mist and the snarling laughter of Dianas who ruined her family.

Winnie spent four years hung up on what came before. Right now, she wants to know what waits ahead. There's no will-o'-wisp to lead her to safety now, but she doesn't need one. Nor does she need a secret map or coded clues, or even a book about secret messages from an Italian library . . .

Okay, she might need the book. But not yet. Not *at this precise moment* after she survived a night she shouldn't have—as did everyone she loves. You either trust the forest or you don't. You either trust yourself or you don't.

Which is why Winnie rolls her shoulders once, cracks her neck with a satisfying *crunch!* to ripple across the cold parking lot. Then she eases her hands into her pockets and sets off for home.

The sun rises ahead of her. The wind off the Little Lake kisses her face.

Winnie finds her house empty and a note from Mom about Rachel being in the hospital: *I got a ride with Darian. Bring the Volvo when you can. I LOVE YOU SO MUCH—Mom*

Winnie also finds a half-made batch of pancakes. She eats them, despite the fact that two of the four are mostly still dough on the inside. They are delicious nonetheless, and after hours on her feet, the calories are all Winnie needs to crash into a deep, *deep* slumber.

She doesn't sleep long. Just until the titmouse outside rouses her with songs for Peter. But the few hours were all Winnie needed to feel as stitched back together as Jay was after the mist.

It makes Winnie's heart ache to think about him—about the fact that Jay cannot heal unless he has the mist because the boy she once loved is physically gone, his cells rebuilt into something that isn't human when examined beneath a microscope.

His sparrow-shaped heart is the same, though. His integrity and his reliability—those never went away.

Winnie showers, though she keeps the water cool this time. After a night of heat and flames, she has no desire to burn as bright as phoenix. She simply wants to feel clean, awake, alive.

She does at least tend to her changeling bite. It's not pretty, but the anticoagulant no longer loosens her blood, and all those tiny monster fangs didn't dig deep enough to require stitches.

As for her collarbone, Winnie finds no burn there. There isn't even a blister. It's just smooth skin, as if the locket never turned to flames. As if it is and always has been nothing more than a necklace with a photo of herself and Darian on the inside.

The photos are still in there. Intact, if a little bit dirty.

Obviously, though, this locket is much more than it seems. And just as Aunt Rachel knew it belonged to Grandma Harriet once upon a time, maybe Rachel also knows why Grayson Friday had one just like it.

Winnie adds those questions to her ever-expanding list.

It is almost noon by the time Winnie stomps outside in her Converse and Save the Whales hoodie—her bent glasses perched atop her nose. The bear flag ruffles at her, watching her departure with wary eyes. *You are definitely a bear,* it says, *but not of the Wednesday variety.*

As she aims for the Volvo at the curb, her calf twinges. Her head throbs from the brightness of the day. And the crow on the roof laughs and laughs, which makes Winnie think of the crow from the forest, with her gray hair and commanding voice.

There's an important Venn diagram to be drawn about that woman at some point soon . . . But later. After the first two questions on her list have been dealt with—one that will take her east. A second will take her north.

Clouds part. Sunshine teases Winnie with a brief promise of warmth. Tree branches reach over her, fracturing shadows onto the Volvo. Darkness, darkness, light made by new leaves grappling for spring. Then she is encased in her family's car and revving it up to hyperspeed.

A cardinal sweeps by. Winnie thinks of the will-o'-wisps. She wonders if they will re-form again tonight or if this morning's mist erased them forever.

Though most nightmares re-form nightly unless slain, sometimes they do not, disappearing forever instead. Some speculate this is a conscious decision by the spirit, while others postulate it is an unintended failure of the mist—

like faulty genetic code in the natural world. Others still suggest perhaps the nightmares simply senesce and eventually die with time.

Maybe that was what happened to the will-o'-wisp outside the forest. Maybe it was dying of old age, not an injury. Either way, Winnie hopes Jay's boot really did end its pain.

And she's glad—so, *so* glad—that the other will-o'-wisps deemed her friend instead of foe.

Once Winnie reaches the high school, she parks (very carefully) beside a red Porsche that used to belong to Marcia Thursday. Minutes later, the bell rings to mark the end of the main school day. Now everyone will go to the Sunday estate.

Winnie glimpses her square of new best friends leaving school. They pile into a familiar minivan a few rows over, but Winnie doesn't get out to say hi. She's relieved when neither the twins nor Fatima notice her in the Volvo. Winnie will explain *all* of this to them eventually, but only when she herself knows the full story.

And only when her triangle of old best friends tells her it's okay.

When at last Erica struts out of the high school, Winnie pushes into the midday. Spring wind pulls at her shower-damp hair. Erica notices her immediately, although her runway stride doesn't miss a beat. In fact, she moves as if nothing unusual happened last night. As if she really did go home after Joe Squared and sleep until this morning.

Amazing how much makeup can hide, though. How mascara can make Erica's eyes seem to sparkle or how lip gloss can plump a mouth pressed tight as Erica strides right up to the Porsche with Winnie standing beside it.

Winnie holds up a hand before Erica can say anything—not that she thinks Erica *will* speak first. It's just that Winnie wants to ensure she gets her words out before her old Thursday friend can steer this conversation. "You know why I'm here, E. I want answers from you about Jenna, about the Band-Aids and the magic, about the Dianas that were in the forest and all the stuff that went missing from my room. But"—Winnie waves her hand emphatically—"I don't want you to explain it now."

Erica's eyes twitch. Her lips somehow pinch more tightly. "Is that so, Winnie Wednesday? And when exactly am I supposed to *explain* all these things you're throwing at me?" She makes air quotations around the word "explain."

But Winnie ignores the gesture, as well as the tone of Erica's comments. Winnie won't be tricked into an argument. She knows how clever and commanding Erica can be when it comes to words—a skill learned from her mother. Instead, Winnie answers the actual question Erica put forth: "You'll explain it all tonight when Jay and I come to the cabin after your clan dinner. *Then,* you're going to tell us everything we want to know about what happened. And in turn, we're going to tell you everything we know."

"And what if I don't show up?"

"I'm pretty sure we know where to find you."

Another twitch of Erica's eyes, another pucker of lips that shine bright as moonbeams. But then the curtain rises. The Marcia-like persona slips away. Erica swallows. Her nostrils flare . . .

And it's as if Winnie is watching her friend's lockbox open up right before her. As if she, Winnie, had the key all along and all she had to do was check to see if it fit.

The glimpse of grief doesn't last long. Merely a peek through the keyhole before Erica flips her hair over her shoulder and declares, "Okay, Winnie Wednesday. I guess I'll see you and Jay tonight at the cabin. I hope you're ready, though, for what's in store."

And that's all she says—a statement that isn't quite a threat but is most assuredly more than a promise.

Erica slides into the red convertible. The door slams. In seconds, it purrs sultrily away, quiet as a dryad slipping through the forest. Or a hound prowling on the hunt.

C H A P T E R

49

Winnie finds Jay where she knew he would be: at the Friday estate on the hunter training grounds. She saw it on the schedule in his desk last night, scribbled in Grayson's handwriting. *Training session on Thursday at 1PM.*

It isn't one o'clock yet, and Winnie is glad for it. She wants just a few moments alone before other Fridays descend upon her, howling and calling her "Wolf Girl."

She has just rounded the burned-out tower, its crumbling bricks almost beautiful today beneath the burgeoning sun, when she spots Jay at the archery range. He preps the day's work for his hunters, ancient targets lined up across patchy grass at different heights, different distances, different angles.

Like Winnie, he has cleaned up. He wears fresh training gear—black joggers and a hoodie—and although Winnie can't tell from this distance if Jay's face is more haggard than usual, she suspects the answer is no. After all, while everything might have changed for her, this is just another day for him. He has had four years to adjust to this normal; Winnie has only had a few hours.

How does he do this all the time? she wonders. *Just continue on as if he didn't spend last night fighting for his life?* Hunters might never have hit him before, but that doesn't mean he has always evaded other nightmares.

In fact, why else would he have an impossible vial of red mist in his drawer unless it was to save him each time he nearly died?

Winnie passes the obstacle course, its swaying ropes and wooden platforms silent beneath a cold wind stealing from the spirit's forest nearby. Up ahead, at the tables beside the archery range, Jay has arranged compound bows and quivers of bolts. One for each of his hunters.

It's strange how such a seemingly small detail—the tidy placement of tools *right* where he wants each person to stand—can reveal so much about him. How good he is at what he does. How much he cares to do it well.

And how, even if he never looks at the audience while he plays his guitar, he will always pour his nightmare soul into the music.

Jay hears Winnie at last, jerking around to face her, a compound bow gripped in one hand. It is *his* bow, she notices, that he lent her a few weeks ago when they first went into the forest to train together.

The sun slides over him. No darkness, only light. And a muscle feathers in his jaw as she approaches. His eyes—those gray, gray eyes . . . They throb with something more than mere exhaustion.

She can't tell what. She used to know everything Jay was thinking; now she can't tell a thing. She is hopeful, though, that in time she'll learn the new tics and traits of him. He is so much more than just an illustration in her sketchbook, after all.

"Did you sleep?" she asks once she is a few paces away. She has to tip up her head to meet his eyes.

"A few hours," he answers. "You?"

"A few hours," she agrees. And then she shakes her head, because this isn't at all what she came here to say. What she *wants* to say is a very simple phrase that she can easily diagram on the whiteboard.

I (subject) like (predicate) you (direct object) too (adverb).

Just do it, she prods inwardly. *You went into the forest after him. He can probably guess how you feel. Now just say it out loud, Winnie.* She doesn't say anything. Instead, she shoves her warped glasses up her nose and fights the urge to click her teeth.

Jay meanwhile continues to stare with such intensity that it's actually getting uncomfortable. Winnie's also pretty sure if he grips his bow any tighter, it will snap in two.

Just do it, just do it.

"I like you too," she blurts. It comes out loud and harsh. Definitely *not* the suave presentation she practiced in front of her mirror. But it's too late to stop now, so she just blunders on: "I also liked you four years ago, which was another reason it hurt so much when you ditched me. Because I *liked* you, Jay. I mean, I *really* liked you. And while yeah, I understand why you didn't want to stay friends with me, I didn't know that at the time, so—"

Jay moves so fast, Winnie barely processes that he has lifted his bow and taken aim—much less that he has nocked an arrow and let loose. She only realizes, in fact, once the arrow hits the farthest target directly in its heart.

Flecks of foam spray from its vinyl chest.

A *lot* of foam, as if the force of impact is more than that poor human-shaped torso was ever meant to sustain.

Jay shoots two more arrows, one after the other with a speed that isn't quite human. And Winnie suddenly understands in a fuzzy part of her brain *why* he stopped running in the Nightmare Masquerade 5K. *Never startle a nightmare.*

A heartbeat later, Jay is tromping off toward the target as if he wants to murder the thing with his bare hands.

"Are you . . . *mad*?" Winnie asks his retreating back. When Jay doesn't answer, she chases after, hurrying over new grass and old mud. "Are you mad?" she repeats once they're beside the target and Jay is very, *very* forcefully removing the first arrow from the dummy.

"Not at you," he snaps. The arrow rips free. Shredded foam and vinyl fly into the breeze. Then Jay rounds toward Winnie, now clutching the arrow with the same bone-breaking ferocity he'd clutched the bow.

Winnie can literally see the shaft bending within his fingers.

"I'm mad at me, Winnie. I've been mad at me for four fucking years be-cause all I have wanted to do was tell you the truth about what happened. Instead I wrote stupid songs—"

"I really liked your song."

"—and tried to pretend I didn't know how much I was hurting you. I'm sorry, okay?" He doesn't actually sound sorry as he says this. He instead sounds furious, and now there are spots of pink rising onto his cheeks.

His gray eyes shine pewter, and Winnie is pretty sure if he doesn't re-lease that arrow, it *will* break in half. So she reaches out and cups his fist.

With both her hands, she closes her fingers around his. "Jay," she says quietly.

He doesn't relax.

"I'm not going to pretend I forgive you, but you're not the only one to blame here."

He still doesn't relax. If anything, a confused tension rises up his spine. His forehead pinches.

"I should have noticed what was going on with you, but I didn't. I didn't notice it with Erica either. I should have looked at someone other than myself for once and realized maybe they had problems too. But I didn't, and I'm sorry."

"Please don't apologize." Jay wags his head. Some of his posture relaxes. "Please, Winnie. I don't want you, of all people, to apologize to me. Not after . . . after everything."

He doesn't specify what *everything* might be, but he doesn't really have to. Plus, Winnie isn't actually sure he could summarize it all if he tried. She certainly can't. There are so many circles on her Venn diagram now—so many Ping-Pong balls and open questions that can be traced back to four years ago . . . and then likely even farther back than that.

Between them, they have two *very* full lockboxes.

So Winnie simply says, "How about neither of us apologize, then?"

Jay's muscles soften a little more. Enough so that she can gently pry the arrow from his grasp and drop it to the sunlit earth.

And enough so that she spies her chance to crack a joke. Something the old Jay would have laughed at. Something to diffuse the final tension stretched between them. "So is *this* one of your make-out spots, Jay?"

He stares at Winnie for several seconds, incomprehension dulling his eyes to brushed steel. Then he laughs—a sound that is brimming over with the boy Winnie once knew. "Oh shit, Winnie." He shakes his head. "You're really hung up on that, aren't you?"

She blushes. "Well, is it?"

"No." He tips his head to one side, still grinning. "It could be, though."

"Ah," she replies, and her heart punches into overdrive. "So . . . if I kissed you right now, you would like that?"

Another laugh, and a nod. "Yes." He bites his lip. "I think I would like that."

And just like that, Jay changes before Winnie's eyes. He is no longer the hunted version of himself, as she has grown so used to. Nor is he the hunter, ready to let loose wherever the bow is aimed. It's as if he has spent days, weeks, years running and now the game is up. It's time to turn himself in and submit to the sweet relief of finally, *finally* letting go.

Winnie knows the truth of him. He knows the truth of her.

Jay closes the space between them, but where she thinks Jay will lean in and kiss her—where she *wants* him to do that, because she's afraid her heart might pummel out of her rib cage if she has to wait any longer—he instead reaches up and slides off her glasses. He's careful not to snag them on her ears or in her hair. And he's careful as he folds them into the pocket of his hoodie.

While Winnie appreciates that he is being respectful and cautious and possibly even a little bit romantic, she is way too impatient to put up with this. Four years was more than enough time to be kept waiting, thank you, and Jay is so close now. All she can smell is bergamot and lime. All she can *see* are those eyes of forever gray.

Yes, I will agree to make out with you, but then I will take my sweet time actually doing it.

Winnie hooks a finger into Jay's hoodie and yanks him against her. Then she rolls onto her toes and brings her lips to his.

It's both exactly like she remembers from when he kissed her in the snow four years ago . . . and also *nothing* like that at all. The same explosion rocks in her stomach, in her chest, in her brain, but now she is older. Jay is older. They are adult bodies flush against each other, and the kiss isn't ending after a single *Mississippi* surrounded by snow.

Instead, Jay is sliding his hands behind Winnie's back and she is sliding hers behind his, where *god*, she can feel every line of him. All those planes and grooves she saw three nights ago—now she gets to touch them. To pull and tug at his hoodie while his lips pull and tug at her.

For a brief fraction of a moment, while her teeth collide with Jay's, she is angry. Because yes, he *should* have told her the truth four years ago so then they could have been doing this all that time instead of secretly wanting each other from afar.

But her anger fades as quickly as it arrived, replaced by an inability to breathe and an uncertainty she actually *needs* to breathe. Jay tastes like toothpaste, and he feels like a Lead Hunter with a nightmare curse throbbing inside his veins.

Which apparently Winnie is very into.

Best of all, though, he feels like the friend she has loved since the day she met him eleven years ago, on a carpool ride to the Sunday estate.

Why don't you ever lock your front door? he used to ask.

And she used to answer: *Why do you always lock yours? No one is going to break into the Friday estate.*

You don't know that. There are bad people, even in the Luminaries.

Yes, Winnie thinks, *but there are also good ones.* She presses harder against Jay. Fresh wind rustles over them.

A crow caws above the forest.

HEMLOCK FALLS TESTING PORTAL

THIS PAGE IS NO LONGER OPERATIONAL.

All citizens have been tested. No werewolf mutations were found, and the nightmare's corpse was confirmed dead by Dr. Mario Monday on April 11 at 7:14AM.

Thank you for doing your civic duty and keeping Hemlock Falls safe!

Click here for information on the upcoming Nightmare Masquerade.

THE CROW

The crow watches as three friends enter a garden shed. They were children last he saw them together. Now they are almost grown: the bear, the bell, and the sparrow.

The final scraps of sunset knit over them, mingling with twilight blue.

He cannot hear what they say once they are inside the green clapboard walls filled with lawn mowers and fertilizer, yet relief settles through him all the same. He thanks the spirit for granting him sentience these few moments while the friends reunite. And he thanks the spirit that his secrets and clues eventually got the bear where she needed to be.

He misses her so very much.

He also hopes she figures out the rest of his messages. The ones that will lead her to the other crow—the human one who hisses through a golden beak.

As the last of the sun's rays vanish behind Hemlock Falls, a lone lamp flickers to life inside the shed. The real crow shakes his wings. He has forgotten why he flew here. He never travels this close to the hungry trees. It is cold here. The air is too thin.

The crow caws once, to no one in particular, before setting off for the glittering lights of downtown. If he's lucky, the woman with the apron will toss him a stale burger bun and tell him he has kind eyes.

Her own eyes are so very sad—and sometimes he thinks he might know why . . . But the inkling never lasts. And ultimately, the crow doesn't really care. After all, death is a part of life in Hemlock Falls.

Even for the crows.

ACKNOWLEDGMENTS

Thank you, forever and always, to the LumiNerds who have supported Winnie and #UghJay since the beginning. The entire Luminaries world would have stayed hidden on my hard drive for the rest of time if you all hadn't shown up for that Sooz Your Own Adventure in 2019.

To Erin Bowman, who helped me *finally* crack through the last sticking points in this book: you were my first reader for *The Hunting Moon* and your ideas helped me turn it into what I knew it could be! Thank you! You are truly a wonderful friend, and I'm so grateful you're in my life.

To all my other incredible friends: Alex Bracken, Leigh Bardugo, Victoria Aveyard, Amie Kaufman, Jodi Meadows, Shanna Hughes, Rachel Hansen, Meghan Vanderlee, Elena Yip, Beth Revis, Rae Loverde, and Cait Listro—I couldn't write this book without your eyes, brains, and unwavering support.

To Colette, Sandra, Travis, and my ever-amazing Mom, Dad, sister, and brother: thank you for helping me wrangle the two-year-old and meet my most daunting deadlines.

And of course, a huge thank-you to the early readers who cheered me on and helped me find all the story spots that needed work: Donald Quist, Callum Carr, Kaite Krell, Samantha Tan, Sanya Macadam, and Asteria.

I owe so much to the incomparable team at Tor Teen, who have supported me and my books for so many years now. Go Team Luminaries!!! You're a huge group, and you all deserve all the thank-yous an author can possibly give: Lindsey Hall, Aislyn Fredsall, Anthony Parisi, Isa Caban, Eileen Lawrence, Lucille Rettino, Alexis Saarela, Giselle Gonzalez, Sarah Reidy, Megan Barnard, Lesley Worrell, Greg Collins, Rafal Gibek, Ryan

Jenkins, Jim Kapp, Michelle Foytek, Rebecca Naimon, Erin Robinson, Alex Cameron, Lizzy Hosty, Will Hinton, Claire Eddy, and Devi Pillai.

I must also thank my husband for being an incredible partner, an even better dad, and always, always going the extra mile to help and support me. Cricket and I are lucky to have you.

And Cricket, oh, Cricket. Where to begin? You turned two . . . and then three during the creation of this book. Watching you grow has been the greatest adventure of my life. I hope one day, when you're old enough to read this, you will know just how much I love you.

ABOUT THE AUTHOR

Susan Dennard is the award-winning, *New York Times* bestselling author of the Witchlands series (now in development for TV from the Jim Henson Company) and the Something Strange and Deadly series, as well as various short stories and other tales across the internet. She also runs the popular newsletter for writers, *Misfits and Daydreamers*. When not writing or teaching writing, she can be found rolling the dice as a dungeon master or mashing buttons on one of her way too many consoles.

Twitter: @stdennard
Instagram: stdennard